PRAISE FOR SCOTT THORNLEY
AND ERASING MEMORY

"An all-too-human sleuth ... MacNeice
seems a character w... s two
more MacNeice books on the way, but with Thornley's elo-
quence and his character's appeal, the two should be at the
beginning of an even longer run." — *Toronto Star*

"The reader is ... compelled to go on, in part because that
killer, if not a superior, twisted mind, is a first-class jerk and
we love to see such people get their comeuppance."
— Philip Marchand, *National Post*

"Thornley's intelligent and evocative prose, combined with
his depictions of complex police investigations, brings to
mind one of Canada's most prominent, bestselling crime
writers, Peter Robinson." — *Quill & Quire*

"For crime fiction junkies, Scott Thornley's first novel,
Erasing Memory, a beautifully written police procedural set
in a fictional version of Hamilton, just whets our appetite
for more.... Please tell me this is the first of a series."
— Stevie Cameron, author of *On the Farm: Robert William
Pickton and the Tragic Story of Vancouver's Missing Women*

"MacNeice is a splendid addition to the pantheon of [literary]
detectives ... A first-class mystery." — *Vancouver Sun*

"An auspicious debut for author Scott Thornley." — *Salon*

PRAISE FOR SCOTT THORNLEY AND *THE AMBITIOUS CITY*

"Terrific... Thornley blends history into a really good cop-shop story... Read this and then look for the first MacNeice book, *Erasing Memory*." —*Globe and Mail*

"No writer grabs the violent new zeitgeist more firmly than Scott Thornley with his second book, *The Ambitious City*." —*Toronto Star*

"Captivating... Along with a terrific plot, Thornley produces prose that is both hard-hitting and thoughtful... I'm already anticipating MacNeice's next investigation." —*Edmonton Journal*

PRAISE FOR SCOTT THORNLEY AND *RAW BONE*

"This is stellar police-procedural writing that takes in characters, history, and, most of all, place. Dundurn is beautifully and sordidly rendered in all its glory as MacNeice tracks a killer with a message... Those who like solid clue-hunting will love this series." —*Globe and Mail*

RAW BONE

RAW BONE

A MacNEICE MYSTERY

SCOTT THORNLEY

SPIDERLINE

Published in Canada in 2018 and the USA in 2018 by
House of Anansi Press Inc.
Published by arrangement with Random House Canada, a division of
Penguin Random House Canada Limited

www.houseofanansi.com

House of Anansi Press is committed to protecting our natural environment. As part of our efforts, the interior of this book is printed on
paper that contains 100% post-consumer recycled fibres, is acid-free,
and is processed chlorine-free.

22 21 20 19 18   1 2 3 4 5

Library and Archives Canada Cataloguing in Publication

Thornley, Scott, author
Raw bone / Scott Thornley.

A MacNeice mystery
Reprint. Originally published in 2015.
Issued in print and electronic formats.
ISBN 978-1-4870-0323-4 (softcover). — ISBN 978-1-4870-0324-1 (EPUB). —
ISBN 978-1-4870-0325-8 (Kindle)

I. Title.

PS8639.H66R39 2018   C813'.6   C2017-905990-4
C2017-905991-2

Library of Congress Control Number: 2017961330

Cover and text design: Alysia Shewchuk
Typesetting: Sara Loos

 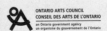

Canada Council   Conseil des Arts   ONTARIO ARTS COUNCIL
for the Arts   du Canada   CONSEIL DES ARTS DE L'ONTARIO
                                      an Ontario government agency
                                      un organisme du gouvernement de l'Ontario

*We acknowledge for their financial support of our publishing
program the Canada Council for the Arts, the Ontario Arts Council,
and the Government of Canada through the Canada Book Fund.*

Printed and bound in Canada

RECYCLED
Paper made from
recycled material
FSC
www.fsc.org   FSC® C103567

For Shirley

Beauty.
Does it live forever?
Yes, it lives forever.

From "Beauty" by Richard W. Halperin

[1]

SHE WAS LEFT THERE SOMETIME BEFORE THE HEAVY SNOWS AND early December freeze-up, far enough from shore that coyotes couldn't reach her and in water shallow enough that the massive carp and cruising pike wouldn't feed off her. In this early spring, the snow that remained in the city was all grey and honeycombed — littered with paper, plastic wrappers, cigarette butts and abandoned bags of dog shit — but on the bay side of Cootes Paradise, such sights were foreign. Among the grey rocks and black trees, there were still large patches of white snow sharing the ground with the dead leaves of endless autumns, or laying like cotton balls deep in the branches of evergreen. From beyond the trees, the low sonic hum of traffic on the highway came in waves, like a bow crossing the strings of a double bass.

The ice was so thin that the right buttock and right hand had broken through and were frozen in place. The flesh appeared waxy and grey, either from decomposition or exposure to the air. Two young men had spotted the hand while cycling cross-country through the park—initially they thought it was a rubber glove.

MacNeice trained his binoculars on the slab, blocking out the raucous banter from the cluster of cops at the end of the bay. He studied the protruding hand. The fingers appeared slightly swollen but relaxed. From the elevated trail where he was standing, he couldn't tell with any certainty, but he felt sure the hand belonged to a woman.

The marine unit was taking its time. They had decided it would be better to cross Dundurn Bay—and certainly more exciting—than to haul a skiff around the bay in a trailer and paddle out from shore. He'd sent Detective Inspector Fiza Aziz with them to oversee the body's removal.

MacNeice leaned against a maple and waited for the sun to break through the clouds scuttling across the bay. The damp smell of early spring filled his nostrils and, even though it had more than a hint of rotting vegetation, he found it pleasant. He exhaled, then trained the glasses on where he thought the head would be. Like it was breathing, the slab gently rose and fell.

Someone was coming along the path toward him; he recognized the footfalls. "What have you got?" MacNeice asked, studying the ice.

"Not much," DI Michael Vertesi said.

MacNeice lowered the binoculars and glanced at the cops on the road. "Michael, give those men something useful to do. Get them busy searching the surrounding area, along these trails, and up that road in both directions."

"On it." Vertesi pulled his collar up against the chill and walked back along the trail.

MacNeice looked through the binoculars again as the sun broke free of the clouds, and he caught sight of the body floating in counterpoint to the rise and fall of the ice. Long hair, hard to tell what colour, was drifting out from her head. Through the ice, her body resembled yellow marble. He sighed and let the binoculars hang down against his chest.

His cell rang. "MacNeice."

Over the noise of the engine, which he could hear approaching, Aziz said, "We're not far, Mac."

"Richardson's on her way from home and Winston's—the commercial outfit they use to retrieve and deliver the body—will be here shortly. Tell your team they'll have to bring her to the shore here." He glanced back to see Vertesi pointing up the road and two of the uniforms heading off in that direction.

"They tell me this is a jet boat that can function in five inches of water, so that shouldn't be a problem."

"You don't sound too certain."

"Well, we've also got two divers in wetsuits and two fire-fighters with pikes, axes and a chainsaw."

"The sun just gave me a glimpse underneath. I don't know how thick the slab is, but I think the body's somehow holding it in place. I can't see anything of her left side, so make sure they understand she's probably tethered."

"You're sure it's a woman?"

"I can see long hair."

The engine sounds grew louder and he looked out to the open water and spotted the police boat racing in a wide arc around the spit of land to the east. "I can see you now. You'll be fine."

"How bad is it going to smell?"

"Probably not bad. She's been down there for a while, so the body is cold." He put the phone in his coat pocket and walked down to the water's edge where a fringe of icy lace hemmed the ragged shoreline. A shiny black GMC van with WINSTON spelled out in gold serif letters was lumbering slowly and heavily down Valley Inn Road. It stopped beside the cruisers, but no one emerged.

MacNeice watched Vertesi walk over to the driver's side of the retrieval van, then focused the binoculars beyond the narrow spit where the police boat had dropped power and was surfing forward on its own wake. As it turned into the small bay, he could see Aziz in a bright yellow life jacket. As he got closer, the wheelman swung the boat about, shifted to neutral and let the boat drift gently toward the slab. It came gracefully to a stop just shy of the ice.

One of the divers climbed onto the stern-mounted step deck, pulled the neoprene hood over his head and put his black gloves on. The cop at the wheel shut the engine down and the bay returned to silence. The firefighters used pikes to hold the boat in position as the other diver dropped anchors fore and aft.

Aziz and the crew chief came out of the cockpit and stood on the port side, and Aziz shouted to MacNeice, "Sergeant Nelson Rivera is commander of this unit. The divers are Constables Dodsworthy and Zanitch."

MacNeice called to the diver on the step deck, "Dodsworthy, can you tell how thick the ice slab is?"

"Probably four to six inches in the middle, three or so at the edge," he said. "I'll go under and see what's happening."

Zanitch brought Dodsworthy the tanks and helped him suit up. Dodsworthy put the mask and breathing line on and grabbed a large underwater flashlight. He made sure it was working, nodded and slipped silently into the water. Everyone waited, then the diver's shiny black glove appeared at the opposite edge of the ice. He pulled down hard; the heavy slab, perhaps eighteen feet long, dipped slightly before his black hand slid back into the water.

MacNeice had been half expecting, half hoping, that the frozen buttock and hand would sink—but they didn't. When Dodsworthy reappeared and hoisted himself onto the step deck, the first thing he said was "She's stuck pretty bad." He turned MacNeice's way and shouted, "Her left leg is tied to a marine anchor, her butt and hand are stuck solid in the ice. If I pull her out, I think she'll rip."

"What do you recommend?" Aziz asked.

He thought about it, looking down at the hand in the ice. "I'll slide across the surface and use the chainsaw to cut her free. The ice is only about five inches thick where she is and she's the only thing holding that slab in place."

"Has the decomposition gone so far that she'd actually come apart?" Aziz asked.

"She's actually in pretty good shape," Dodsworthy said, "probably because she'd been on the bottom, buried in the muck, not getting torn up by the ice coming and going all winter. You can't see squat even with the flashlight—it's all by touch." They settled on having one diver on the ice and the other underneath to catch her when she sank, or to keep her from drifting away.

Vertesi came back carrying two Styrofoam cups. "From the Winston's boys, it's a double-double; that's all they had."

"I'm chilled enough to forget that I'm picky. Thanks." MacNeice held up the cup toward the van; the driver flashed the lights in response.

Zanitch was into his gear and disappeared quickly under the ice, resurfacing a short while later with the heavy anchor. Rivera took it from him, ensuring the line was slack before placing it on the decking. Zanitch dropped quietly beneath the ice again. With the help of the firefighters, Dodsworthy eased himself onto the ice. On his belly, he began snaking toward the hand. A rope was looped from his left arm back to the boat where he had tethered it to the chainsaw. Once he was spread-eagled in front of the hand, he nodded and pulled the chainsaw toward him.

The operation took several minutes and was not without its surprises. Riding the icy slab was difficult enough, but when Dodsworthy dug the blade of the chainsaw into the ice, he leaned on it for balance as much as cutting power, and the slab suddenly split in two, sending man and machine beneath the surface.

The body, however, was free of all but a two-foot chunk around the hand and it wasn't long before Zanitch had brought her to the stern of the boat and the firefighters lifted her into a wire mesh Stokes basket. With the divers aboard, Commander Rivera reversed the police boat slowly toward shore.

MacNeice turned to Vertesi. "How much coffee do they have?"

"Two thermoses. We've put a dent in one of them."

"Tell them to save the second thermos."

"Okay, should I tell 'em what for?"

"De-icing."

Vertesi looked over at the boat. "Understood."

[2]

DR. MARY RICHARDSON, DUNDURN'S CHIEF PATHOLOGIST, ARRIVED as MacNeice was pouring hot coffee on the ice around the hand. It dissolved easily and the firefighters placed the hand gently on the tarpaulin.

"Have you any of that coffee left?" she asked.

"A little. Would you like some?"

She nodded and walked down to the water's edge, wrapping her long, grey woollen coat around her and crossing her arms against the chill. Turning around, she registered that the cops, divers and firefighters all seemed to be standing about waiting for something to happen.

One of the retrieval men came forward with her coffee. "Double-double, doctor."

"Exactly the way I take it." She smiled warmly, accepted the steaming cup with both hands and came back to MacNeice. "With the retrieval van here, I shan't need your men. Also, do you have a privacy screen?"

"Better than that, a tent." MacNeice turned to Vertesi, who gave a thumbs up and disappeared behind the police van.

Sipping her coffee, Richardson gazed out across the bay to the distant city. "Just look at that view."

MacNeice agreed that it was beautiful even on a grey day. He turned back to see Vertesi erecting the bright white tent. When it was up, he signalled that he was going up the hill to check with the cops that had been doing door-to-doors.

Rivera and Zanitch were about to slide the body in the basket into the tent when Richardson turned and said, "Please remove her from that contraption and place her on the groundsheet."

MacNeice stood aside, glancing at the anchor and line. "Also, before you go, Sergeant Rivera, cut the anchor line on this ankle to the same length as the line that had broken free. And, if you can, please identify those knots for me." He pointed to the elegant criss-crossing of figure-eight ties cinched tightly to both ankles.

After Rivera and Zanitch removed the basket, placed the body on the tent's white plastic groundsheet and cut the line, Rivera studied the knots. He shook his head, stood up and held the tent flap open for Richardson. She put on her surgical mask and latex gloves and stepped inside, holding her case.

Rivera dropped the flap. "I have no idea what you call these knots," he said to MacNeice. "And other than cutting 'em, I wouldn't know how to undo 'em. They may be marine knots, but nothing you'd see locally." He gestured toward the anchor. "Don't know if it's important, detective, but that anchor wouldn't have been spec'd for any boat from around here. That's gear they use for deep-sea oil rigs up in the Bering Sea." Rivera turned the anchor over with his boot heel. "It'd be enough to secure a sixty-foot glass cruiser."

He shook hands with MacNeice, Vertesi, and Aziz, who handed him the life jacket. With their pikes, the firefighters eased the boat away from shore. Rivera started the engine and powered out of the small bay, swinging east in a tight curve along the north shore of Dundurn Bay. A great plume of water gave some suggestion as to their speed.

"They've gone off joyriding," Aziz said.

MacNeice smiled. "I would too if I were them."

Richardson called from inside, "Mac, join me. Bring Detective Aziz with you."

MacNeice held the flap open. "Are you ready for this?"

Aziz said, "I think so. You?"

"Never."

They found the coroner kneeling in front of the body. She tapped the tarp, indicating that they should join her. "You won't need a mask. For the moment, she's too cold to offend."

This was the first time Aziz allowed herself to really look. The woman's flesh was waxy, with mottled colours varying from pale peach to grey, black to bone white, but in a perverse way, beautiful, like alabaster. She had the urge to reach out and touch the thigh but restrained herself, turning her attention to Richardson.

"Notice anything?" With her mask crumpled below her chin, Richardson was smiling at MacNeice.

"Bruising about the neck," MacNeice said.

"Yes. It was broken from behind, by the looks of it. Someone with exceptionally strong hands crushed the windpipe back to the vertebrae and snapped it. Relatively painless and swift. Anything else?"

"Her eyes and mouth are closed," MacNeice said. "Wouldn't they be open if she was strangled?"

"Yes, and they likely were when it happened. Someone closed them, and I'm curious to know why. What are your thoughts, Aziz?"

"We were just talking about the knots on her ankles— they look so . . . distinct."

"They are. And?"

"The one that was tied to her right leg looks like it was chewed through, ten inches or so from the ankle."

"Likely a muskrat, though why it took a notion to attack the rope, I couldn't tell you."

MacNeice was attempting to look beyond the discoloration and small wounds on the body to see her the way she was before she was murdered. Five foot six or so, slim, with breasts in proportion to her body. She had no tattoos or piercings. Her hair, a dirty blond or light brown, was shoulder length and, while matted, looked natural. There were no rings on the fingers of either hand. Her big toe had been bitten, but otherwise her feet were well formed and undamaged.

"What can you tell me about her, MacNeice?" Richardson asked.

"She wasn't a prostitute or destitute."

"Why do you believe that?"

"She has no tattoos, no rings, ankle bracelets, no signs of piercing other than her ears, and those holes appear overgrown. Her pubic hair is natural—untouched, I mean."

Richardson was smiling at him again, resting one gloved hand on the corpse's forehead as if she was checking for a fever. "What else?"

He pointed to the pale hand. "Her fingernails..."

"They look cared for," Aziz offered.

"Exactly," MacNeice said. "And the feet look as if they'd never known stiletto heels or poorly fitted shoes—no bunions or calluses...No nail polish on her toenails."

"Let's turn her over," Richardson said. "Do you have gloves?"

MacNeice pulled the latex gloves out of his jacket pocket. "I do."

"Oh come now," Richardson said, knowing that MacNeice did not like to touch the dead. "Disassociate, detective. She won't mind."

As the coroner held the head and shoulders, MacNeice took the lower back and buttocks. "On two," Richardson said, and they moved her onto her side. There was an ominous squishing sound that made Aziz gulp.

"Yes, a bit wodgy that," Richardson said. "It's her internal organs. Her lungs have liquefied, and everything else has turned to aspic—that's "jelly" to you, Mac. It's all being held together by this rather lovely skin."

MacNeice leaned closer, surveying her from her armpit to her calves.

"What do you see?"

"It looks like there's a very faint spiralling."

"She may have been wrapped up in that nylon rope." Richardson moved her hands like she was winding it around her. "I'll know more when I get her on the table."

"Have you looked at her teeth?" MacNeice asked.

"I have and they're like the rest of her, undamaged, unaltered." On her own, Richardson eased the body down onto its back. "If you'll give me three days, I'll complete the post-mortem—but don't get your hopes up. What time hasn't done, the water has." She laid a hand gently on the cold shoulder.

"How old do you think she was, and do you have any idea how long she was down there?" Aziz asked.

Richardson stared at the face. "Mid- to late-twenties. And I'm guessing three months." She closed her bag and stood up.

Aziz turned to MacNeice, taking out her camera. "I'll shoot those knots around her ankles, the bruising on her neck, and the anchor—anything else?"

"Her hands and face."

MacNeice followed Richardson outside. "Thank you for coming, Mary. Call me if you discover anything new."

"Of course." Richardson glanced once at the bay, then walked off to her car.

The Winston's men rolled the stainless steel gurney across the gravel and stopped next to the tent. Several minutes later they emerged, the body inside a black plastic bag that was strapped down and covered neatly with a deep burgundy blanket. Her exit from Cootes Paradise was much more dignified than her entrance.

As MacNeice and Aziz walked toward the Chevy, Vertesi came running down the hill, the sides of his unbuttoned overcoat flapping behind him. MacNeice said, "Here's a question for you, Aziz: What's *wodgy*?"

"I knew you'd ask. It's ancient English slang... I'm not sure, but I think it means 'bulgy' or 'lumpy.' "

"Here's another one for you..."

"Remember, Mac, I'm not really a Brit. I only lived there a while."

"Can you recall any missing persons reports from three or four months ago that fit this woman's description?"

"Nothing remotely close... only a couple of teens, I think."

Vertesi came to a stop in front of them, his olive skin flushed almost rosy. "Man, I should've been doing that earlier when I was freezing—it feels good to run." He told them he'd spoken to the residents of several houses; no one remembered anything. But he'd found out there were often boat parties in the small bay, which got loud and out of hand. "I don't understand why someone would dump her here—why not in the middle of the bay, or a mile or two out in the lake?"

"Good question."

They stood together, looking out at the water. The largest of the ice slabs was nudging the west shore; the others drifted aimlessly out in the bay. On the gravel, the pieces that had encased the dead woman's hand now looked like dirty Styrofoam.

A quiet rain began to fall, and within a minute or so the city disappeared as the surface of the bay came alive, dancing in the downpour.

"I'll finish up here," Vertesi said, buttoning up his overcoat. "No sense all of us getting soaked. I'll see you at Division."

Beside him in the passenger seat, Aziz reviewed the images on her point-and-shoot as he drove. When she was done, she said, "I've got some shots of her face that Ryan can retouch. Once he fixes the discoloration and replaces her hair with something like its original colour, we'll be able to circulate them to see if we can get an ID. Maybe he can help with the knots too. I've got several good shots of those." She glanced at MacNeice, then back at the images on the screen. "Is your intuition speaking to you?"

"No, though I'm certain those knots are whispering something. When firefighters and marine unit cops can't recognize them, that's interesting. Thugs tie thuggish knots—this was craftsmanship. I think the person who tied them didn't think about it either: that knot came as naturally to him as tying his shoes."

WHEN THEY GOT back, Ryan was alone in the cubicle where he had become a permanent fixture, serving the computer research needs of every homicide detective in the city. Though currently assigned to Swetsky and Williams on the double murder of an elderly couple in their home on Mud Street, he had a reputation for saying yes to every request. On the fabric wall above his computer was a little sign that looked like a '60s Jefferson Airplane poster in hot pink, electric blue, and black, with psychedelic lettering that hadn't been seen in his lifetime: TAKE ON MORE.

"Ryan, find out everything you can about the knots Aziz has shots of. What they're called and especially who uses them. And we need multiple prints of a decent portrait of the deceased woman as quick as you can manage," MacNeice said, taking off his coat.

He walked over to the empty whiteboard. "Someone from somewhere else tied those knots. Just to get things going, let's imagine he arrived on a lake freighter; he has time to kill, he rents a boat and takes a woman for a ride in late November or early December. He comes back, she doesn't."

Tap, tap, tap — Ryan's fast fingers hammered out a bebop rhythm that continued for a minute and then paused. "Constrictor knots," he said, "once common in the UK, not often used today because they're very difficult to untie. Oystermen used constrictor knots for binding sacks of oysters and cockles, either to keep them from falling out of the sack or being stolen." Ryan printed photos of the knots from the camera and his online source and compared them, then nodded—a dead match.

The images of the woman and anchor followed; he passed the lot to MacNeice, who taped them to the whiteboard. He always found this first posting difficult. The young woman was beyond shame now, but she was exposed—naked and taped to a whiteboard—next to the exotic knots and the anchor that had held her on the bottom of a brown-water bay for months.

"We can begin by checking boat rentals from the local marinas," Aziz said.

MacNeice nodded. "Let's also check out the Royal Dundurn Yacht Club. Aziz, does she look like she's from Dundurn?"

"Do I?" Aziz asked, smiling up at him.

"Not what I meant," said MacNeice. "She just looks to me slightly out of place, or maybe time."

"Meaning, anyone her age from around here would probably have a tattoo of a butterfly, a bluebird or a dolphin, painted fingernails and toenails, piercings and a bikini wax job."

"Exactly. Maybe she's from somewhere tattoos and piercings aren't the fashion."

"You mean Mennonite or Mormon communities?"

MacNeice shrugged and continued to study the face.

BY DAY'S END MacNeice and Aziz had shown Ryan's retouched photographs of the woman, the anchor and a foot-long piece of the nylon line at every marina in the area. Only one person, the owner of Dockyards Marine Supply, could recall an anchor being sold in late November. The sale was notable because most pleasure craft were out of the water for the winter.

He agreed to pull the receipt records by the next day but cautioned Aziz that pick-n-go sales were often paid for in cash, so the only record might be the inventory or a clerk's memory. As far as the nylon line was concerned, every marina sold the same nylon line, "like chewing gum at the corner store," the owner said.

Vertesi had headed for the yacht club. As he walked toward its entrance, he became certain that whatever the attraction of the Royal Dundurn Yacht Club was, it wasn't the building. The wide and low white aluminum facade, with its white picket fence perched on top — an attempt to mask the facility's heating and air conditioning units — would double quite nicely as an industrial facility for the manufacture of fast food placemats. Nonetheless, out front there was a proper nautical flag mast, while the marina and Dundurn Bay lay beyond. And, of course, the power of the name to inspire association not just with the city's yacht set but the very Age of Sail had to be a strong draw.

When he presented a photo of the dead woman to Melody Chapman, the young facility manager, she tilted her head this way and that, as if the tumblers of recognition might fall into place with a little agitation, but in the end she shook her head. "With the economy being so bad though, some members do rent out their boats for cash." She glanced through the window as if she might catch one doing so at the moment. "We frown on it, but the best we can do is insist that those renters are not allowed to use the facilities — not even the washrooms — unless they're coming into the Nautical Pub for lunch."

"Is it okay if I walk around and see if anyone else might have noticed something?" Vertesi asked.

"Of course," Chapman said, "though not that many people are around yet. You have to be pretty committed to go out on the water this early in the year."

She was right, the place was deserted. Then Vertesi spotted Ernie Reese, the club's ancient gas jockey, checking the pumps. Reese looked at the photo for a long moment but then shook his head, saying he'd never seen her. Vertesi asked him if there were boats at the RDYC that would take runs into Cootes Paradise Bay across the way, especially late in the season.

The old man looked out to the far shoreline, rubbed his chin and delivered a response that identified him as a born and bred Brightside north-ender. "Strictly speaking, eh—no fuckin' way—unless you're talking a tin outboard or one of them dinghies or inflatables that'll take ya anywheres, not in style eh, but shit. Mind—we don't see mucha that in here, eh."

[3]

AFTER SENDING AZIZ BACK TO DIVISION, MacNEICE DECIDED TO make a final stop in the north end. Somewhat wearily, he climbed the stairs to the Block and Tackle Bar, overlooking the bay at the corner of Bay and Burlington Street. Built in the 1880s, the BTB was originally a roadhouse where lake sailors and merchantmen could have a pint and a room for two dollars a night.

It smelled of spilt beer and suffered a music mix that a banner proclaimed as "Where Authentic Celtic Meets New-World Country." Judging by the customers — none of whom looked like sailors, Celtic, country or otherwise — they were more likely lured in by a sign declaring, "The lowest on-tap price-per-pint in the fair city of Dundurn."

The owner, William Terence Byrne — also known as BTB — was standing on the porch with his arms crossed. After MacNeice introduced himself, Byrne led him into his back office, a crowded little affair that boasted more cases of Guinness than functioning office space. There was, however, a roll-top desk with three chairs. As the owner shoved the paperwork from the desk onto one of the cases, he eyed the detective. "I know you from the TV. You're DS MacNeice, if I'm right."

MacNeice nodded and put the manila envelope containing the photo of the dead woman on the desk, resting his hand on top of it. He asked about the bar and the rooms for let upstairs.

"Well, as you can see," Byrne said, "it's a humble but authentic Irish pub, and some of them fellers takes rooms from time to time when their women chuck 'em out." He glanced at the envelope. "If you got somethin' on one of my roomers in that envelope, I'll be a monkey's uncle. I've never thought they could do anything to get arrested, let alone warrant a visit from the murder squad. Hell, half a them boys don't have teeth and the other half can't see for Jesus, and all of them are deaf, so far as I know — you heard how loud the music is in there. And they like it that way. It gets turned down at eleven because of the neighbours and the six rooms upstairs, which I keep clean and tidy."

MacNeice enjoyed the brogue. "How long have you been here?"

"You mean here at BTB, in Dundurn, or Canada?"

"All three."

Byrne cracked open the case beside him and pulled out a tall, slim can of Guinness stout. "You want one, or you can't, I suppose, 'cause yer on duty."

"Correct."

He popped the can. "I've been in Canada since 2006. I sold the family farm when me ma died, twelve hectares near Dublin. Made a small fortune... well, not in North American terms, no." He took a long swig of the dark liquid and licked the caramel foam off his lip. MacNeice noticed the downturned lines on either side of his mouth, how they contrasted with the laugh lines heading toward his temples. "Truth be told, I was had by a developer who wanted to do a working-class housing estate. But then, call it the 'luck of,' I got out just at the right time, 'cause the economy tanked. The developer decamped to Majorca just ahead of a lynching by the buyers he'd defaulted on."

"So why here?" MacNeice asked, as he continued to study the man. Judging by the yellow stains on the inside of his middle and forefingers, he was a right-handed heavy smoker — which would explain why he'd been standing on the porch without a jacket, even though there was a red down-filled coat on the back of the door. Shorter than medium height, he was too slender for his own good, with the pinkish complexion of someone whose body was close to mutiny due to decades of abuse. If his body wasn't speaking to him, Byrne's eyes should have — the whites were almost yellow and that wasn't a trick of the lighting.

"Well, I could have gone to America or Australia, but to my mind they're both full of macho men or fundamentalist Christians. So I chose Canada." He said he landed in Dundurn and then bought the bar, which was a dump. But he'd been slowly investing in it, hoping that the rumour of Dundurn's turnaround would soon come true. He took another drink, wiping his mouth with his hand. Then he leaned to tap the edge of the envelope. "Okay, your turn, detective."

"Fair enough." MacNeice picked up the envelope. "The woman whose photo I'm about to show you died, we believe, about three months ago, in late November or early to mid-December. I want to know if she may have been to your bar, or possibly rented a room upstairs."

"You sayin' she was a tramp and this is a flophouse?" He squared his shoulders in mock offence.

MacNeice put the photocopy on the desk in front of Byrne. "Not at all. I believe she may have been passing through, off a ship or off the highway."

Byrne's shoulders relaxed and he picked the photo up, studying it closely. "She's pretty — well, she was pretty," he said, meeting MacNeice's eyes. "What happened to her?"

"All I'm prepared to say at the moment is that her death is suspicious."

Byrne put the photocopy on the desk and ran the fingers of his right hand tenderly over her face.

"So you do recognize her."

"Me, ah, no, I can't say I've ever seen her before. No. She was pretty, that's all. It's a shame." He cleared his throat, then cleared it again and looked at MacNeice. "Anything else I can do for you?"

"Yes, you can give me the desk register for the rooms upstairs for November and December of last year. I assume you do keep records?"

"Yeah, well of course, I gotta keep records like I gotta keep the kitchen clean." He put his hands on both thighs as if he was about to stand, but then didn't.

MacNeice picked up the photograph and held it in front of Byrne again. "You're quite sure you've never seen this woman?"

"I haven't seen her before." He picked up the can of stout.

"I'll need your written consent to remove the records from the premises, or I can come back with a warrant for them."

Byrne began shoving papers around on the desk and then opened the drawers before he stood to look about the clutter as if for an answer. "The registers are somewhere in here . . . so, if it's all the same to you, come back tomorrow with a warrant like, and I'll give 'em to ya. Is that okay with you?"

"It is." MacNeice put the photocopy in the envelope and stood up. "Not that I'm accusing you of anything, but if those records are missing, or if they've been altered even in the slightest, I will be prepared to have you charged with tampering, and trust me, you won't want that to happen."

At the door MacNeice hesitated, then took out his cellphone. "I'll take your cellphone number in case I have to call." He held the phone up, waiting.

Byrne gave him the number.

MacNeice punched it in and pressed the green button. A moment later, Byrne's phone rang.

"Just checkin' on me, I see, detective," said Byrne.

MacNeice met the man's eyes. "I'll be here with the warrant at eight tomorrow morning."

WALKING BACK TO the Chevy, MacNeice thought about Byrne's response to the photograph. While it may have been an absent-minded gesture, or just part of the man's theatrics, he hadn't reacted the way one would if the face meant nothing. Glancing back at the BTB, MacNeice couldn't picture that young woman walking in there for a beer, let alone to rent a room. But, in the absence of evidence, one is left with intuition: a hand's gentle passage across a photograph of a beautiful face would suffice for the moment.

In the Chevy MacNeice took a deep breath and took out the photograph. Ryan had done an admirable job. Though black and white, he'd recreated the porcelain skin of her face and the gentle curve of her cheekbones framed by her hair. She looked like she'd just closed her eyes and was about to open them and smile. MacNeice put the photo back in the envelope. He called Ryan and asked him to find the residential address for Byrne. It turned out that Byrne owned a small cottage just a few blocks south of the bar.

MacNeice called Deputy Chief Wallace to fill him in and to ask for a warrant for the records, another to search the bar and Byrne's residence, and wiretaps on Byrne's cellphone and the land lines of the bar and home. And, while he was at it, unmarked surveillance on the bar.

"Based on what?" Wallace said.

"A hunch."

"Christ, MacNeice, you know judges don't like hunches. Can you give me anything better?"

"An educated guess."

Wallace sighed. "Leave it with me. There's a surveillance team I can redirect. They'll be there in five minutes or so. Brief them when they arrive."

MacNeice opened his CD wallet and took out Thelonious Monk. He slid *Solo Monk* into the CD player and, as he waited, let the light-fingered playing carry his thoughts down to the water and over to the shallow inlet across Dundurn Bay. The striding piano stripped away a myriad of concerns and allowed him to focus on the possibility of Byrne as a killer. It didn't work. Byrne didn't have the strength to crush the girl's neck, let alone lift her and the heavy anchor over the side of a shallow draft boat. An aluminum or cedar strip runabout would have been unsteady, too, like trying to throw her out of a canoe. And, as far as a second man to help him went, he'd have had to be younger than those he'd seen at the bar. They were doing all they could just to lift a pint of beer.

A rusted-out blue Ford Windstar approached slowly from the south. The driver flashed the headlights once before turning onto the side street. He did a slow U-turn before parking comfortably between two driveways, one home to a tired old Chrysler and the other, a worn-out Lincoln with one of its rear wheel hubs rusted and resting on a jack, within sight of the BTB entrance and side door. MacNeice drove around the block and came to a stop behind the van. When the driver emerged, he was wearing a black wool watch cap, blue jeans, cross-trainers, and a grey hoodie under a beat-up Harley-Davidson leather vest. He slid into the passenger seat — Constable Edward Radnicki.

MacNeice gave him a detailed description of Byrne: fifty years old, give or take, five foot seven, mousy brown hair, brown eyes, approximately 130 pounds, skinny, heavy smoker, wearing a grey blazer, baggy denim jeans. "He lives a few blocks up Bay," MacNeice said, handing him a note with Byrne's name and address. "I want him watched until a warrant is served tomorrow morning. And, taking into account the clientele you can imagine frequenting the BTB, I'd like a report on anyone that looks out of the ordinary."

"No problem." Radnicki jogged back to his vehicle.

Back at Division, he found a message from Wallace that the necessary paperwork would be on MacNeice's desk before morning.

AS HE SAT in his usual spot at the end of Marcello's bar, it wasn't to the body or the Block and Tackle Bar or William Byrne's shaky performance that MacNeice's thoughts turned. What came back was the moment in Cootes when the sun broke through and all the black tree trunks turned to zinc; even the smallest branches glistened silver-gold. It was early March and entirely possible that he wouldn't see precisely that quality of light for another year. When it had happened, the sparrows around him paused and fluffed their feathers as if they'd noticed too.

He recalled looking back at the bay through the rain as he and Aziz had driven away. Like tiny islands, the remnants of ice that had imprisoned the body lay forlorn, left to drift and dissolve in the brown water. The landscape forgets over time; the bay had already forgotten. MacNeice wouldn't. The morning, the ice, the hand and buttock, the once-lovely, near-frozen woman had all found their way to the stack of shadows where they'd be waiting for him. While the zinc trees and the happy sparrows were no match for those shadows, he'd cling to them for a time.

His mind drifted back to when he was twelve or so, taking Silver, his golden retriever, into the birch, spruce and pine forest for the first time, climbing over the pink and quartz-veined bedrock with its crispy lichen and blueberry bushes— the latter picked over by his mother or by black bears—to go skinny-dipping on the other side of the Georgian Bay island labelled D-25 by the government bureaucrats that had sold northern properties to the public in the 1950s.

The secret beach he'd found was out of sight and earshot of the newly acquired rustic family cottage on the adjacent D-24, though if a beach required sand, there was none, just the mucky bottom of leaves and vegetation blown in from Georgian Bay.

He'd stripped off, dumping his T-shirt and shorts on top of his underwear, socks and runners, and stepped slowly into the water, trying not to disturb the bottom. Not because he was squeamish, but so he could look for the schools of minnows that would dart about him like copper slivers.

He wasn't called Mac yet. That nickname was reserved for his father. The boy was known by his first name, Iain, which he hated, in part because most people couldn't spell it.

As he was floating on his back, a great blue heron flew low overhead to land nearby. Startled to see the boy, it flapped furiously to gain altitude, its shoulders rotating backwards, then it veered to the right and down the inlet. Feeling the wind from the wings wash over him, he felt more alive than he ever had before. The great bird's belly feathers had been only three or four feet above him, its long legs, feet, and talons thrust down toward him, like brakes, before tucking up as it escaped.

He'd stood up, elated, straining to catch sight of the bird, but it had flown off in search of a solitary place to spear fish. He'd climbed out of the water, walked past his clothes and into the forest. Lying down on a thick bed of star moss that blanketed a gulley between two granite shoulders, he'd put his hands behind his head and looked up at the canopy. He'd inhaled deeply, the smells foreign to his home in Dundurn, the strongest of which were pine and spruce. But there were others he couldn't name or describe, other than to say they smelled sweet and wet. The boy had made himself a quiet promise that MacNeice realized he'd never kept: to spend as much time as it took to record everything he had smelled on that August afternoon.

The sun fell in fragmented glints as the water dried, droplet by droplet, on his skin. Silver came bounding up from the water, shaking himself and showering the flinching boy before lying down next to him to chew on a fallen branch.

He'd listened to the calls of grey gulls passing overhead, to the chatter of a red squirrel somewhere nearby, to Silver's happy groans as he munched on the stick, and slowly his breathing relaxed and he fell asleep.

Over the rest of that summer, he'd gone back to his beach, hoping the heron would return, and though he would see many herons, none ever again came so close.

The reverie led him directly to the last time he'd visited his secret beach, with Kate. They'd skinny-dipped and then made love on the bed of star moss. The sudden thought of his late wife was enough to break the reverie. MacNeice was back at the bar at Marcello's with the remains of pesto pasta in front of him, and visions of a woman frozen in the ice. He shoved the plate aside and picked up *Montaigne's Essays*, a book of Kate's he'd taken off the shelf before coming to dinner. She'd read it twice in the two years before she died. Perhaps that was why it was something he'd always found an excuse not to read.

"Detective MacNeice?"

MacNeice looked up at a woman with black hair and black-framed glasses that encouraged you to focus on her deep brown eyes.

"I am." He glanced at his book, closing it with an index finger to mark the page.

"I thought so." She sat down on the stool beside him, holding up her empty wineglass to signal Marcello.

She was wearing a dark blue suit and a satin blouse the colour of butter. It was open at the neck, where a pearl teardrop hung on a fine chain. Her fingers were long and slender—no rings—and the natural nail polish looked fresh, driving his thoughts back to the fingernails of the dead woman.

"Samantha Stewart—everybody calls me Sam." She looked at him expectantly, and when he didn't react, she said, "You were my first interview out of journalism school. You had arrested a young man suspected of killing his girlfriend and their baby."

He recalled the case. The man's name was Anthony Billingsworth—*angry Tony*. His father took the stand on his behalf and kept repeating, "Anthony's a good son, Anthony's a good son." But the more he said it, the less it appeared that even he believed it. Tony had crushed his girlfriend's skull with a baseball bat and drowned his three-month-old baby in a kitchen sink full of dirty dishes. Though he finally confessed, he never explained why he did it.

The boy and his dog were well and truly gone.

"I remember the case, but I'm sorry, I don't..."

"I wouldn't expect you to. Your wife had died only a month or two before we met, then I left for a job at the *Chicago Sun-Times*."

"Ah, and now?"

"I've moved back home and I'm freelancing. Newspapers have hit hard times." Marcello put down a glass of white wine in front of her and, turning to MacNeice, said, "Grappa?"

MacNeice nodded. "You could freelance anywhere. Why come back to Dundurn?"

"Boy, you still cut to the chase." She smiled at him briefly. "It's cheaper and safer than Chicago."

"That's true."

She retreated to the Billingsworth case. She reminded

him that he'd noticed something about the way Tony looked whenever he spoke about his girlfriend.

And he had: angry Tony was trying to convince everyone that he was desperate to find the killer because he'd failed to protect his family. MacNeice finished his grappa. "Once, Tony said almost in passing that the baby wasn't his— though that was not in doubt. He was insanely jealous and convinced himself that he wasn't the father. After he was convicted, he killed himself in prison a year later by shoving toilet paper down his throat and up his nostrils."

"I didn't know that was possible."

MacNeice pushed the glass away. "It is if you're determined. He was determined." An awkward silence descended and MacNeice signalled for the check.

All at once, Sam said, "So I was engaged, the relationship went sour, my dad had a heart attack back here, and I decided it was time to come home." She'd kept her eyes on the bar, but now she said, "You're studying me." And he was.

"Sorry."

"Well . . . ?"

"You mean, what conclusions am I drawing?"

She nodded, but there was no trace of a smile.

"I'd just wondered why you weren't telling me why you really moved home. Now I know."

BACK AT HIS stone cottage, MacNeice poured himself another short grappa, then went to stand at the window. Outside, the forest was still stuck in winter. The remaining mounds of snow were hugging the tree trunks—iridescent blue in the deep twilight. His thoughts returned to the encounter at Marcello's. Since Kate had died, he'd had thousands of conversations with women—often, but not always, through police work. The closest he'd come to feeling attraction had been with Fiza and that had very nearly spun out of control.

He chuckled briefly, looking out at the web of branches caught in the light spill from his window, surprised that Samantha Stewart occupied his thoughts. He emptied the glass, tucked it into the dishwasher, out of sight, and went to bed. His thoughts drifted, never landing—the benefit of grappa—and he sank into sleep.

[4]

WHAT ARE YOU PECKING AT IN MY GARDEN?

"To be honest, I have no idea. Seeds, I think," the bird said under its breath.

I've never seen you here before. I know you see me, as I see you—I think I made you nervous but I didn't mean to.

"Nervous? No, you don't make me nervous."

Sleek, chimney-smoke grey, the size of a robin—minus the orange pot-belly—a narrow black beak; engineered for speed, and yet here you are pecking away in my garden. Possibly you recognize, in that birdbrain of yours, a kindred spirit.

He picked up *Birds of North America* and found the entry for gray catbird: plain dark grey with a black cap and a long, black tail, often cocked, *Dumetella carolinensis*.

The book says you're a singer, a mimic thrush from the family Mimidae.

"You look sad," the catbird said. "There's something you hang on to, or can't let go of."

If I were ever to wonder about the moment when it all came unstuck, it might be when I started talking to a bird.

"I know. It's not easy for me either." The catbird tilted its head and hopped under a bush. When it came back, it turned in his direction. "If I could lick my lips, I would. A young grub is the sweetest."

I'm sure.

"But, back to you: something has caved inside of you. What was it?" The catbird suddenly appeared on the top of the chair across from him. It stretched its head toward him and hopped onto the table, stopping beside the grappa bottle. "Ah, I see."

What do you see?

"This." It turned its head toward the bottle. "Instead of dulling the pain, it drops the veil and turns you inside out."

Would you like to try some?

"Just a drop."

He poured a little from his glass onto the white metal table. The catbird hopped close. Bending forward, it tilted its head to look closely at the liquid.

"It's not water."

No.

"It smells strong." The catbird snapped its head down to the grappa, tapping the tiny puddle, hitting the metal surface, then swiftly lifting its head and shaking it furiously before fluttering its wings.

More?

"Absolutely not."

Tell me about yourself, your life. I've always wondered about a bird's life.

"You have?" The bird lifted a wing, nipping and grooming the wingpit.

Always. As a kid, I thought if I could come back, you know, after I died, it would be great to come back as a raven.

"Smart birds, but nasty bastards—you can't trust them." The catbird fluffed its wings before setting down on the surface, letting the metal cool its belly.

Tell me about flying.

"Aw, now you've hit the one thing I really love to do, especially on a windy day like today." The catbird swayed as it spoke. "You soar and glide, climb and dive with such ease."

I'd love to feel that.

"You could . . . any time." The bird tilted its head at the empty shot glass. "But you need to leave sorrow on the ground. Have you ever seen a bird, a swallow or even those filthy gulls, flying sorrowfully?"

No.

"It's not possible. Joy and sorrow don't fly together. You stink of sorrow. You're sinking into yourself."

Really?

"But if you trust me, I'll show you how." The bird flew low to the side of the stone cottage, where it landed on a branch and waited. "Coming?"

I'm coming, I'm coming.

He got up from the chair and realized he was unsteady. He had to hold on to the table for a moment, then he walked over to the bird.

The catbird hopped onto his shoulder. "Okay, out to the driveway. It'll be easier if we go up the mountain first to catch the draft."

Are you sure I can do this?

"You will fly away from sorrow right now. I don't care what happened, I don't care how long you've been suffering—life is too short to spend it feeling sorry for yourself."

I don't think of it like that.

"No, you think sacrificing your happiness is noble, an answer to loss or to the fact you were incapable of stopping loss from happening. You know what the answer to loss is?"

No.

"Fucking flying. Flying so high and fast, so wildly, so this way and that," the catbird did a shimmy with its shoulders, digging needlelike talons into his shoulder, "so free that you laugh out loud with the joy of it."

Tell me what I have to do. And I didn't know birds could swear.

"Right . . . but you accept that I speak English. Okay, lean forward and lift your legs."

I'll fall on my face.

"If you say so. I say you'll fly and we'll sail up across this road, then down the mountain and back again. Think about it: You're already having a conversation with a bird, so how much harm could there be in trying?"

Leaning forward, he lifted one leg, then the other, and to his surprise he didn't fall. He didn't fly exactly; he was just bobbing a few feet in the air like a tethered balloon. The catbird was laughing hard, hovering just above his shoulder. Its eye—a glossy black bead of polished granite—reflected the trees and sky.

"Technically, we're not flying yet. And actually, what we're doing is harder, so let's go."

Do I flap my wings—my arms, I mean?

"You're not doing that now, so no. You can use them to change direction, but you don't have to work at it. Trust me, half of flying is simply believing you can."

But you're a bird, he thought, and then he lifted higher and moved effortlessly forward. As the bird sheered to the right, gliding over the trees and sliding down the mountain, he followed—fast. He started to laugh and was soon laughing so hard the tears were streaming from his eyes. Ahead of him, the catbird was laughing too. He was surprised at how lush the forest was and how, from this height, he could see the breezes sweeping off the mountain, making the treetops dance. The bird shifted its shoulders and in a second was flying just to the left of his face. It kept looking over at him; he kept looking back.

"You see, you're flying. You know what else? Your eyes are bright, that sadness that filled them is gone, your cheeks are rosy, and when you're not laughing, you're smiling. This is what being alive is. Before this, you were breathing, but I wouldn't have said you were alive. It's important to know the difference."

I do! I do.

The catbird had disappeared; the lesson was over.

He found himself cloud high, but then the earth appeared to be reeling him in like an exhausted trout. He raised his knees and pushed out, hoping that would change his direction, but he was dropping faster now. He may as well have been falling from a tall building. Below him, people were pointing upward and screaming; those closest to the monument started running, trying to get clear of the human missile before it smashed into them or splashed into the stone.

The last thing he recalled was the sweet smell of chocolate-mint ice cream.

[5]

AS VICTORIAN PARKS GO, GAGE PARK WAS MUCH GRANDER THAN A factory town deserved. But then, such was the optimism of Dundurn's early industrialists. If the citizens were inspired to dress up for Sunday promenades, the park had served its purpose in bringing at least a pretense of civility to the city. Even now, in late spring, summer and early fall, young brides and grooms gathered with their wedding parties in Gage Park to record their happy day. The grounds had faded, but the place had its fine points; the fountain and the band shell still stood for something.

But on this morning in March, with a frost blanket on the grass, James "Salty" Conner, a one-time worker with Streets and Sanitation, lay under a pine tree on the east side of the grand promenade. Beneath him were three layers of

corrugated cardboard, and he was tucked inside a dark green
sleeping bag donated by the Catholic hostel. It had been
given to him once the staff had accepted that Salty felt safer
living rough than bunking in God's dormitory, surrounded
by drug addicts and alcoholics.

It would be at least another hour before the sun came up,
but Salty had learned to be a light sleeper, and the sound of
a squeaky wheel was all it took to wake him. He fumbled
in his pants pocket to find the jackknife with the worn picture of a Mountie on its handle. He opened the blade and
waited. The squeaking grew louder and Salty worried that
the cough he'd been fighting all week would give him away.
He fought the cough down, rolled over and peeked out from
his refuge at the level of a mouse.

On a path four feet away, he saw the legs of a man appear.
Salty held his breath, fearful his exhalations could be seen.
The intruder stepped off the path and walked across the
frosted lawn, towing a red wagon with wooden side pan-
els, a large bag strapped to the wagon. Salty eased up on
an elbow for a better view. He found it odd that someone
from the street would use a kid's wagon when a shopping
cart could hold so much more stuff. He squinted, trying to
make out the man pulling the wagon, but it was too dark
and what he could see unnerved him. The man seemed
to be looking about, making sure that he was alone. He
stopped the wagon, dropped the long black handle, adjusted
the bundle and walked off through the trees toward Gage
Avenue.

Like most men living rough, Salty protected what little
real estate and valuables he could claim. Why would this
guy dump the wagon here? If the man's bundle was garbage,
why bring it into the park—you could just abandon it on

Main Street and nobody would care. Salty closed the knife but kept it in his hand. He'd wait awhile to make sure the man wasn't coming back, and then he'd go see what was in the bundle.

Though he hadn't intended to fall asleep, he did. Waking up in the daylight to the chatter of sparrows perched in the tree above him, Salty took the taped-together wire-rimmed glasses from his coat pocket and peered again at the wagon. In the dawn light, the cargo looked silver.

Maybe aluminum coils, like the ones they used for exhaust ducts, Salty thought. They're light enough that you can jump on them till they're flat, then sell them for scrap. He studied the opposite treeline and up and down the wide lawn for any movement. The frost was already melting, but Salty could still see his breath. He stood up and took a long theatrical stretch, just in case someone was watching. He pulled off his toque, rubbed his scalp, and scratched the thin white hair at the back of his head. Then he leaned down to fold up his sleeping bag to keep it dry inside.

He approached the wagon slowly. When he was within twenty feet, he ruled out the idea of aluminum coils, but he still couldn't make out what was in the wagon. He veered to get a look from the side. Sunlight was breaking through the trees to the east and from that angle, the wagon's load made no more sense than it had from behind. Maintaining his distance, Salty shielded his eyes from the sun. As the bundle emerged from the glare, it moved.

Salty jumped back, letting out a deep gravelly yell. The bundle was still. He stepped forward slowly until he was eight feet from the wagon. Putting on his glasses, he bent over from the hip to get lower than the breaking sun and studied the huge silver lump.

The silver was duct tape, encasing a person. What little flesh he could see appeared in narrow slivers. The eyes and nostrils had been left clear. The eyes blinked and opened wide; the body jerked slightly but couldn't move enough to scare off a fly.

Salty stepped closer. There were tears falling from the eyes and cascading down the duct tape, pooling on the edges of the tape. Salty knew fear when he saw it, but this was something worse. He coughed to clear his early morning rasp and raised a hand. "Okay, mister, okay; I'm gonna get somebody — just wait." He nodded several times before turning and setting off at a half-trot toward Main Street. Salty stopped, hesitated and ran over to his sleeping bag. Picking it up, he unzipped it and hurried back to the wagon, where he draped it over the body. He leaned over in front of the eyes. "That'll get ya warm. Okay, I'll go get help."

When he reached Main Street, Salty waved down a passing cab and told the driver to call for an ambulance and the police. The driver looked at him suspiciously but made the call to his dispatcher before driving off. Salty paced back and forth on the sidewalk as he waited.

Within five minutes a Dundurn rescue truck came speeding down Main Street. Salty waved it down and before long was confronted by four firefighters, one carrying a large blue bag.

William Doolittle, the crew captain, said, "Good work," to Salty. "You did the right thing. Is that your sleeping bag on top?"

"Yeah, I thought it would keep him warm. I don't think he has any clothes on."

"Okay, we'll get it for you. For now, just stand off to the side. Understood?"

"Sure, I understand. I'm broke but I ain't stupid."

Joe Calleja, one of the firefighters, squatted in front of the wagon so he could look into the eyes of the person inside. "This is not cool, man. As practical jokes go, this one's freaky-fubar." He turned to the men standing behind him, their helmets pushed back on their foreheads. "Hand me the scissors, the surgical ones in the second pocket."

Doolittle unzipped the med bag and retrieved the scissors. He handed them to Calleja and leaned down to make eye contact with the lump. "The only way to do this is pull it off fast. It's gonna hurt like hell wherever you've got hair, so just think happy thoughts."

The eyes started blinking and the man began to whimper. Doolittle was surprised the man could still breathe, let alone emit any sound.

Doolittle glanced back at the others. "Petravich, get your phone — I want a video of this."

The younger man took out the phone and framed the shot, giving a thumbs up. Doolittle wasn't sure what he would do with the video, but if this turned out to be a prank, it would provide a record for the courts if the guy wanted to press charges.

Calleja looked up at his captain. "Why's he blinking so hard?"

"He's probably telling us to cut the chatter," Doolittle said. "Nice wagon — Roadmaster woody wagon — cool ride. Calleja, get him out of there."

There was vertical banding on his face, but it was obscured behind the dozens of horizontal bands that wrapped around the body. Slices of exposed flesh — purple and swelling — appeared along several narrow slits in the tape. "Man, you are done up tighter than a ... Let's just say it's tight." On his knees, Calleja sat back, resting his butt on his boots.

"What do you need?" Doolittle asked.

"A knife. I have to get an opening in this thing before I can use these scissors."

Doolittle handed him a folding knife.

Calleja tapped the space between the face and the top of the knees; he heard a hollow sound and pushed the tip of the knife in and cut an opening roughly an inch long. He handed the knife back to Doolittle and picked up his scissors. They could hear sirens approaching from the west.

"Okay, I'm gonna start cutting around your neck first, so you can breathe easier. Then I'll go between your knees. Got it?"

The eyes blinked rapidly and now they all could hear the urgent whimper. "Mmmn, mmmn, mmmn."

"I'll take that as a 'hurry up.' "

"Mmmn, mmmn, mmmn."

From Main Street, two cops came running across the grass, followed by two paramedics shoving a gurney.

Calleja cracked his knuckles, stuck a finger inside the small opening, and widened it before inserting the scissors. With some difficulty, he cut a three-inch horizontal flap. "Christ, there must be four layers of this shit here. There's no way scissors will cut it." Through the slice he could smell ammonia. "Pissed yourself?"

Blink blink.

"No problem, I'd a done that and worse."

He cut a vertical line three inches long, then with both hands on the flaps of the opening, he said, "Okay, this is when you go to your happy place — this is gonna hurt, but I'll be quick."

Rapid fire blinking.

Calleja pulled the flaps outward, hard and fast.

They all heard it. The guy inside the duct tape heard it too. A metallic *clink*.

Doolittle and the guy taped to the wagon were the only ones who knew what the *clink* meant. Doolittle screamed, "Grenade. Get down! Down!"

He grabbed Calleja's shoulders and dragged him several yards away before throwing him face down and flat on the ground. Doolittle pancaked on top of him and covered their heads with his helmet. The others had scattered. The grenade went off with a terrifying blast that sent shrapnel, bone, gut, and flesh as far away as the trees on either side.

As the roar faded, Doolittle rolled off Calleja. "Report. Report. Report — who's hit?"

No one answered for several seconds. Then, from several directions he heard: "I'm hit." "My legs, I'm down." "Me too."

Doolittle slapped Calleja hard on the back. "You okay, brother?"

"Yeah, but my leg…"

"Lemme see."

A shard of the wagon's wood panelling protruded from the back of Calleja's left thigh, just above the knee.

"I need to check on everyone else before I come back to you," Doolittle said. "Don't move."

Two of the wagon's wheels were melted on the axles, the other two were nowhere in sight. The tape now held a stew of guts and what appeared to be lower leg bones. Smouldering shreds of tape and fragments of panelling were everywhere. A black cloud was drifting lazily off to the west.

Standing up, Doolittle saw that a long splinter of panelling had penetrated his left hand. Instinctively, he cupped the hand to reduce the tension. He looked over at the two firefighters who were farthest away from the blast. Both were on their butts. One had a slash on his right cheek that exposed the cheekbone. The other appeared dazed, but there was no sign of blood. "Petravich," he called, "take care of Davis. Bandage that cheek—tight now. Get to it."

One of the cops was face down; the hair on the back of his head was torn away and, with it, part of the skull bone above the right ear. Blood was spilling from that ear. His partner was kneeling, dazed. There were lacerations on the back of his jacket, but he was wearing a Kevlar vest and he seemed to be unhurt.

"You. What's your name?" Doolittle shouted.

"Uh, my name?"

"Your name!"

"Penny...Constable David Penny."

"Okay, get a pressure pack for his head wound from the blue med-bag. When you're done, check with me—got it?"

"Yessir...I mean, yes."

"Tell me your partner's name?"

"Constable Len Szabo."

"Szabo. Good, okay Penny, quickly now." Doolittle wrote *Szabo* on his sleeve with a ballpoint pen.

The paramedics were face down in the grass. The taller one was bleeding badly from the upper back and left shoulder. He was trying to roll over but was too stunned to figure out how. Doolittle knelt by him and told him to stay still, before stepping over to look at the second man. He was unconscious but breathing. Doolittle smacked his cheeks until he came around.

"Name? Gimme your name?"

"I'm okay...I'm okay."

"Didn't ask that. What's your name?"

"Oh yeah . . . Latimer—Jason Latimer."

"Well done. Latimer, you may have a concussion, but right now I need you vertical and working—can you do it?"

"I think so, yeah. What happened anyway?"

"Later. Right now, your buddy needs you. He took some shrapnel. Get your kit open and do what you can—I'll take care of the rest. Can I count on you?"

"Yeah, okay, yeah, I'm up." Latimer wobbled over to the overturned gurney to retrieve the medical bag.

"What's your partner's name?"

"Jimmy, uh, James Tobias, sir."

Doolittle wrote their names next to Szabo's on his sleeve and looked over at Salty, who was sitting on his corrugated cardboard, staring at what was left of the wagon. "You okay, old man?"

He'd already lit a butt. "You owe me a sleeping bag."

Doolittle looked back at the blast site where, along with everything else, the sleeping bag had disintegrated. It was scattered everywhere, pieces smoking on the charred grass or impaled twenty feet up on branches or reduced to dust floating away on the breeze.

"Okay, pal, you got it."

Doolittle listened for sirens. He couldn't hear any yet, but his ears were ringing so much he wasn't sure.

Carefully feeling the palm of his hand, he could detect the point of the splinter just under the skin. On the other side, however, it protruded out between his index and middle fingers for five inches or so. His hand was numb and there was very little bleeding. He took hold of the shaft, took several deep breaths and pulled it so it wasn't pressing on his palm. That opened the entry wound enough that the blood began flowing. Quickly, he moved it back to where it had been. "Now, that hurts," he said out loud.

Doolittle was lightheaded as he made his way back to Calleja. He could hear sirens approaching from several directions; the cavalry was on its way.

Calleja asked, "How's the old guy?"

"He's fine—just pissed off that his sleeping bag's gone." Doolittle was focused again on his hand, where blood was still oozing. "Got this wagon splinter through my hand. I'll need a tet shot, same as you."

Calleja managed a laugh before shifting his hips to get a better look at Doolittle's hand. "That's not wood, Dooey," Calleja said. "That's bone. Definitely a tet job."

Doolittle studied the shard. It looked convincingly like pine or maple, until you studied its porous core.

Calleja eased himself down. "Man, you saved our asses— all our asses."

"Not all our asses, Joe." He was looking at the burnt-out wagon.

"In what, five seconds?" Calleja closed his eyes.

"That's all you get." Studying the bone sticking out of his hand, Doolittle said, "It's weird though. Three tours in Afghanistan, where I could have been blown away every day and wasn't. Then I come to Gage Park and this happens."

He looked up to see three cruisers bouncing over the grass, followed by four ambulances. From the east, a hazmat truck tore through an opening in the trees and slid to a halt on the wet grass, thirty feet from the wagon.

"Dooey, remember when he was blinking—remember that?—and those groans?"

"Yeah."

"He was trying to warn us." Calleja's mouth was quivering, either from shock or grief. "If I'd cut an opening for his mouth first . . . That's why he was crying, Dooey. He knew it was gonna blow."

[6]

T WAS 8:12 A.M. WHEN THE DUTY SERGEANT RANG HOMICIDE. VERTESI took the call. Aziz swung around to read the look on his face, which was dark and getting darker. He held the phone away, covering the mouthpiece. "Explosion in Gage Park, one dead, several injured, our guys included."

She looked at MacNeice, who had been busy packing a briefcase with the warrant and a portable recorder for the Block and Tackle Bar.

Vertesi put the phone down. "This is weird. We've got a guy on a kid's woody wagon, all wrapped up in duct tape. The firefighters were cutting him out of it when they triggered a grenade." The surviving casualties were either at St. Joe's or Dundurn General—no word on their status. Vertesi added that there was an old homeless guy who saw the whole thing from under the tree where he was bunking. "He's unhurt and on his way here for an interview, 'and breakfast,' downstairs."

MacNeice snapped the briefcase shut and looked down at the fine scratches on its worn surface. He recalled the moment Kate gave it to him. She thought it was what a newly minted detective needed. He was grateful but couldn't imagine ever using it. Now, years later, it was a through line to the countless scenes of shattered lives. "Michael, get over to St. Joe's—they'll have the walking wounded there. Interview anyone who's conscious. After that, start doing door-to-doors along Gage Avenue to see if anyone saw something suspicious before or after the blast. Fiza, find out what you can from the old man. I'll go down to Gage Park before I hit the Block and Tackle."

Vertesi grabbed his coat, slapped the top of his cubicle divider and ran off toward the stairs.

"I'm off too," Aziz said. Notepad in hand, she turned and was gone.

Ryan had swung around on his chair to watch them leave. As if sensing panic, the lights on several of his machines were blinking blue and green behind him. He turned to MacNeice, who gave him a grim smile and said the first thing he could think of: "Protect the groove, son. It's going to get weird." He threw his coat over his shoulder and disappeared down the corridor, clutching the scarred briefcase.

YELLOW POLICE TAPE blocked curious citizens from entering the park from Main or Gage Avenue, from the south end past the band shell and anywhere along the eastern boundary. A second ribbon of tape meandered everywhere the shower of wagon, flesh, gut and bone had flown. A dozen Tyvek suits were walking slowly about with large, opaque Ziploc bags, placing little plastic numbers on the grass—a seemingly endless supply of numbers—wherever they found evidence. Pieces of the wagon and fragments of the grenade were numbered and bagged separately from the body matter. Each bag was marked with its corresponding location number in a red or black Sharpie. Red: bio-matter; black: everything else. The red-numbered bags were stacked at the edge of the site, close to the black morgue van. This pile was the size of a toddler and distinguished by the soft sagging of the forms. The stack of black-numbered bags was larger and angular, as if what was inside had resisted.

At the centre of all this activity was a blackened and circular four-foot hollow that resembled the pit from a weekend-long pig roast. Angry streaks of torn grass and soil splayed outward in a starburst for three more yards or so. Anyone who had stayed standing would have been ripped apart by shrapnel. Clearly, the trick wasn't running; it was knowing when to hit the ground. Instinct said to try and outdistance the blast. By the abandoned wads of bloodied gauze, MacNeice could see how far each man had run before he'd been knocked down.

MacNeice walked over to where the old man had been sleeping, under a tree on the east side of the clearing. Three layers of flattened corrugated box remained, alongside two Styrofoam food containers—presumably empty. MacNeice squatted down and looked across to the black starburst. "Ringside seat."

To his left, he could just see the intersection of two paths. The wagon-puller had a choice there, to go right or left, but instead, he'd pulled the wagon onto the grass. Wheel lines were still visible where his heavy load had dug into the ground. Salty Conner said the man had dropped the wagon's handle and walked off toward Gage. But did he keep walking or take cover somewhere to watch the show?

MacNeice went over to the path. It curved away north before joining another spoke that led to the delta of King and Main Streets. But that's where the man had come from, not where he was going, and there were seven uniforms, heads down, walking slowly toward that corner. MacNeice turned and went the other way. He looked back to the corrugated pad and took several steps to ensure he was in line with the detonation site. To the north, he could see that the wagon-puller had positioned his load on an axis with the east-west path and the promenade that led north to Main Street. The guy likes geometry, MacNeice thought, and walked through the trees on the west side, pausing at another spoke.

He looked in both directions: *think like him*. He turned to see if the epicentre of the explosion was still visible — it was, but barely. Slowly, he walked north, away from the band shell. When he found a clear sightline to the blast site, he realized that if the bomber had stood here he would be in plain sight. He turned and walked south again.

Along the northern edge of the band shell, he found a place where he could see the wagon pit while he remained hidden. Stepping away from the wall, he did a slow pirouette, looking for any sign of roughed-up ground or cigarette butts or even gum wrappers. If his theory was correct, the killer would have been standing there for a long time before the explosion, with no control over when the grenade was triggered. The dirt behind him looked freshly disturbed, and MacNeice noticed something on the back of the band shell wall. He leaned closer, took out his cellphone and framed the image: a happy face with the words "Justice, Finally" written above it.

It could have been there for months, since the last summer music festival. But still, move one foot in either direction and the blackened starburst would disappear. MacNeice jogged back along the path. To the first Tyvek he came across, he said, "Where's your boss? Point him out to me."

Within minutes there was a two-man forensics team at the north end of the band shell, one inspecting the roughed-up dirt, the other dusting the graffiti and the back of the descending shell in the unlikely event that the perp wasn't wearing gloves. MacNeice waited off to the side, where he was certain the man wouldn't have stood.

"Interesting," he heard the one dusting the wall say to his partner.

"What have you found?" MacNeice called.

"The guy who wrote this was wearing gloves, but not leather or wool."

MacNeice stepped closer as the man showed him one of the handprints.

"What am I looking at?"

"I'd say the same synthetic gloves I'm wearing. The wagon handle was too charred to get anything, but we might luck out with a piece of wood from the sides, or even some of the duct tape. If we find the same print, you haven't got the man, but you'll be sure he was here."

"So this is fresh."

"Yes. Going by the width of the palm print, the guy's got big hands. Look here."

MacNeice leaned to get a view of the wall.

"Here's the heel of his right palm—see the width?"

"Yeah, I think so."

The tech held his own palm close to the print and said, "I'm six-one, with fairly big hands, but look at this—he's got an inch on me."

The man on his knees said, "There's a couple of your shoe prints, detective, and the rest of the ground is pretty messed up, like he was shuffling back and forth from the cold or something. Except here—see?"

"What is it?"

"Size twelve, I think...a fresh print."

MacNeice thanked them and walked back out to the path heading south to the Gage entrance to the park. He studied the gravel and dirt pad near a phone box. There was nothing that he could see and the rest of the area was paved. Stepping back onto the path, he considered the possibility that the wagon-puller had headed north after the explosion, but that way he might have walked right into a cop.

The residents bordering the park would soon be heading off to work or errands. MacNeice ran back to the uniformed squad leader and told him that it was important to have officers immediately knocking on doors from Main to Lawrence on the west side of the park and to pay particular attention to the apartment building and houses facing the park's exit at the Cumerland Street intersection. Did anyone see someone exiting the park right after the grenade went off—either a person running away from the explosion, or a big man walking casually away as if nothing at all had happened?

"DI Michael Vertesi from Homicide will be here soon. Have your team coordinate with him."

As MacNeice got back into his car, the skies opened and rain pounded the roof. It was like being inside a snare drum and at first he just sat and listened. The rain would make a mess of the scene and the footprints by the band shell would soon be splattered and gone.

When it let up a little, MacNeice drove slowly up Gage to Lawrence and pulled off the road next to the railway tracks to survey potential escape routes. Everything seemed possible here — east, west or north — if he had a vehicle. He could have climbed the mountain and made his way along the tracks, using the trees for cover. But Cumerland, adjacent to the park entrance, appeared to be the quickest and easiest way out.

As he was turning to head back down to King Street, a deafening thunderclap took MacNeice's breath away and, a moment later, a lightning bolt flashed off to the right, so close that it lit the interior of the car. On the far side of the tracks, a tree exploded and fell, igniting a small fire in the shattered trunk that, for a few minutes, appeared to ignore the rain. Biblical, truly biblical.

He put in a call to the dispatcher to have either the fire department or the railway check the downed tree and eased the Chevy northbound on Gage, heading toward the Block and Tackle Bar. Passing the band shell and crime scene, he could see white tents over several sites with forensics personnel huddling inside.

APPROACHING THE BAR, MacNeice hesitated, then drove north to the waterfront. He parked at Macassa Bay and waited for the rain to run out. When it finally did, he locked the Chevy and walked toward the shore trail. The wind was coming in hard off the bay. It was colder than the day before and the rain that had fallen was already freezing, making it slippery underfoot.

MacNeice fastened his coat buttons and coaxed the scarf higher on his neck. The trail led to a lump of land the city had reclaimed as a waterside park. After it was revealed the infill was toxic and not fit for residential development, the developer avoided a lawsuit by gifting it to the city. From Burlington Heights, it looked like a coyote's head, jaw wide open, howling to the wind. Deserted in winter, the surrounding slips for powerboats and sail were all empty.

A young couple passed him, bundled against the weather. They nodded cheerily in his direction as their tan and white terrier raced along clutching a miniature orange Frisbee in its teeth. MacNeice walked to the end of the coyote's nose, which jutted deep into Dundurn Bay. He squinted against the driving wind, looking out to the spit of land Rivera's police boat had roared around after the body was found. It was a short boat ride away, maybe five minutes, give or take, depending on the weather.

Turning around, MacNeice faced the intersection that led directly to the Block and Tackle Bar.

During the day, Macassa would be the last place you'd bring a dead body for a boat ride, even in December. The pleasure craft that anchored here in the summer were mostly gleaming white fibreglass. Their owners wouldn't risk going deep into Cootes Paradise, because getting that brown gunk off a white hull would be hard work. And the farther you went into Cootes, the more unpredictable, shallow, and weed-infested it became — especially late in the year. Nobody would want to feel the humiliation of being towed out of trouble.

An aluminum boat could do it, though who'd moor a tin boat in a marina of glimmering fibreglass?

MacNeice walked somewhat stiffly over to the coyote's lower mandible, where there was a narrow inlet used for launching boats. Beyond and above it to the west were parked or decommissioned freight cars sitting on the cold, rusty ribs beyond the active lines that connected to Toronto.

Sitting stately and proud on top of it all, on what had been a pristine bay-view lot, was Dundurn Castle.

MacNeice recalled from some long-ago class that it was the castle's owner, Sir Allan MacNab — war hero, rebellion quasher, politician, and railway magnate — who promoted and presumably profited from the railway's development, even though the rail lines put an end to his unimpeded view and severed the family's private access to the bay and the lake beyond. Sir Allan didn't care. He'd simply go up on the roof with his bagpipes to drown out the unearthly clamour of heavy metal below. The fog of steam and coal-black smoke hadn't bothered him either. He was a dedicated champion of progress and captain of industry.

Walking down to the water's edge, MacNeice startled six Canada geese that had taken shelter in the inlet. Flapping frantically, they paddled the water until they were airborne. Banking east, they gained speed and altitude, their honking fading and finally lost in the wind.

"The perfect place to launch," MacNeice said out loud.

Was she alive when they left, pushing off for a romantic tour of the Burlington shore? A romantic tour in late November or December? Stranger things have happened. She most certainly would have been wearing several layers of warm clothes. MacNeice's joints ached as he climbed the bank and walked on the frozen-stiff grass back toward his car.

Strangling a woman in an aluminum boat wouldn't be too difficult. But stripping her, wrapping her in a nylon line tied to a heavy anchor, lifting it and the body over the side, sliding it silently into the water without a loud *kersploosh* — well, that would take considerable strength. Not to mention a cool head free of panic.

If she screamed as someone was passing by? Too risky. She had to have been dead before the boat ride, her neck snapped somewhere else. Night comes early in December. If he'd attacked her in the parking lot, he would appear like any other man stealing kisses in a parked car.

MacNeice climbed into his car and started the heater. His hands were finally thawing when a black Saab with a kayak on the roof pulled in to park. He watched the driver take the kayak from the rack and put it on the frozen grass, then retrieve a life jacket and paddle from the trunk. Not far from him was a concrete dock, but it appeared that he was going to launch from the land. MacNeice turned off the car, put his keys back in his pocket, took the envelope and walked over to him.

Short and fit, the man was wearing a black neoprene body suit with a hood topped off by a Montreal Canadiens toque. As MacNeice approached, he was pulling on a fluorescent green life jacket.

"You appear to know what you're doing, so I won't ask, why go out on such a cold day?"

"It's not so bad today, and I'm used to heavy water. So's the boat."

"What is it exactly?"

"It's a Beaufort sea kayak."

MacNeice explained who he was, then asked, "Can I show you a photo of a woman I'm trying to identify?"

The kayaker was willing but didn't recognize her. When he asked what happened to her, MacNeice told him she died in Cootes Bay the previous November or December. The man shrugged and said—as he slipped on his neoprene gloves—that wasn't water he'd want to die in. MacNeice nodded, returning the photo to the envelope.

MacNeice braced himself against a sudden gust of wind. "Just out of interest, why don't they make those suits in fluorescent yellow?"

"I have no idea. I wouldn't wear one if they did." He lifted the kayak into the water, held it still with his foot and, laying his paddle across the cockpit to stabilize it, he slipped inside, adjusted the vinyl apron's elastic around his waist, making himself one with his boat.

He was about to paddle off when MacNeice called to him, "Do you know where the nearest marine supply store is?"

"Right over there" — he pointed with the paddle — "three blocks east on Burlington, the Dockyards." With a half-dozen strokes, he was out on the bay and turning into the wind, the waves breaking over the bow and sheering off either side before they reached the cockpit.

As MacNeice was getting back into the Chevy, his cellphone rang. He fumbled with near-frozen fingers to retrieve it from his pocket and answered on the fourth ring. It was Ryan. He'd had a call from the overnight surveillance of Byrne's house. He'd left the bar just after midnight, walked home, stayed inside until morning and received no visitors.

"Nothing else?"

"Byrne made one call at 12:18 a.m. A male answered, 'Hello.' Byrne replied, 'Don' call me, I'll find you.' The man responded, 'Yeah,' and hung up. It was over in four seconds, not long enough to trace."

MacNeice had just put the phone down when it rang again. Looking across the bay to the spit of land getting blasted by wind and rain, he picked up.

It was an angry William Byrne. "I was expecting you here at eight."

"I'm on my way," MacNeice said. He punched in Mary Richardson's number, turned away from the view, and eased the Chevy slowly toward the entrance.

"I was going to call you, detective."

"News, I hope."

"There was one small thing." Richardson's voice echoed; she was likely standing next to the morgue table. "I cannot speculate as to the reasons why it was done, but under ultraviolet there appeared to be evidence of tape over her eyes and a wide patch across her mouth halfway to her ears.

"Tape, like duct tape?"

"That would leave a different adhesive residue. This was more likely common packing tape, the kind couriers use. With magnification, we've detected rectangles that suggested the killer used two-inch tape. Where there had been tape, there was no peach fuzz."

MacNeice looked back across the water to Cootes. There were things to reconsider; among them, his initial theory that the killer had arrived by freighter. That one was fading faster than a radio signal on a lonely highway. To begin with, it was impossible to see the steel plants from here, and it was unlikely that anyone disembarking from a ship would know anything about the tiny bay at the other end of Dundurn Bay. To make it more difficult, Cootes was invisible from the southeast. Heavy anchors, exotic knots, tape on the mouth and eyes — somehow it was all too ornate for a merchant seaman.

WILLIAM BYRNE WAS standing on the porch of the old port hotel, smoking a cigarette, when MacNeice came to a stop in front of the bar. As he climbed the stairs, Byrne rubbed the butt out on the railing and flicked it onto the road.

"There's actually a law that deals with littering, Mr. Byrne."

"Then I'm guilty as charged."

MacNeice presented the warrants, one for the November and December registries, another for a search of the premises.

Byrne led him to his office, where he sat down and read both documents carefully. Then he tossed them on the desk and asked MacNeice which he'd like to do first: search the place or look through the registry books. MacNeice took the two black imitation leather books.

"You got September through December there, but I've also added January and February. I hope that's enough. I'd give you March, but I'm using it."

"I'll return them as quickly as possible," MacNeice said, tucking them into the briefcase. "Take me on a tour. If I feel a more thorough search of the premises is necessary, we'll be back."

Byrne retrieved a two-inch ring with a set of keys from the drawer and together they left the office, squeezing past the remaining cases of Guinness. On the left was the kitchen. Its door swung both ways, a circular greasy window keeping the waitresses from pushing through with their orders and whacking someone, mostly Byrne, heading to the office. On the right was a door with a small Private sign. It was the storeroom for the bar and the hotel rooms.

The kitchen was clean and staffed by two men, one in his twenties and the other middle-aged. "Hard workers, from the Philippines," Byrne said. The younger one was dipping healthy portions of haddock in batter while the older one emptied a massive tin of mushy peas into a pot. "Do one thing well, Pa told me, and you'll be a happy man. Fish 'n' chips is what I do well. We don't do burgers or fried chicken—there's plenty a places to find that."

The storeroom contained an industrial washer and dryer for the bed linens and towels, kitchen and bar supplies, a stack of toilet paper, tiny bars of Ivory soap, and extra towels, sheets, blankets, pillows and pillowcases. Like the office, there was no room to spare.

The bar was empty, inhabited only by the sour smell of spilt beer from all the nights before this morning. MacNeice moved into the middle of the space. The washrooms were on either side of the stairs leading to the rooms above. The entry wall featured — what else? — grimy block and tackle, fishnets, framed black and white photos of large trawlers. Several featured docks — somewhere other than Dundurn — where large fish were hung for weight and length with men smiling and smoking pipes, wearing heavy sweaters or rain gear and waving to the camera. The windows that faced the street looked untouched from when they'd been installed in the 1880s.

Byrne watched MacNeice as his eyes took in every detail. He drew the detective' attention back to the end of the bar and the cash register. "I usually keep the registries here the till. It doubles as the check-in counter."

Byrne led the way up the stairs. On the landing there was a heavy door that he said was deadlocked between one and six a.m. The only way out was the fire escape on the south side of the building, and if someone returned after the bar was closed, they'd be locked out of the building until six a.m. "Saves me having an all-night clerk in slow seasons like this and keeps the sleepwalkers from coming down for a drink after I've gone home."

"Not exactly code, Mr. Byrne. I would recommend you have a night clerk if you're going to rent these rooms."

MacNeice turned and opened the washroom door next to the stairs. Shiny painted white walls, a toilet stall, shower and two sinks set into a laminate counter. On the wall was a mirror and, next to it, soap and paper towel dispensers. Both appeared to be empty.

The corner room Byrne wryly referred to as the "Presidential Suite" had a shower stall that was so stained with use and age that it looked like nicotine plastic. Its faucet dripped, hitting the contained aluminum base with a *plit, plit, plit.*

The enamel was all but worn off the sink, and the mirror was so dull you wouldn't bother looking for yourself in it. While cheap to begin with, the double bed was worn out, sagging from its hard life. There was a single night table of worn pine, with burns on the edges and circles from endless bottles. A nice touch for the port flophouse theme was an imitation hurricane lamp on the table, its metal base rusting. The bedcover emphasized a cigarette burn near the thin pillows, and underfoot, the carpeting was prickly and stiff. It reminded MacNeice of walking on the frozen grass at the bay. A pale yellowy green curtain covered the window, casting an uneasy tint across the room.

The room across the hall — with no such lofty designate — had only a sink, a 1950s armoire and an identical bed and night table. The lighting was provided by two four-foot fluorescent tubes behind a dirty acrylic lens. The colour scheme was hospital blue. It was a toss-up as to which room was the more depressing.

"No televisions?"

"There's TV downstairs, and beer, if you catch my drift. We don't have room service."

MacNeice nodded. *Abandon all hope ye who enter here.* He told the barman to carry on, and Byrne swung the key ring theatrically around his index finger to isolate a key. He appeared to be enjoying the tour.

Byrne opened the next door. MacNeice stepped past him into a wall of musty air. The room was fitted out with a double bed and two straight-backed wooden chairs, a metal nightstand, and, overhead, a bare fluorescent tube. A brown curtain was drawn over a small closet. When he pulled it back, he found three shelves with curling paper. Two dead flies lay together on the middle shelf. Byrne brushed them off and they fell to the cracked red and black checkerboard linoleum floor.

"Comfy, eh? I mean, yer here to sleep. It's not a drawing room for receptions."

"Next."

The rest of the rooms were rented. Given how quiet it was, the three tenants were presumably still asleep. Byrne smiled, knocked sharply at the first door and announced, "Police," before turning the key. Startled, an old man in pyjamas sat up and put his glasses on. "Mornin'," he said, as if Byrne and MacNeice standing before him was the most natural thing in the world.

MacNeice asked him how long he'd been rooming at the bar. The old man reached over to a cup on the bedside table, put his hand in and retrieved his dentures. He positioned them and worked his jaw once or twice. "Well, I dunno... What do you think, Billy, three, four months now?"

Byrne shrugged his shoulders. MacNeice turned to the old man again. "So, what's your name?"

"Freddy Dewar."

"When was the last time you had a decent breakfast, Mr. Dewar?"

Freddy looked over his glasses at the detective. "What, you mean like bacon and eggs and hash browns?"

That was exactly what MacNeice meant. "How about you come along with me and you can eat while we chat?"

The old man's face brightened. "Sure. Gimme a few minutes and I'll be right with you."

The other two roomers had awoken when they heard Byrne call, "Police." They were both new to the bar. The first had arrived two days ago. An Italian immigrant in his thirties, he was looking for work as a carpenter. He retrieved his passport and landed immigrant status papers from a heavy corduroy jacket and handed them to MacNeice. The detective made a mental note of the name and handed both back to him.

The last of the roomers stood up shakily as they came through the door. He was a heavy man in his late fifties. His wife had thrown him out of the house the week before because of his drinking.

If there was anything left in the rooms from late November or December, it might be very tired evidence, worn down by disinterest, disinfectants, and stale air.

Byrne walked MacNeice to the front door and out on the porch, where he lit up another cigarette. MacNeice was going to ask the question anyway, but this seemed to be the best time to do it.

"Do you own a boat, Mr. Byrne?"

"What for?"

"You mean, why am I asking, or why would you want a boat?"

"The former."

MacNeice watched Byrne, patiently wondering if the barman would answer, curious to know what he might be thinking.

"I've an old eighteen-foot aluminum boat. In season, it's tied up at the far end of Macassa, far enough away from the yacht club that people won't be embarrassed."

"And where is it now?"

"In the garage beside me house and it stays there till the beginning a May, when I put it in the water to go fishing again." Byrne looked at his watch, snuffed the cigarette against a column and turned to go inside.

"There'll be a unit down here for the boat and a forensics team to do a thorough search of the premises—they'll be as efficient as possible so as not to interrupt your business."

Byrne exhaled dramatically but said nothing.

When he'd gone, MacNeice called Aziz to get the additional warrant to have the boat picked up.

[7]

THE COMMITTED CHICK WAS DEDICATED TO ALL-DAY BREAKFASTS and never-ending coffee. Freddy Dewar read the menu, taking his time over the cartoons of cavorting yellow chicks and photos of the specials. He settled on Chickin-lickin-blues, pancakes with two strips of bacon, maple syrup, and blue-berries—whipped cream on the side—and said yes to the bottomless cup of coffee.

Though it was a lie, MacNeice said he'd already eaten and ordered tea with milk—referencing the chick in a bowler hat with an umbrella tucked under its wing. He pulled a notepad from his briefcase and set a pen down on top of it. "Tell me about your life, Freddy."

"I don't recall ever being asked that question." Dewar smiled. He absent-mindedly ran his fingers over the crease in the paper napkin, and then he started at the beginning. Born in Halifax, Freddy was eighty-four. He joined the merchant marine at fifteen, surviving the war ferrying supplies, equipment and men across the Atlantic. Afterwards, he tried settling down in Halifax, but it didn't take. There was no steady work on land for a stoker. He eventually came west to Dundurn and worked with the city's road crews patching cracks in the summer and spreading sand, and later, salt in the winter. For a few years, he signed on to the lake freighters, but he found working the lakes deadly boring.

Freddy paused as the waitress put the stainless steel teapot and china mug in front of MacNeice. He said he went back to spreading gravel in Dundurn and a year later married Florence — Flo — a girl he'd met at the Woolworth's lunch counter. She worked next door in the lingerie department of The Right House. They had a daughter together — Edith.

The waitress slid the plate of pancakes in front of Dewar and filled his cup with coffee.

"Three years ago, almost to the day, Flo died of a heart attack. She was seventy-six. I sold the house on Province Street, including its contents, and moved to Edith's dairy farm near London."

He had his own room at the farm and the food was fine — there was always plenty of it — but there was nothing for him to do. His daughter was a teacher and her husband farmed from sunrise to sunset. They didn't have kids, so he couldn't even babysit. Before the first snow came, he moved back to Dundurn with nothing but a duffle bag and the nest egg of his savings account.

"Why would you live at the Block and Tackle rather than take a small place of your own?"

"I considered it. But I'd have to get furniture — everything from a bed to a lawnmower — and it didn't make sense since

I could be dead in a year or two." The napkin's crease was now crisp; he patted it gently, a job well done. "I stayed at the bar a couple a times when I was working freighters, eh. I like the old guys there, always somethin' to talk about, something to watch on TV, and I'm crazy about Fish 'n' chips. Reminds me of a place in Southampton during the war. That was the best you could hope for: getting there in one piece, then Fish 'n' chips and a pint. Funny eh? Unlucky, and you were fish food; lucky, and you ate good fish . . . Anyways, it's pretty clean, and I've only ever had one thing swiped — my duffle bag. And I don't know why anyone would want that old thing. My name was on it — F. A. Dewar — and stencilled below was "Stoker." The thing has to be sixty years old or more."

"When was the bag stolen?"

"Pearl Harbor Day — last December 7th."

MacNeice watched the old man mop up the remaining syrup and cream with the last section of the pancakes, creating an elegant series of looping blue and gold and white swirls on the plate. Freddy had a steady hand, absent of any tremors of age. When he was done, the waitress came by and scooped up the plate in one hand, pouring Freddy a top-up with the other.

At last, MacNeice produced the photograph of the young woman. Before showing it to Dewar, he told him that she had died violently out on the bay. He said there was a chance, a remote possibility, that she may have had a beer, or fish and chips, or even stayed a night or two at the bar. He laid the photo on the table and waited.

Freddy wiped his mouth with the napkin, adjusted his glasses and looked down at the face.

"She's a goner in this picture?"

MacNeice nodded.

"You been to the bar, detective? I mean when they're serving?"

"I have."

"Well there aren't many women who come in for a beer, let alone dinner. The ones who do are geezers like me and some don't bother putting their teeth in."

"Her face isn't familiar to you then?"

"Oh, I didn't say that. No, I've seen her all right." He tapped the photocopy with a crooked right index finger. "I can't say where . . . but not at the bar. I can tell you the hair's wrong. You've made it straight, eh, and this gal's hair was wavy." He handed the photocopy back to MacNeice.

"Try and recall where you saw her, Freddy, and why you'd remember her at all—especially her hair."

"Oh, that's easy. An early life at sea, eh. The only thing we ever talked about was girls. We had pin-ups taped everywhere." Freddy sat up and said, "Betty Grable, that's it. Her hair was blond and wavy like Grable's."

MacNeice was struck by how animated the old man had become. "Anyways, ever since then, I've liked looking at girls—though not without clothes Our pin-ups always had something on, a bathing costume, a fancy dress . . ."

MacNeice asked again, "Can you recall where you saw this particular young woman?"

Freddy sipped his coffee, taking warmth from the mug, thinking hard, but finally gave up. "I can't."

"Give me an idea of your typical day. Do you go for walks?"

"Oh yeah, I walk everywhere. Over to the main library . . . I can spend a day there. Or down to the water, sometimes the botanical gardens or just along Burlington to see the ships coming and going. Mostly, folks pass you by like you was invisible, eh, and I don't blame them."

AFTER BREAKFAST, MACNEICE dropped Dewar back at the BTB. He wrote his cell number on the back of a card. "You've seen her face, Freddy. When you remember where you saw her, call me right away."

On his way back to the division, MacNeice drove slowly past Byrne's house. A patrol car was already parked in the driveway, facing the street with its engine running. The uniform inside spotted the unmarked Chevy passing slowly and nodded.

[8]

THE NAME APPEARED FOR THE FIRST TIME ON NOVEMBER 14, NOT as a roomer, but scrawled across the spot for Day/Night Clerk, the final box in the column: Duguald—no last name. The entries prior to that had been Byrne, and on December 28, Byrne was back. MacNeice put the name on the white-board under the Block and Tackle Bar.

"Ryan, what's the etymology of *Duguald*? Please tell me it's Irish."

"I'll check." *Click click click* pause . . . *click* pause. "Irish, sir . . . means 'dark stranger.' "

"You're serious?" MacNeice looked up from his desk as the young man spun around in his chair.

"Completely. There are different ways to spell it, but that's what it means. It's Gaelic." Ryan spun back to the computer, where he was searching the missing persons files of several forces, looking for a lead to either the body in the bay or the one blown up in the wagon.

Standing back from the board, MacNeice let his mind wander, flipping the red marker over and around the fingers of his right hand, the way Clint Eastwood would a silver dollar.

Did the name trace back to the Black Irish and the myth surrounding the fate of the Spanish Armada after its catastrophic defeat at Gravesend? Many of the men who survived that battle and its desperate retreat—the long way around the British Isles through gut-wrenching storms—were shipwrecked off Ireland's northwest coast. Most were slaughtered on the beaches, stripped of anything useful and rolled back over the cold stones into the sea. Those not put to death were taken into service as soldiers by the Irish warlords. As the story goes, these men married or otherwise impregnated the fair and freckled girls of Kerry and Antrim. The product of their coupling was born: fair and freckled, dark and fair, or simply dark. Born with them was the story that Black Irish were the descendants of Spaniards that had washed ashore. The myth refuses to die, but then great myths never do.

"Black Irish" may also have been an ancient English slur suggesting the treachery of the Irish. If so, it was a classic case of the pot calling the kettle black. Putting the marker back in the tray, MacNeice cautioned himself not to read too much into the name.

Aziz appeared, espresso in hand, hanging her wet coat over the leading edge of the cubicle.

MacNeice sat down at his desk again. "Tell me, how are the casualties doing?"

"Michael says the paramedic will live, but it could be weeks before the doctors will know if he'll be able to return to work. The damage to his upper arm and shoulder will heal, but a portion of the lung on that side is gone. As for Szabo, the neurosurgeon was able to stop the bleeding and reduce the pressure in his brain. But he's in an induced coma and no one is giving a prognosis. Both these men have young wives. The cop has two small children, a two-year-old girl and a baby boy. The paramedic has only been married a year."

The phone rang. Ryan had taken to wearing a headset and answering the team's phone without having to leave his keyboard. "Boss, it's Forensics calling about a boat."

MacNeice picked up.

"It's Nathan Ho, sir, senior scientist up at the Mount Hope Forensics. Can you tell me what I'm looking for?" Byrne's aluminum boat had been taken to one of the decommissioned RCAF hangars at Dundurn's regional airport.

"DNA — anything female. Hair, pubic hair, clothing, a lost lipstick tube, an eyelash, a fingernail."

"What I can already tell you is that this really is a fishing boat. I've found dozens of small silvery scales and a fair amount of dried slime."

"Is there an anchor?"

"A twenty-pounder. It appears to be old, what fishermen call a bass river anchor. It's attached to a coiled half-inch white rope ... about thirty feet long." MacNeice could hear him walking around the boat, his voice booming in the hangar. "There's another anchor too," Ho said, "but it's not so fancy. It's a makeshift job — an industrial-sized juice can with a heavy-duty galvanized eyelet set in concrete and a similar length of the same rope."

MacNeice asked Ho how long it would take to do a thorough sweep, but Ho was reluctant to promise anything specific. He was about to hang up when he volunteered something else. "The guy that towed it in said it's not local. The numbers on the side are American and the draft is so shallow, it really is meant for bass fishing on a river, not Lake Ontario or even Dundurn Bay. We're checking the registration now."

It wasn't just that a shallow draft boat couldn't make it across the bay in November or December. To dump a body wrapped in a rope with a heavy anchor overboard would take a man much more robust than Byrne. But, when the winds of winter were howling over the water, crossing with three people might have drowned them all. No, MacNeice didn't think Byrne was the prime suspect, but he wasn't ruling out that Byrne knew who was.

When MacNeice turned, Aziz gave him the update on her interview with Salty Conner. She had taken a Google Earth aerial view of the park beyond the promenade and asked the old man to point to where the wagon-puller entered the park and where he went after leaving the wagon. Salty drew the line with his finger from east to west, saying, "Came in this way, left that way." He tapped the paper, indicating south.

"I asked him, 'What makes you think he went south and not north?'" She glanced at her report. "He looked at me like I was a bit batty and said, 'I'm not Buck Rogers, lady, I'm just saying I think he went that way.'" Not knowing who Buck Rogers was, Aziz asked again if he was just guessing. "Salty tapped the south end again and said, 'Because I'd turn that way, 'cause the cops would come up from Main.'"

"Smart man."

Salty had also told Aziz he thought the wagon-puller knew the park, because he didn't hesitate. "He just dropped the handle and kept on going. He knew where he was headed."

MacNeice leaned against his desk, studying the board. He asked Aziz if she had a sense of the wagon-puller yet. Without hesitation, she replied, "A cool-headed man, and calculating. What do you think?"

"I agree with you. Do you think he's done yet?"

Aziz shrugged. "I'm not sure. The killing was so artful that repeating it might prove irresistible — just to show how truly clever he is. Alternatively, if it was about exacting punishment on one individual, there's no reason to worry that it will happen again."

The phone rang. Ryan answered and turned quickly to MacNeice. "It's Vertesi, sir, calling from the door-to-doors."

MacNeice picked up the phone. On the other end, Vertesi raised his voice to be heard over the rain. "Boss, I think we may have something — the apartments at Cumerland and Gage."

MARTHA AND BOB Goode lived in the fourth-floor corner apartment, fronting on Gage Avenue. Retired from a maintenance job at the university, Bob was happy to have the attention of both MacNeice and Vertesi, who stood beside him on the narrow balcony overlooking the park. Though sheltered from the rain, they were getting hit by a bracing spray, like standing too close to Niagara Falls on a windy day.

Goode said, "I was out here, having a smoke — Martha don't allow me to smoke inside. That's when I sees it, like a flash and then a loud bang — jeez, it was loud. All of a sudden this black cloud floats up over the trees. Then I could hear some screaming from somewhere — I don't know where exactly, maybe one of the other apartments. But, like you can see, we're right above that park entrance over there."

He called his wife to come out and see what was happening, but she was in the bathtub and hollered that unless the building was on fire, he should leave her alone.

"I was just about to go inside and give her what for, when I see this guy wearing a long, dark coat and a hat—the kind with the flaps on the ears—pushing an old shopping cart." Goode said he was certain it was old because one of the front wheels was spinning this way and that and it all seemed a bit rusty. MacNeice nodded, and the man carried on. "It was loaded with bags full of stuff—junk, most likely. The guy's waving a hand like he's swatting flies, like he's mad at someone, but there was no one with him. I thought he was one of the mentals—you know, the ones they let out of the hospital in the '90s, so I didn't pay too much attention to him. The park has a lot of nuts—nuts 'n' punks. You don't go in there at night unless you're one a them."

Then he heard the sirens screaming across Main Street and he went in to get Martha out of the bath. He didn't want her to miss the action.

"Did you see which direction he went?" Vertesi asked.

"Yeah, he crossed over to Cumerland, right down there." He pointed to the corner.

MACNEICE AND VERTESI left the building, pulling up their collars against the rain, which was now whipping in gusts like horizontal needles.

MacNeice glanced at the corner. "Let's take a walk down Cumerland."

"Why don't I get the car?"

"We're not going far."

Directly behind the apartment building was a narrow strip of grass that ended at a chain-link fence bordering the

rail line that skirted the mountain. On the other side of the
rail line was an old one-storey red brick building edged so
close to the tracks, there was no fence at all. Behind that
building was a feral clump of trees and shabby undergrowth.
As he walked along the tracks, MacNeice studied the gravel
and stone on either side, avoiding the puddles, looking for
any shoe prints or cart tracks that had survived the rain.

"You think the buggy man's our man and he dumped the
buggy here?"

"Here . . . or the other side of Cumerland. The buggy was
a disguise, and he didn't need it after the park."

They stepped into the clump of trees. There was plenty
of garbage and plastic bags tangled in the groundcover, or
hanging like overripe fruit on bare branches — but there was
no abandoned shopping cart. MacNeice turned around and
started walking back in the direction of Cumerland Street.
Soaked to the skin and more concerned about pneumonia
than crime busting, Vertesi trailed behind.

"If he went this way, he couldn't be seen from the apartments above." MacNeice gestured toward Goode's building. Most people don't study homeless people closely, and
avert their eyes when they act out. It's one of the reasons
the homeless stay homeless.

Crossing Cumerland, they walked the rail line south
behind an old brick factory that had been repurposed into
offices. The loading docks facing the rail line hadn't been
used in twenty years. Everything likely arrived at this
place by FedEx. Fifty feet along, the dirt path beside the
line curved off to the right as the tracks eased left. A few
yards farther, MacNeice spotted a cart shoved roughly into
the bushes. He put his latex gloves on and grabbed the handle, pulling the cart back onto the path. The bags Goode
described were still in the buggy.

"What the hell? How did you know it would be here?" Vertesi said, as he gathered his coat about him and squatted to check the front right wheel. The weld had failed and the wheel was hanging off to the side.

"Our man needed some way to walk out of Gage Park. He knew the grenade explosion would bring people to their windows and porches. A guy that comes running out of that gate would be noticed. But who'd ever think a mentally challenged homeless guy was the bomber? More likely they'd think—if they thought anything about him at all—that he'd been scared off by the blast." MacNeice studied the bags. "Judging by the weight of the cart, you'll find those bags are filled with paper."

MacNeice stepped back, looked along the track to where the path curved the other way. He didn't believe the buggy man went any farther than he needed to. "That path crosses the next street to the west: that's where he parked his car." He pulled his point-and-shoot camera out of the pocket of his coat and took several photographs of the cart. "We'll get these processed and show them to Goode."

Seeing how drenched Vertesi was from two hours of door-to-doors in the rain, he told him to retrieve the Chevy and wait inside the car for the forensics team to arrive. When the young man brought it rumbling in from Cumerland, spitting gravel as it left the asphalt, MacNeice guided him as close to the cart as possible and then walked away, slapping the roof as he passed.

Vertesi rolled down the window. "Where you going, sir?" Vertesi called. Whatever MacNeice said was lost in the rain as he disappeared in the direction of the park.

MACNEICE HEADED FOR the north side of the band shell. Once he got there, he turned around and timed his walk back to the park entrance at the Cumerland intersection. Three minutes, plus or minus thirty seconds. If the buggy man waited to witness the explosion, Goode would have spotted him three minutes later. If he'd lingered, it might have been four or five. MacNeice crossed the street and stood looking up and down Gage Avenue, then glanced up to see Goode waving at him from his balcony.

"What do you think?" Goode called.

"How long after the blast did you see the buggy man come through the gate?"

"Oh . . . jeez." Goode massaged the stubble on his chin while staring down Gage in the direction of the blast site. "It's gotta be, I'm pretty sure, it's gotta be like five minutes or so. Why?"

"Thank you, Mr. Goode. You've been very helpful. Stay dry."

Goode laughed. "Look at me and look at you."

MacNeice smiled at the man. His hair was plastered to his skull. Rain ran down his face and neck, under his scarf and was inching down his back. He could feel it ricocheting off his shoulders, hitting his chin. He waved at the man, then walked back to the Chevy. After he climbed in, he asked, "No one else saw what Goode saw?"

"No. Everyone else seemed to be watching the smoke coming from the explosion. Add to that the sound of emergency vehicles screaming along Main and up Gage . . . Nobody saw him."

MacNeice wiped his face and smoothed his wet hair back. "Salty Conner and Bob Goode are the only ones who actually saw the explosion and the killer."

The Chevy's heater fan was maxed out, forcing Vertesi to raise his voice. "So the buggy man's the wagon-puller."

"I believe so. He was able to stick around to see it happen because he'd planned how to get away unnoticed."

MacNeice's cellphone rang. Aziz.

"Mac, Ryan's found someone who could be the bombing victim. His name is David Crawford Nicholson. He's a high school English teacher at Our Lady of Mercy, out past Kenilworth. He's forty-seven and lives alone with his sixteen-year-old son, Dylan, who reported that his father hadn't been home for two days. The school's VP confirmed Nicholson hasn't shown up for work, didn't call in sick, and his car's sitting in the school's parking lot."

[9]

DYLAN NICHOLSON MET AZIZ AND MacNEICE AT THE DOOR OF HIS home on Tisdale Street South. At sixteen, he was already well over six feet tall, lanky and fit, sporting a curly mop of sandy hair. He was wearing a light grey Indiana sweatshirt, khaki cargo pants and well-worn Converse high-tops. Never certain about teen fashion, MacNeice nonetheless realized that the young man was out of step with his generation, which he found refreshing if only because it suggested a degree of independence.

"You said you guys were from Homicide?" Dylan appeared uncertain as to why they were there. Clearly he wasn't ready to believe anything as horrible as that could have happened to his father.

Aziz said, reassuringly, "We're detectives, Dylan, and we're investigating where your dad might have gone."

Dylan ushered them into a living room of nondescript furniture and comfortably worn brown carpeting. There were sports magazines, mostly basketball, on the heavy wooden coffee table, sharing space with neatly stacked hardcovers. On top, with several flagged pages, was volume one of Winston Churchill's biography, and just below it was a new biography of Lyndon B. Johnson.

Original oil paintings hung on the walls—all landscapes of somewhere else. On the fireplace mantel were two MVP awards for basketball, two medals from the regional championships and, beside them, a photo of a player shot from behind, number nineteen, dunking the ball over the heads of two defenders. He appeared to be floating, his legs relaxed, his free left arm hanging as if he felt no tension, uncertainty, or concern. Given the hair fanning out from the player's head, it had to be Dylan.

MacNeice walked over to the mantel to take a closer look. To the right of the image, almost hidden by the bodies rushing to the net, was the man in the missing persons photo, slightly overweight, barrel-chested and tall. What was left of his hair—mostly on the sides—was bushy and grey.

"That's your dad in the background."

"Yeah, he volunteered as an assistant coach," Dylan said, "even though he'd never seen a basketball game till I started playing."

"Looks like you had no problem making that shot," MacNeice said.

Dylan shook his head, embarrassed. "Well...yeah, it was a good game."

"You're being modest, Dylan. Isn't Mercy the best in the city?"

"Okay, yeah, we are." He pushed his hair away from his eyes. "We've got a great bunch of guys."

"I read the paper, Dylan. I'm told there are division team scouts coming up from the States and talk of a potential full scholarship for you. That must make your father proud."

"Wow, you noticed that? Yeah, sure, he's proud, but he's told me not to get ahead of myself 'cause I have my senior season with the Panthers first."

"Have you got a better photo of your dad you could give us?" Aziz asked.

Dylan told them that he had already given the police a photograph of his dad taken the previous summer in their backyard. His father had organized a barbecue for the team, hoping it would become a pre-season tradition. He shoved his hands into the pouch of his sweatshirt and glanced at MacNeice. "This is totally not like Dad...I mean, he's just a regular dad."

"Where's your mother, Dylan?" Aziz asked.

"She deserted us when I was four. Since then, we haven't heard from her and we don't know where she went." The hurt of her leaving registered briefly on his face. "Dad had to be both parents for me, I guess."

MacNeice was struck by his use of the word *deserted*. It was likely a word he'd been taught, one loaded with his father's bitterness.

"Do you know of anyone..." — Aziz was struggling for words that wouldn't alarm the boy further — "who might have had a dispute with, or grudge against, your father?"

Dylan shook his head. "As far as I know, he has no enemies. He loves teaching. Every day we discuss school on

our way home . . . It's like we're both students at Mercy."
He smiled at the thought of it. "Dad has a wicked sense of
humour. Even though he looks so nerdy, he isn't."

MacNeice heard the front door open, and turned to see
a middle-aged woman closing her umbrella and leaning forward to get a view of the living room. Surprised to see two
strangers, she put down a small paisley bag and stepped into
the living room.

"This is my aunt Doris," Dylan said. "These are police . . .
I'm sorry, I've forgotten your names." Dylan's cheeks flushed
red.

MacNeice offered his hand. "Detective Superintendent
MacNeice, and this is Detective Inspector Fiza Aziz."

"I'm Doris Nicholson. I've come to spend the night, if
necessary. I just don't know what's happened. This is so
utterly out of character for Dave." She took her coat off and
hung it on a hook in the entrance. Turning back to them,
she said, "I've called the local hospitals . . ." Noticing that
Dylan's head was down, Doris looked at both detectives and
shook her head slowly.

Aziz asked her the same question she'd put to the boy.

Doris remained standing near the living room doorway.
"He's just a decent, hard-working man who's had to manage
everything since his wife left him twelve years ago." The
corners of her mouth tightened, then she asked Dylan if he
would take her overnight bag upstairs. As soon as he was out
of earshot, she whispered, "Jenny Grant, Dylan's mom, was
a sweet young thing, and certainly attractive, but I always
thought she was a tramp."

It was an ugly word, but neither of the detectives let their
reaction show. Encouraged, Doris went on. "I have no idea
where she got to, of course, or any details of why she left,

but I know Jenny's parents and brother still blames David for the breakup." She adjusted her dress; Doris wasn't done. "A woman that leaves a child, I mean, I find that despicable."

"Do you have children?" MacNeice asked.

"No, I've never married."

"To be clear, Ms. Nicholson," MacNeice said, "it's your belief that if your brother had any enemies, it would be Jennifer Grant's family?"

"Yes . . . Well, I know they were very angry with David, so much so that he was forced to forbid them from seeing Dylan." Her tone was thick with righteousness.

"Is there a photo of Jennifer Grant that we could borrow?" MacNeice asked.

Surprised, she said, "Why ever would you want one? She's been gone for years."

"Because it might also be something we can help with."

"Well, I don't know about that. David brought the police in back then and they couldn't find her." She shrugged. "Well, David and Jennifer's wedding picture is on Dylan's dresser." Hearing Dylan on the stairs, she turned to him and called, "They want to borrow your parents' wedding picture. Will you fetch it?"

MacNeice winced at the tone of the request, and especially at the word *fetch*.

Dylan had come to the bottom of the stairs. "I'll get it back, though?"

Aziz smiled reassuringly. "Absolutely, and without delay. Thank you, Dylan."

The boy turned and headed back up the stairs.

"Doris, Detective Aziz and I will need to see your brother's room."

"I'll take you up."

"Actually, we need to do this alone. Just direct us to it."

"I see. Well then, it's the first door on the right, upstairs."

The room suggested a man who might be an obsessive-compulsive. Everything was folded, organized, categorized. White, blue, checked, and two Hawaiian shirts hung next to blue, brown, and dark grey trousers. Three suits — blue, black, dark grey — all inexpensive two-button jobs. A rack of ties, stripes and solid colours in the palette of the wardrobe, hung on the inside of the closet door. If David Nicholson had left never expecting to return, his room would still be too tidy. Each drawer of underwear, socks — all black or brown — chinos and jeans, and sweaters were folded precisely. The sense of order struck MacNeice as more boarding school than army. On the dresser were framed photographs of Dylan, mostly happy summer snapshots covering his pre-teens. Dylan paused in the doorway as he was looking at them, then went back downstairs.

Twenty minutes later they emerged with Ziploc bags containing the man's toiletries, shaving kit, brush and comb, toothbrush and nightshirt, which they found tucked neatly under the pillow. It was an XXL burgundy T-shirt with white lettering on the front: "English Teachers Do It Literally."

MacNeice was grateful Dylan didn't ask why they wanted these things, as there was only one answer to give: DNA testing. When Dylan saw them with his dad's T-shirt, he took a deep breath, then told them it was a gift to his father from his last graduating class.

At the door, Dylan handed MacNeice the photograph of his parents on their wedding day, but didn't take his eyes off it.

"We'll take care of this, I promise," MacNeice said as he glanced down at the image. The first thing to strike him was how pretty Jennifer Grant appeared in her wedding gown. David Nicholson was big and blustery, puffed up like a young professor, not in a tuxedo but a donnish dark tweed suit. Dylan's mother was petite, with a round face and reddish hair. There was no veil or elaborate hairstyle. Her smile was wide and open. There was no indication of the approaching disaster of their marriage in either of their faces, but then there seldom is.

"Dylan, we'll also need the spare set of keys to your dad's car. It'll be removed from the school parking lot and searched to see what we can find out." Dylan opened the drawer of an end table and retrieved the keys and handed them over.

As they stepped outside, MacNeice turned back to him. "You said that you and your father drive home from school together every day?"

"Yeah, even from practice, since he became an assistant coach."

"Any ideas why his car is still in the lot?"

"I thought that was weird. We came home together, just like always, and had dinner. I just assumed he went back to Mercy after I was asleep, or he had an early morning meeting he didn't tell me about . . . " Dylan hesitated. "But, for sure, he would've left me a note. Dad's a big-time note guy."

"Is there a notebook of his in the house, a journal perhaps?"

"No . . . Dad writes on anything he gets his hands on. One time, he wrote the grocery list on the back of a parking ticket." Dylan shook his head.

Aziz said goodbye and headed down the stairs. MacNeice shook Dylan's hand. He tucked the wedding picture under his coat and walked quickly through the rain to the Chevy. Once inside, he handed the photograph to Aziz and looked back to the house. Dylan was still at the door, but when MacNeice nodded in his direction, he closed it.

"I've got a very bad feeling about this," MacNeice said, turning on the engine and the windshield wipers.

VERTESI WAS WAITING for them at Division. "The buggy handle has been checked, and there were no fingerprints, boss. And the bags? Like you thought: full of paper, two weeks of *The Standard*; again, with no prints."

MacNeice wasn't surprised. Why would the buggy man go to those lengths and leave any traces of his identity? He looked at the whiteboard, sighed quietly, then turned and watched as Aziz put the Ziplocs and the framed photograph on the desk.

She said, "I'll get these items down to Forensics. Get a comparative DNA check with what was left of the man in the wagon."

MacNeice nodded, then handed the photograph to Ryan. "Meet Jennifer and David Nicholson on their wedding day, roughly twenty years ago. Copy the image, and please be careful to put the original back in the frame. It may be all the son has left of his mother. Four years after they were married, Jennifer disappeared and no one has heard from her since. The cops were involved in tracking her, but nothing came of it."

Ryan took the photo. "I can try to trace her, boss. I've got a program that will age her wedding photo to show us what she might look like now."

IT WAS PAST nine when MacNeice finally said good night. He was too tired to make the trek to Marcello's and decided instead to throw some pasta together with Mrs. Provenzano's sauce, followed by a grappa — or two — before bed.

He was just finishing dinner when he thought, again, of Dylan. MacNeice couldn't shake the feeling that body in the wagon was David Nicholson's, though he hadn't a clue why anyone would kill the man. If Dylan's father was dead, would his aunt be willing to move in, or take him to live with her? Was there someone else in the family who would adopt him? As he twirled the last of the spaghetti through the sauce in slow figure eights, he made a mental note to inquire, discreetly. Otherwise Dylan would be sent to live in a foster home until he was eighteen. Having lost his mother to desertion, and his father to a grisly murder, would his choice be to live with a frosty "fetch this" aunt, or with maternal grandparents he hadn't seen in years, or with foster parents — total strangers?

MacNeice rinsed the dish and cutlery, the pot and pan, then put them in the dishwasher with those from the day before and the day before that. As he put the container of grated Parmesan back in the fridge, Dylan was still in his thoughts. Where had his mother gone and why? And why she'd never reached out to him? The woman in the wedding photo didn't look like someone who'd desert a child. And why would she also abandon her parents and brother?

From his small collection of fine grappas, MacNeice chose a Nonino so rare that he rarely gave himself the pleasure of it. Barely a glass gone in the many months since Marcello gave it to him for his birthday. Bottle and glass in hand, he went to the living room to watch the rain as it lashed furiously at the window. The branches of the trees beyond were waving frantically, like they'd just witnessed something horrific and were desperate to tell someone.

[10]

AT 8:40 THE NEXT MORNING, THE MANAGER OF DOCKYARDS MARINE Supply called for DS MacNeice. The clerk who handled the purchase of an anchor in late November was back at work following a bout of pneumonia. With Aziz and Vertesi off doing interviews with the teachers and staff at Mercy High, MacNeice went alone. The clerk was easy to find; he was coughing and swearing among the racks of equipment.

His name was Jamie Corbeau, and MacNeice was able to avoid a handshake because the clerk was on his knees, stocking the shelves with small, shiny outboard propellers. When he'd finished, he led MacNeice back to his "office," a corner of the loading dock with two chairs.

"I understand that you recall selling an anchor and some nylon line in late November, early December?"

"Yessir. But it wasn't one, it was two anchors."

"To the same customer?"

"Yep. I remember, see, because this guy first tells me he wants an anchor for a small skiff. I asked him to define 'skiff' and turns out he's talking an eighteen-foot aluminum flat-bottom runabout. I show him some eleven-pound pieces, but he's going for weight. I explain to him he doesn't need weight for a small boat, but he says, 'Oh yeah, I do.' He wanted two sixty-six-pound galvanized claw anchors fit for a boat at least sixty-foot long."

But a sale is a sale, Corbeau said, and this was pick-n-go stuff at the end of the season, so he wasn't about to argue, especially since those two heavyweights had been on the inventory for years. The customer paid cash and left with an anchor in each hand and a bag of nylon line under his arm.

"Do you remember what he looked like?"

"Not really."

"Did he have an accent?"

Corbeau scratched his head and closed one eye to suggest he was thinking real hard. "Yeah," he said at last. "He did. I'm no good at accents, but maybe English or somethin'. And he was big, like you but thick, like a wrestler—you follow me?"

MacNeice sat in the Chevy afterwards, looking out to the waterfront's rusting behemoths, the industrial hulks that once were alive with thousands of men making tractors and combines. The second anchor presented a problem. He punched in Wallace's number. When the deputy chief picked up, MacNeice told him he needed a dredging unit for the small bay in Cootes Paradise. The sound pressure on the line changed, like Wallace was holding the phone away from his ear and looking hard at the receiver. Then he went on a tear about how there was no wiggle room in the department's budget. MacNeice waited for him to finish — waited until Wallace finally asked, "You've got a serious hunch there's another body down there?"

"I do."

"If you don't find a body, for your sake I hope you find sunken treasure."

PULLING INTO THE division parking lot, MacNeice was surprised to see DS John Swetsky and DI Montile Williams getting out of Swetsky's car. They had been partnered up with the OPP on a double homicide on the edge of Dundurn's jurisdiction. All killings are senseless, but the slaying of an elderly couple out on Mud Street had set a new record for dumb. Two brothers, who lived nearby, showed up late to the couple's garage sale. The objective: stealing the cash from the sale, which amounted to about twenty dollars. The murder weapon: a nine iron from an ancient set of golf clubs that nobody had wanted.

MacNeice turned off the ignition and was about to open the door when Swetsky opened it for him. Startled, he said, "John, what brings you two back to town?"

Swetsky stuck out his hand and hoisted MacNeice out of the Chevy. "Came back to see the wife, have a decent meal and grab some clean clothes." Williams stood behind him, a large duffle bag slung over his shoulder.

"But we've also been watching the news, so we thought you could use another hand," Williams said.

"They'll let you go?"

"We've got one kid in custody, and the other is on the run," Swetsky said. "I can wrap it up over the next couple a days."

Williams shook Swetsky's hand and headed for the division entrance. Swetsky said, "You've got Montile now, and I'll pitch in soon as I can, Mac."

"Do you have a line on where the kid is?" MacNeice asked.

"His dad says he's trying to make it to Tijuana. There's a record of him crossing into the States at Fort Erie an hour after the killings, so he's got a good sixteen hours on us. His photo and a description of the vehicle are on every patrol car from here to Mexico."

Swetsky gave MacNeice a goodbye slap on the shoulder and walked off to his car.

"Be careful, John," MacNeice called after him.

MACNEICE UPDATED THE whiteboard, then stood staring at the woman from Cootes, the wedding photo, and the barbecue shot of Nicholson in a Hawaiian shirt as if the images would speak to him. At last he put the marker in the tray and turned to Ryan.

"Keep searching for Jennifer Grant, but first track down members of her family." And, because MacNeice knew he always underestimated how fast Ryan was with his array of computers and blinking boxes, he added, "Also, scan the incoming inquiries about the Cootes woman from the various police services responding to her photo and description." There had already been three inquiries, all ruled out because the missing women had tattoos. Looking back to the board for guidance and spotting the images of the Gage Park blast site, he said, "Go to the military sources for M67/C13 fragment grenades and see if one's gone missing."

Ryan mumbled a yes, his fingers already flying.

"As for street availability . . ." MacNeice looked at Vertesi. "Get onto the vice and drug unit—see if they'll squeeze their snitches for word about military ordnance that may have changed hands recently."

"On it." Vertesi turned back to his desk.

The phone rang; it was Freddy Dewar calling from a pay phone at the corner of James and Robert. MacNeice put him on speaker.

"I remembered, you know—I told you I would. Well, that young lass, I remember now. She worked at the Royal Dundurn Yacht Club." He said the name slowly, pronouncing each syllable.

MacNeice looked sharply toward Vertesi, who whispered, "No way," and flipped open his book to find the manager's name.

"Freddy, you didn't mention that you were a member of the yacht club."

"Oh my, no. But I walk that way a lot, and yesterday it hit me: She came up to me when I stumbled on a curb and asked if I was okay. After that, since we were both going the same way, I walked her to work. She told me she had a job in the yacht club restaurant."

"Do you recall when this happened?"

"Late November, I figure, because I slipped on some ice."

"There's a Portuguese bakery near you, north side of James, south of Robert. Head over there and order a coffee. We'll be right down."

FREDDY WAS SITTING in the back corner of the restaurant, tucking into a custard tart, when MacNeice and Aziz arrived. Seeing Aziz, he sat up straight and wiped his lips with the napkin.

"What an old fool I am. My memory is as clear as a bell about what happened in the '40s and '50s." His brow furled and the corners of his mouth tucked into the folds of his cheeks. "I don't recall much more than I said on the phone, except she sounded Scandinavian."

"How can you be certain of that?" Aziz asked.

He smiled at her. "Merchant seamen get to know accents. I think she was either Swedish or Norwegian. I'm sorry now that I never asked her."

"Can you remember anything else about her — her demeanour or personality?" MacNeice asked.

"Well, she was very attractive, that much I do remember." He busied himself with folding and refolding the napkin and seemed happy to hear Aziz say the tart looked so good she'd get one for herself. As soon as she left the table, he ate the rest of his and wiped his mouth and chin before laying the napkin neatly over the plate.

"Freddy, does the name Duguald mean anything to you?"

"Well, it's Irish . . ." Freddy pondered.

Aziz returned with a tart, a knife and two napkins. "You're going to share this with me, Mac. I know you haven't eaten." She cut the tart in two, put half in a napkin and pushed it toward him. Then she lifted her half and bit into it, eyes closing the better to savour the taste.

MacNeice turned back to Freddy. "So . . . Duguald?"

"Sure, there was a guy by that name at the Block and Tackle. A night clerk . . . well not much of a night clerk, missing most of the time . . . maybe drunk or asleep somewhere. I don't know. He was a relative of Billy's from the old country."

Aziz set her tart down reluctantly, to take notes.

"So he had an accent?" MacNeice asked.

"It was thicker 'n molasses in January," Freddy said. "And he talked so fast that no one but Billy could understand him."

Aziz was eyeing the second half of the tart. MacNeice slid it toward her without comment.

"Duguald was friendly, though, always joking . . . had an eye for the waitresses, but I never saw anything happen. He was just looking and smiling at them like most of us do, but when an old man smiles at a girl, he's just a harmless old man."

"How old do you think Duguald was?"

"Oh, I'd say maybe mid-thirties. So he had more reason to look at the girls than I did." Anticipating the next question, Freddy added, "And I never seen the girl from the yacht club at the bar either."

"So where did Duguald go when he left the bar?"

"All I recall is Billy saying, 'Duggie had to ship out'—I remember that, you see, because that means somethin' to me—and I asked him somethin' like, 'Duguald's a seaman then?'" He finished his coffee, leaving the question dangling for several seconds. "Billy says, 'Oh, Duggie's bin lots a things.'"

"Tall, short, heavy?"

"Solid. Yeah, I think that best describes him. You know, I never heard his last name or, for that matter, where he came from or where he was going. One day he's there, next he's gone. The place is like that eh, people comin' and goin' all the time. Except for the customers; we're there for the beer or the Fish 'n' chips. As regular as stars at night."

"You're a poet, Mr. Dewar," said Aziz.

Freddy flushed and tapped his fingers on the table like he was playing the piano.

MacNeice offered him cab fare back to the bar, but Freddy said he preferred to walk, as the heavy rain had kept him inside the day before.

"For now, keep this conversation confidential, Freddy," MacNeice said.

"Yes, sir. Loose lips sink ships." He stood, shook their hands, pulled his coat on and waved goodbye to the young waitress.

MacNeice finished his coffee and got up to pay.

"No need," Aziz said. "I paid when I picked up the tart. Worth every penny, too."

[11]

MELODY CHAPMAN USHERED THE TWO DETECTIVES TO HER OFFICE, taking the back route through the kitchen corridor so the yacht club members wouldn't see them. She was a slim woman in her late thirties who smiled easily — but too often. Smartly dressed in a pale blue suit, she waved for them to sit down opposite her desk. The office was modest modern, with touches of the old world that presumably made the clients comfortable. There were photographs and paintings, all of ships Dundurn Harbour hadn't seen for hundreds of years, if ever. MacNeice walked over to study them. The beautifully framed reproductions included a stirring painting of the *Bluenose*, raked over at an angle and tearing south along the east coast.

"Do you know sailing ships, detective?" Melody's name was apt; her voice floated merrily through an octave.

"Sadly, no. But I like to look at them."

"How long have you been manager here at the yacht club?" Aziz asked.

"Five years, and before that I was assistant manager for three." She flicked something invisible from her sleeve.

Aziz retrieved the photocopy from an envelope. "DI Vertesi already presented this photo to you — do you recall?" Aziz waited for Chapman to look at it before setting it down on the envelope.

"Of course I recall," Chapman said. "I told him I didn't recognize her, though I did say she may have been a renter, a boat renter I —"

"Oh my."

Both women turned to look at MacNeice. He seemed captivated by a painting of the British ship HMS *Victory* in 1803 — according to its brass plaque — full sail against a windswept sky, three decks of cannon at the ready, smashing through an impossibly blue sea. "It would be wise for you to look at the photo again, Ms. Chapman." He continued to study the painting.

"I, I don't understand . . ." Melody's hands dropped to her lap.

Aziz tapped the photo in front of her. "Detective Superintendent MacNeice believes you do know her, that she worked here at the yacht club and that you were likely the one who hired her."

MacNeice came back to the desk and sat down beside Aziz. Melody Chapman smiled nervously as he looked at her, expressionless and waiting.

No one said anything for nearly a minute. Melody lowered her eyes to the photocopy and kept them there. Then Aziz said, "Perjury carries significant consequences. If found guilty, the cost to you will be this office, this job and, I suspect, any job remotely like it in the future."

Melody raised her hand in surrender. The lyrical bounce was gone when she spoke. "Her name is Anniken Kallevik. She was a foreign national doing a working tour of Canada. She'd applied for and accepted a position here as wait staff for the restaurant during the summer months only, June 1 to September 21. It's the busiest season for the club." Having gained some control of her voice, she turned her eyes to her hands now folded in front of her. "Anni was going to travel across country and take up a similar post in British Columbia, at Whistler." Melody swung around in her chair and opened a filing cabinet drawer, retrieving a fat folder. Laying it on top of the dead woman's photo, she flipped through until she came to an employment application. She took it out, closed the folder and placed it before Aziz.

MacNeice had turned to stare at the painting, attempting to contain an impatient fury inflamed by hearing that the body from Cootes Bay was known to this woman. "But Ms. Kallevik didn't leave in September, did she?"

"No. Two of our full-time staff quit the club and we were short, so I asked her to stay on and she agreed. Her Whistler resort position wasn't going to begin until December 1, and she was willing to help us out."

Aziz looked up from her notes. "You lied twice about knowing her. Why?"

"I don't know." Melody shifted uncomfortably. "Yes, she worked for us and she was very good, but then she left and I just feel that..."

"You felt like that was the end of your obligation, and that what happened to her afterwards was not your concern nor that of the RDYC—does that about sum it up, Ms. Chapman?" MacNeice said.

Her face flushed, and she looked first to Aziz then back to MacNeice. "Yes."

MacNeice held a hand out for the employment application. Chapman passed it over as if it was burning her fingers. Stapled to the corner was a photocopy of her passport. She was smiling. Unusual to see a smile in a passport photo, he thought. Glancing through the record, he saw that Kallevik was twenty-six and had graduated with a master's degree in biology from the University of Stavanger in 2013. Since then she'd been travelling the world, working in the hospitality industry. Her address in Dundurn was listed as the Global Youth Hostels, a youth hostel on Ferguson near King William.

Melody, who had been watching him, tried to find a good spin on things. "I was trying to save the club from embarrassment. There was nothing we could contribute other than her name, and I thought there was no reason to drag the club into it. Anni was a hard worker, cheerful, always on time and yet, like most temporary staff, she kept to herself."

"Did anyone come calling for her at the end of her shift?" Aziz asked.

"Sometimes a young man, also from Norway. She had been travelling with him. He was working somewhere nearby, but I don't know where."

"You see—there was something else you could contribute," MacNeice said. "What did he look like?"

"He looked like a hockey player, kind of wide shoulders, tall, blond." She couldn't recall anything else about him.

"We'll want to interview any staff that were here during Ms. Kallevik's stay and we may extend that to your members."

"Whatever we can do to help. I'm truly —" Melody stopped when MacNeice abruptly stood up.

He didn't want to hear her apology. He picked up the employment record and photo of Anni Kallevik—previously known only as "the corpse"—and left the office. He crossed the hall and entered the members only area of the club, where he was sure to be noticed before leaving the building.

Aziz found him waiting under the canopy, his hands driven into the pockets of his overcoat, the photo and form tucked under his arm.

Her cellphone rang. She took the call, but the wind was too strong to hear the caller—Vertesi—so she stepped back inside the building, where a middle-aged man told her, "No cellphones in the club, miss."

Aziz pulled the badge off her hip and showed it to him. "Go ahead, Michael," she said as the man backed off.

"The DNA results are back. Nicholson is the man in the wagon."

"Thanks, Michael. We'll go straight to the house." Aziz hung up.

MacNeice had been watching her from outside and held the door for her. "Nicholson's a match," he said.

Abandoned at four by his mother, Dylan Nicholson was now an orphan at sixteen.

[12]

AZIZ WAS ON THE SOFA, NEXT TO DYLAN, WHILE MacNEICE SAT opposite in a chair. The aunt seemed determined to busy herself in the kitchen with making tea, though none had been offered or requested. It was clear that whatever the news was, she didn't want to hear it. Dylan leaned forward, elbows on his knees, like he was waiting for the coach to coach. MacNeice said, "Dylan, your father has been killed. He died in an explosion. We don't know who did this or why, but we'll do our best to find out, I promise you."

The boy took a deep breath to steady himself. "The explosion in Gage Park . . . was that my dad?"

MacNeice said, "Yes."

Dylan nodded several times and turned to Aziz as if he wanted to make sure she'd heard too. She reached out, put a

hand gently on his shoulder. His nodding slowed but didn't
stop. Aziz slid closer and put her arm around him.

At that gesture, perhaps the only time a woman had held
him that tenderly since he was a toddler, he leaned into Aziz.
His mouth opened and a line of spittle fell from the corner.
Dylan wasn't aware of it until it reached his hand. He raised
his arm and wiped the sleeve of the Indiana sweatshirt across
his face, and then, slowly, he pulled the hood over his head.
Moments later, tears spilled down his cheeks. Aziz turned
to MacNeice with tears in her own eyes but stayed put, her
arm around Dylan.

From the kitchen came a muffled shriek. MacNeice went
in to find Dylan's aunt clutching the kitchen counter as the
kettle's whistle blew. He turned off the burner, moved the
kettle to one side and, taking her by the shoulders, led her to
a chair at the kitchen table. He waited until she'd composed
herself enough to look at him.

At last, she said, "So Dave's gone?"

"Dave's gone."

"How, how could this happen... to such a decent man?"

"I will tell you all we know. But first—and I apologize for
being so blunt when this is so brutally fresh for you—my
concern is for that young man in there."

"Dyl...Oh God. Dylan so worships his dad."

Both of them could hear the boy, who was now sobbing.
Aziz's voice was soft and low, trying to comfort him.

Doris was strangling the tea towel.

"Right about now, Ms. Nicholson, Dylan is coming to
grips with the fact that he is alone in this world—just as
his world is opening up to him as a young man. I'm certain
you believe, as his father clearly did, that he's a wonderful
boy with a bright future."

"Oh . . . yes. Dave wants —"

"I'm sorry to interrupt you, Ms. Nicholson, but I want to know if you will adopt him."

"But —"

"Let me finish." He put a hand gently on her arm. "If there is no family willing to take him into their lives, Dylan will go into foster care. Do you understand what I'm saying?"

"Of course, but —"

"I don't know you or your circumstances, but in the next few minutes, it will dawn on him that he could soon be homeless. It's not my place to ask you to do anything, but there is no one else. You are his remaining family on his dad's side."

"I want to do what's right . . ."

MacNeice stood up, went to the counter, poured hot water from the kettle into the waiting mug, soaking the tea bag until the water was dark, then lifting it out and dropping it into the sink. "Do you take milk, sugar?"

"Just milk . . . thank you."

He took the carton of milk from the fridge, poured some into the mug, stirred the tea and put the mug down in front of her. "In a half-hour or so, there'll be a team here from Children's Services. Initially, they'll provide crisis counselling for Dylan, but they'll also want to know who's responsible for him now that his father is gone. If you don't step up, he'll be placed in the care of the Children's Aid. From there he'll go into foster care until he's eighteen. Think about that, please, Doris."

He left her there and went back into the living room, where Dylan was still on the sofa, his hooded head down on his knees, his shoulders trembling. Aziz had a hand on his back.

MacNeice sat quietly, waiting patiently until the boy surfaced. Aziz's eyes never left his.

In time, they heard a car approach outside. MacNeice stood to look out as the dark grey sedan stopped, backed up and parked. Dylan heard the car too. He lifted his head, peering out from the hood, wiping his nose and eyes on his sleeve. He slid the hood back—his face was deep red and his hair looked as if he'd stuck his finger in a live socket.

Aziz removed her hand from his back and rubbed her eyes, as if weary from a long day.

Dylan took three deep breaths, and asked, at last, "What happened to my dad?"

"Your father was bound with tape to a wagon and left in the park." MacNeice spoke softly and slowly. "He couldn't speak or move. Emergency Services arrived and tried to free him. What they didn't know, and your dad couldn't tell them, was that there was a grenade rigged to the tape. When they tried to free him, the grenade blew up."

The boy seemed stunned by what he was hearing, but he didn't dissolve into tears. He took a long, deep breath and asked, "Why would someone do something so cruel to someone who never harmed anybody?"

"That's what we will find out, Dylan."

They could hear footsteps on the front porch stairs now. Dylan looked from MacNeice to Aziz.

"That's Children's Services, Dylan. They're here to help," Aziz said.

"What am I supposed to do now? Can I go on living here?"

"If you and your aunt are willing to make this work, then perhaps you will live here, or at her place," MacNeice said. "Otherwise, you'll be placed in foster care."

"For how long?"

"Until you're eighteen."

The doorbell rang. Aziz got up to answer it.

MacNeice put up a hand. "Ask them to wait for a couple of minutes."

It was as if Dylan had been slapped awake. "Can I still be on the Panthers, have my friends . . . my teammates?"

The doorbell rang again. Aziz answered, but stepped outside, closing the door gently behind her.

Dylan's aunt came into the living room from the kitchen, turned and went upstairs without saying anything or even looking the boy's way.

Aziz came back, followed by two more strangers who were now a part of Dylan's life. Dylan remained seated, looking fearfully from MacNeice to Aziz before shaking hands with the social workers.

"Dylan, later today there'll be a forensics team here to search the home for any evidence that could aid us in our investigation," MacNeice said. "They'll be as considerate as possible, but they have a job to do. We're leaving now, but you have my card. Call me if you think of anything that will be useful." He glanced toward the social workers, who stood looking down at Dylan with expressions of solemn compassion. Turning to the medals and photograph on the mantel, MacNeice said, "I'd like to come to one of your games."

The boy tilted his head, maybe thinking it was a strange thing to say at such a time. "We're through for the year," he replied. "We practise all the time, but next season starts next November."

"Who's your toughest rival?"

"Oh . . . the Golden Ghosts, for sure. They'd say the same about us too." He seemed to be sitting a little straighter.

"Look for me in the stands when the championships come around again."

"Serious?"

MacNeice reached over and shook Dylan's hand, pulling him onto his feet. "Think about what I said. This will be a very hard time for you — the hardest you've ever experienced." Standing back, he pointed to the photo. "Look for me, I'll be there."

Dylan nodded. "You'll find out who did this to my dad, sir?"

MacNeice said, "We'll do everything we can." Then he said goodbye to the two social workers. He opened the door for Aziz and they stepped outside.

In the car, doing up her seat belt, Aziz looked over at MacNeice. "Well...it staggers me, the things we don't learn at the academy."

"You didn't need to be taught that, detective."

She smiled at him, then turned away to hide her tears.

Before he drove off, MacNeice rolled down the window to see if he could make out what was happening in the living room. Dylan was still on his feet, his head down. The care workers had their backs to the window. There was no sign of the aunt. With his foot on the brake MacNeice put the car in gear and glanced up to the second-storey window. Doris Nicholson was peering down at him from behind the sheers. When she realized he'd seen her, she stepped away.

Aziz blew her nose. "What do you think will happen to him?"

"My guess is he'll be in care by this evening." He took his foot off the brake and eased down Tisdale toward Main, the wipers on the Chevy doing a feeble *fwub, fwub, fwub* against the rain.

[13]

MAcNEICE DROVE SLOWLY THROUGH THE CITY AS IF HE WASN'T sure where to go. They didn't speak, and both seemed distracted by the sound of rain on the roof, by the wipers that couldn't clear the windshield fast enough.

Aziz shifted so she was looking at MacNeice—the one thing in her field of vision that wasn't moving, his brow furrowed and his jaw locked tight. "You okay, Mac?"

He glanced toward her with a brief but unconvincing smile. "I need a bit of a breather." If it weren't for Aziz sitting beside him, MacNeice would have gone for a long walk to let the rain wash over him until all his thoughts were clean or gone.

The rain eased as they zigzagged through the city. "Let's go down to the bay," MacNeice said.

Minutes later, he eased the Chevy into the deserted Macassa Bay parking lot, splashing through shallow puddles before coming to a stop at the bay side. Together, they headed along the trail to the end of the snout, where they looked across the water to Cootes Paradise. They could see smoke from a diesel engine, belching black roses above the trees before the wind swept them away to the west. The enormous barge was carefully combing the small bay's bottom, like a gorilla attempting to lift a tiny flower from a pond.

"I hope they don't find Anni's tall Norwegian friend," Aziz said.

From somewhere in the train yard to their left came the colliding ripple of shunting cars. Then the mist turned to rain again and they both jogged back to the car.

Safely inside, MacNeice turned the key, saying, "Let's go see what Byrne has to say about Duguald."

AZIZ REMOVED THE hotel booking records from a large manila envelope, placing the originals on William Byrne's desk. She sat down with a bull-clipped photocopy of the ledger on her lap. Byrne sucked on his teeth, shrugged and looked over at MacNeice.

MacNeice tapped the cover of the top ledger before sitting down. "Who is Duguald, Mr. Byrne? Where is he from, what's his relationship to you, when did he leave Dundurn, where did he go and how did he get there — and if he didn't leave, where might we find him now?"

"Duguald Langan. County Meath, not far from Dublin. Duggie's my second cousin. As to the rest, I haven't the foggiest. Why, what's he accused of doing and, while I'm at it, what's become of me boat?"

"Langan is listed as your night clerk from November to late December—he's a person of interest." MacNeice let his eyes wander over the desk. "Your boat will be returned when we've finished with it."

"Where does Mr. Langan live?" Aziz asked.

"Beats me. Duguald's been travelling since he was seventeen, working freighters out of Dublin."

"Did he arrive here on a boat?"

"No. He wanted to see a bit of Canada first, so he landed in Halifax and took the train across. He stayed here for a while and might've booked himself onto another ship or gone home to be a carpenter and bricklayer."

"Without letting you know he was leaving?" Aziz asked.

"Duggie is like that. I don't expect more of him."

"Did he have access to that boat of yours?"

"He's a damn fine fisherman, so yeah, I let him take the boat out."

"Over to Cootes?" Aziz asked.

"Nuttin' there but carp. No, he'd be gone from first light to last some days. Come home with a haul of lake and brown trout he'd caught off Secord." Byrne leaned against the wall. "Once, he snagged so many, my chef made it a special with fries—they sold out over lunch."

Aziz looked up from her notes, keen to interrupt Byrne's trip down memory lane. "What was the name of the ship that brought him to Halifax?"

"Ya know, detective, I can't recall him ever telling me the name." Byrne wasn't leaning on the wall anymore. "Though I remember it sailed out of Helsinki and was registered in Taiwan—funny, the things you do remember."

"Was your second cousin ever in trouble with the law back in Ireland?" MacNeice was studying the worn oriental runner on the floor.

"Not that I know of. He's a good lad, a bit quick-tempered, but then single men his age often are."

"And what age would that be?"

"Twenty-eight."

Aziz asked whether Byrne had a photo of the young man. He didn't; nor did he have the address in Ireland where Duguald or any of his family lived.

"Why is that?" Aziz asked.

"Duggie left home early for a life at sea, and neither side of my family is given to staying in touch with the far-flung relations."

MacNeice's fuse was running short. "Describe him to us."

"Whaddya mean?"

Aziz put her pen down with a slap. "Is he tall, short, heavy, slim, built like you or more like DS MacNeice? Does he have tattoos, as seamen often do? Any scars? Is he bald or does he have a full head of hair — if so, is it fair or dark? Are his eyes green, grey, hazel, brown, or blue? Did he walk erect or hunched over — any limp or oddness in his gait?"

Byrne reacted like he was being smacked. When she'd finished, he exhaled. "I wasn't in love with the fella, we were only related. Lemme see . . . he's taller than me for sure, but not as tall as him." He nodded in MacNeice's direction. "He's heavier, though — like I said, he's a big boy." Arching his eyebrows like he was running through Aziz's list, he added, "Duggie has dark hair, lots of it. He says the ladies like it that way because they can run their fingers through it, if you follow."

"He's a lady's man." Aziz kept her eyes on her notebook.

"How should I know? We didn't double date. He was my night clerk and when he wasn't clerkin', he was out fishin'."

"Tattoos or other distinguishing marks?"

"He has a tattoo of the flag of Ireland on his chest over his heart, and a bathing beauty on his forearm that he can make shimmy when he flexes his muscles. Duggie is fit, but not the kind of fit you get in a fancy gym."

"You said that Duguald is dark. How dark?"

"Well, no offence, but not as dark as you, detective."

She let the comment slide. "Did he ever bring one of his girlfriends back to the hotel?"

"Nope. Never met a one."

MacNeice leaned closer to study the memorabilia tacked to the corkboard: postcards and brochures from the Emerald Isle. He removed both postcards to check the backs—nothing written on them; they'd never been used. "Where is Duguald now, Mr. Byrne?"

"You asked me that already. I dunno."

"Yes, but you suddenly remembered so much about him, I thought you might have gotten lucky there too."

"You mean you thought you'd get lucky."

MacNeice smiled. "Why don't you show us where Duguald stayed."

Byrne shrugged and led them upstairs to the room with sickly green curtains. He leaned against the door jamb after the detectives went in.

Without turning to him, MacNeice said, "Leave us now. We'll see you downstairs when we're finished." He put on his latex gloves.

"Okay, but no funny business you two—not witout payin' first." He winked at Aziz, raising his eyebrows as she put on her gloves. She turned on him with a cold stare and the man retreated.

MacNeice opened the oppressive green curtains, sending a fog of dust particles floating toward the bed. The window was so filthy, it filtered the already grey light from outside.

They tore the bedding off the double mattress, lifted and turned it, then slid it off the frame and checked the structure and its stained headboard. Nothing. They put it back. They lifted the mirror and the cheap print of Boston Harbor off the wall to see if either had been tampered with. They tipped the chair, checked the drawer in the bedside table and lifted the edges of the crusty carpet, sending more dust flying up in their faces. They removed the shelf paper from the closet—nothing. Aziz ran a hand over the wallpaper and scanned the subflooring for any lumps or loose boards.

MacNeice sat on the bed frame while Aziz stood on the chair to check the fluorescent light fixture. Its diamond-patterned screen came off, but there was nothing behind it other than the tubes. She climbed down and sat beside MacNeice, who was staring at the curtains.

"Those curtains put me in mind of Wilde's final words."

Aziz dusted off the dead insects that had fallen on her when she removed the fluorescent cover. "You mean either they go or I do?"

"Exactly."

MacNeice stood up and went to the window. He lifted the right side curtain and felt along the bottom hem from the outside in, then checked the left. That's where he found it, tucked inside the hem: a piece of paper torn from a bar tab, neatly folded to make it smaller. In pencil were seven single digit numbers—4, 3, 7, 5, 2, 6, 1—and beside each, an initial with another number: B50, W100, S75, Z400, A50, R100, G500.

"That's rich." MacNeice held the paper up to the light and laughed. Sitting down again beside Aziz, he told her about a case he worked as a young cop. It had involved an old guy that everyone—cops and crooks alike—called the Fox. "He was the real deal, right out of the pages of a Damon Runyon novel, a street-smart bootlegger and bookie, horse racing mostly." MacNeice handed her the chit. "Each of those numbers represents a horse in the race, the initials are the person who placed the bet, and the number next to the letter is the amount of the bet. It's garden-variety bookie accounting. But hidden in the hem — that's the Fox — pure genius."

He told Aziz that the Fox had had a faulty heart. One day, following his umpteenth attack, he was in a single bed recovery room at Dundurn General — tubed to the hilt with monitors measuring everything — when MacNeice and another young cop were told to turn the room over and be thorough about it. "He had allegedly been running bets with the other cardiac patients out of the critical-care unit. The fresh widow of one of those patients found a note about a bet in the drawer of the table next to his bed as she was clearing out his effects. He'd put it there perhaps because he knew he might not wake up, or that if he did, he might not remember — and nobody really trusts a bookie. She called the cops."

MacNeice smiled as he remembered. "The Fox had somehow managed to get out of bed long enough to slide his record of the bets into the hem of the curtain." MacNeice and his sergeant never found it, even though they tore the place apart, including the bed — they had the Fox moved onto a gurney for the purpose. He had a clear plastic oxygen mask over his nose and mouth and he was smiling the whole time. "When we came up short, the sergeant lifted the mask off the Fox's face — the nurses went crazy. Sarge asks him, 'What's so funny?' "

"How did you learn about the hem?"

"Years later, the Fox finally had one too many heart attacks. My sergeant showed up at his funeral, either because he had a soft spot for a smart crook or he just wanted to make sure it wasn't another scam. The Fox's wife told him about the chit in the hem. She didn't know it was there either, until he had asked her to retrieve it so he could collect on the bets."

MacNeice looked over at Aziz. "The sarge says, 'Well, I'll be damned!' The Fox's wife laughed, then whispered to him, 'Maybe you will be. But if you are, you're sure to see him again.' "

Aziz laughed. She took one last look at the chit and handed it back to him.

"Pass me the photocopy of the register pages."

She took them out of the manila envelope and he laid them out on the bed's wooden slats. They compared the letters on the chit to the night clerk's entries; there was a clear match in style, complete with a stroke through the seven.

"Fisherman, seaman, carpenter, bricklayer, night clerk, and bookie," MacNeice said, sliding the chit into the envelope with the pages.

"So it appears... But why would he leave it here?"

[14]

THEY RAN THROUGH THE RAIN TO THE CAR. ONCE THEY'D PULLED away from the bar, MacNeice called Ryan and asked him to find Anniken Kallevik's travelling companion, the tall Norwegian. "I need to know if he made it to Whistler."

"You think Duguald Langan killed them both?" Aziz asked after he hung up.

"I don't know, but I don't think Duguald just wandered off."

Back at Division, Aziz photographed both sides of the chit, slid it into a Ziploc evidence bag and took it down to Forensics.

"When you're ready, sir, I've sourced the missing persons file on Jennifer Grant," Ryan said.

"Thanks...Right after you find my Norwegian."

MacNeice taped a copy of the chit and wrote "bookie" under Duguald Langan's name, then drew a dotted line to Anniken Kallevik's picture.

Ryan had soon found two Norwegian males, both twenty-three years old, working in or near Whistler, one in a bar at the Whistler Inn and the other with the ski patrol at Blackcomb. Only the bartender, Markus Christophe, was tall and blond, but since he worked nights, he was still in bed. Ryan was on hold with the inn. "He'll be up by six p.m. our time. Do you want me to ask them to wake him up, sir?"

"No. Just get the best number to reach him. And find out when he was hired."

After a minute or so more on the phone, Ryan put a hand over the receiver. "He arrived on November 15th and started at the bar the next night."

Though MacNeice's gut was telling him otherwise, this news meant there might not be anyone at the bottom of Cootes after all.

He heard Vertesi and Williams coming before they were halfway up the stairs, bantering about the rain. Williams said, "It's like the tropics out there, without the heat, the palm trees and the bikinis."

"So what, you're not from the tropics?"

"Stallion, my ancestors have been living in Canada since yours were hanging out in caves over in Sicily."

"Calabria — the mountains of *Calabria*." Vertesi was the first to notice that MacNeice was there. "Hey, boss," he said, shaking the water off his coat.

"To some, Nicholson was a saint. Nobody had anything negative to say about him," Williams offered, shedding his equally drenched coat.

Vertesi pushed the wet hair off his forehead and said,

"Yeah, but even the ones that thought he was a mensch admitted they didn't know him all that well."

"Even though he'd been teaching there a long time." Williams shrugged as he said it, like either it was a sad comment on the man or that Nicholson's colleagues weren't being honest.

Vertesi tapped David Nicholson's name on the whiteboard. "Somebody really didn't like the guy. That school's in shock, so it's hard to tell for sure what they think. All of them asked about Dylan."

"Whatever questions we might have about his dad, that kid is a hero at Mercy," Williams offered.

Vertesi opened his notebook. "Elana Roane was the only teacher to mention Nicholson's wife leaving him. She said . . . " He looked for the precise quote. " 'I thought his wife was lovely and she appeared to adore Dylan, who was in Mercy's junior kindergarten.' Roane was really surprised when she bolted."

"Tell him what she said then," Williams nudged.

Vertesi returned to his notes. "David was a bit darker back then. She said *moody* would best describe him."

Referring to his own notes, Williams added, " 'He seemed much sunnier afterwards, so I just thought it was a bad marriage. At Mercy, Dylan and his father were inseparable.' "

"Understandable, with the mother deserting them," Aziz said as she returned.

MacNeice's head was resting on his hands. He seemed to be studying the fake grain of his desk. "Ryan, let's hear what you've got on Jennifer Grant."

"Quite a bit, sir." Ryan spun his chair around and began tapping away on the keyboard. MacNeice felt some comfort in the sound. In seconds, the photocopier was printing out the missing persons report.

MacNeice turned to Aziz. "Fiza, find out if Dylan is still at home." She nodded and turned to her phone.

"Boss, should we start checking old report cards?" Vertesi asked.

"No. There's no way he was killed by a high school student."

Aziz put the phone back in its cradle. "Nobody answered at Dylan's, Mac. I'll try again in a few minutes."

Ryan handed MacNeice the report, and MacNeice quickly scanned it. He shook his head. "Nicholson and Jennifer Grant's family filed MPRs on the same day but with different divisions. One week later, Jennifer called her parents from Silver Lake in Los Angeles. Said she just needed a break and was staying with a girlfriend who'd moved there from Dundurn. The grandparents said she seemed to be happy. Jennifer apologized for not telling them and admitted that she hadn't told David either." He looked up to see the raised eyebrows of his team. "Jennifer promised to stay in touch by cellphone. Her parents told Nicholson, along with her promise that she would be returning to the city in a few weeks. With that, the case was closed until two months later." MacNeice turned the page. "Her parents called the police again because they hadn't heard from Jennifer, she wasn't answering emails and her cellphone message box was full. They'd called the girlfriend she'd been staying with, and the girlfriend said that Jennifer had left two weeks earlier to go up the coast before heading home." He flipped through the pages and back again. "The rest is about what the cops did—standard stuff, engaged the LAPD, sent her photograph and description to law enforcement agencies across the continent. LAPD searched the girlfriend's condo and found a bag of marijuana she claimed was Jennifer's. They speculated that Jennifer might have disappeared into the drug culture."

"Long way to go for a few joints," Vertesi said.

Williams added, "And a big leap from finding a bag of weed that might have actually been her friend's to opium dens in East LA."

"I suspect it was a convenient assumption at the time," MacNeice said, and returned to the notes. He turned the page to the Dundurn Police Department's confidential summary. "After interviewing her husband, parents and brother, DPD concluded that Jennifer Grant was a 'wild child' tired of parenting and disinterested in teaching—their conclusion based primarily on the fact that she didn't inform her husband or the school that she was leaving. Though they never closed the case, it's safe to say it's cold."

"Frozen." Williams shook his head in disgust.

Referring to a note on his desk, Ryan said, "It wasn't hard to find her parents. They own Grant Greengrocers out in Dundas. They still own the shop but it's mostly run now by her brother, who was also a teacher before he took early retirement." Ryan handed the address to Vertesi.

"It's strange, now that Nicholson has been identified as the bombing victim by the media, that the grandparents haven't called Dylan," MacNeice said.

Aziz's cellphone rang. She listened, then put it on hold and turned to MacNeice. "You spoke too soon, Mac. They're at the house. The grandparents. I've got Dylan on the phone. Children's Services brought them in because Dylan's aunt refused to take responsibility for him." She clicked back onto the line and then hung up, after promising Dylan that she'd tell MacNeice what was going on.

"It was a reasonable assumption that his grandparents are the next best option before foster care," MacNeice said.

"The only trouble with that is that Dylan hasn't seen them or his uncle Robert in years because his father had severed contact with them. When Dylan asked his dad why, he was told his uncle blamed Nicholson for Jennifer's disappearance and her parents agreed with him."

MacNeice stared at the photo of David Nicholson in the Hawaiian shirt. "The poor kid. The way this is going, he will end up in foster care."

The main line rang and Ryan picked up. "Sir, there's someone asking for you, but he won't give his name."

MacNeice nodded, and answered. "MacNeice."

A man said, "There's a café bar on Locke near Pine — you know the place?"

"Yes."

"Be there in a half-hour."

"What's your name and how will I know you?"

"Don't worry about that. I know you. And if you're as good as they say, you'll be able to figure it out. I knew David Nicholson well enough to know there's a different story than the one you're probably hearing."

"And what might that be?"

The caller laughed or coughed, his voice crackling through nicotine or alcohol-clogged airways. "Come on, detective, that's something we'll discuss in person."

Once MacNeice explained, both Vertesi and Williams offered to back him up.

"No reason why three of us need to check this out. I'll be back soon."

HE PARKED ACROSS the street from the bar, then tried to peer through the rain into its interior, but it was too dark.

Standing on the threshold, he shook the rain off his coat. The bar was a long, narrow and immediately familiar space, shaped like a shoebox. There were elevated booths on the right and a long counter on the left. It was just after four, and locals out for an early evening or a late lunch occupied all but one of the booths. At the bar three men were talking to the bartender, and two others were pretending not to listen. The bartender was working the ornate handle of an on-tap lager into a pint. After she glanced at him, she whispered something that made two of the men look his way and nod. In the last booth a man sat alone with his back to the door. He didn't look around. MacNeice made his way to him.

"See, that wasn't too difficult. I've ordered you a lager."

The man was in his mid-forties, his face lined not from age but from working outside in all kinds of weather. An ancient waxed Barbour raincoat leaned stiffly against the wall of the booth.

The bartender brought the lager over and placed it in front of him. "Cheers, detective," she said, then walked away with an exaggerated wiggle.

"Out of interest, how did you know when to order the lager?"

"Easy. You had thirty minutes to get here. At twenty-six I asked her to pour another glass. Cheers." He chinked his glass against MacNeice's while it was still on the table.

Studying the pint for a moment, MacNeice at last smiled and lifted his glass. "Cheers." He took a long draw before putting it down. "Name?"

"Graham McLeod. I'm a landscape architect and contractor. I was once Jennifer Grant's fiancé."

Watching MacNeice for a reaction—there was none—McLeod drank and wiped the foam from his lip with his thumb. "We broke up for all the wrong reasons and a few of the right ones." He put his large hands flat on the table and took a deep breath. "We stayed friends after, but when Jenny started dating Nicholson, that ended too."

"Why was that?"

"The obvious. Nicholson was uncomfortable with her maintaining a relationship with a former lover, let alone a fiancé. He was jealous for years, and even after they were married, he was convinced that she was seeing me on the sly. She wasn't."

"Until?"

"What do you mean?" McLeod sat back in his seat.

"We're not here now because Nicholson was jealous for no reason. When did you reconnect?"

McLeod tilted his head, studying the detective. "A year before she disappeared, she called me. She said he'd struck her and after she ran into the bathroom and locked the door, he kicked it in. He'd punched her so hard in the stomach that she threw up. If it hadn't been for her vomiting, she thought he would have beaten her senseless." He spoke slowly, as if he was pulling a file from somewhere back in his head, but he wasn't finished.

MacNeice took out his notebook and pen. McLeod finished his lager and waited for him to look up again.

"She called in sick at the school. I told her to meet me here." He wiped his mouth and looked around the bar. There were tears in his eyes that he wanted to hide from MacNeice. In a moment, another pint arrived. McLeod took a first sip, then said, "She had a welt on her cheek, and when she lifted up her sweater, there was a deep bruise on her stomach."

"Did she report the beating?" MacNeice asked, making his notes.

"No. She was too embarrassed or ashamed. She didn't want it getting out that Nicholson was abusive. I asked if she wanted me to talk to him, but Jenn didn't want that, in part because she was worried about what Nicholson might do to me, and what he'd do to her afterwards. She told me that this wasn't the first time it had happened. Worse, if I'd spoken to Dave, he'd have been convinced she'd been seeing me all along."

MacNeice was nursing his lager, considering whether McLeod could be responsible for Nicholson's death.

"I insisted we take photographs of the bruises. I went out to the truck and got the camera I'd been using out at the botanical gardens. I took her into the washroom." He nodded to the narrow hallway beyond the bar.

"What did you do with the photographs?"

"Nothing. I was going to show them to the police after Jennifer disappeared, but then she called me from Los Angeles. She sounded happy. In a few weeks, she said, she'd like me to come out and join her."

"And Dylan?"

"Dylan was four. Nicholson made it sound like the kid was deserted. No way. She loved that boy."

But McLeod couldn't explain why she hadn't come back for her son. The woman she was staying with had come home one day and found a short note. McLeod recited it: "On my way back, to where I once belonged. Thank you sooo much for taking care of me. Love, Jenn."

"I'm told she had a wild streak," said MacNeice. "Do you think she just took off?"

McLeod hung his head for a long time, studying the foamy head on his beer. When he looked up, he said, "When we were in our twenties, we did a lot of weed. Does that suggest a wild streak?"

"Alcohol? Heavier drugs?"

"Never anything to excess. Sure, we would get drunk together from time to time. I'd take her out to one of my projects and we'd lie down on a rock or on the grass, sipping bourbon and looking at the stars. But we'd also be laughing and planning our future together. She wasn't wild or addicted to anything. If anything, she was worried about how much I liked to get high, and with good reason. But I've straightened out my act. I work too hard to manage anything stronger than a few lagers."

"So what did you think happened?"

Again his eyes welled up. "You know . . . her note, the Beatles lyric about getting back? I took it to mean she'd gone off to find herself." Again he looked briefly around the bar. "I imagined her living somewhere in British Columbia on a back-to-the-land farm, or gone to Australia, because once, when we were high, she talked about teaching somewhere in the Outback because they needed great teachers. Two years after she disappeared, I got married."

"Are you still married?"

He smiled. "No. I realized I had married someone who looked a bit like Jenn, but she wasn't her. We got divorced after a couple of years. No kids."

McLeod said he took to searching Jenn's name on Google, thinking someday she would suddenly pop up. "I'd be okay if I found out she was living somewhere, married with a dozen kids, just as long as she's happy."

MacNeice sensed McLeod was working hard to persuade himself that was true. "Do you think she's still alive?"

The man exhaled sharply, coughed hard, then took a long pull on his lager. "I have to . . . I have to."

"Did you kill David Nicholson?"

McLeod stared at MacNeice, maybe trying to decipher if he was serious. "No, man, I didn't kill him."

"Why ask me to come here? If you have nothing to hide, why not give your name and meet me downtown?"

"Because this is where I last saw her—right where you're sitting." He inhaled whatever emotion was rising in his throat.

MacNeice drained his lager. "Why did your engagement to Jennifer Grant fail?"

"We'd fallen in love mostly under the influence of one drug or another. We woke up six months before the wedding and decided to clean up our act before the big day. Within a month we were barely talking. Suddenly, the differences in our lives seemed greater than what held us together. We were dreaming different dreams." He pushed the glass aside for a moment. "Then she married David and I realized what a huge mistake I'd made." He slid the glass back and cradled it in his hands.

MacNeice grabbed his coat and stood up. "Meaning your dreams weren't different?"

"Not at all." McLeod handed the detective a slightly crumpled card on which he'd written his home and cell numbers.

MacNeice gave him his card in return.

McLeod said, "Hope the weather clears up, for both our sakes."

"I'll come by and get those photographs from you."

"No need. I've got them here. The negatives too." He reached under his Barbour and pulled out a manila envelope labelled "McLeod Landscaping" with an embossed Jack pine logo.

MacNeice took it and thanked him. He left McLeod ordering another pint.

He waited until he was back in the Chevy before he opened the envelope. The four eight-by-ten-inch black and white prints were worn around the edges, but there was no wear or tear in the images. A frightened-looking woman gazed into the lens. The blue black of the bruise on her left cheek was clear, and in a profile shot, McLeod had zoomed in on the bruise. His face and the camera lens were reflected in the bar's bathroom mirror. The next set of prints were of her stomach. The blow had landed just below her rib cage, again on the left side.

"He was right-handed," MacNeice said to himself.

She held the sweater up, the flash catching the glint of the wedding ring on her finger. At the bottom, her navel fluttered out of focus. She was nervous, or frightened, or maybe even turned on by being in a closed bathroom with a former lover. He put the photos back in the envelope, then called into the division. "Aziz, we're going back to Nicholson's house. I need to check something out."

"What are you looking for?"

"I want to look at the second-floor bathroom door. I'll tell you why when I get there." He started the engine. "Where's the boy?"

"The Children's Aid have got him: he wouldn't go with the grandparents. The caseworker says they'll try to put him in foster care somewhere near his school, but she couldn't guarantee it. And there's something else . . ."

MacNeice's stomach tightened.

"I took a call from the uniform on the barge. They found something and sent down a diver to check it out before they try to raise it. They'll know within the hour."

"Vertesi and Williams?"

"They've just left to interview Dylan's grandparents and uncle."

"I'll be there in ten minutes. Meet me in the parking lot." They would go first to the Nicholson house, and then out to Cootes Paradise.

[15]

HE AND AZIZ STOOD INSIDE THE FRONT DOOR. THE SILENCE INSIDE the house was oppressive. It hung like humidity. The pillows on the couch were still askew from their visit, the same books were on the table and yet nothing and everything had changed.

MacNeice turned on the second-floor hall lights and they went upstairs. "Aziz, check the father's room again: see if something speaks to you."

She put on her gloves, crossed the threshold and looked slowly about the room.

MacNeice glanced into Dylan's room. There were sweaters and jeans folded hastily on the bed; presumably, they'd be picked up later. Retrieving his Maglite, MacNeice walked over to the bathroom door. He scanned the exterior frame, feeling along the edge of the painted wood for a seam or a joint out of place that might show where it had been repaired years before. Nothing stood out.

He went into the bathroom and closed the door, jiggling the handle to see if there was play — there wasn't. He shone his flashlight up the wall next to the door frame; everything looked normally worn, needing a new paint job. And there it was, near the handle: a stress crack in two of the small white wall tiles. The vertical framing was different on that side of the door, slightly wider and also shallower than the rest.

He found Aziz sitting on the bed in the master bedroom, opening a small metal box she'd found in the drawer of the nightstand. It was empty but for three keys on a wire key chain. Two looked like spare door keys, but the third was a smaller gold key with a distinctive round head with an engraved envelope on it — a P.O. box key. She handed them to MacNeice and went back to searching the drawer.

MacNeice left the room with the keys, wondering why a high school English teacher needed a P.O. box. Neither of the door keys fit the side door lock, so he went through to check the garden door and the front door — the keys didn't fit those either.

Aziz came downstairs as MacNeice stood staring at the keys. "Could they be from a house they used to live in?"

"They've lived here Dylan's whole life. Why would you keep keys that old?"

"Sentimental?"

"A post office box key isn't sentimental." He put them in his coat pocket and held open the front door.

SOFT RAIN FELL in sheets on the caramel water of Cootes Paradise. The dark grey barge looked gigantic and menacingly out of place. Diesel smoke burped intermittently from the stack, and the two Volvo diesel engines shattered the damp tranquility like a Harley on a quiet street.

Seeing the Chevy slow to a stop on the low road, the cop on board climbed into the black inflatable, along with one of the divers in a wetsuit. Aziz and MacNeice were standing at the gravel shore when it slid, motor up, to a soft landing. The cop in the bow introduced himself. "Corporal Danny Fournier. And this is Marine Unit Constable Jun Takeuchi." Fournier glanced back at the barge. "It's a male, sir. He was tied to an anchor."

Takeuchi climbed over the side and swung the dinghy parallel to the shore, holding it as they got in. Once they were settled, knees together like they were attending a church picnic, Takeuchi swung the inflatable around, shoving it farther into the water. He slipped quickly on board, lowered the engine, pulled the cord, and they glided through the rain. Aziz had her head down and her collar up, trying to protect herself from the downpour, but MacNeice lifted his face into it. The closer they got, the larger the barge loomed above them. As Takeuchi held the dinghy alongside the ladder, he said, "Mind your step and please hold on to the railing—the ladder is slick."

The platform, with its great sheets of black non-skid steel, glistened from cranes to wheelhouse. The smell of diesel and grease dominated, augmented only slightly by the scent of the bay and its surrounding vegetation. Underneath it all was the distinct and creepy-sweet odour of human decay. The shiniest drenched surface by far was the black plastic sheeting that covered the body. MacNeice and Aziz stood together as Takeuchi pulled it back to reveal the head and shoulders. He paused there as if considering whether to go all the way, and MacNeice impatiently gestured for him to remove it all.

At first MacNeice couldn't make out what he was seeing. It was as if a large black leaf had settled on a black, partially deflated, balloon. Then the face came into terrible focus. Steel wire was wound tightly around the neck, embedded in the flesh, with two small makeshift handles protruding. The hair — matted with mud on one side — was full and there was little distinction between it and the face colour — both were black. The upper torso was covered in a dark blue fleece pullover under which was a grey or possibly white jersey. The lower torso was — with the exception of black briefs and one white athletic sock — blue and grey and naked. The underwear was twisted, a testicle showing.

Blue nylon rope was still coiled around the body, spiralling tight enough that it bit into the torso, then disappearing in the fleece where the body bloated around it. The divers had set the anchor beside the body's right shoulder, still tethered to the line. Aziz turned and walked to the side of the barge for a moment, staring out at the water.

MacNeice took out his camera and bent over the body. "Did your dredging bring up anything else?"

"No, sir, though we kept going, thinking we'd be able to find his pants at least." Takeuchi looked out to Dundurn Bay. "They could have been tossed farther out, on the way over or back."

"Roll up the sleeves of that sweater," MacNeice said.

Takeuchi crouched to pull the soggy sleeve up on the left arm to the elbow.

"The right arm, too, please."

Takeuchi leaned to pull at the sleeve, which bled water into the diamond treads of the deck near MacNeice's feet. A few inches above the wrist, red high heels and shapely legs gave way to the striped bikini, flat stomach and large breasts of a woman with her arms raised, her hands lost in a deep red mane of hair—the classic pose of a bathing beauty.

"Hello, Duguald," MacNeice said softly.

"It was done in Japan," Takeuchi said, leaning closer. "See here, by the right shoe? In Japanese, it says, 'Studio Tadanori, Tokyo.'"

"Apparently, he could make her dance," Aziz said without turning to look.

Someone behind MacNeice said, "Yeah, well I think she's done with dancing," which sent the barge crew into uneasy snickers.

To be absolutely certain, MacNeice asked Takeuchi to show him the chest. Taking out a long knife from a sheath below his knee, Takeuchi cut the spiralling line in three places, put the blade as far up inside the jersey as he could reach, and thrust up. The tip appeared through the cloth, then the sweater and jersey parted in a long V, as if he'd pulled an invisible zipper. Takeuchi peeled the sweater and jersey away to reveal the upper chest. Rain pelted Duguald's blue and grey flesh. Perhaps it was the light, or the damage and decay of being so long on the bottom, but the flag appeared more Italian than Irish—dark red rather than orange.

DRIVING UP THE hill with Aziz quiet beside him in the passenger seat, MacNeice called and alerted Mary Richardson to expect another body from Cootes Bay, then checked her progress on David Nicholson.

She said there wasn't any. What remained in the wagon had been so riddled with shrapnel and burnt from the blast that it was effectively charred mincemeat. She could say that he'd had lower leg issues, likely varicose veins, but even that was speculative given the damage.

"And you should know that I checked the young woman's fingers to see if there was muscle memory that might indicate she wore a ring—but there wasn't any," Richardson said. "Tell me about the latest one." Her voice echoed in the large, cold lab.

"Well, he isn't Norwegian—he's Irish. There's a garrotte wrapped tightly around his throat. And, judging by the matting of the hair on one side, I'd guess he was slammed hard on the anchor that held him on the bottom. There goes my theory of who killed Anniken Kallevik."

"Theories are fickle," Richardson said. "The damn things are never as loyal to you as you are to them."

[16]

WILLIAMS POINTED A MARKER AT JENNIFER GRANT'S WEDDING photograph taped to the whiteboard. "Here's the thing: Her parents don't feel David Nicholson caused their daughter's disappearance, but her brother, Robert, not Nicholson, was the one who went out to California looking for her, following leads up and down the coast for almost a year, putting flyers on poles across LA, all around Silver Lake, and even Malibu. And it was Nicholson who, two years after she went missing, severed all ties with the Grants and refused to let them have any contact with their grandson." Williams quickly sketched what else he and Vertesi had learned from Jennifer's family: Nicholson had considered himself the victim—deserted by his wife, the mother of their son—and he'd never explained to her family why he blamed them for her flight.

Their legal attempts to gain access to Dylan proved fruitless. The court sided with Nicholson because Jennifer's parents admitted they had spoken to her after she'd gone, but hadn't told him. Dylan's grandparents grew embittered and, ultimately, defeated. They began to question their own opinion of their daughter—maybe she *had* deserted her son.

"Their problem has always been that phone call they received from Jennifer in California," Vertesi said. "She sounded so happy. When they pressed her to find out when she was coming home to be with her son, all she said was, 'I don't know, not just yet.' " Jennifer had never confided in her parents about her difficulties at home, and even they had to admit there appeared to be a strong bond between father and son.

"And Jennifer's brother? What did he have to say?" MacNeice asked.

"Haven't spoken to him yet," Williams said. "He was off at the Food Terminal, picking up vegetables."

MACNEICE WAS TAPING up cropped photos of Duguald's face, chest and arm when his phone rang.

"Sir, I've got Markus Christophe," Ryan said, "calling in from BC."

MacNeice picked up. "Thank you for calling back. We were going to call you in the morning."

"I was worried when they said it was the Dundurn homicide police that wanted to talk to me." His English was excellent.

"Do you know Anniken Kallevik?"

MacNeice heard a sharp intake of breath. "What has happened to Anni? Is she okay?"

"I'm sorry to tell you she was murdered. Her body was recovered from a small bay —"

The receiver was suddenly muffled: MacNeice heard the young man scream something, likely in Norwegian, after which the phone dropped to a hard surface. MacNeice could hear water running and the sound of a fist hitting something—a wall, a counter? He waited several minutes more, through an echoing silence. When Christophe picked up the phone again, he spoke in a whisper.

"I don't understand. Are you certain it's Anni? I can't believe it . . . No, maybe she drowned, ya?"

"We're certain. Her neck had been broken."

"Christ . . . no. No one would do that to her. Not to Anni. No one would hurt her." Christophe cleared his throat and then coughed. "Sir . . . you must be mistaken. You've found someone else."

"Anniken Kallevik was working at the yacht club when she died, and her photograph was identified by the manager there."

"No. No . . . " His voice trailed off. It sounded like he was going to put the phone down again.

"Mr. Christophe," MacNeice said sharply. "Take a few minutes, and then call me back. We need your help."

"I will call you . . . I need to . . . "

"I understand." MacNeice disengaged.

In ten minutes, the phone rang again. MacNeice knew by the greeting that the young man had gained control of himself.

"Tell me about your relationship with Ms. Kallevik," he said.

"Ah, we are friends, yes. We met in university and shared many interests."

"Was it a romantic relationship?"

"No . . . not ever. She's like a sister. We see the world, we laugh and learn before we go home to get serious . . . about life." He cleared his throat. "We agreed to work our way across Canada. We would end up here at Whistler for the winter, go down the coast to California, on to Chicago and New York, then we go back to Norway."

"But the plan changed."

"Anni was offered more work at the yacht club. I wanted to go west, as we had agreed. She said she'd come later to Whistler. I keep expecting her, but her phone has been dead for months now, so I didn't know where she was." MacNeice could hear the guilt rising in the young man's voice. "I called the hostel, but she was gone. I just thought she was some-where in between, and any day she'd walk into the bar here and ask for a beer."

"When did you leave Dundurn?"

"Oh . . . the first day of October. I got a ride to Calgary with a German girl from the hostel. I helped pay for gas, ya. From there I took the train through the Rockies."

"The name and location of the hostel?"

"Global Youth Hostels. It's downtown, on James Street."

MacNeice wrote the name down and, below it in cap-ital letters, CHECK FOR BELONGINGS, then passed it to Aziz.

"Was Ms. Kallevik seeing anyone, a boyfriend?"

"I don't think so. She would have told me."

"What about her family?"

"She has her mother and father and two sisters. Her par-ents have a farm, ya, a nice place. Before we left, she had told them not to worry or expect postcards and phone calls but to think of her as they would Roald Amundsen, who was born not far from their place." The phone was muffled again; several seconds passed. "Ah . . . Anni wanted to return home, ya, like an explorer, with all the treasures and stories of her journey."

"But...Amundsen disappeared." MacNeice regretted the words the moment they came out.

"Not a good comparison, I think." Christophe broke down again. When he recovered, he said, "I will come to Dundurn and help. After I've...When I can, I will take Anni home." He caught his breath. "Will you call her family or should I?"

"Do they speak English?"

"Yes...not a lot, maybe not well but, ya, a bit. Her sisters do."

"That call will be hard. Let's make it together."

MacNeice told him they'd patch him in from Whistler. Given the time changes involved, he suggested 6:30 a.m. Pacific time.

"I have the number," Christophe said, and dictated it.

"Do you have any recent photographs of Anniken that would help us in our investigation?"

"I will send them to you—travel pictures, ya, all smiling." He inhaled deeply.

MacNeice gave him the email address. "We won't release her identity until we've spoken to the family. For the time being, please consider this conversation confidential, understood?"

"Ya."

Though another silence fell, MacNeice had a sense that Christophe wasn't finished. "Is there anything else, Mr. Christophe?"

"Well...I was just thinking...I promised her father I would watch over Anni."

As the young man lost control again, MacNeice said, "We'll call them in the morning. Thanks for your help."

MACNEICE WASN'T EXPECTING anything like the emotional reaction he'd got from Markus Christophe as he walked into the Block and Tackle bar to break the news about Duguald to his cousin. Six old men—four together and two single drinkers sitting at separate tables—turned toward him. A hostess was polishing pint glasses behind the bar. She didn't bother to look up but seemed to know who was approaching—probably knew the moment his shoe hit the first step of the porch—her red lips curled into a tight smile as she waited for him to say something.

MacNeice wasn't in the mood for games and walked right up to where she stood behind the bar. Though she'd once been pretty, not even the optimism of rouge and pink eye shadow could alter the defeat in her eyes.

"Detective," the hostess said through her teeth.

Before he could reply, Byrne came striding from his office. MacNeice wondered if she had pushed a button under the bar to alert him.

"Where's me boat?"

"Let's go into your office, Mr. Byrne," MacNeice said.

"Here to shoot the breeze again, MacNeice?" Byrne said. "You must be growing fond of me."

MacNeice shut the office door behind them, then turned to Byrne. "Duguald Langan is dead. His body was pulled out of Cootes Paradise today—from the same place where the young woman was found."

Byrne sat down. "Sweet Jesus—you sure?"

"Well, his face isn't as you described it anymore, but his tattoos are. Yes, we're certain."

"Poor lad…poor lad." He rubbed his hands on his thighs, looking down at the floor. "And here I thought he just took off like the County Meath gypsy he was, eh."

It was difficult to tell whether Byrne was being genuine or not. If not, he was doing a better job of faking it than MacNeice would have given him credit for.

"I'll need you to identify the body. There'll be a detective here tomorrow morning to take you to the morgue."

"I guess that's necessary, is it?"

"It is." MacNeice moved over to the side window where beyond the black branches of the trees, he could see the slate grey water. "One more thing..."

Byrne sat waiting.

MacNeice turned away from the window. "You were aware that Duguald Langan was running numbers?"

"Whaddya mean?" He rolled his chair back and stood up.

"Duguald was a bookie and he was working out of your bar."

Byrne filled with a fury that almost burned away the bleary fog of his eyes. "I don't believe it. The police always have it in for a lad like him."

"So what was your role in that enterprise?" MacNeice said.

"Look around you: Does this place look like fertile ground for bookmakers? The thought is pitiful. I lose one of my kin, and you're here with these accusations..." Byrne seemed too angry to finish his sentence.

"Someone will be here for you in the morning," MacNeice said, and walked out.

HE WAS RUNNING through the rain when his cell rang. "MacNeice, hang on a minute." Inside the Chevy he said, "What have you found?"

Aziz said, "Two duffle bags full of clothes, hiking boots, postcards, and a dozen small trinkets she'd picked up on her travels, including a little plastic Mountie. She had a cellphone charger—but I didn't find a cellphone—toiletries, a small bag with a point-and-shoot camera, folding binoculars . . . no computer. The hostel manager remembered her. She was going to leave the first week of December. She had packed her own bags. When she went missing, he put her bags in storage. He's seen so many backpackers, it didn't occur to him to be worried. Since then, at least thirty people have stayed in that room."

"Did he mention a boyfriend?"

"Never saw her with anyone. I asked the woman who covers nights. She knew that Kallevik worked mostly days and some evenings, but says that after her Norwegian friend left, Anniken was always alone. Both of them remembered that she was always writing in a diary. I assume that's with her purse and cellphone. I've sent the bags to Forensics, and I'm just writing up my notes."

He could hear the fatigue in Aziz's voice. "Do your notes tomorrow, Fiza. Go home."

HE PULLED AWAY from the Block and Tackle, his head full and heavy from the day. By the time he reached King Street, though, he realized that Fiza was on his mind.

There were so many things that hadn't been said between them. Feelings they both knew were true but off limits—a betrayal of their working relationship, the department, and (he couldn't help feeling) Kate. He'd already experienced what could happen when his mind was on Fiza and not on his work—and the devastating impact that could have on Fiza. He made a conscious effort to block the thoughts of her swirling in his head, and found relief of a peculiar sort in thinking instead about Dylan Nicholson's future.

As he parked behind Marcello's and checked the time, he figured that the boy was likely finishing his first dinner with a foster family somewhere in the city. Taking out his cellphone, MacNeice called Children's Aid. Since it was after eight, it took some time to connect with a live voice, who at his insistence patched him through to the agency's executive director. When he told her about the post office box key, she agreed to set up a meeting but insisted a caseworker be present during the interview, as the boy was still very upset.

The caseworker would call MacNeice when Dylan came home for lunch the next day. He gave the executive director his cellphone number and hung up. He looked past the fog of the windshield to the welcoming light of the restaurant's back door, then made a run for it through the steady rain.

[17]

SHE ARRIVED BETWEEN THE SALAD AND HIS SECOND COURSE, THE grilled branzini.

"Do you mind?" she said, her hand on the stool to his right.

"Not at all."

"Sam Stewart, MacNeice. In case you forgot."

"I didn't." Lie.

"Given up on Montaigne?" She smiled.

"Tonight, yes. Tomorrow is another day." MacNeice had slid Kate's favourite book a few inches to his left. The day had so crowded his capacity to absorb words, he hadn't even been able to face reading the newspaper. Finding himself somewhere between adolescence and dementia, he could only doodle.

First to fall had been the front section of *The Standard*. He put Groucho Marx glasses and a moustache on the prime minister, the US president, the pope, Angelina Jolie and the toddler she was carrying. Tackling the former mayor of Toronto made him chuckle; his honour instantly became Fatty Arbuckle, the silent film star. Before MacNeice had finished his appetizer, he'd defaced every portrait in the paper.

"I have an article in *The Standard*. Did you read it?"

"I didn't see it."

She took the newspaper and started flipping the pages.

Busted, he thought.

Pausing over his artwork, Sam tapped the headline about the president's ongoing campaign for health care reform. "That's mine. I can see you weren't into it, though. But President Groucho is on the right side of history."

"Sorry."

He looked away toward the wall-mounted television as she turned the pages back, commenting particularly on the women, "Angelina looks particularly good with a moustache, but the Queen . . . well, that's just cruel."

They were quiet for some time. Marcello refilled his glass. If Samantha assumed that he was actually considering a subject they could discuss, he wasn't. But he felt the need to say something.

"Are you dating?" It was the best he could come up with.

"Are you asking?"

This was worse than the silence.

"I'll take that as a no," she said at last.

He was aware she was smiling but resisted looking her way. He decided the best way to survive the conversation was to enjoy his wine and his food and then get the hell home to the sanctity of his cottage.

"It's never easy to be in a place like this in the shape you're in—I was just trying to lighten you up. Perhaps if I'd said, 'A duck walks into a bar, orders a martini and notices Albert Einstein nursing a beer on the next stool . . .' "

MacNeice waited for the punchline, and when it didn't come, he glanced toward her. Her elbow was on the bar, a hand supporting her head as she looked at him.

"What happened then?"

"No idea. A handsome man who puts a moustache on the Queen could finish it better than I."

"Are you working me for a story?"

"If you had read that article instead of defacing it, you'd realize I'm on a different beat." She offered her glass of white wine for a toast. "And, please, let me say you're handsome without you thinking it's a come-on. Cheers."

They clinked their glasses and fell into silence again. MacNeice was aware of Marcello, polishing glasses behind the bar, far enough away to appear to be interested in the hockey game on screen, but close enough that MacNeice was fairly certain he was eavesdropping.

He cleared his throat. "Why aren't you seeing anyone?" Then he immediately tried to take the question back. "I'm sorry, it's none of my business."

She grinned at him, enjoying the moment.

"I do have one question—well two. Are you flirting or making fun of me?" MacNeice asked.

"Both."

She was wearing a dark blue suit and a grey cashmere sweater with a low V-neck showing modest cleavage. It struck him as somewhere between business smart and night-club sexy—though he realized he wouldn't really know, since his nightlife was non-existent.

"Mind if I ask you a question? Have you dated at all since your wife died?"

Instantly, his face felt hot and the last bite of branzini stuck in his throat. He coughed slightly and took a sip of wine to wash it down. He was happy that Marcello was busy making a cappuccino at the end of the bar. The loud hissing of the machine's frother gave him time to compose himself.

"No . . . I haven't." He glanced up at the television and pretended to be interested in the game, though from that angle, he couldn't make out who was playing.

"I'm not much for dating either."

Sam told him she hadn't dated anyone since returning to the city. In part, because of work and the need to generate freelance contracts with American syndicates, but also because she'd bought a condo and was obsessed with furnishing it.

"It's at James and Bold, an 1880s stone two-and-a-half storey. Mine's the top one-and-a-half." She explained that the half-storey was her office, and the roof patio made her think of Paris.

"That's a stretch for Dundurn." He looked at her to be sure she was serious. She was. For the first time since she came into the bar, he felt that they had made a connection — a mutual affection for the city.

"It has to start somewhere, probably with people like me who believe the first step is just that — a belief that Dundurn is great."

He smiled.

"I can jog to the botanical gardens, the mountain or along the waterfront. I can walk here in any kind of weather to enjoy the food and the company."

He was surprised to see her face flush as she cleaned an area of her bowl that she'd already cleaned. MacNeice offered his empty plate to a passing waitress and shifted on the bar stool to face Samantha. "What else?"

"Okay. I loved Chicago, but I can go everywhere here and feel safe. Even into the north-end. When I was a kid, my mother told me that was strictly off-limits."

MacNeice accepted an espresso and grappa he hadn't ordered, noting the look on Marcello's face and admitting to himself that a few minutes earlier he'd been exhausted and desperate to leave. He wasn't anymore.

"Don't you feel like this is an exciting time for Dundurn?"

He nodded. "Tell me something else."

"About...?" She wiped her mouth with the napkin.

"What do you love?"

She looked at him to make sure he wasn't teasing, or flirting, then pushed the hair from her face. "I love intensity... I mean in people, but also in places. I love art and music and books and wandering around the great cities of the world."

Her face became softer and she lowered her voice. "I love wine and food, and I love a man who asks me what I love."

He was twirling his grappa glass on the marble bar, noticing how light from the spotlight above splintered around the glass. He wondered, *why now, why her? What about Kate? What about Fiza?*

"And, I have a recurring dream about walking on cobblestones between ancient houses, a black and white dog follows happily along, but I haven't any idea of where I am — somewhere in Europe."

MacNeice forced himself back into the moment. He looked down at Samantha's hands, watching how they rose and fell as she spoke — punctuating, emphasizing. MacNeice knew about dreams and was certain he'd pay for this flirtation the moment he was asleep. "How are you getting home, Sam?"

"It's not that far. I've got my umbrella at the door."

"I'd be happy to drive you."

After glancing at the slashing rain on the restaurant window, she accepted.

As he pulled up in front of her building, she laughed. "It was almost like my first date in Dundurn."

"Mine too, in a long time." He eased the Chevy up to the curb and stopped, keeping it in drive, his foot firmly on the brake.

"Would you like to come up, Mac?"

Though it was almost eleven, he said yes. Soon he was climbing the stairs behind her. He smiled, noticing her slim ankles. God is alive in the details, he thought. Sam paused at her glossy blue door. "You'll see blue's a bit of a theme," she said sheepishly as she opened the door and turned on the lights, easing herself out of her shoes. MacNeice removed his too and put them neatly beside hers. Samantha took his coat and hung it next to hers on a wall rack. She asked him if he'd like a glass of Chablis. "I opened it when I thought about making dinner at home. I don't want it to go to waste, but I don't want to drink it alone."

He agreed that would be a bad idea. As she went into the kitchen, he took in the room. What wasn't white—the door frames with their panelled doors—was pale blue. Except for the sofa, which was a cobalt blue that reminded him of Matisse, but he wasn't confident enough to say why. The wide-planked flooring appeared to be the original cherry, bearing the scars—nail and screw holes—of the building's past.

The galley kitchen was separated from the living room by a counter. Scattered across it was *The New York Times* and nestled between its sections was a near-empty glass of white wine. On one of the stools was a notepad and pencil. MacNeice resisted the urge to scan what was written.

On the walls were French industrial drawings, schematics of machinery, most of which dated from the 1930s, but MacNeice found two from the mid-1800s. These were fine line reconstructions of circular staircases burnt to ash in the châteaux during the French Revolution. These were complex drawings, so sophisticated that one could be forgiven thinking that they were art and not a how-to guide for restoring what had been lost.

"My father was a structural engineer and I've always loved that kind of drawing. They remind me of him," Samantha said, handing him a glass as she came to join him. "Cheers."

"Indeed, cheers."

HE WOULD RECALL later that the evening ended the next morning, but he was less certain about the actual moment it began. He was sure of the music — Art Tatum, his choice, from her collection of LPs, played on a high-tech turntable. He remembered the moment she put her hand on his as she poured the first glass from the second bottle of Chablis, and her laugh. Apparently he'd said something funny, though whatever that was, he couldn't recall.

He remembered the kiss. He was at the door and he'd meant it as "thank you" and "I hope to see you again," but it led immediately to another kiss followed by an embrace — initiated by her. He remembered not wanting her to let go, but not knowing exactly what to do.

Was it too much wine or the years spent living without physical contact? He didn't know, but he woke up with an untroubled mind, an utterly relaxed body and a foreign tingling in his groin. His eyes took in everything, the room and the duvet pushed down to their ankles, her body and on the bedroom wall another drawing of another ancient staircase. He could see that he had made an attempt to put his clothes neatly on the chair, but his socks looked like they'd been tossed. He had no idea where he'd put his underwear.

She stirred beside him and rolled onto her back. "Good morning, Detective Superintendent." She looked at him and smiled before closing her eyes again. Moments later, her phone buzzed urgently from the nightstand. She propped herself on an elbow to scan the display, then said, "Sorry, but I have to take this."

She slipped out of bed and walked to the window, the phone to her ear. She listened, said "okay" and "understood" and hung up.

Turning back to him, she said, "I have to pack. I'd proposed an in-depth article on the Greek banking system's risk management practices before and after the economic collapse. At first my editor said no, but then I found a disgraced former bank president who was in a prison near Athens. He agreed to give me an interview in return for his wife and grown son receiving the equivalent of five thousand US dollars. My editor just told me that the paper will cover it, so I have to catch the next flight to Athens."

"When are you back?"

"It depends on how co-operative people are. I can't just take what the imprisoned banker says as the truth: I have to corroborate it. Maybe a week, maybe longer." She came over and sat on the edge of the bed, and he reached out to run a hand along her thigh. "Please don't do that," she said. "It makes me not want to go."

[18]

THE CALL TO ANNIKEN'S PARENTS TOOK ALL OF SIX MINUTES – including the time it took for Markus Christophe to translate English to Norwegian and back again. The two daughters were both away, one doing her residency at a hospital in Oslo, the other in Frankfurt on business. Anni's mother was in hospital following a hip replacement. Her father had just arrived home from the market when the phone rang. MacNeice told him what had happened to his daughter, and then Christophe repeated his words in Norwegian, his voice charged with emotion but steady. When he stopped, there was a pause that lasted at least thirty seconds.

Then, over the crackling line, the father said, in English, "My Anni is gone?"

MacNeice asked Christophe to ask if there was someone nearby so that he wouldn't be alone. But before he could interpret, Mr. Kallevik said, "We will be well. Okay . . . okay. Well . . . goodbye. We talk soon, Markus. Goodbye." The long-distance line burped twice. He was gone.

"Markus, are you still on the line?" MacNeice asked.

"I am."

"Do you know how to reach the sisters?"

"I call my fiancée — she knows them. And I will phone him later too." He cleared his throat. "The Kalleviks are strong people, ya — farmers in Norway must be strong." He excused himself and blew his nose. "I come to you, ya? I come for Anni's body. We should be going now . . . back to Norway."

IT WAS JUST after noon when his cellphone rang. MacNeice realized he'd been daydreaming about soft flesh and warm sunlight.

It was Dylan's caseworker, and before she let him speak, she outlined the rules: MacNeice would have five minutes, no more, since Dylan had to eat lunch with his foster family. Second, MacNeice was not to upset him.

She passed the phone to Dylan.

"Hullo." The boy's voice was filled with fear and uncertainty.

"Have they put you up close to your school?"

"Yeah, pretty close."

"So how is the foster home?"

"It's okay, I guess."

"I just have one question for you, Dylan. It will help our investigation. In the night table next to your father's bed, we found three keys in a metal box. One of them is a post office box key. Do you know anything about them?"

"Keys?"

"Yes, in a tin box: a post office box key and two others, fairly old. Neither of them fit the doors of your house."

"I saw them once, but I was just bored and snoopin', so I never asked Dad about them."

The caseworker came back on the line to inform MacNeice that the conversation was over. When he protested, she said softly, "Dylan doesn't want to talk anymore. He needs time to adjust…to a different life. I'll keep you informed, if you like, though I'm limited in what I can share."

MacNeice thanked her, put the phone down and slipped Nicholson's keys in his pocket. He told Ryan he'd be back in an hour, and headed for the stairs.

AT THE MAIN post office, he asked to see the manager. When a middle-aged man with thinning hair emerged from a back office, MacNeice introduced himself, then put the key in front of him.

Without picking it up, the man said, "It's a P.O. box key."

"Right. I want the name that it's registered under and the location of the box."

"No can do. Without a warrant I can't give you a name. And to get information out of me, you'll need a federal warrant, requested by the RCMP."

MacNeice looked at the name tag on the man's shirt. "Tell me, Mr. Tekatch, do you have kids?"

"Yeah—two, a boy and a girl—but you're still gonna need the Mounties."

MacNeice pointed over the manager's shoulder to a box wrapped up, down and sideways in two-inch packing tape. "That box behind you…"

Tekatch turned. "So?"

"This key," MacNeice said, "belonged to a man who was a teacher and father. He was stripped and duct-taped tighter and more completely than that box, to a child's wagon. He was left in Gage Park. As a first responder was cutting him out of the tape, a grenade taped to his chin exploded. Several men were injured, some very seriously, and the teacher —"

"I read about it."

"Well, his son is now an orphan. And, when I left him yesterday, he made me promise to find out who killed his dad."

"Jesus . . ."

MacNeice picked up the key. "All I'm trying to do is keep a promise." Offering the manager the key, he added, "Don't give me anything other than the name that goes with this, but if that makes you uncomfortable, just give me the names of everyone who rents a P.O. box."

Tekatch looked around to see if his staff were watching, and when he was sure they weren't, he swung around to his computer and began clicking away on the keyboard. After a few minutes, six pages of single-spaced names, organized five columns across, spilled out of his desk printer. He collected them and brought them back to the counter. "So we're clear, detective, this could easily cost me my job." He passed them to MacNeice, along with an envelope. "These are last names only, nothing else. You find the name, I'll give you the location of the box. Fair?"

MacNeice took the pages and started flipping through them, looking for Nicholson. His name wasn't there. "Tell me, could someone rent a box under a pseudonym?"

"You need a government-issued photo ID to get a box, but to be honest, with some effort you could probably get around that."

MacNeice thanked the manager, asked for his card, put the list and card in the envelope and left the building. It had started pouring again, so he tucked the envelope inside his overcoat and jogged the rest of the way back to Division.

NOT ONLY WAS there not a Nicholson, Nicolson, or Nickelson on the list, there wasn't a Grant, either. MacNeice made himself an espresso and went through the list again, worried he'd simply missed it. He hadn't.

As he pondered another approach, Aziz arrived from Forensics. "All they have are clothes, travel brochures, souvenirs, toiletries, and fingerprints. And on the computer, camera and cellphone, no mention of Duguald." She looked over his shoulder at a page of small type. "What have you got there?"

"The P.O. box key list," he said. "The last names of every renter in Dundurn. Nicholson didn't use his own name, or Jennifer Grant's."

Their eyes met for a moment and a flash of guilt sliced through him. He quickly looked back at the page.

"So maybe he invented a name?"

"Not impossible, I'm told. Wait, he was an English teacher who loved history. If he was using a pseudonym for some reason, he likely defaulted to some recognizable figure. You take three pages and I'll take three."

"What am I looking for, Mac?"

"Great writers, authors, poets, living or dead—no, probably dead."

They found twenty-three candidates among the 1,453 names on the list, at least trusting that the two of them knew enough about literature.

From Cooper to James, Fitzgerald to Johnson, they were all very common names except for one: Marlowe. MacNeice circled it. Aziz reached for the Dundurn phone book and found three Marlows, none with an *e* tacked on the end.

"A contemporary of Shakespeare — it has to be him. Shakespeare would have been way too obvious." MacNeice pulled Tekatch's card out of the envelope and dialed the number.

Within a half-hour, MacNeice and Aziz were on their way to check out Box 3220 at the post office on Railroad Avenue. Standing in front of the box, he handed Aziz the key.

Aziz unlocked it. Inside, they found three envelopes, all bills addressed to Nicholson.

"Why wouldn't he just have them sent to his house on Tisdale? I mean, why come all the way out here?" Aziz asked.

MacNeice shrugged. "Check the address . . . It's not Tisdale. It's another property, 1012 Ryder Road."

THEY DROVE EAST on Main Street until they were in farm country. Large farmhouses sat solidly on treed lawns next to the highway, some of them no longer attached to their farms, but spruced up for folks who loved country living without all the manure and flies. Ryder was a north-south access road beginning at the foot of the escarpment on one end and stopping at the lake on the other. On either side, a half-mile apart, were two modest homes used by itinerant labourers who came to work in the local orchards. However, on the east side of the road, there weren't any fruit trees or vineyards, and the surrounding land, like the house, looked abandoned.

There was a small, weedy yard and gravel driveway at 1012 Ryder Road. The windows were boarded up, and the white plastic imitation aluminum siding was yellowed by the sun. The roof shingles were curling from neglect. And yet the front and back doors were steel, still carrying the primer and lot number. Neither had ever known paint. Both had been hit with graffiti, but there was no sign that anyone had broken in.

Aziz looked up and down the road. "Not exactly a romantic cottage in the country."

MacNeice didn't respond—he had a sinking feeling about the whole set-up. He tried one key, then the next on the front door. With the second, the heavy door swung free of its steel jamb with a loud groan, sending a knifelike shard of light into the otherwise black room.

He turned to Aziz. "Flashlight and latex gloves." He retrieved his own from the inside pocket of his coat and waited as she put on gloves and took out her pocket flashlight.

MacNeice switched on his flashlight and stepped inside. He was struck by the smell of exhausted space; if it could, the room would gasp with the arrival of fresh air. There was nothing rancid, rotting or organic in the atmosphere; it was simply devoid of life. Aziz tried the switch and, surprisingly, a ceiling light just above MacNeice's head clicked on. He put the flashlight away and surveyed the space.

There were two wooden chairs, a worn-out sofa and an equally tired linoleum floor cracking in the middle, presumably from the plywood subfloor he could feel sagging beneath him. The bedroom had a single bed with a bare mattress, heavily stained in the middle and dirty all over. There was no other furniture—not a dresser or a chair—just the filthy bed. Though hinges were mounted on the door frame, the bedroom door was missing.

The kitchen cupboards and ancient Frigidaire were empty, and the stove showed signs of a heavy infestation of

mice. On the floor, scattered like tiny leaves, were the aging
husks of dozens of cluster flies and ladybugs. They crunched
underfoot and sent Aziz back into the living room, where
she chose a clearing devoid of dead bugs to stand.

MacNeice checked the bathroom. The tub had a permanent dark ring inside it and the toilet and sink were soiled
almost black. He tried the flusher and it worked. Though
there was no hot water, cold ran from both faucets. The
bathroom window, like the others, was boarded up from the
outside but also featured an iron grid on the inside. "Check
the thermostat, Fiza. On the wall just outside the bedroom."

Aziz tapped the small screen several times. "Sixty degrees.
The place is heated, for God's sake."

MacNeice opened the cellar door, which separated the
bedroom from the kitchen, and flicked the switch. It worked
too. He walked down the wooden stairs into a brightly lit
space with a concrete floor. In the centre, a small table
and a bookcase filled with classics from Shakespeare to
Hemingway flanked an upholstered chair that sat opposite
a sturdy wooden chair. On top of the table was a half-empty
bottle of single malt with two glasses, one dusty, the other
with amber residue in the bottom.

The only sound was the hum of a decades-old gas furnace soldiering on for no particular reason. He looked at
the small ensemble of furniture, the books and whisky, and
called, "Fiza."

As she came slowly down the stairs, she said, "Oh, I hate
this. Seriously, this is truly creepy. I want to go home." She
crossed the floor to him and looked down at the table. "What
is this place?"

Images of Jennifer Grant's bruised face and stomach
flashed before him. "Christ!"

Terrified by his sudden reaction, Aziz instinctively grabbed his arm. "What? Shit. You're scaring the hell out of me, Mac. This place is fucking awful."

He couldn't remember the last time he'd heard her swear. Taking out his flashlight again, he stepped in front of the chair, squatted and shone the beam on the grey painted concrete floor. He got up and walked over to the outside wall, where he squatted again and looked back.

"What are you seeing?" Aziz was looking the way people do when they're standing on a rock in the middle of a river. She could see nothing but the concrete floor.

"As seasons come and go, concrete floors that don't have expansion joints—like this one—will develop stress cracks, often very fine." He walked back and forth, shining his light along the surface, before finally laying it on the floor and rolling it along with his foot. "Look at this. Watch the cone of light."

"It looks perfect to me."

"Keep watching." With his next step, the cone rolled and distorted slightly. "Did you see it?"

"I think the shape changed as you rolled it."

He left the flashlight in position, knelt down and ran his hand over the stress crack and into the cone. "Beyond the crack, there's a slight rise." He stood up and rolled the light toward the front of the house. For seven or eight feet, the shape of the cone didn't change, but then it did.

"What does it mean?"

"This floor's been re-poured or repaired, then refinished and repainted. See, there's another crack here." He picked up the flashlight and ran the beam the length of the crack to the outside wall. He looked back at Aziz. "Something's under here," he said.

"It could have been a plumbing issue ... or bad workmanship."

"I don't think so." MacNeice squatted down beside the glass with the amber residue and passed his light over its surface. "There are prints on the glass. We'll check those against Tisdale and Nicholson's car. For now, let's get out of here."

Aziz was up the stairs and outside before he'd made it to the first floor. He found her waiting in the Chevy. MacNeice climbed into the car and called Division to request a full forensics team with a jackhammer and shovels. Ending the call, he started the engine and turned on the heater and defroster.

They sat in silence looking at the sad little house. To everyone passing by on the lonely road, it would appear to have been abandoned or boarded up for demolition to make way for something grander. But it was the secret retreat of David Nicholson, a place where he would read and drink in the middle of an empty basement in a house in the middle of nowhere.

Aziz shook her head. "Nothing good or kind or loving ever happened in there." She took off the latex gloves, shoved them into her pocket and unbuttoned her coat.

MacNeice wiped away the last of the windshield fog in front of him but said nothing.

"I know you've got a theory," she said. "So what is it?"

"Jennifer Grant came home. She promised she would and she did, for Dylan's sake. There was no record of her returning by air, so Nicholson met her at the train or bus station and brought her here. This was solitary confinement—her crime was running away."

Aziz wrapped her arms about herself and looked away toward the escarpment. When they finally spoke again, it was about the weather and how oppressive the rain was and how it seemed like London in a very bad year.

After a half-hour had passed, the radio phone burped to life. The forensics team had overshot the road and were making their way back; the jackhammer was coming separately and would arrive in ten minutes.

While they waited, Vertesi and Williams called in to report on their interview with Jennifer Grant's brother. MacNeice put his cell on speaker mode.

"Boss, he seems like a loving brother. The only flag is that when he was eighteen, over twenty years ago, he joined the Royal Dundurn Light Infantry. He was in the militia for three years," Vertesi said.

"It's not like he stuffed a grenade down his shorts to sneak it home back then," Williams chimed in. "And anyway, they would have been using the pineapple ones — the kind some hero's always falling on in the war movies."

Vertesi picked it up. "He said he has no ill feelings toward David Nicholson, and I believed him. His explanation as to why Nicholson didn't pitch in with the search in California was that he was focused on caring for Dylan and making a living to support him. As far as he was concerned, Nicholson was a great father. And he thinks that his sister simply ran off to live in California, that she wasn't really concerned about her son or her own family. Basically he thinks his sister was a free spirit and hasn't been found because she doesn't want to be found."

Aziz glanced at MacNeice, who was staring through the rain at the house. "I have another theory," MacNeice said. "I want you both here at 1012 Ryder Road."

WITHIN MINUTES, THE first of the black Suburbans came tearing down the road and pulled onto the grass beside the Chevy. Five people climbed out. The driver came over as the others were donning their haz-mat suits and pulling equipment out of the trunk. He leaned down to MacNeice's window while stepping into his yellow Tyvek. "What have we got here, sir?"

"The house belongs to the bombing victim, David Nicholson, but he didn't appear to want anyone to know about it. I think we need to excavate the basement." MacNeice got out of the car and handed the front door key over. "Until your jackhammer gets here, do a thorough search for prints on the first floor and basement."

VERTESI AND WILLIAMS showed up with lunch: burgers and milkshakes from the Secord Dairy. When the jackhammering finally stopped, they waited until the steel front door opened and the team leader appeared, pulling off his yellow hoodie and sliding down his face mask. He stood on the front step and stared at them but made no indication of what they should do.

"That doesn't look good," Aziz said.

"Let's go." MacNeice opened the car door.

When they were lined up in front of him, the team leader shook his head. "I need to give each of you a mask, not because it's rank in there, but just in case. This is a no-shit spooky one." He walked over to the Suburban, popped the trunk and came back with four masks and goggles.

"Seriously? Goggles?" Williams screwed his face up. "I look like a dweeb in goggles."

"No goggles, no look-see, detective. Trust me, you'll thank me for them. We don't know what's in the dust down there."

After Williams put the goggles and mask on, the forensics leader pulled the hoodie over his head again and adjusted his mask, then turned back to them. "Ready?"

They all nodded and followed him to the basement, past a couple members of the team who were scanning the bedroom. The jackhammer operator was dismantling his rig. Standing beside a pit roughly ten feet square were two members of the forensics unit, both female. Large and small chunks of concrete were piled neatly against the outside wall, along with a door that might be the one missing from the bedroom. The women moved back a few paces to provide them full access to the pit.

MacNeice stepped toward the edge and looked down. He inhaled sharply. When Aziz came to stand beside him, she took one look and buckled. Williams caught her before she hit the floor. They all stared at what the digging had revealed: a mummified female body in a soiled wedding dress complete with its train and veil. The nose and cheekbones were flattened. MacNeice glanced toward the door. The forensics leader noticed and said, "Yeah, it was on top of her, and on top of that was the gravel and concrete." The dead woman's hands were folded across her stomach, pressed deep into the folds of the dress, which MacNeice recognized from the wedding photo Dylan had loaned him. On the left hand was a wedding ring. Her flesh was dried and leathery over the bones, covered with concrete or gravel dust. The lips were pulled back as sharply as an incision, exposing grey teeth.

Neatly stacked beside her was dirty clothing. "Soiled — feces and urine, some blood," one of the women on the forensics team offered. Folded the way it would be if someone were packing for a long trip — underwear, socks, T-shirts, jeans, a cotton dress, a light sweater. Beyond the clothes was a small carry-on bag and a suitcase. Next to the head was a coil of rope with something stuffed in the middle.

"That's a gag. There's blood on it with an incisor stuck to it. Looks like it wasn't knocked out—just rotted out while the gag was on." The team leader's voice was flat.

Aziz adjusted her mask and goggles. "She must have been kept in this house for a while."

The jackhammer operator was perched on his generator. "Oh yeah," he said, "she was here for a while." He went over to the door and lifted it, pivoting it so they could see the other side. The days and weeks were scratched into the wood, the seventh day crossing over the previous six. "She made it to 101. If she started keeping score on a Monday, her last day was Thursday." MacNeice looked down to the right of her hip, where a green garbage bag was stuffed between her and the wall of the pit.

"That's garbage, sir. Appears to be biscuit wrappers and empty cereal boxes."

"He wanted her alive but not very," Williams said wryly.

"She was being punished," MacNeice said. "What's that under her head?"

"Looks like a book in bubble wrap, sir," one of the women said.

"After we lifted off the door, we wanted you to see it before we disturbed anything further," the team leader said.

MacNeice nodded and put on his latex gloves. "Lift the book out for me."

The woman stepped carefully into the pit and gently raised the skull, trying not to disturb the matted hair or stained veil. She retrieved the book, and as she let the head down, they heard the sound of something clicking or snapping. In the quiet of the basement, the noise was sickeningly loud. Aziz wasn't the only one who winced.

MacNeice took the package from her. Removing the bubble wrap, he studied the cover. "It's a diary." MacNeice opened the book and read aloud: "This will be my wife's last will and testimony." It was dated 07 08 01 and signed by David Nicholson. Below, in a jagged scrawl was another signature: "Jennifer Nicholson."

THE BOOK SAT in an evidence bag on the floor between Aziz's feet as they drove back to Division. He noticed her glancing down at it from time to time, though she said nothing. When he was parking, she spoke for the first time. "He deserved to die." She opened the door and got out. MacNeice leaned over and picked up the book.

As he climbed the stairs behind her, he said, "What amazes me is that someone so brutal could also be a great father."

"But, it happened... it happens," Aziz said. "Or at least that was the image he fought to preserve."

MacNeice had a thought that made his skin crawl. "Dylan was also his prisoner—he just never knew it."

"How so?" She was taking off her coat, draping it over the cubicle wall.

"Dylan and his mother both did whatever David Nicholson wanted them to do. She was forced to obey. Dylan complied out of love and affection. Doesn't it seem strange now to think how many people said that Nicholson was Dylan's best friend, that they were inseparable, and that a father who didn't care about sport suddenly became an assistant coach on the basketball team so he could support and encourage his son? Now I have to think it was all about control." He put his coat beside hers. "Double espresso?"

She nodded, smiling at him for the first time since the basement.

When he returned with the coffee, Aziz said, "Ryan has some news—it's not good."

Ryan was sitting at his computer station, his feet up on the casters of his task chair, his hands on its leather arms. "Sir, Constable Szabo died this afternoon. The head injury triggered a cerebral hemorrhage late last night."

Aziz held the cup to her lips with both hands as her eyes welled up. "That young man did *not* deserve to die."

MacNeice put his latex gloves on, removed the diary from the evidence bag and bubble wrap, and sat down to examine it.

The handwriting was precise—consistently within the lines—and smaller than he expected from the tall man he'd seen in the barbecue photograph. The neat entries were dated to the minute, leaving MacNeice with the impression that Nicholson knew it would be discovered eventually and that he wanted people to be impressed that it was neat—that he was neat.

MacNeice began at the beginning:

— *August 6, 2001. 4:37 p.m. J wants to know why we're here. It's disingenuous of course—she knows exactly why, so I ignore the question. Have managed to establish 7:00 p.m. as my pick-up time for Dylan at Daycare—splendid! This means I can continue to arrive here between 4:30 and 4:40 every day. I neither need nor want more.*

— *4:48 p.m. She wants to go home. Promises she'll behave. I tell her this IS her home, and that I will come once a day.*

She will remain tied to the bed until I arrive, and while I'm here, she will be allowed to move around the house until her lessons begin. "F*** you!" she says. I tell J that every time she swears—a nasty habit that I'm determined will not infect my son—she will lose food privileges for the day. J screams, "F*** you!" I introduce her to a dirty dishcloth that was here when I took possession of the house. Rolled up, it makes the perfect gag. Today's lesson was postponed due to bad behaviour.

— *August 7, 2001. 9:40 p.m. Daycare closed early for cleanup, so I had to miss today. Dundurn Missing Persons called me and her parents to say there was no record of Jennifer Grant returning by air, rail, or bus. Of course they don't know she came back by car. That part was so easy. J wants to begin teaching next month—what a laugh! J wants to be with her son, begs to be with Dylan. Why? "I love my son, I'll do anything you say; just let me be with him." I tell her D is not her son anymore and he will grow up knowing his mother deserted him. Tears now . . . oh my, such tears. "When a woman weeps, she is setting traps with her tears." Dionysius Cato.*

— *August 8, 2001, 4:15 p.m. On the bright side, J understands now that I'm serious. I have removed the gag for the visit. J eats Cheerios from the box. She smells like excrement— for good reason. She has defecated in bed, soiling everything, and has to be punished. We move downstairs for the lessons—permanently, I think, as the stench above is too much for me. She'll sleep and spend her day in the bed until I come—but I will limit her liquid intake to eight ounces of water a day. Dry food means, hopefully, a dry bed. What a pig she is. How did we ever, ever, ever, find ourselves together?*

– 4:42 p.m. J fondles her breasts, groans, a come-on from a
bad actor. I laugh. J cries. AGAIN! I tell her she's pathetic
and I mean it. Who would want this woman if they could
see her now? Begging, pleading . . . If I were in her shoes,
I'd like to think I'd be stoic and resigned to my fate. Not
her. She's still squirming, conniving, looking for a way
out. Right now, she thinks I don't notice, but she's studying the basement windows to see if I've forgotten something. I haven't.

– 5:00 p.m. Our lesson is a success I think. Yes, she continues
to beg me to let her go, but as soon as I reach for the dirty
dishcloth, she sits silently, whimpering in a sweet but
pathetic way. I read Auden and James. She listens—and
I hope learns—from the beauty of the language.

– 5:45 p.m. Before I leave, J cleans up—well, she scrapes
the bed with a spatula and puts the filth in a garbage bag.
She's quite domesticated now, and only two days have
passed. J has so much more to learn—I'm quite excited
about this. I tell her so, and say that I've decided to call
this the Great Reform Program. J sees neither the humour
nor the gravity in that statement. But she will.

– 5:58 p.m. Have determined to hose J down every Friday—
must do for my own sake. Pity, there's no hot water. Will
make do. Have taken to wearing rubber gloves.

MacNeice stopped reading, put the book down, and
slowly peeled off the gloves. His breathing was shallow
and his heart was racing. He couldn't go on—at least not
right away—and he wouldn't except for the chance the
diary would provide clues about the person who wrapped
Nicholson up in duct tape with a grenade under his chin.

Catching the look of despair on his face, Aziz said, "It's that bad?"

"Worse." He rubbed his face and eyes hard.

"Well, I've got something of interest in that respect: an email from a Constable Jeremy Hopewell, concerning interviews he's doing on Tisdale. Something was troubling him and, after he got home from his shift, he reread his notes of an interview he did with a woman across the street from the Nicholsons.

"Her name is Grace Smylski, and it turns out that her son, Tom, is the same age as Dylan. They've been friends since grade one and Tom's also on the Mercy basketball team. About a month or so after Dylan's mother disappeared, a man showed up at the Nicholsons'. There was a loud confrontation on the front porch, and the stranger shoved Dylan's father against the wall.

"Grace told the constable that she couldn't see what happened next, because of the tree in front, but when she ran across the street, David Nicholson was lying on the porch with a bloody nose and the man was driving away."

"Ask Hopewell to confirm that she's at home and get him to meet you there in a half-hour," MacNeice said. "Let's see if she can describe the man or recall the kind of vehicle he was driving." He took a sheet from his pad and wrote, "Jennifer Grant's body found, basement of Ryder Road." He taped it next to Nicholson's photo, then, feeling sickened by the proximity, he moved the note two inches to the right.

Williams and Vertesi got back as Aziz was heading out.

"Get this," Williams said. "Inside the suitcase there was a *Star Wars* Jedi Knight toy still in the box. Guess Dave didn't think Dylan would appreciate having it."

"Which one of you has the skin to read something grim?" MacNeice pointed to the diary.

Vertesi shrugged, and Williams looked over at the whiteboard.

"I won't lie about how sick it is," MacNeice said. "I want it skimmed — don't get hooked. Remember the man who wrote this is still being picked up by crows, seagulls, and pigeons."

"I'll do it," Williams said.

Vertesi said, "I'm in too. If you need a breather, I mean."

"I'm not looking for the details of what was done to Jennifer Grant — that much we've already discovered," MacNeice said. "I want anything that would point us toward Nicholson's killer — and Szabo's. Again, the man was a monster — don't let him in your head. Understood?"

"Yeah, I'm cool."

"Sure, me too...I guess."

[19]

BYRNE'S BOAT WAS GETTING THE STAR TREATMENT AT MOUNT HOPE.
Surrounded by computers on folding tables and microscopes on rolling cabinets, the runabout was suspended by
chains a few feet off the ground. There were four research-
ers on site and Nathan Ho said two more were down at the
Barton Street facility doing DNA. "Basically, gene matching."

He suggested MacNeice look at something inside the boat
and took the controls of an overhead crane that tilted the
boat toward them. Large floodlights were positioned to shine
on the aluminum interior — the effect, at first, was blinding.

"See here, sir..." Ho used a metal pointer to indicate an
elliptical dent in the hull's surface. "This blow isn't typical
of the damage caused by running a boat over rocks; this
was caused by something heavy dropped inside the boat. It's

recent, within the last four months. It's here we found hair—not blond, but black. And not female . . . This is male hair."

He took MacNeice over to one of the microscopes where the hair, seen through the lens, appeared to be a half-inch thick. "It's oval in section—Caucasian hair. It was stuck in place by the blood that had pooled around it and dried like cement. The blood washed away when the boat was cleaned, but this hair held fast. Whoever cleaned the boat didn't notice."

"So what caused the dent?"

"Not the anchor—it has the wrong profile. This was something heavy, like a sledgehammer."

Then Ho showed MacNeice another strand the team had found, a grey line that snaked across the lens.

"Woman's pubic hair." Ho clicked twice on the keyboard. "Now look," he said.

There were two lines snaking side by side. "Two hairs from the same woman, as best we can tell. One is from this boat and the other is from the body you brought out of the bay."

"A match?"

"We're waiting on the DNA, but yes, a dead match."

Finally, Ho offered MacNeice the view through a large illuminated magnifying glass. A small turquoise stone was centred on a black felt pad. It was conical on one side and facet cut on the other. "Pointy end goes in a ring or an ear-ring or maybe a brooch."

"Interesting," MacNeice said. "The young woman didn't have rings or pierced ears, and there was no evidence of any piercings on her body."

"Maybe it's not related then? I don't know." He turned the light off in the magnifying glass. The stone sat—a lonely turqouise speck in the middle of a black sea.

PULLING AWAY FROM the lab, MacNeice called Richardson.

"He's on the table now, Mac. There's not much I can tell you at the moment," Richardson said. He could hear suction hoses going, and Junior humming something in the background.

"Mary, is he wearing an earring?" MacNeice asked as he merged with the traffic heading back to Dundurn.

"Yes, left ear...a modest affair." Her voice was almost a whisper, suggesting she had the phone propped between chin and shoulder. "Small turquoise stone...nicely set in a thick silver hoop...and, let me see," he could hear the ruffling of her lab coat, Junior still humming over the gagging of the suction hose, "diameter, slightly less than an inch, thickness, shy of three-sixteenths—does that suggest anything?"

"And the other ear?"

More rustling, sounds of exertion. "No stone, just a flattened ring. Likely happened when his skull was crushed."

He thanked her and asked if she'd taken delivery of the body of a woman who'd been dead for more than a decade. "She was buried under concrete in a basement."

"Arriving shortly. We've got another half-hour or so of sucking this young man's insides out, but there's plenty of room here, so we won't turn her away."

AS HE DROVE, MacNeice's thoughts were racing between the basement on Ryder Road and Nicholson's diary, when what he wanted to focus on was Dylan Nicholson. Devastated by the loss of his father, and the manner of his death, he was about to discover that his mother was tortured, starved, and murdered by his father. That his father was a monster, not his best friend.

While there already was an army of social workers and psychologists available to Dylan, MacNeice couldn't escape feeling some responsibility for how he learned the news. He wanted to be the one to tell him.

Before he could make the call to arrange that, though, MacNeice's phone rang.

"It's me, Mac, on the Smylskis' porch," Aziz said. "Not only did she remember that the man was big and athletic-looking, she saw him drive away — in a truck carrying soil, garden tools, and a small birch tree wrapped in burlap."

"How could she remember that?"

"She thought he was coming to do landscaping for Nicholson, and she was looking for someone to work for her. She was heading across to ask him about it when the fight broke out. By the time she was on the sidewalk, the truck was heading toward Main Street and Nicholson was struggling to get up. Remarkably, Mrs. Smylski can recall what Nicholson said about the man too. 'Oh, him, he's a nobody.'"

"It's not every day that your neighbour gets decked."

"Exactly. She said Nicholson was seething — wiping the blood from his face — but managed somehow to sound casual about it. I've been asked to stay for lunch and meet Tom. As Dylan's best friend, he may be helpful."

MacNeice thanked her and said goodbye. Instead of heading back to Division, he swung the Chevy onto King Street, heading for the west end. At the next light, he pulled out Graham McLeod's card and punched the number into his phone.

A PALE GREEN bubble trailer was parked in the wide turning circle that led to the lilac dell. It and the truck next to it were the only signs that anyone was in the botanical gardens.

As MacNeice stepped out of the Chevy, McLeod opened the trailer door and waved him in.

Edging past the mud-caked rubber boots on the trailer's step, MacNeice ducked and entered.

"Yeah, sorry—anyone over five-ten has gotta watch their head."

Under the rear elliptical window was a drawing table, with plan drawers below, custom fabricated to fit both the width and curve of the space. In the belly of the trailer, there was a small table and two chairs. Opposite was a shelf with a two-burner electric stove with a steaming coffee pot on top. Two mugs were waiting beside it. With its door closed, the trailer appeared bright, almost spacious.

McLeod noticed MacNeice taking it all in. "It's intimate," he said. "But, on a day like today—or a month like this one—I can get a lot done here and it's always better to be on site rather than trying to remember what was here back at the studio."

McLeod didn't seem nervous or concerned to have a homicide detective across from him, and MacNeice was content to let McLeod set the pace, making conversation about his work over coffee. When he'd finished his cup, McLeod asked, "You had something you wanted to discuss?"

"Tell me why you didn't mention the altercation with Nicholson on his front porch?"

The younger man took the mugs and placed them both in a plastic bowl under the shelf, then straightened and met MacNeice's eye.

"Maybe because I didn't want you thinking I was a suspect." He leaned against the trailer wall. "I went over to Nicholson's after she'd been gone for two months. Something about the way he said, 'No, I haven't heard from her,' really ticked me off." McLeod came and sat down again at the table. "He made some crack about knowing that I'd been seeing his wife, and maybe I should tell him where she got to. I mean, it all happened so fast. I shoved him and turned to leave, but Nicholson grabbed me by the shoulder. I hit him square on the nose and he went down like a beach umbrella in the wind."

"Were you surprised he didn't lay charges?"

"Not really. David wouldn't want word getting out that I'd slugged him."

"Did you confront him about hitting her?"

"No...I figured that would jeopardize Jenn's trust in me. And if she came back, he'd take it out on her. I couldn't risk that."

"She's dead, Graham. She died roughly a year after she showed you those bruises."

McLeod stood up, slamming his head on the ceiling. Without a coat and wearing only moccasins on his feet, he went outside in the rain.

MacNeice looked around the trailer, which suddenly seemed smaller. He retrieved McLeod's battered Barbour and went after him.

He was standing on the edge of the dell, the rain beating off his shoulders, his hair flattened to his skull. MacNeice put the coat over his shoulders. With the rain pelting his face, it was hard to tell if he was weeping, but his voice cracked when he spoke and he coughed several times. "I guess I've known all this time. She wouldn't leave Dylan—no way. Jenn loved that kid."

MacNeice took him by the shoulders and turned him back to the green bubble. "Have you got anything stronger than coffee?"

"Yeah...some Guinness, bottom drawer of the plan files."

Inside, MacNeice hung the Barbour and his own raincoat. He guided McLeod back to his chair, found a hand towel and gave it to him so he could dry his face and hair.

The bottom drawer was marked "Plan B." MacNeice smiled, took out two cans and pulled the tabs on both. They sat sipping Guinness in silence, McLeod cradling the can in both hands, looking down as if studying the label, the small print or the harp logo. When he'd drained it, he dropped the can in a small wastebasket, pulled the drawer open and took out two more.

"Not for me, Graham. I'm driving."

McLeod sat heavily, setting both cans down in front of him. He pulled the tab on one. "How did she die?"

"I can't reveal the details, but it was homicide."

McLeod's eyes welled with tears, but he made no sound. He was forcing down the grief either out of pride or the fear that if he gave in to it, he'd fall to pieces right there.

MacNeice finished his beer and put the tin in the bin. He looked out the window and waited for McLeod to pull himself together.

"It was Nicholson," McLeod said at last. "It was him...I know it was." He wiped his face and blew his nose into the hand towel. "She called me from LA, called her family. I can't speak for the Grants, but it never occurred to me that she wouldn't ever come back." He looked down at the floor for a moment. "I tried to believe she was happy somewhere out there, you know, on the edge of the continent." He smiled then, ruefully. "No, it's worse: I convinced myself that one day, out of the blue, I'd get a call from Jenn asking me to come out to join her. We'd live happily ever after."

"I think she came back for her son," MacNeice said.

"If he didn't want Jenn, why wouldn't he let me have her? I should have taken those photos to the cops. I was going to, you know. She was terrified I would and I was worried that I didn't. Man, it was such a relief to give them to you."

"Do you have any idea who might have killed David Nicholson?"

McLeod was knotting the small towel around one hand. "Honestly, I don't know. If I did, I'd buy the guy a beer."

"A young constable was killed by the same blast. He leaves a wife and two kids. If there's anyone you know who might have hated Nicholson enough to kill him, I need to know."

"Shit, no. Sorry, I really don't know."

MacNeice left him there in the trailer, with his guilt and his grief.

Driving slowly out of the gardens, he glanced through his rear-view mirror at the little trailer. A green bubble in the rain, it qualified as the second loneliest place in the world. First place would have to go to the sad little bungalow on Ryder Road.

[20]

WHEN MacNEICE GOT BACK, IT WAS 2:35 P.M. WILLIAMS WAS ONLY four weeks into the diary, but he had already taken a walk, had two double espressos, drunk a jug of water and swallowed three ibuprofen for a headache that he couldn't shake. So far, there was nothing to indicate who might have wanted to kill the English teacher. Instead, Williams had three pages of notes, all of which focused on dates or the increasing punishments Nicholson had inflicted on his wife. He gave MacNeice a quick overview. Nicholson had kept his pledge to hose his wife down once a week. When he aimed the water at her face, she'd cover it with her hands. He'd spray it between her legs until she closed them, then aim at her breasts, which she tried to cover with her forearms and so on—for him, it was a game.

"That hose was underneath her, coiled like a snake," Vertesi said, executing a narrowing spiral with his hand.

Williams flipped to a page he'd marked with a purple Post-it and read aloud: " 'J should thank me, but she won't. I'm getting the filth off her while she's getting some exercise.' The water would have been ice cold, but he never mentions it. That poor girl would have wished she were dead every minute of every day — and she's still got...," he flipped through the rest of the pages, "roughly eleven weeks to go."

Vertesi swivelled in his chair to tell MacNeice that he'd offered to take over, but that Williams wouldn't let him."

Williams said, "One sorry brother in this unit is enough, and you white folks...well, I just don't know. I definitely think it's safer that a black man be reading this shit. Lord knows, we have a lot to answer for, but when it comes to weird, nobody does weird better than a white man."

"I've been out in the botanical gardens with Graham McLeod," MacNeice said. "When I told him Jennifer was dead, he took it very badly. I think we can rule him out."

"Nicholson made one reference to McLeod knocking him on his ass. He already had her locked up in that house, and after the incident, Nicholson punished Jennifer by giving her a dozen lashes with the garden hose. I'll read it to you." Williams thumbed to a marked spot. " 'For McLeod. Because I'm told landscapers do it with hoses.' " He rested his hand on the page to hold his spot. "She passed out after four lashes and that scared him. Nicholson wasn't sure exactly what damage he was doing, so he decided to abandon the treatment rather than lose his prisoner...I think he was having too good a time."

Williams got up and headed for the washroom. When he returned, he sat down the way one does when preparing for really bad news, then picked up the diary.

MacNeice's eyes settled on the images of the bandshell tacked to the whiteboard. The phone rang behind MacNeice.

Ryan picked it up on the second ring. "I've got Freddy Dewar, sir. Do you want to take the call?"

MacNeice nodded.

Dewar was calling from a pay phone. With the sound of traffic, he had to raise his voice to a level he probably hadn't used in years. He sounded excited.

"Detective, I think I have something for you. Last night, I was sitting at my usual table in the bar, just finishing my Fish 'n' chips, when a big man came in to talk to Byrne." He paused either to catch his breath or wait until someone passed by. "They disappeared into the office. Byrne looked back at me before closing the door. That was odd, I thought."

"Go on."

Freddy explained that the two men stayed in the office for a half-hour or so, during which the waitress brought Freddy his apple crumble. He'd asked her about the guy meeting with Byrne. The waitress said she'd seen him before. She thought his name was Bishop and that he was another expatriate mick."

"Meaning?"

"She said that once the micks have had a few, they think her bum is public property." Dewar laughed. "In my day, girls never used to talk like that."

"Did you notice when he came out?"

"Yeah, and that was funny too. Byrne took him out the side door so he didn't come back through the bar. Anyways, that was it. I just thought I'd better ring you."

MacNeice thanked the old man, reminded him to keep a low profile, and then walked over to the whiteboard, where he wrote "Bishop" next to Byrne's name. He added a question mark.

"Michael, call your contact at Vice and Drugs — ask them if they've got a file on someone named Bishop, a big man, possibly an Irish national."

"Will do... What do you think he's involved in?"

"I'm guessing bookmaking. Horses, I think."

MacNeice stared at the whiteboard some more, his mind flitting in two directions. Then he picked up his phone and dialed. It rang twice before McLeod answered, slurring a little.

"Yeah... Who's calling?"

"You're still out at the gardens?"

"Yeah. Just cleaning out my Plan B drawer."

"Promise me you'll take a cab home."

"I think I'll sleep here tonight. What else?"

"Did Jennifer ever mention another man in her life, besides you and Nicholson?"

The long pause was punctuated by the sound of a Guinness can being crushed. Just as MacNeice was regretting the question, McLeod said, "I heard that shit about her being wild. Ridiculous. She was straight and narrow, you know. That was the thing about Jenn. That was the reason she left me. I was wild back then, but she was the straightest person I've ever known."

MacNeice heard a chair fall and the zip-fizz of another Guinness from the Plan B drawer being popped. Then McLeod let out a long, ragged sigh. "I don't know. It's possible, I guess. Funny, Mac — do you mind if I call you that?"

"Not at all."

"I wanted to be the one she turned to. I was waiting for her. Shit, people thought I was gay because I didn't want to date anymore after my marriage broke up. I was just waiting. Now, I've got nothing to wait for."

"So you think it was possible she took up with another man?"

"Sure . . . I guess. Sure. I mean, who wouldn't? You saw those photos. I wouldn't have blamed her."

After he hung up, MacNeice circled his note — "We're looking for another lover" — and turned again to the whiteboard for inspiration.

Ryan came over and tapped his shoulder. "The duty sergeant says Markus Christophe is waiting downstairs."

MacNeice looked over at Aziz, who said, "I'll fetch him. We'll be in the interview room." She was up and out of the cubicle before he could respond.

[21]

MARKUS CHRISTOPHE HAD CAUGHT THE RED-EYE OUT OF Vancouver and it showed. His eyes were ringed with red, a fact made more noticeable by his pale skin. When he stood to greet MacNeice, his bearing impressed the detective. Slim and rugged, the young man was at least six foot five. His straight blond hair was long enough that he'd tucked it behind an ear on one side, which emphasized his rectangular face and wide mouth. He offered a firm but very brief handshake.

Christophe told them he had called Anni's sisters from a pay phone in the Toronto airport. They still hadn't told their mother.

"They don't say as much, but they blame me for her death," he said. "Her business-woman sister, whom I don't know, said her father had only given permission for Anni to go because I would be by her side. I knew that. I was there when he said it to her." He paused. "What can I do here? If I can help in any way, I will stay and help. If I cannot help, will you release her body so I can return with her to Norway? I have taken all my earnings from the bank and will pay for the flight."

"Why didn't you stay with her?" Aziz asked.

"Ah...you see..." He searched for the right words. "We both felt so safe here in Canada. It's not like home, but in a way it is. The club..." He tapped his fingers on the table, searching for the correct name.

"The Royal Dundurn Yacht Club," MacNeice said.

"Exactly, yes. The yacht club was short-staffed and asked her to stay. Anni felt somehow she would be deserting them...Funny, but she did. She convinced me that she would follow later, to Whistler. I would work there and wait for her. Then we would go down the coast of America before going home." He finished his coffee. "Ya, well, that was the plan."

MacNeice told him the coroner's office would release her body soon and that DI Aziz would assist him in the arrangements for its transportation to Norway. "Would it help if I were to speak to Anni's sisters?"

"I don't think so. They want justice done of course, and the sister who is a doctor wants to know the details—but she wants it in a report. After reading that, if she needs to speak to anyone, it will be the person who did the examination." He laid his hands flat on the table, a gesture that carried with it the terrible finality of the situation.

"Mr. Christophe, if we could download your correspondence with Anni, there's the slight chance we might see something we've missed between her cellphone and computer. If you're comfortable with us searching your devices, we could do it while you wait—it won't take long."

Christophe reached for his backpack. He took out a small laptop and his Nokia cellphone and offered them to MacNeice. Aziz took both and left the room.

"Why don't you wait here for DI Aziz," MacNeice said. He stood and took Christophe's hand. Before letting go, the young man said, "Please find the person who did this. I need to know why he killed her."

MacNeice hesitated for a second, then said, "We've discovered the body of a man in the same area as we found Anniken's."

"Who is—was he?"

"We believe we know, but it's not conclusive."

"Anni didn't mention any man." He shook his head. "I won't tell this to her family... not yet."

"Please don't."

AS MACNEICE SHUT the interview room door behind him, Aziz was coming toward him from down the hall. Her eyes were wide; she had a hand over her mouth. MacNeice reached out to her, a hand on her shoulder. She looked up at him, stricken. "Swetsky's been shot."

"Where is he?"

"At St. Joe's. It was that kid they thought had run across the border. He wasn't in Mexico, but in a barn at a farm down the road from his parents'. Swetsky took a round from a .30-06 in the hip. It smashed part of the hip bone, though apparently he insisted on walking to the ambulance. He lost a lot of blood, and he's in surgery now. They expect it will take several hours."

MacNeice realized he hadn't taken a breath since she began. He inhaled deeply. "Any other casualties?"

"One of the OPP officers took a round in the shoulder, and the boy's mother was hit in the thigh. He'd come to hit his parents up for money and was in the basement when the OPP arrived. When Swetsky showed up too, the kid took his father's hunting rifle and decided to go out in a blaze of glory."

"Did he?"

"Swetsky put two rounds into him, and an OPP policewoman's shot took him down. She wasn't hurt."

"Has anyone called John's wife?"

"She's at the hospital."

"Let's head there together for when he's out of surgery. I know it's not ideal, but I want you to wait with Christophe until Ryan is done, and make sure he has somewhere to stay. And before I can go to the hospital, I need to break the news of his mother's death to Dylan."

"Does Children's Services know?"

"Not yet. They may not want me there, but I should be the one to tell him."

Aziz nodded. "Why do we do such grim work, Mac?"

He reached out and squeezed her shoulder again. "Don't go there. We're walking across a frozen lake in a blizzard. We don't know how wide the lake is, whether the ice is too thin or if there's shelter on the other side. We can't go back. We just have to keep walking. It's as grim as that, and as essential."

[22]

WITH ITS PALE YELLOW WALLS, THE OFFICE OF THE EXECUTIVE director of Children's Services was warm enough, though the authority of its occupant spoke firmly through the charm. The power was apparent on her desk with its sleek black monitor and keyboard. It was there in the two silver pens, standing like missiles, in a thick silver base featuring a small gold plaque lauding her meritorious service. It also spoke in what wasn't there: stacks of papers, a lipstick-stained coffee mug, notepads, inbox/outbox correspondence, pencils, pens, a stuffed teddy bear—the clutter you find on most desks. The only thing to indicate that someone actually worked there was a tidy pile of file folders held in place by a glass slab *objet d'art*.

He'd been shown into the office by the executive director's assistant and told to take a seat in one of three leather chairs arranged opposite the matching sofa. MacNeice noticed one of these chairs was more worn than the others, and assumed it had been brought from the lobby for the meeting. He wondered how many people it took to inform a teenager that his father had very likely murdered his mother.

He stood as the executive director came in, a tall woman who crossed the room gracefully with an extended hand. "Detective Superintendent MacNeice, I'm Sally Bourke-Stanford."

Though her hair was grey, her skin was unlined, suggesting she'd rarely spent time in the sun. There was a large emerald on her right ring finger, and she wore a grey cashmere scarf over a blue-grey suit with a tight masculine cut. She motioned for him to sit, and instead of sitting down beside him, she sat on the arm of the chair next to him and crossed her hands. He had to suppress the urge to smile at the way she was establishing that he was in her territory.

The assistant arrived with a tray carrying four cups and saucers, a ceramic teapot and matching milk and sugar containers and put it down on the glass coffee table next to her boss. "Will that be all?" she said.

"Yes, thank you, Mary."

Bourke-Stanford settled into her chair and leaned toward MacNeice. "I want you to know that we do appreciate your interest in the welfare of this young man. Before Dylan and his caseworker arrive, I wanted to convey her concerns — and therefore mine." She picked up the teapot. "Do you take your tea with milk and sugar?"

"Just milk, thanks." Bourke-Stanford handed him his cup, then poured hers. "I was told by the caseworker that you had

created a significant rapport with Dylan...at a terrible time."
She sat back, holding the cup and saucer in both hands. "I
agreed to have you here for this very difficult meeting—an
unprecedented situation in my experience—but I want to
set the parameters."

"Understood."

"You'll greet Dylan, as you would normally do, but his
caseworker will deliver the news. If Dylan asks you a question directly, you are free to answer, but my job is to watch
out for his welfare, and if you unduly upset him I will inter-
vene. This is not an opportunity for you to grill the boy. Do
you understand, Detective Superintendent MacNeice?"

"I do. One question though: Is Dylan's aunt coming with
him?"

"We had asked her to be here, but she has refused."

MacNeice nodded. He was not surprised and, though
he didn't say so, he was relieved. "If he asks what happened
to his mother, I hope your caseworker has a way to..."
MacNeice saw her frown and realized that neither the caseworker nor Bourke-Stanford would tell Dylan the whole
truth.

"Our mutual commitment is not to destroy this young
man," she said. "We'll choose our words, detective, and he
may not ask. At least not right away."

Putting down his cup, MacNeice noticed the boxes of
tissues on the coffee table's bottom shelf.

The boy entered the room with his caseworker and a
child psychologist, who introduced herself as Francine and
then took the far chair. MacNeice found the change in him
dramatic: his posture, so erect when they first met, was a
defeated slouch. He took his place on the sofa and avoided
looking in MacNeice's direction altogether.

Bourke-Stanford clearly was skilled at dealing with children in trauma, but with each attempt to engage him, Dylan's head dropped deeper toward his chest to the point where all anyone could see was his hair. The director exchanged glances with the caseworker, Jean, whose only response was a subtle shrug.

"Dylan, can you look up at me?" the director asked, waiting as the seconds passed.

He shook his head once — it appeared to MacNeice a signal of defeat — and looked not into her eyes, but somewhere beyond her shoulder.

"It is impossible, Dylan, for any of us to understand the pain you are feeling, but each of us can help you — if you're willing to let us."

The caseworker reached over and put a hand on his shoulder. Dylan pulled away slowly until she removed it, and he lowered his head again.

"How are you finding your foster home?" Bourke-Stanford's tone was trying for upbeat.

"Good."

"And school? Are you adjusting to being back with your friends and classmates?"

"Yeah, I guess."

"And basketball?"

Dylan raised his head, looked directly at her and asked the obvious question. "Why am I here?" He looked around the room, waiting for someone to answer.

The director put down her teacup and said, simply, "You have been through a lot, Dylan, and I'm sorry to say that it's not over for you. What you're going to hear today is going to be very painful."

He sat back on the sofa and crossed his arms as his face emptied of colour. The caseworker shifted on the sofa to turn to him and said, very gently, "Dylan, the police have found your mother's body."

He nodded, and kept nodding, slowly at first, then faster, and his legs began to bounce in time. Everyone waited. MacNeice wondered if Children's Services really had a strategy here, because if they did, it was lost on him. Then Dylan began to sob, and as he did he looked to each of them directly. When his eyes met MacNeice's, he shook his head but didn't speak. The caseworker reached for the tissues, placing several in Dylan's hand. At last he blew his nose and wiped away the tears with his sleeve.

Crumpling the tissues, he finally asked, "How'd she die?"

The caseworker started to speak, and Dylan raised his hand like he was swatting away a fly. "I want to hear it from him." He was staring at MacNeice, more tears spilling from his eyes. "You found her, didn't you?"

"I did, Dylan. You remember the keys from your father's bed table?"

"Yeah, you asked me about them but I didn't know what they were for."

"Those keys led us to a post office box and then to a small house on the edge of Dundurn. We're pretty sure your father kept your mother prisoner there. And when she died, he buried her there in the basement."

Bourke-Stanford turned away as abruptly as if there had been a sudden knock on the door. The psychologist cleared her throat. The caseworker was looking at MacNeice with a combination of horror and confusion. Only Dylan remained . . . remained what? On the surface, he was calm — or rather, MacNeice thought, frozen, like an ice-age man discovered in a receding glacier. All movement in his legs stopped, the nodding and sniffing stopped, even the tears stopped.

Somewhere deep in his throat, words formed. No one could make out what they were until he'd repeated them several times. "No way...No way...NO FUCKING WAY."

The caseworker put a hand on his shoulders, but he shook her off and stood up. Pointing at MacNeice, he screamed, "You're lying to me. You are...You're lying."

The caseworker looked to the psychologist, who put a finger to her lips. Bourke-Stanford reached across and touched the psychologist's arm. Francine turned and whispered to the director, "Just listen."

Dylan was standing over MacNeice, staring into his face for the answer he wanted to hear. Finally he asked, "Why... *why* would he do that?"

MacNeice stood and wrapped his arms around the boy. Dylan buried his head into the detective's shoulder and his legs buckled, so that MacNeice had to hold him up. He spoke so softly that the other three strained to hear him. "I don't know, Dylan. We just don't know. Stand up now—I want to tell you what I do know about your father."

Dylan found his legs but kept his forehead where it was, resting on the detective's chest. "What?" he whispered.

"Whatever love your father had to give, he gave to you. He gave you all the love he had available...You are living proof of that. And, there's something else..."

The boy pushed away and looked up at MacNeice. "What else?"

"Your mother never deserted you. Your mother came back for you. She loved you."

MacNeice met the executive director's eyes over the boy's head and she nodded.

[23]

AFTER HE LEFT DYLAN, MacNEICE DROPPED BY THE HOSPITAL TO check on Swetsky, who was out of surgery and managed to smile when he saw MacNeice looming in the doorway of his room. He tried to prop himself up but had to abandon that idea along with his need to explain why he'd ended up with a bullet in him. MacNeice just held a hand up and said, "You can tell me about it later, but I'm warning you: I'm not going to listen to you taking the blame. No one died. This was a good day. So rest and recover, and when you're feeling better we can talk."

The rain pelted the car as MacNeice pulled into the division parking lot. He found a spot as close to the back door as he could, and ran in.

Halfway up the stairs, he met Aziz coming down, taking two stairs at a time. She stopped dead when she saw him. "Freddy Dewar's been assaulted and he's been taken to the General."

As he followed her back down the stairs, he said, "What do we know?"

"Freddy went out for his daily constitutional, carrying his Canadian flag umbrella. He headed east along Burlington and turned down to Guise. Just before he got to Catherine Street, someone pulled him into the trees and worked him over with a bat or a brick and left him there. One of the rowers cycling to the club found him, but only because he stopped to pick up the umbrella, which was rolling about on the road. Freddy was unconscious."

"How is he?"

"Three broken ribs, a broken wrist, nose, and cheekbone. All his front teeth are gone, but the ICU resident said they were false anyway."

At the car, MacNeice stood for a moment, collecting himself, as Aziz climbed in. When he got in and started the engine, he said, "I should have told him to stand down."

"Mac, he wanted to be useful again. And maybe this attack has nothing to do with him calling us about the man he saw."

MacNeice shot her a glance that said they both knew that couldn't be true.

Dr. Aaron Rosen met them at the door of the ICU. "We've set the wrist and stitched up his torn lip. The broken nose and cheekbone will heal on their own, as will the ribs, in time. He's on an IV drip for the pain, oxygen to ease the pressure in his lungs and rib cage. We're watching him closely for any sign of pneumonia—so, no bets on him yet, but I'm optimistic."

"Can we speak to him for a moment?" MacNeice asked.

"He's in a tent and he's groggy. You can have five minutes, that's it."

Freddy was barely recognizable and looked to be unconscious under his oxygen tent. MacNeice and Aziz were about to leave when one eye opened. A moment later, so did the other. Both were bloodshot.

"It's Mac, Freddy. I'm here with DI Aziz."

The old man tried to smile Aziz's way, an unsettling sight — his upper gum was raw and there were no teeth.

"We'll let you sleep, Freddy, but one question: Did you recognize who did this to you?" Aziz asked.

He slowly turned his head their way. "Big fellas . . . used a billy club — couldn't do it with their fists. Didn't know them."

His eyes closed and he smacked his lips. MacNeice stuck his head into the hall to spot the nurse, who was already approaching. "I think he's thirsty."

"He's getting his fluids through a tube, but I'll give him some crushed ice," she said, shooing them both out. "Your time's up, detectives."

As they walked to the elevator, MacNeice said, "When we get back, Fiza, send a uniform over to the bar to collect Freddy's kit, and make sure the officer tells Byrne or the bartender that Freddy was mugged, probably by kids. I don't want Byrne to think this has anything to do with the homicide case, just that it was another mugging in a rough end of town. And I want Freddy out of the city for a while. He needs to be near water and good fish and chips. Maybe Port Dalhousie — he'd have the lake, the Welland Canal. There's got to be a place for him out there."

When the elevator doors opened on the lobby, instead of heading for the exit, MacNeice turned toward the morgue.

"Since we're already here, let's go see how the coroner is doing with Jennifer Grant."

But as they walked down the white-tiled corridor toward the stainless steel doors, he wished he hadn't suggested it. He realized that he was disturbed by the thought of Jennifer Grant's remains on a table anywhere near her husband's. It seemed cruel that after enduring a decade of his visits to Ryder Road—between basketball practice and dinner with her son—her bones were not to be free of him now.

Mercifully, there was only one body in the autopsy area, and it was covered with a plastic sheet. Junior was using a long-handled brush with stiff bristles to clean the floor. When he saw MacNeice and Aziz, he nodded toward Richardson's office.

Richardson looked up from a folder on her desk as they came in. "She's been dead twelve years and six months, give or take a week." She got up and slid three photographs of the body into the clip rack, followed by two X-rays. The way the flesh still clung to the bones, it appeared as if a powerful vacuum had sucked the life and everything else out of Grant.

"She was entombed very quickly following her death," Richardson said. "Her insides suggest the diet was meagre— basically cereal. She wasn't only starved, she had to have been refused liquids, because she was severely dehydrated." She tapped one of the images. "Before she died, she probably looked not too much different than she does here."

As if being starved wasn't sufficient, Richardson pointed out the signs of torture. There were rope burns so severe they scarred the flesh of her wrists, rib cage and ankles. "It looks like she spent the end of her life in constant bondage. And she'd been hit several times across the back by something with a metal head. The marks suggest the metal threading of a broom handle or hose."

"A hose," MacNeice said. "It's in his diary."

"Ah." Richardson put down her pencil and crossed her arms. "I don't want to think about that." She began pulling the images from the clip rack. She returned the photos to the file and picked up her pencil, poised to write. "Who shall I release the remains to when it's time?"

MacNeice thought of Dylan and how impossible the idea of arranging his mother's funeral would be for him. Aziz stepped in when MacNeice didn't respond. "I'm sure it will be her parents. I'll send you their contact information once I'm back at Division."

Outside in the parking lot, it hit him. "Fiza, I just realized I've been struggling with the fact that David Nicholson got exactly what he deserved. It's made it hard for me to concentrate on finding Constable Szabo's killer."

Aziz replied in Arabic.

When he asked for the translation, she said, "Let's just get out of here."

He turned out of the lot into traffic, and they drove in a silence that lasted for a good five minutes. Finally, Aziz cleared her throat. Looking out the side window, she said softly, "It's from the Qur'an. It means, 'He punishes whom He pleases, and He grants Mercy to whom He pleases, and towards Him are ye turned.' " She glanced at him. "And for that, I can only live in hope. Nicholson played a vengeful god but wasn't finally punished by God."

"Maybe he was, Fiza. I think Nicholson knew his killer. He knew that he was being punished when that grenade was taped under his chin. He thought salvation had arrived when the firefighters showed up. He was definitely praying to someone — and he certainly heard the answer when the pin was pulled. He had five seconds to ask the question,

'God, why me? I've been a good father.' Maybe, just before that fifth second, he realized what God's answer was."

"So who do we think killed him?" Aziz asked. "We've considered the Grants, the father and brother, and the landscape designer, McLeod. With all three of them, you have to ask, why now?"

"From what I saw of McLeod's reaction to the news that she'd been found, he knew nothing about her imprisonment, torture, and death. If he had, Nicholson would have been dead years ago."

Aziz curled into her seat. "So maybe she had another lover. Jennifer Grant made two bad choices in men, first McLeod and then the worst—Nicholson. She was unhappy, which I don't think would have improved her judgment."

The on-board phone rang and MacNeice pushed the hands-free button. Deputy Chief Wallace's voice crackled out of the speaker: "I've got a press conference on the Nicholson case tomorrow morning. What do I need to know?"

"The son is reeling from the news. Safest thing for Dylan at this point would be for you to announce at the end of the conference that an unidentified body has been found in the basement of a home on Ryder Road."

"All right, I'll be careful not to link them as of yet, but I need to be able to say we are making headway in locating the killer." Wallace paused. "We are, I trust?"

"Yes," MacNeice said, and hung up.

His thoughts turned to Dylan. There was no way to keep the identity of the body quiet for long, but the revelation would put pressure on Dylan Nicholson, the one true innocent in the unfolding story.

He dialed Sally Bourke-Stanford's office number, even though it was after office hours. But she picked up after three rings.

"Sally, I wanted you to know that Deputy Chief Wallace will be holding a press conference in the morning about Dylan's mother. He won't name her, because Forensics is still confirming that the DNA, fingerprints and handwriting found on site match those of Jennifer Grant and David Nicholson. But her identity will come out soon, especially as it'll be tied to Nicholson's death. Do you have Dylan on a suicide watch?"

Bourke-Stanford's tone was grave. "Before I leave this evening, I'll personally call the foster parents and his case-worker to alert them of your—our concern for his safety."

RYAN WAS STILL working when they got back to Division, though it was past eight. He had made progress narrowing down the date of Anniken Kallevik's disappearance from Markus Christophe's emails—finding a message that must have been sent from an Internet cafe. He read out, " 'Wonderful day ahead. I'm going to see a horse race in Toronto, then to dinner.' That was one of the last emails she sent to him. When he replied and asked who she went with, her response was, 'Just a friend. It was the end of the season. The horses were beautiful, but it was so cold we stayed bundled up drinking hot chocolate. I won $30 betting on Glory Girl in one race and lost $25 on Hard Candy in the next. I didn't bet anymore, so I'm still ahead $5.' " They corresponded in English, presumably to increase their proficiency.

Ryan had found out that the last day of thoroughbred racing was December 13. Her responding email was dated December 14. There would be two more emails, one in which she forwarded news from home and the other answering Christophe's request that she make her way to Whistler before the New Year, so they could keep to their original schedule and head down to California. Ryan showed them that one on screen, dated December 22 and cheerfully annotated with pictograms: "Yes big brother Λ. I'll be there soon;-) AK Bisous."

Christophe sent her a total of twenty-two emails after that, and twice as many text messages; all went unanswered.

MacNeice asked Ryan if he'd already requested the video-tapes from the track's surveillance cameras. He had, but they were recycled after three months—nothing existed from December 13 except direct video replay of the actual races.

Studying the photographs on the whiteboard, MacNeice reminded himself that the friend might have been from the hostel, the yacht club or both. But he didn't believe it. Anniken went to the races with a man who knew racing—Duguald Langan. That she didn't mention his name suggested that she knew Markus might insist that she be on the next train to BC.

By the time MacNeice picked up his coat, at 9:18, the rest of the team had gone home. As he headed for the stairs, he looked back once at the whiteboard and remembered the image that wasn't there yet—the one of Jennifer Grant's naked corpse on Mary Richardson's wall.

THAT NIGHT, SLEEP came slowly for MacNeice. The city had installed a new lamp on the road near his cottage, which effectively projected the rain streaking down his window onto the wall beyond the bed. It took discipline to see the images as raindrops and not snakes or endless tears.

Normally, he would never bring grappa to bed. Much better if he put the glass in the sink as any responsible drinker would do. But there he was, glass in hand, his eyes glued to the light up the road. Black branches crowded about the glow, for warmth, he imagined.

Warmth. He tried bringing Samantha to life, but she emerged only in fragments: mopping up the sauce on a plate, or her naked silhouette at the window of her bedroom in the morning light. Soon she would be looking out the window to morning in Athens. Like loose wires shorting out a fixture, Fiza's face appeared in his mind.

He got up and pulled the curtain shut and sat down on the bed. Sipping the grappa, he wondered what Kate would make of the new lamp. She'd hate it, for sure. Kate needed total darkness to sleep. Finishing the grappa, he put the glass in front of the clock radio, fragmenting the digital display. When he was exhausted, his mind always slid back to her. He lay down and closed his eyes, and wondered, yet again, when exactly it was that he'd lost Kate. It wasn't when she died—it was way before that. Even *before* the morphine drip, drip, drip, that disappeared the pain but left you in a coma until you stopped breathing.

"So when do you think it was then?"

Ah, you're here. I knew you were. I think I lost you when we were told the cancer was terminal.

"I suppose."

The lump on your collarbone; it suddenly appeared, the size of a dime, then a nickel. I told you it must be a fat globule.

"That was cruel, Mac. Never tell someone you love she has a fat globule."

I was too terrified to say what I really thought. That was the best I could do. Do you remember, Kate? That very spot—it was one of my favourite places to kiss.

"I know, and I never asked you why."

Because it had a special quality; it was open…but hidden, and there was always this smell.

"Scent, darling, not 'smell.' "

A scent then, like perfume but not perfume. You. It was a private pleasure, like kissing the small of your back or behind your neck; you couldn't watch me, so they were—

"Stolen kisses. I always loved the idea of that."

Kate, when do you think I lost you?

"It began with a lump the size of a dime."

[24]

BEFORE HE ENTERED THE TEAM CUBICLE THE NEXT MORNING, MacNeice knew something had happened. It was as if a tremor was emanating through the concrete floor: his chest tightened as he stepped out of the stairwell door. "What is it?" He looked at each of them, wondering who was going to speak first. Ryan, uncharacteristically, didn't turn around or say good morning.

Williams stood up. "I've found something, boss. You want me to read it, or just give you the book? I've marked the pages with orange tabs."

"It's big," Vertesi chipped in.

"Hand it to me," MacNeice said, as he sat down wearily at his desk and put on the gloves. Williams carried the diary to him. Taking a deep and, he hoped, discreet breath, MacNeice opened it to the first tab.

Williams smiled grimly. "It's November 22nd. She's got less than a week to go. Two days later, he notices her calendar on the back of the door. He punished her for that even though she had stopped tracking the days: she didn't have the strength. He refers to the punishment as being for 'past sins.' She dies four days later."

MacNeice looked down again at the sickeningly neat script.

- *5:12 p.m. I thought J was made of sterner stuff. She stopped eating two days ago (little stools, mouth ulcers, coughing blood!). Had to carry J downstairs for her lessons—that wasn't easy, the stench.*

- *5:35 p.m. Thought that now was the best time to confront J with S. Disappointed! She opened her eyes a little, but said nothing. She hasn't spoken for a week or more. Perhaps I've waited too long . . . hope not. We'll see.*

- *5:50 p.m. Tried force-feeding Cheerios, but she coughed them back up. I ask how she thought she'd get away with it—S, I mean. No response. I'll try tomorrow.*

- *November 22, 2001. 4:29 p.m. A New Day for Truth. J force-fed Ensure—I wait.*

- *4:31 p.m. Throws up—much blood—feed her some more. I wait.*

- *5:25 p.m. It stayed down. Try some more . . . it came up almost immediately. Nevertheless, J seems more alert—I ask again about S. Her eyes are closed now all the time but she smiles. MISTAKE. Smacked her for smiling.*

— 5:41 p.m. I think she got the message: she's not smiling anymore. I say, "I hope it was worth it. Is it worth it to you now?" No answer.

MacNeice looked at the Post-it hanging off that last sentence and then at Williams, who took the diary back and laid it on the table. He pressed the palm of his hand on the closed book as if it would otherwise open of its own evil accord, then peeled off the latex gloves and set them down on top. "You don't need to read any further, Mac. He never mentions 'S' again. She never speaks or even opens her eyes again. He keeps trying to feed her Ensure, but her system's shutting down. I'm amazed she lasted that long."

The day she died, Williams told them, Nicholson had exams and got to the house late. "After hosing her down, he put her in the wedding gown. He'd dug the pit over the previous two weeks after researching how to lay concrete in the Our Lady of Mercy school library. The equipment was all rented under his pseudonym, Christopher Marlowe. He paid cash."

MacNeice looked at them all. "I want all first and last names beginning with S of the male teaching staff at Mercy, past and present, including the principal."

The phone rang and Ryan picked up. Without even asking, he handed it to MacNeice. It was Sally Bourke-Stanford. "Dylan left his foster parents' house early this morning through the bedroom window. He took a gym bag with all of his clothes."

"Have you called his grandparents, or Grace Smylski? Her son, Tom, is Dylan's best friend.

"Not yet—I just found out. His caseworker went to the school first, then called me to say he hadn't shown up for class."

"I'll get an amber alert issued, and we'll check the bus and train terminals and all roads out of Dundurn in case he decided to hitchhike somewhere."

MacNeice ended the call, then said, "Aziz, give me the keys to the house on Tisdale, fast."

HE WENT ALONE, parking down the hill so the boy wouldn't spot the Chevy and bolt. Before climbing the steps to the front door, he turned to see if Grace Smylski was watching — she wasn't. A moment later he was easing the storm door open and sliding in the key. The heavy oak door gave way in a hush of stale air. Inside, he paused to look around the living room — nothing had been disturbed. The wood floor- ing creaked as he moved down the hallway. The door lead- ing to the basement stairs was open. In the kitchen, there was a Dr Pepper on the table. He felt the can — it was empty but still cold.

MacNeice went back into the hall and listened for any sounds from the second floor. Hearing nothing, he made his way to the top of the basement stairs. He could see there was a light on. The stairs were hopeless — they squeaked with every footfall.

"Who's that, who's there?" Dylan's voice.

"It's me, Dylan. Mac. I'm coming down."

"Haven't you done enough? Get out of here."

MacNeice stepped into the rec room. Dylan's gym bag was on the floor by the sofa. The door to the furnace room was open. MacNeice crossed the room swiftly and there was the boy, standing on a three-legged footstool. He had a belt buckled around his neck and he was struggling to secure it to a hot water pipe. He wasn't distracted from his task by MacNeice.

"Go away, detective. You've done your job. That's it, isn't it? Your job: find the bodies, find the killers and fuck the rest."

"You need a hand with that?" MacNeice asked calmly.

"What? Oh yeah, like I'm some tool. I know you can stop me. But I will do it, I will."

"I never said I wanted to stop you. Like you said, I'm the one who finds the bodies. You're still alive." He stood in front of Dylan, looking up at what he was trying to do. "I assume you're using your dad's belt—that's poetic. Give it to me. I'll tie it off at the bracket. That pipe's too wide." With some force he took the belt out of Dylan's hands and looped it around the vertical bracket, pulling it tight to make sure it would hold. "You're good to go," he said.

There was now very little play in the belt, the noose forcing Dylan to stand on tiptoe, which made the stool even less steady. MacNeice backed off and leaned against the door frame.

"What are you doing?" Dylan's face was contorted with anguish, and the pressure around his neck was painting his cheeks a dark red.

"I'm here to watch you go, if you're determined to do this. You should at least have one friend."

"You're not my friend. Man, you think I'm crazy? You don't care about me."

"Okay, so at least I'll be here to pull you down after it's over. But for the record, I do care about you."

"Well I don't care about you!" The stool wobbled. To steady it, Dylan lifted his head so that he faced the ceiling, his feet flat on top of the stool.

"You do, though. That's what's difficult for both of us, Dylan. You do care about me. And I started caring about you the moment I saw that photo of you on the mantel upstairs— that and the wedding photo of your mom that you kept in your room."

"Don't talk about that." He was crying now and began to gag.

"You're going to choke to death that way too, Dylan. It'll be quicker if you kick over that stool." MacNeice stepped forward. "Here, I can do it for you."

"Get back—get away from me." The boy's voice cracked and he went back up on tiptoe to release the pressure on his throat so he could spit and swallow.

"Weird thing is, I actually had a proposition for you."

Dylan couldn't look directly at him, but he tried. His expression reminded MacNeice of a porcupine he'd seen caught in a leg trap—the mixture of fear and rage in its eyes—and it sickened him. He went back into the rec room and picked up one of the basketballs. He slammed it against the wall; it bounced back to him across the tiled floor and so he did it again—the noise was startlingly loud.

"What are you doing? Stop that. What do you want? Why are you here?"

Mac looked back into the furnace room. "Like I said, I had this proposition."

"You were tricking me at Children's Services, weren't you? At least now, you should tell me the truth."

MacNeice lobbed the ball back into the rec room. "No, Dylan, I believed every word of what I said. But if I had been through what you've been through, I wouldn't believe me either. That was why I knew to come to the house. You wanted to finish it where it began, here in this house, across the street from Tom."

"What do you mean?"

Dylan's legs were shaking with a fatigue that ran up the whole of his body to his hands locked on the belt around his neck.

"You've lost everyone who loved you; and worse, you've figured there'll be whispering and cheap shots in the hallways of Mercy High," MacNeice said. "And that's just the short term. You'll never have a parent there to see you graduate, get married, have your own kids. Your whole idea of who your parents are is upside down and I can't argue with that, because it's true. But you've left Tom and your teammates out of the picture. They don't strike me as cut-and-run friends."

"What do you know about them?"

"I know Tom is your best friend and that you've known him your whole life. I know, when it comes to basketball and life, good times or bad, win or lose, you will have each other's back."

"So?" He was sniffing, trying to keep the snot from running down into his throat.

"Let's think about Tom for just a minute. First he'll be angry you hanged yourself and that you didn't confide in him — *your best friend*. But then he'll begin feeling guilty that he was useless at helping you survive what you were going through and he'll start blaming himself. The guilt will deepen and it'll stay with him till his grave. But there's no point in you feeling guilty about Tom feeling guilty. And maybe the biggest hurdle for Tom is his sense that you betrayed him when you didn't turn to him. That's his problem though, isn't it?"

MacNeice walked back into the rec room and thumbed through a small stack of NBA game and highlight DVDs before calling, "I saw an empty Dr Pepper can upstairs. Are there any more of those?"

At first Dylan didn't answer — maybe he was trying to figure out what MacNeice's strategy was — but then he said, "There are two left."

"You want one? I imagine you must be as thirsty as I am at this point."

MacNeice went upstairs. He found the two Dr Peppers and a half-full package of Fig Newtons in the fridge. He took the cans and cookies, went back downstairs and settled on the sofa. "You still with me, Dylan?"

"You wouldn't let me do this—they'd put you in jail."

"Who'd know?" There was a pause and he heard the stool rocking. "I'll just say I got here ten minutes too late."

He put the Fig Newtons on top of a magazine, opened his drink and took a sip. Looking at the posters—LeBron James, Kevin Durant, Blake Griffin, Dirk Nowitzki, and Chris Paul—he asked, "Why isn't Bill Russell on your wall?"

Long pause, then Dylan asked, "Who's he?"

"He was the Celtics centre who changed the game forever, I'm told."

"I thought Shaq and Kareem did that."

"Nope. I have it on good authority those two wouldn't even have happened if the door hadn't been blown open by Bill Russell."

"Well, I don't care anymore."

"I look at these walls, the magazines, DVDs, the balls, the photo that was on the mantel and is likely now tucked in your bag, and I'd have to say I don't agree. You do care. At your funeral, Tom Smylski will say that basketball was what you cared about most." Then he added, in as matter-of-fact a tone as he could produce, "Basketball could save you now, Dylan."

For close to three minutes the only sound was the intermittent rapid rocking of the stool and Dylan's coughing and spitting. Soon, whether he wanted to anymore or not, the boy would hang because he couldn't balance anymore.

"So what is your proposition?" Dylan struggled to say.

MacNeice took a long, deep breath, his eyes welling with relief.

"I refuse to speak to a man on a stool with a belt tied around his neck. Sorry, Dylan, but you need to come and hear me out. If you reject my idea, I promise you I'll help you climb back up on that thing."

"What's the move in all this?"

"Only you and I are here, so what we say happened is what happened. If you accept my proposition, you'll agree to at least outlive me and be the man I know your mother wanted you to be."

"What do you know about my mother?"

"More than you, maybe more than her parents and certainly more than your father—all of which I'm willing to tell you."

Another pause. "Okay."

MacNeice went into the furnace room and unlashed the belt from the bracket. He helped the boy off the stool and undid the buckle from his neck, then dropped the belt on the floor. He held Dylan by the shoulders. "I know it took courage for you to agree to listen. The truth is that's only a fraction of the courage you'll need if you accept my deal." He walked him to the sofa and handed him the last of the Dr Peppers.

"We're going to talk about Bill Russell, about sacrifice, about competition and how that might save your life. But for the moment," he said, "just enjoy your Dr P and the fact that you're still breathing." MacNeice clinked Dylan's can with his, took a sip and swallowed. Then winced.

Dylan was studying the detective's face. "Do you even like Dr Pepper?"

"Hate it." He laughed. "What's more, I don't believe Pepper's a doctor." MacNeice sat back and waited for Dylan to recover a little.

"Would you really have let me do it?" Dylan nodded toward the furnace room.

"What do you think?"

"Sir, I think...you're seriously weird."

"That may be," MacNeice conceded. "May I tell you about someone I loved who died a few years ago and the impact her death has had on me. You okay with that?"

"Sure...I guess."

MacNeice began at the beginning, with his first sight of Kate, their first words, the first time their conversation wasn't awkward, the first moment he admitted what had been true for him from the beginning: that he loved her and wanted to be with her forever.

He told Dylan about how he'd reduced his life to its simplest form: work and Kate. About how, in the years they were together, she'd opened him up to music, art, reading and travel, and how even though their lives were completely different before they'd met, they managed to fold themselves around each other. How, in time, Kate made him better than he was, more of a man than a cop, and how he didn't really know what she saw in him, other than a potential that she alone could identify. Anytime he asked what it was exactly, she'd smile and touch his cheek, and suddenly the question didn't matter. Life was good and complete.

"But I learned 'forever' can't be measured in years when I got the call that Kate's tests had come in and it was bad news. I felt the life being sucked out of me. The doctor was a family friend and he wanted to speak to me first so we could tell her together."

Dylan's head was down on his chest, and tears were sliding down his cheeks.

From that point, things went fast, MacNeice said. Days filled with waiting, days of chemotherapy that poisoned her and made her weak and angry and then just weak. He told Dylan how he'd looked for alternate treatments, plants, roots, Chinese herbs, and how each glimmer of hope was dashed by a further slide in her strength. Finally, she gave up.

"Kate was semi-conscious for two weeks before she died. When her breathing stopped, a tear fell into the hollow below her eye. I've never been religious, but I put my finger in the little pooled tear as if it were holy water and touched it to my lips and my forehead. It was the last drop of her life left."

"Harsh," Dylan said under his breath, and wiped his face with his sleeve.

"What I know is, Kate died sure of my love for her. She left this world knowing we shared something worth a lifetime, and while it was cut short, she lives on in my experience of her."

He could see that these ideas had gone over Dylan's head, so he told him how close he felt to her when he visited her grave out in the country, how he'd speak—out loud—about the weather, the birds and chipmunks, the sky and the scuttling clouds, the amber sunsets, about his current passions in music, his joy in listening to her practise violin, especially when she didn't know he was listening. "In those moments, to me she's alive again, just sleeping."

He told Dylan about the dreams, the ones that hovered over him like nightmares, where he was desperate to find her and couldn't. He said things to the boy he'd never said to anyone. He was hoping Dylan would recognize something in it for himself. After all, rage and overwhelming grief had taken him into the furnace room. Those were emotions MacNeice knew well.

"I've been told, by men I grew up with, that I should move on," MacNeice said. "That I should look ahead, not back — and there's much to be said for doing so. But I've resolved to let nature guide me. You know, when you see a leaf floating down a stream, and you watch it and follow it, at some point it leaves the current and circles around before coming to stop on the bank. Eventually, it sinks to the bottom and joins the leaves that took the same journey years before."

"Yeah . . . I've done that."

"That's me. I am a leaf swirling around now in a little eddy, not quite stopped, but no longer captive to the current." MacNeice put his hand on Dylan's shoulder. "Perhaps everything I've just said — or nothing — applies to you. But I want you to consider that not even death can alter the fact that your mother loved you."

Dylan was looking down at his empty can and nodded slowly.

"So let me tell you about the proposition. Not surprisingly, it involves basketball and Bill Russell." MacNeice waited until the boy turned to him. "It also involves a friend of mine, a guy who played basketball when he was your age, who loves the game as much as you do, and needs your help."

[25]

THE SCENT OF PATCHOULI PRECEDED UNDERCOVER OFFICER ZENO Trakas down the corridor. Vertesi's contact from Vice was every bit the sight that he was the smell. He wore a pale ochre suit with wide lapels, a Mediterranean blue silk shirt, and a gold medallion hanging from a heavy gold chain around his neck. The medallion floated in a bed of black chest hair that rose all the way to his neck. Trakas rolled a toothpick with his tongue from one side of his mouth to the other as he enjoyed the wide-eyed stares of MacNeice, Williams and especially Aziz. Smiling at her, he lifted his massive eyebrows and said, "You like what you see, eh?"

"Detective, you are an...exotic."

Suddenly the shtick dropped and Trakas said, "Enough of that. Okay if I sit?"

Vertesi pushed his chair toward him, and Trakas turned it so he could face all of them and settled in. He took the toothpick from his mouth and shoved it into his jacket pocket. Leaning over his legs like he was about to draw a diagram on the carpet, Trakas wiped away an imaginary speck from his cream-coloured leather shoes. "So you want to know about grenades? Who has them, how do you get them, and who got one delivered to him in Dundurn?"

Vertesi said, "Exactly."

Trakas's beat was weapons traffic, mostly handguns, Uzis, and assault rifles crossing the border at Fort Erie. His cover was an actual family connection in the port of Kalamata in southern Greece, through which many of the weapons coming from and going to the Middle East were smuggled. He smiled broadly, displaying a gold incisor. Noticing MacNeice's reaction to the tooth, he put his beefy fingers in and pulled it out. "Cap. No big deal." He slipped it back in his jaw and winked at Aziz.

"Okay, so there's BBT. Barry and his brother Shawn Bailey, twins out of Ithaca—that's a Greek name, by the way—they hooked up with a kid from Dundurn, named Luther Tirelle, a Jam-Can who went down to Cornell on a full scholarship."

"Football?" Williams asked.

"Stereotyping, detective." He made a tsk-tsk sound through his teeth. "Luther went to Cornell on a business scholarship, but dropped out after second year because he wasn't learning anything."

"Meaning he was a lousy student."

Trakas shook his head at the absurdity of such clichés coming from a black man. "No, Luther had the highest scores in his class, and his profs were grooming him for big things in business. Instead, he founded Bailey and Bailey and Tirelle—BBT—but that means something else on the street…Anybody?"

"Bacon, bacon, and tomato?" Williams said.

Trakas didn't take the bait. He looked up at Vertesi and over to Aziz, who both looked back, then swung his head toward MacNeice.

"Big Bang Theory," MacNeice said.

"Exactamundo. If I had a cigar, sir, it would be yours."

Trakas told them that Tirelle's mission with Big Bang Theory was to supply the Canadian side of the border with superior quality and reasonably priced weaponry for all occasions.

"The money goes south, the weapons come north, and the gangs of the Golden Horseshoe hit the streets evenly weaponized, because they were all buying from the same supplier—BBT."

Trakas cast a look around the cubicle to make sure they were keeping up with him. "Now, to the grenade in question. Grenades are an infinitesimal part of BBT's business, there's just not that much demand. This one took out two people. Interestingly, Luther is as upset about that as we are. I got him on the phone right after I heard a grenade had exploded in Gage Park. I reminded him that not one incident of gangs and grenades had ever been recorded. And that now, especially with the death of that cop, everyone was going to bear down on the border, thinking the gangs are going crazy."

Vertesi looked up from his notebook. "What if it was a Canadian grenade?"

Trakas dropped his head, took a deep breath and said, "It wasn't. I can tell you the military base it came from, south of the forty-ninth. And here's some news: it wasn't one grenade, it was two. Luther sold the two grenades to one customer for five K. Which is a deal, 'cause one goes for three K. So why the deal, you might ask?"

"I'm asking," Williams said.

"Luther knew the guy who bought them and gave him a family discount. Get this: Luther says this client has no connection to gangs, the Mob, or terrorists. Luther won't tell me who it is—he's certain the cop was an accident, by the way—but he's still pissed at the guy."

"Where's Tirelle now?" MacNeice asked.

"He's nowhere you're interested in."

"He's an accessory to murder. If he's here or even in the States, why not arrest him?"

"With all due respect, sir, stick to homicide. We're taking down the cross-border shoppers, and we know pretty much—with this exception—what's coming in and we're getting better at tracking where it goes. I need Luther Tirelle and the Bailey boys just where they are. Luther's in the mountains of Jamaica and he doesn't need to come back to run his part of BBT. He does it all online."

Trakas stood up, shook everyone's hand, hiked up his collar and then paused at the exit of the cubicle to say, "That smell?" He inhaled deeply. "For you, at least, it'll fade."

He smiled—in character again—took the toothpick out of his jacket pocket, slid it between his lips, and followed Vertesi to the exit.

MacNeice went into the corridor and opened a window as Williams raced to the other side of the office, where he opened another. Aziz took a small hand sanitizer from her briefcase and doused her hands with it, rubbing them together as if she had come in contact with an infected alien.

When Vertesi came back, MacNeice was writing BBT on the whiteboard. The young detective smelled his chair before deciding it was safe to sit down.

Aziz gave him the hand sanitizer. MacNeice added the name Luther Tirelle and a question mark on the board. "Let's find out where Tirelle went to high school."

"Already on that, sir," Ryan said. Thirty seconds later: "Geez Louise. Here's his graduation photo, and can you guess where it's from?"

"Our Lady of Mercy High," MacNeice answered.

"Exactamundo! Sorry, sir, I couldn't resist, but yes, Tirelle's a 2002 Mercy grad." Ryan clicked several times, then summarized what he'd found: "Luther Tirelle, twenty-seven, grew up in Dundurn, Ontario. He lived with his mother, then, after she went back to Kingston, Jamaica—no reason given—he moved in with his grandmother, who stayed on in Dundurn until 2009, when she moved to Oakville, Ontario, to live in a home by the lake—purchased for her most likely by her grandson. His ambition in high school? Win a Nobel Prize for business innovation in the new economy."

"Like that's going to happen," Vertesi quipped.

"Not so fast, wasn't Nobel into explosives," Williams said.

MacNeice said he was interested to know if there were any extracurriculars mentioned during his years at Mercy. The only thing Ryan could find online was noted below his name; it simply read, "Go Panthers Go."

"So Tirelle is another reason for you two to get over to the school," MacNeice said. Vertesi and Williams nodded as they picked up their raincoats.

[26]

THE VICE-PRINCIPAL, CELESTINE BRION, WELCOMED VERTESI AND Williams into her office. Haitian by birth, she still spoke with a soft, lilting Creole accent. Guiding them to two chairs placed in front of her desk, she sat down herself and folded her hands together on top of a red file on the desktop. "This has been devastating for all of us at Mercy," she said, "not only because of what happened to our colleague, but because of Dylan. He told his coach and his teammates that his mother was the body that was found...It's unspeakable." Coffee arrived, carried in on a tray by the school secretary, and Brion opened the door of her credenza to retrieve a package of chocolate biscuits. "They're from Montreal, baked near where I grew up. They make coffee taste especially good." Both detectives took their biscuits and their coffee—black, no sugar—and sat like students before her. The coffee and treats were enjoyed as if time wasn't an issue. After Brion cleared the cups, she said, "That's the way all meetings should begin, no?" She sat behind her desk, put her hands together again and said, "I've only worked here for three years, but Mr. Westbrooke has been principal for fifteen. He wanted me to tell you that he will answer any questions you might have that I can't help you with."

"Ms. Brion," Vertesi began.

"Detective, we've shared coffee and Creole wafers. I think you can call me Celestine."

"Thank you. We have two missions today, Celestine. One, as I mentioned when I called, is to review the first and last names of the faculty and staff. If we feel it will be helpful, we'll want to interview anyone of interest. But we also need any information you or Mr. Westbrooke can give us on a former student, Luther Tirelle. He left for Cornell on a scholarship in 2002."

"Oh my, a sports scholarship?"

Williams raised his eyebrows and glanced toward Vertesi.

"No, actually it was a business scholarship," Vertesi said. "We'd like to speak to anyone who may recall Tirelle, any teachers he was close to."

"Can you tell me why?"

"No . . . just that Mr. Tirelle may be able to assist us in our investigation."

"Well, here's the easy part." Brion opened the red folder and retrieved the stack of paper inside, which she placed in front of them. "These are all the names of male staff at Mercy since 2000 with the initial S, either in their first or last name. Quite a few of them are no longer teaching here. I've provided additional anecdotal information and anything else

I thought might be useful. For example," she reached across and with a red fingernail pointed to the entry for Harvey Sharp. "Mr. Sharp is in a wheelchair."

With the vice-principal's help, Vertesi and Williams soon eliminated seven of the ten male staff: two of them were too short to have been the bomber, another had only been teaching for a year, Mr. Sangha because he was South Asian and Mr. Singleton because he was Trinidadian, Mr. Sharp because of the wheelchair, and one had died of lung cancer. Of the remaining three, two were over six feet, but one of those, the shop teacher Sam Madden, weighed roughly three hundred pounds and walked with a pronounced limp. Unlikely. Both of the remaining S candidates had been at the school for at least ten years: Steve Bernard, Mercy's religious studies teacher, who graduated from a seminary but didn't enter the priesthood, and an English teacher, Mr. Swinton.

Something in the way the vice-principal spoke Swinton's name caught Williams's ear. "Tell us about Mr. Swinton."

"Well, we don't discuss these things, obviously, and he has never said anything, but I believe our Mr. Swinton is a bachelor by choice."

"Are you saying Swinton's gay?"

"Well, he's a *very* committed bachelor."

"You mean he's a womanizer?" Vertesi asked.

"Well, the opposite, really," she said, looking uncomfortable. "I'm going to go ask the principal to join us."

After she left the office, Williams turned to Vertesi. "So, lemme see, we've got a gay guy forced to stay in the closet, a graduate seminarian, and an obese, limping shop teacher."

The meeting with the principal proved slightly more productive. Westbrooke told them he had helped Luther Tirelle apply for his scholarship. "Luther was exemplary, not

only top of his class, he actually topped the entire graduating class of 2002. His interests were primarily academic.
Though he played basketball, Coach Knox kept him mostly
on the bench."

"Has Tirelle maintained contact with anyone at Mercy?"
Williams asked.

"Apart from a brief trip back from Cornell when he spoke
to the senior student body about self-discipline and creative
thinking, I don't believe so. As often happens, once students
leave the city, we rarely hear from them. I found out that
he'd dropped out of Cornell after two very successful years,
but I haven't been in touch with him since and, as far as I
know, no one else has, either."

"Was he particularly close to any of your staff, sir?" Vertesi
asked.

"Who wasn't he close to? Luther had that spark every
teacher looks for in a student. I wish I could be more helpful...Perhaps if you told me why you're looking for him?"

Nice try, Williams thought, and Vertesi gave the stock
answer.

Westbrooke took that to be the end of the discussion and
stood up. "There are several photos of Luther in the halls.
If you're interested, Ms. Brion can point them out to you."
With that, he shook both their hands, thanked his vice-principal and was out the door.

"Celestine," Williams said, "all we need now is a brief
word with Mr. Madden, Mr. Bernard, and Mr. Swinton."

She nodded. "I'll find a room where you can meet."

A half-hour later, they left the building, convinced that
the man who blew up Nicholson and killed Constable Szabo
wasn't currently teaching kids at Mercy.

[27]

MacNEICE AND AZIZ HEADED OVER TO THE BLOCK AND TACKLE BAR: it was time to tell Byrne about the evidence found in the boat and advise him to hire a lawyer.

As MacNeice reached for the handle, the door of the bar flew open so suddenly that he had to step aside for a large man in a hurry.

"Pardon me," MacNeice said.

The man snapped a look his way, gave him a brief nod and headed down the steps. MacNeice turned to watch him. The man carried his significant bulk with an athletic and even jaunty bounce, and as if on cue, when he reached the street, a large silver Mercedes suv with black-tinted windows lurched to a stop, and the big man climbed into the rear seat. The suv moved south and turned down the first side street. Its licence plate was easy enough to remember: MACHT4.

"Cute," Aziz said, also having followed the man's progress. "A nice play on *mach*, or 'speed,' and *macht*, German for 'power' or 'force.'"

"Hold on a minute, Fiza," MacNeice said. He took out his cellphone and called Division. "Ryan, run a plate for me: Mother-Albert-Charles-Henry-Thomas-4. It's a silver Mercedes, a big, lumbering retro job."

Ryan began clicking away. "I know the model — G-Class — but I always imagine it in desert camouflage as Rommel's North African staff car."

"Desert's too hot," MacNeice responded. "Might work better for Rommel's defence of the Atlantic Wall."

"Oh yeah, no a/c back then. Here you are, sir: MACHT4 is registered to Canada Coil and Wire Inc., 1400 Burlington Street East, Suite 210."

"Find out who owns Canada Coil and how many employees it has, and text the info to me as soon as you can. Thanks." He hung up and said to Aziz, "Freddy's a typical patron here. That man isn't. Neither are his wheels."

"Maybe he's the man Freddy saw."

Before MacNeice could respond, William Byrne opened the door to the bar. "You two want your refreshments out here, or inside, where it's warm?" He didn't wait for an answer, just let the door go.

Inside certainly was warmer, but there was a lingering smell of fish and chips, vinegar and spilt beer. Two geezers nursed pints in the corner by the window, staring out at nothing in particular. A trio of younger men had their faces glued to the muted television screen, watching a replay of a football game from the past season. Judging by the two large half-empty plastic jugs of beer on the table, it didn't matter to them who was winning. On the sound system, Frank Sinatra was doing it his way but, happily, at early-afternoon decibels. Byrne led them toward his office

Approaching the door, he said, "First things first: Where's me boat? You have no right to seize a man's boat and not even tell the owner what it's suspected of doing. If you want to go out fishing, get yer own bloody boat."

MacNeice ignored the theatrics. "Who was that fellow who was leaving as we arrived?"

Byrne opened the door and headed for his desk. "He's another customer, fairly regular, always enjoys a pint and the Fish 'n' chips. I've never took note of his name, because he always pays cash."

Following him in, MacNeice took his coat off and draped it over the back of the chair before sitting. Aziz did the same and, making a show of settling in for the long term, took out her notebook.

Before a word could be said, MacNeice stood up again and walked over to the small north-facing window to stare out at the sliver of the bay between the buildings and trees. Somewhere unseen, but across the water, was the tiny bay called Cootes Paradise.

Byrne looked at Aziz, then up at MacNeice, then back at Aziz.

"Do you have a criminal lawyer on retainer, Mr. Byrne?" MacNeice asked from his spot at the window, his question leaving a little fog circle on the glass. It was so flatly delivered that Byrne didn't react at first, as if he didn't understand the meaning of what the detective superintendent had said. MacNeice breathed on the glass and drew an exclamation mark in the fog. The question hung in the air. Finally Byrne swallowed hard and asked MacNeice if he was serious.

MacNeice turned away from the window and looked down at him with searing contempt. He returned to his chair, dragging it around the side of the desk and closer to Byrne before he sat. Their knees were almost touching. Tiny beads of sweat were beginning to form on Byrne's upper lip.

"What do you think is going to happen next, Mr. Byrne?" MacNeice said.

Byrne wiped his upper lip. When MacNeice just stared at him, he finally answered the first question. "No, I don't have a criminal lawyer on the payroll. I'm an honest man who's just trying to get by, and I don't appreciate being —"

"Shut up."

Aziz flinched and Byrne looked like he'd just been slapped.

MacNeice leaned into him. "For the next five minutes, the wisest thing you can say is nothing. You need to grasp how seriously you're implicated in the murders of two people. I will consider any smartass comment you make a refusal to co-operate and you will be cuffed and taken to the station."

MacNeice reached over for the briefcase by Aziz's chair, unclasped it and pulled out a folder. From it, he pulled three photos and slapped them on the desk in front of Byrne: the first of an Irish or Italian flag tattoo on bluish flesh, the second of a bathing beauty tattoo on an arm. "This one was done in Japan, apparently. I'm told it was a terrific tattoo." The last image was of the bloated black head and blue-grey upper torso of Duguald Langan, formerly of County Meath, Ireland. MacNeice took one more image out of the folder: the porcelain face and matted hair of Anniken Kallevik.

Byrne's bleary eyes had opened wide, not in shock or horror, MacNeice thought, but in disgust. MacNeice pulled out a plastic bag with the betting chit in it. He placed it over the photo of Duguald's head and shoulders. Next to that, he set down a photocopy of a room registry page for November.

Byrne looked up at Aziz and found no sympathy there. He looked at the chit and the registry page, shrugged, and sat back in his chair.

"And now for your boat." MacNeice pulled out a stack of images of the boat, each a blow-up revealing something Forensics had discovered in it. One by one, MacNeice set them down, with commentary: "Pubic hairs, female; head hair, male; a turquoise stone." MacNeice held the next shots up for Byrne: Duguald's ear with its flattened ring, and his other ear with the matching stone. The last shot was of two identical anchors. "At least three people, possibly four, went out for a ride in your boat—two of them didn't return.

"The pubic hairs came from Anniken Kallevik—one from the boat, the other from her body. They're a dead match. The anchors and line were purchased at the same time, and that purchase makes this premeditated murder." He sat back in his chair.

He tapped the photo of Duguald's bloated head. "This young man had developed many skills in life, and one of those was as a bookie. Is that why he died? How did Duguald know Anniken Kallevik? Why was she in that boat? If I feel you're not being honest in your answers to these questions, Mr. Byrne, you'll be out that door and taken to the station quicker than you can say *fish and chips*. And my sincere recommendation is that you find yourself a criminal lawyer." He looked at his watch. "So that's my five minutes. Do you have anything you want to say?"

"I need a drink," Byrne said, jumping up from his chair.

"Sit down. Detective Aziz will get it for you. Water?"

"No. Irish whiskey, a double."

Aziz came back with a double shot of whiskey in a heavy glass, which she handed to him. Byrne looked down at the amber liquid. He took one and then several more sips from the glass, his hand shaking slightly. At last, he said, "Duguald was in love. There was no telling him to back off—he was that stupid about her. He couldn't see what was obvious. She was educated and doing her grand tour, and getting deeply involved with Duggie—a young lad who'd never made it out of fifth form—wasn't going to happen."

"How'd he meet her?" Aziz asked.

"He had business at the yacht club and bumped into her in the hallway."

MacNeice asked him what business Duguald had and who with.

"A woman named Melody was the go-between for the bets of some of the club's members. It was supposed to be done on the sly, eh. None of the yacht club folk were supposed to know about Duggie, and he didn't need to know who was actually placing the bets, just their initials. This was a win-win for everybody: he took the percentage owed a bookie and gave a small percentage to the woman, and she was also getting a slice from the members. But, pretty soon, more members wanted in."

By the time he bumped into Anniken, Byrne said, Duguald was feeling confident that he was finally on his way to building a real nest egg, something he never had in the old country and couldn't get at sea. During the day he'd run the bets from the bar, and at night, he'd steal away from the front desk and wait for Anniken to finish her shift, so he could walk her home. "He told her the north end wasn't safe and he could protect her. The thing was, Duguald didn't want just to have sex with Anniken—he'd travelled the world and had sex enough for two lives, he told me. He wanted to take care of her, to be in her company, no pressure, so that finally, he hoped, she would grow fond of him."

"What led him to bookmaking?" MacNeice asked.

"I don't know. But a month into it, he told me, 'Bookmaking is simple; it's just numbers and relationships—mostly relationships.' I wouldn't trust a bookie, and I told him so, but his answer was, 'You'd trust me though, wouldn't ya?' " Byrne acknowledged the point. "I would trust him. I did. And it wasn't about Duggie being family. I wouldn't trust any of his people to pick up a packet a fags. But Duggie had real presence, and his looks were movie-star level, like a young Liam Neeson, but shorter and darker."

Aziz looked up from her notes. "How did he convince people he knew anything about horse racing? He'd been at sea, not at the track."

"The lad did his homework. As soon as he got here, he was studying the horses—their history, trainers, jockeys, and lineage." Byrne finished his whiskey and set the glass down near the photo of Duguald's head. "In a few months, he was making more money than I was at the bar, and he thought that the people at the yacht club, who initially never knew who the 'Irish bookie' was, were his friends."

"His friends didn't mind losing money?" MacNeice asked.

"Maybe some did, but for the high rollers at the yacht club, this was 'fun money,' and Duggie had his Irish charm."

"Did Melody continue as his go-between?" Aziz asked.

"No. Eventually the betters wanted to know who was taking their money. She was still getting her cut, from both sides."

"So he bumped into Anniken at the yacht club, but how did he come to start walking her home?" MacNeice asked.

"Melody agreed to introduce him to her, and he offered to walk her back to the hostel. I knew, because he missed his shift that night. It was already light when he got back."

"And you asked him about her?"

"I did. He said they just sat in the hostel lounge all night, talking about the places they'd been around the world." Byrne shook his head. "Basically, Duggie was hungry for a settled life after drifting for years. Bookmaking made him a lot of money in a short time. He was working up to asking Anniken to run away, get married, and see the rest of the world together. He upped his game because he thought he needed a lot more in that nest egg to pull it off."

"Had he proposed this to Anniken?"

"No, and I tried to tell him he was dreaming, that they were from two different worlds. But he knew that. I never met her because Duggie thought she was too fine to bring to the bar. I told him she was going to go back to Norway to become a doctor who'd marry a doctor, not an Irish merchant seaman bookie."

"How did he take that?"

"It was a good thing we were family," Byrne said, "not that Duggie wouldn't pop his own brother. He'd knocked out his father and brother all in the course of one evening, back in the day. He said that for Anniken, he'd live in Norway, where he could fish or be a cabinetmaker or a farmer. He was crazy-stupid for her."

"She had no idea of this plan?" Aziz asked.

"I don't know. I don't know even if she understood his feelings for her to be anything more than platonic, since Duggie never made a move on her. I know he wouldn't have, because to him, Anniken was the Virgin Mary. He was a county boy, a rough diamond, and he believed she had the Virgin's power. He was serious. He really had no way of knowing if she was, in fact, a virgin, but he told me, 'Anni's pure, Billy. She's feckin' pure.'" Byrne looked at Aziz. "He asked me if I knew what that meant and I didn't respond."

Byrne twirled the glass slowly on its bottom. "He says, 'I will be saved by the love of a pure woman, that's what it means, ya dim twat. I'll be once more as pure as the driven snow— no more drinkin', fightin', or whorin'.' " Byrne cleared his throat. "Duggie's whole family are titched with a passion, ya know ... That's why he was a roustabout making his way around the world in the first place. The lad just didn't have a proper outlet."

"So he hoped to be pure ... as pure as a bookmaker could be," MacNeice said.

Byrne nodded. "Then, in the middle of December, I think, Anni told Duggie she was leaving here on New Year's Day to join her friend out west. Something about going to see California, and then home. That hit Duggie hard, and he told me he was forced to expand his business—fast. He wanted to build his fortune so he could pop the question before she left, and then he'd go home with her to Norway if she said yes. It was insane."

"But surely she would have told him from the start that her job was temporary and she was leaving," Aziz said.

"I suppose so. It was always a race with time for Duggie, him saving money and hoping she'd stay longer."

"She didn't know what his business was?" Aziz asked, with some disbelief.

"No clue."

"Was he running bets in your bar too?" MacNeice asked.

"Yeah ... but you've seen my customers. He wouldn't get more than a twenty outta them, and only when their pension or welfare cheques came in."

"So how did he expand?"

"He wouldn't tell me exactly. Then, I don't know what happened, whether it was one of them mucky-mucks at the club or somewhere else, but he ran into trouble. All he would say is that somebody wanted to put him out of business. But he wouldn't stop. I asked him how much cash he'd stashed away. He looks me straight in the eye and says $137,214, mostly in one hundred dollar bills. He figured $200,000 would impress Anni's father—that was his magic number. I knew then that he was in trouble."

"And why's that?" Aziz asked.

"For him to pull down those numbers, we're not talking twenty-dollar bets with toothless geezers over a pint; it's coming out of someone else's very large pocket. Whether they were winning or losing, the clients all knew Duggie was winning. So who was taking their bets before this wild Irish boy shows up? Whoever it was, those fellas musta known their own profits were down. As Duggie was getting more ambitious, he was robbing the boys who'd been working Dundurn all their shrewd bookie lives."

MacNeice's cell burped. He glanced down at the text message that had arrived from Ryan: "Canada Coil and Wire president is Paul Zetter. Number of employees: three."

"So when did you last see Duguald Langan?" Aziz asked.

"Christmas Eve. That night, Duggie winks at me and says he has an important date, to pop the question to Anniken. He left here at seven p.m. and never came back. When I went up to his room the next morning, the place had been cleaned out and he was gone."

"But that's not the end of the story, is it?" MacNeice said.

"For me it is. As far as I knew, he'd pulled it off, and Duggie and Anni were now living on some farm in far-away Norway. Until you came in asking questions about her. I don't know what I thought, but I didn't know Duggie was dead until you told me. Not even then could I really believe it, not till these terrible pictures hit the table." Byrne couldn't bring himself to look at them again.

"Who used your boat?"

"Duggie had the keys because he was going to haul it out for the winter. I don't know who used it. I have another set of keys, but they never left my desk drawer, except when I pulled the boat out meself."

"That man we passed at the door, who is he?"

"I'd already told ya. He comes in from time to time and pays cash for a pint and sometimes a meal."

"So what is he, and why would he come here? Is he another ex-pat?"

"No, he's a Scot. Glaswegian, I suspect."

"So you've spoken to him?"

"Only in passin', once or twice. It's an easy accent to spot, and his is very thick."

"And you really don't know his name?"

Byrne paused, then said, "I think it could be Bishop, or something like."

"And Paul Zetter?"

"Who is Paul Zetter?" Byrne looked at Aziz and back to MacNeice for an answer.

MacNeice said nothing, just collected the images, put them into the folder and into the briefcase. He stood up, took his coat from the back of the chair, and put it on. Aziz also stood and put on her coat, sliding the notebook into the briefcase and then picking it up.

MacNeice went over to the window and peered out at the bay in the distance, his hands deep in his coat pockets. "Mr. Byrne, this meeting was the one chance you had to clear the air of lies and withheld truths, to put some distance between you and the incidents that ended with two people dead in the bay." Turning away from the view, he walked to the door of the office, where he paused, then glanced back at Byrne. "Get a lawyer on board, fast. It only remains to be determined whether you'll be charged with double homicide or as an accessory."

For once, the smart-tongued barman had nothing to say.

Outside, it was grey, damp and cool, but for the moment, at least, it wasn't raining. MacNeice lifted his collar and turned to Aziz. "I'll drop you at Division. Ask Williams to pick up Melody Chapman in the morning and put her in the interview room. I'm going to try to get to Paul Zetter's office before it closes."

MACNEICE MADE IT to Canada Coil and Wire just after five p.m. The door wasn't locked yet, but no one was at the reception desk in the empty lobby. Turning around, taking in the space, he could hear a male voice behind the closed door just to the rear of the front desk. He stood for a moment, looking at the framed photos on the lobby walls, featuring lake freighters and tractor-trailers, loaded with huge coils of blue steel.

The computer keyboard on the desk was spotless, as if it had just been taken out of the box. There was a leather desk pad, a vase with impossibly pink silk flowers, and a plastic tray with two ballpoint pens in it, both with "Canada Coil and Wire" printed on the shaft.

MacNeice walked to the door, knocked once and opened it. A middle-aged man was standing with his back to him, talking on a cellphone. He swung toward MacNeice, held the phone away from his ear and said, "Yeah, what do you want?"

Opening his jacket, MacNeice pulled out his ID, holding it up. "Are you Paul Zetter?"

The man put his hand up. "No, I'm Dave. Just a minute." He told the person on the cell that he'd get right back to them, then said to MacNeice, "He's not in—can I help you?"

His full name was Dave Francis, he said, and he was yard foreman, shipping clerk, and shop manager. He was wearing overalls, a sweatshirt, a worn and oil-stained blue down vest, and steel-toed construction boots with the steel showing through a hole on the toe of the right boot.

"Mr. Zetter has gone home. Wanna leave a message with me?"

MacNeice said, "I'm actually looking for someone named Bishop. He's a big man, likely Scottish-born?"

Francis scratched the stubble on his chin and said the name softly to himself, then shook his head. "What's he got to do with Coil and Wire?"

"I was hoping you, or rather Mr. Zetter, could tell me."

"You sure you got the right place, mister?"

"It's Detective Superintendent MacNeice, not mister, and yes, I'm sure. I saw the man getting into a silver Mercedes SUV registered to this address."

"Well, yes, Mr. Zetter drives one of those. I haven't met any Scottish men around here, but I'm mostly down in the yard, managing shipments. You got a card or somethin'? I'll make sure Mr. Z gets the message."

"Tell Mr. Zetter I'm interested in speaking with him about this man as soon as possible."

"I got that."

[28]

BY ELEVEN THAT NIGHT, THE BOOGIE BIN WAS HOPPING. PINK AND blue laser lights strafed the crowd on the dance floor, ricocheting off the sweat of two hundred young men and women bumping and grinding to house music. In the middle of the floor, a big man had cleared a circle for himself and the tiny brunette who spun and shimmied in front of him.

The space around him wasn't maintained because he was worshipped by the dancing mob. No one had ever seen him before. Just something about the big man made people steer clear of him. His dance partner's instincts had shut down hours before, dulled by test-tube frozen blueberry vodka martinis. She didn't appear to notice that, as her gyrations increased, the big man grew more rooted and still, moving half-time to the beat and then only by sagging one knee or the other.

The big man looked down at his pirouetting pixie, who was wearing a silver-sequined tank top and a cherry-red flared skirt that barely covered her bottom. Even with six-inch heels, she came only halfway up his rib cage. She was old enough to drink, but he realized that she appealed to him because she looked like a twelve-year-old. With that thought, he started smiling—though not so much that anyone sober would think him happy.

The big man was wearing a white cable-knit roll-collar sweater, black jeans, and black cross-trainers. It wasn't the uniform of the Boogie Bin—all about him, young men were wearing tight T-shirts soaked with sweat. Later in the night, he lifted the sweater over his head and tossed it high above the crowd, toward a table bordering the dance floor, where it knocked over a bottle of wine, sending two men in black scrambling and laughing to get out of the way. The big man stuck a fist in the air and nodded toward them.

Bare-chested, he continued his slow, alternating knee-drop dance. Strictly speaking, he was violating a rule the club had posted just inside the entrance: "Nudity Strictly Prohibited." But two of the bouncers, who had watched the sweater fly through the lasers to the table, decided to let this be the one time they'd make an exception.

Sweat streaked down a large blue horizontal rectangle with a pinkish-white X tattooed across his upper chest—St. Andrew's Cross, the flag of Scotland. His bull-like back featured, in large, flourished script, the black-humoured Gaelic toast: "Here's tae us. Wha's like us. Damn few. An' they're a' deid." Centred on the deltoid of his right shoulder was the insignia of the British Special Air Service, with its wings,

sword and suggestively sinister scroll: "Who Dares Wins."
Below it, like Scouts merit badges, were six words:

Belfast
Herzegovina
Mogadishu
Iraq
Afghanistan
Congo

The DJ cranked up the rhythm, and all but one dancer
jumped in unison, the floor sagging as the club's retina-
frying lasers doubled in frequency and intensity. Dry-ice
fog flowed over the stage, oozed onto the floor and into
the crowd, where it rose in frothy clouds to the level of the
dancers' knees, then shoulders. Before long, the pretty pixie
could only be seen by the ponytail on the top of her head,
or by her slender arms when she raised them to touch the
white cross on the big man's chest.

With closing time climbing to a deafening climax, the
thump-thump-thump was exacting a toll. Several couples
bounced off each other and finally staggered, laughing,
off the floor, but still the space around the big man held.
Occasionally the girl's hands would snake up his stomach,
squeeze his nipples and run up the angles of the white cross
to his neck—the extent of her reach.

A minute before closing, he lifted her up. He lifted her
from her rib cage with all the effort it would take to pick
up a newspaper. When her face was in front of his, he studied it. He leaned into her, inhaled her perfume, and licked
the sweat from her neck. On his tongue, the sharp taste of
her sweat had a drying effect in his already dry mouth. He

tilted his head and kissed her, easing his tongue between her lips and into her mouth, moving it about like someone reaching into a purse for loose change. She pulled away from him—then laughed. Wrapping her legs around his waist, she licked the sweat off the white cross and offered her mouth to his again.

SHERRY BERRYMAN'S ROOMMATE found her the next morning, naked, lying on her back in bed. Her head was turned so far to the left that her chin was tucked behind her shoulder. The duvet had been tossed to the floor, along with all but two of the pillows. At first the roommate thought Sherry hadn't come home from the club the night before, but then she'd discovered her keys on the glass table next to the sofa, and her bag on the floor. She'd banged on the door to wake her up for work, and when Sherry didn't respond, she'd gone in. When MacNeice walked past the uniform at the door at 9:18 a.m., the young woman was sitting on the sofa, talking to Aziz.

He nodded for Aziz to carry on and stood looking around the living room. It was large and bright, with a kitchen and island to the left, and beyond, a dining room table with six chairs. The retrofitted office building featured an uninterrupted wall of windows on the north side. A police photographer in Tyvek stepped quietly out of the bedroom to his right and began setting up to shoot the living room, beginning with the bag and keys. He acknowledged MacNeice and then said, "Forensics is waiting for you in the bedroom, sir."

It was a strange scene in a very pink room. Three members of the forensics team in their orange suits stood lined up at the foot of the bed, each with an instrument in hand. Apart from the bruising on her neck and the impossible turn of her head, the lovely young woman in front of them might have been sleeping and would soon wake up to wonder what these people were doing gawking at her naked in her own bed.

"Sir," rippled down the line as he leaned over to study the girl's face, which was turned toward the grey morning outside. He inhaled sharply. From brow to cheekbones, her eyes had been sealed with Scotch tape. The tape dispenser was on the nightstand. There was no sign of torture, let alone one great and final blow. There was a large hickey on her right breast below the nipple, and what looked like a bite mark beside her navel—surely the result of romantic lust, not an assault. Above her teardrop pubic hair was a tattoo of a bluebird in flight, its head tilted downward.

"Is this how she was found, exactly like this?" MacNeice asked.

"Exactly, sir. The roommate didn't touch her and we were told to wait for you."

"Has Richardson been called?"

"Yessir. She's ready for her as soon as we're finished here."

He nodded and looked about the room. Clothing, likely from the night before, was scattered on the plush white carpet and draped over a pink velvet chair. MacNeice pulled on his gloves and picked up a shoe. Turning it over in his hands, he noted the scuffed satin surface. He lifted the discarded tank top, held it to his nose and inhaled a trace of perfume and the vague smell of sweat. There was a trio of photographs on the dresser: one of her on a beach with a girlfriend, another of her dancing with a young black man under a banner that touted Jamaican independence, and in the last one she was in the centre of the shot, about to blow out the candles on a birthday cake. Crowded around her were several young women all laughing and holding glasses of champagne, waiting to see if she could blow them out in one breath. One of them was the young woman now sobbing on the sofa with Aziz.

Hanging on the wall near the bathroom was Berryman's diploma from Brant University, an Honours BA, and tucked into the frame, a photo of her in her gown and mortarboard, holding her degree, beaming for the camera, flanked by her parents, also beaming. MacNeice judged her to be shy of five feet tall, and yet she had an inch on her father, maybe two on her mother. Below the degree, a pink plastic chair was home to a large slouching teddy bear that appeared startled to discover a pair of black lace panties tossed casually in its lap.

He opened the closet door to find an abundance of pink and red blouses, jackets and jeans, and two sparkly tops, one turquoise and the other black. Nothing was on the shelf above, perhaps because it was too high, but on the floor was an array of shoes that complemented the outfits. To the right were several pairs of stiletto heels in different ice-cream colours. There were sequined clutches on a small table inside the closet, and a sheer negligee hung on the inside of the door.

In her dresser were T-shirts, underwear, socks, nylons, and sweaters—mostly pink. Underneath a neatly piled stack of sweaters, he found a battery-operated sex toy. "No books," he said to himself, and turned back to look at the bedside tables—nothing, not even a magazine.

"Sir? Something you should see..." One of the forensic team members was holding up her arm so he could look at her back, causing her head to loll like a doll with a broken neck.

Scratches ran from her shoulder blades all the way to her hips, most certainly caused by robust lovemaking. MacNeice asked, "How large do you imagine those hands to be?"

With a small flashlight, the young specialist studied the scratches closely, saying quietly to himself, "Hmm," and, "Wow." When he straightened up, he looked at MacNeice. "Big is all I can say for sure, from the width of the scratches and the distance between them." He put the flashlight on the bed and held up the first three fingers of each hand. "These digits on each hand. So either he's a small guy with huge hands, or he's a big guy. I'd say he's over six feet... well over." He considered the marks again and said, "The guy was likely six-four, even six-five. And he should have left foot imprints on the carpet. But it's been vacuumed, sir."

"YOU SAW HER eyes?" Aziz said, climbing into the Chevy.

"I did." MacNeice started the engine. "When we found out that Anniken Kallevik's eyes had been taped shut, I thought it was a strange gesture. Superstition or maybe remorse."

Aziz was silent a moment, then said, "Throughout the Mediterranean region, it was the ancient practice to put coins on the eyelids or in the mouths of the dead, but the reasons for it varied." She looked out the window to Berryman's building. "For the Greeks, it was about paying the Ferryman so the body could cross the River Styx, presumably to eternity. Still others thought it was about making sure the eyes didn't spring open again."

Before MacNeice could respond, his cellphone rang. He pushed hands-free. "MacNeice."

There was a long pause before the voice on the other end said, "Hey stranger... I'm home."

Samantha sounded sleepy, maybe jet-lagged, and her tone was intimate. Aziz turned to look at MacNeice. He grabbed the phone and clicked it off speaker.

"Hey, yourself. Can I call you...in ten minutes?" He listened for the response, aware that Aziz was still watching him. When the call ended, he smiled sheepishly and put the cell back in his pocket. He busied himself with easing the Chevy onto the street.

The rest of the drive, seven minutes long, was crowded with silence. They parked, and as they got out of the car, Aziz said, "Sherry Berryman, a paralegal, went out last night, dancing at the Boogie Bin. Her roommate, who's also a paralegal, couldn't go—she had to work. I'll phone the club, but they probably won't be open yet."

When they got to the door, he opened it for her. Reaching for his cell, he said, "I'll be right up." Aziz hesitated, trying to think of something to say, but finding nothing, she went in and up the stairs. At the landing between the first and second floor, she turned and stopped, leaning against the wall. Though faint on such a grey day, his shadow could be seen in the doorway. Her breathing was shallow, not because of the twelve-stair climb, but from the shock of realizing that MacNeice had a lover.

MacNeice's shadow grew larger on the floor and she heard the door swing open. Aziz pushed herself off the wall and ran up the remaining flight as quickly and quietly as possible. Stepping into the corridor, she went immediately to the washroom to splash water on her face. Feeling the fool, she didn't want to look like one.

MACNEICE SPOTTED THE cane as he headed for the cubicle; it was kicked slightly into the corridor, leaning against a chair. He turned the corner to see Swetsky, a doughnut cushion under his butt to ease the pain from his hip. His face was

pale, and his sweater hung loosely over his chest. Seeing
MacNeice, he started to push himself out of the chair. "John,
please stay put. And what are you doing here?" MacNeice
reached down to shake his hand.

"I got out a day in advance. Good behaviour — that or
bein' a pain in the ass." MacNeice turned to the others,
Ryan busy rewiring the computer he'd nicknamed "The
Millennium Falcon" with some new gizmo, Vertesi and
Williams hunched over their desks. "Can you three give us
a few minutes."

"You pissed off with me?" Swetsky said.

"Does your wife know you're here?"

His wife didn't know. She had left him lying comfortably
on the couch, watching television as she went out to shop.
"Comfort comes from a full fridge" was her mantra, which
is why Swetsky usually stretched his sweaters.

"Christ, Mac, I just wanted to fill my head with something
other than alcohol swabs, drips, sleeping pills, pain pills, and
'How're you feeling now? One to ten, rate the pain.' I'll leave
soon; just let me hear the sound of work."

MacNeice placed a hand firmly on his shoulder and
squeezed. "Soon as you're tired, John, you're gone. And I'll
be the judge of that, you crazy Polack."

"Deal. I promise."

Vertesi and Williams had already briefed him on the
developments in the Nicholson case. So MacNeice thought
that now was the time to sound out Swetsky on the idea
he'd had about the young basketball-playing son who was
now an orphan. When he was done, he said, "Mercy is now
down an assistant coach, and next year is going to be critical
for the boy when it comes to both recovering from what
just happened in his life, and maybe drawing a scholarship."

Swetsky was looking off to the whiteboard. He said nothing but started to smile.

"I think he's really talented, John. He's just adrift with grief, and I think you —"

"Enough. You had me at 'basketball.' Besides, I knew about this kid already. He's what I'd call a prospect. The school going to buy it?"

"I haven't pitched Mercy yet. Leave it with me, and thanks."

Swetsky said, "You know I'd love an excuse to get involved, so lemme thank you."

MacNeice turned to the whiteboard and put Sherry Berryman's name next to Anniken Kallevik's. Off to the side, with a dotted line to both, he wrote Bishop's and Zetter's names. As he was finishing, his crew came back, along with Aziz. He turned to them and said, "Another young woman has been murdered, we believe by the same person who killed Anniken Kallevik and, probably, Duguald Langan." He nodded for Aziz to continue.

"Sherry Berryman was twenty-nine. She was described by her roommate, who was the one who found her, as fun-loving: she loved to dance, had no steady boyfriends, and her personality and looks meant that she only came home alone if she wanted to. When I asked the roommate if Sherry was indiscriminate in her choices, her answer was, 'At our age, we all like to have some fun.' The parents of both girls contributed to the upkeep of the apartment, but they were otherwise independent."

"What's the connection to the Cootes case?" Vertesi asked.

"Berryman's eyes were taped shut and her neck snapped, just as Kallevik's were, though Berryman seems to have engaged in a night of drinking, dancing, and fairly intense lovemaking. Kallevik may simply have been in the wrong place, with the wrong person, at the wrong time."

"Does he tape them *before* he kills them?" Swetsky wondered.

"Good question," Aziz said. "We can't say with Kallevik, but it appears not with Berryman."

"This guy's been busy," Swetsky said, massaging his thigh.

No one responded, but everyone's eyes drifted to the whiteboard.

Williams was the first to break the silence. "Boss, Melody Chapman's in the interview room. She's been there for about an hour now."

MacNeice nodded, then turned to Vertesi. "Do you know if Mercy has a basketball practice scheduled today?"

"Yes, sir, one every day, at four."

"Let the coach know we're coming." Looking down at Swetsky, he said, "Head home and rest. I'll pick you up at 3:30."

"Absolutely." Swetsky pulled himself gingerly out of the chair. He picked up his doughnut cushion and cane, and after saying his goodbyes, limped slowly toward the elevator.

[29]

AZIZ ENTERED THE INTERVIEW ROOM AHEAD OF MacNEICE. WHEN he arrived minutes later, Melody Chapman was already clutching a worry ball of tissue.

"Twelve-thirty p.m., DS MacNeice has entered the room," Aziz said when he came in. He noticed she did not look his way.

"Where are we?" MacNeice sat down beside Aziz.

"I just asked Ms. Chapman if she had any idea why she was brought in for questioning."

MacNeice looked at the woman for the answer, but she shook her head several times to indicate her confusion. "No . . . I'm not sure I understand." She used the balled tissue to wipe a tear away.

MacNeice said, "This can be a very intimidating place, particularly for someone like you, Melody."

She nodded and wiped away more tears. Aziz reached over to the side table and handed her a box of tissues. Chapman hesitated, then put down the tattered ball and took out two fresh ones. "I honestly don't know why I'm here."

"But you do. Really, you do," Aziz said.

Chapman's lower lip quivered, but she said nothing.

"We'll spell it out for you if you'd like," Aziz said. "But you'll be much better off telling us what you know and having that on record as your voluntary statement."

They waited three more minutes, while Chapman stared at her clutched hands. Then Aziz said, "We discovered another body in Cootes Paradise, and you know this one too. In fact, Anniken Kallevik and Duguald Langan met because he asked to be introduced to her by his bookmaking associate at the yacht club — that was you, Ms. Chapman."

Her mouth opened, but she still didn't speak, just took another tissue and crushed it in her fist.

"Melody," MacNeice said, "later this afternoon your bank accounts and income statements will be seized. The tiny window through which you have a chance to help yourself, by helping us, is closing. When it does, your silence will suggest a greater involvement in this tragedy than we currently suspect you of. So you can speak with us or spend the night in a holding cell."

There were no more tears. Chapman asked for a glass of water, which she drank quickly, glancing from Aziz to MacNeice, before clearing her throat.

"There were eight members on Duguald's list at the club," Melody said. "I was the go-between in the beginning, but later they wanted to bet directly with him. After that, he was on his own and I wasn't involved."

"But you continued receiving a cut — from both sides," MacNeice said.

"Yes." Her eyes met his for a second before she looked down to her hands again. "I did introduce Anniken and Duguald, but I swear I didn't know about their relationship until one of our members saw them walking up Burlington, holding hands."

"Which member was that?" Aziz asked.

"Paul Zetter."

"Tell us about Zetter," MacNeice said.

"Mr. Zetter?" Chapman hesitated. "He's a successful businessman with connections all over the city and abroad, as far as China. At least that's what he told me. He made a pass at me shortly after I was hired, but I told him I had a boyfriend, which was a lie."

"Why lie?" Aziz asked.

"Paul Zetter is married," Chapman said. "But, he's also, I don't know . . . he's crude."

"And Duguald? Were you attracted to him? Is that how this whole betting thing began?" MacNeice asked.

"No . . . well, yeah, sure." The tissue disappeared in her white-knuckled fist. "He was very attractive . . . very. But he was a wild child, and a bookie. I couldn't afford to get involved with someone like that."

"That's ironic, given the reason you're here today," MacNeice said. "Tell us what you know about a man named Bishop."

Her brow furrowed, as if she was searching through her neural cabinetry to find the name. "Yes," she said at last. "He works for Mr. Zetter. I think he's Scottish — his accent is very distinct. He shows up at the club occasionally to meet Zetter and have a beer at the bar. Once, Bishop and two other men went aboard Mr. Zetter's yacht and they left port for a few days."

"Did Mr. Bishop ever hit on you?" Aziz asked.

"No," she said, shaking her head. "Bishop was someone you just steered clear of, though I know he grabbed Anni once and asked her to dance."

"While she was working?"

"Yes. It was late afternoon and there was no music on the PA system, but I could hear Bishop humming something. Then I heard Anni say, 'No, no, please, sir,' and I came out of my office to find him trying to waltz her down the corridor."

"Did he know Duguald?" MacNeice asked.

"Yes. I think they got here at the same time, off one of the ships."

"Was he involved in the gambling?"

"Not at first, but I don't know what happened after Duguald started dealing with the members directly." She looked at both of them. "I did overhear one of the members refer to 'that greedy little mick.' I asked Duguald about it, but he laughed and said something like, 'The less you know, the better.' "

"What about Duguald's uncle, the owner of the Block and Tackle Bar?"

"I only met him once. I just thought they were friends from the old country."

"Tell us about the last time you saw Anniken," MacNeice said.

"When I paid her out after she'd given notice. I just assumed she'd gone to join her Norwegian friend out West. When Duguald stopped coming to the club, I assumed he either went with her, or he'd been cheating his customers and had left Dundurn for some other port. He told me once that drifting was in his blood."

"Did the members know he had continued paying you a commission?" MacNeice asked.

"No. He told me that would be our secret. The members kept giving me a cut too, to keep me happy...and quiet." Her face betrayed the fact that she knew how corrupt that sounded. "I was relieved when he disappeared. Until Anniken's body was found, I thought I was safe. But now Duguald is dead too...Who would kill them both?"

Aziz closed her notebook with a slap. "Ms. Chapman, you're free to go back to work. If anyone asks about your visit here, tell them we needed to see you about Anniken Kallevik. Don't mention to anyone that you know that their Irish bookie is also dead."

"And the charges against me?" Melody asked nervously.

Aziz moved her chair back. "You're not out of the woods, and the answer to your question depends on how honest you've just been. We can arrange a ride back to the club in a cruiser, if you wish."

"No...I'll take a taxi. I'm sorry for...for —"

"Save it," Aziz said, dismissing her.

After Chapman was ushered away to the elevator by a uniform, MacNeice turned to Aziz. "I owe you an explanation about the phone call I took in the car."

"Actually, no, you don't."

"I wasn't looking for this to happen, Fiza..."

"Are you happy at least?" She stood up, the notebook held to her chest.

"I have no idea. But I do know I should've told you."

She opened the door and left the interview room, thinking about how thoughtless and insensitive this most thoughtful and sensitive man could be.

[30]

LATER THAT AFTERNOON, WITH SWETSKY SETTLED INTO THE FRONT passenger seat, MacNeice drove east toward Mercy on Main Street. As he crossed Sherman Avenue, his cellphone rang.

"Detective Superintendent MacNeice." It was Bourke-Stanford.

"I just took a call from the VP at Mercy. You're going to a basketball practice? I thought we had an agreement that all further contact with Dylan Nicholson would be managed through this office?"

"We did, and we do. I'm taking DS Swetsky to a basketball practice and have no intention of approaching Dylan. This is strictly police work. Call it *observation*. I apologize for not informing you beforehand. I'm convinced that the

answer to Dylan's father's murder is in that school. I want
my colleague to sit in on a practice, in part because I don't
know anything about basketball, but also because this was
the thing the father and son did together most. I'll say hello
to Dylan, of course, but I won't engage him."

Bourke-Stanford was silent for a moment, then said,
"I'll hold you to that, Superintendent. Please don't make me
regret this."

Coach Knox met them at the gym door. Seeing the cane
and the doughnut cushion, he offered them a seat at the
timer's table opposite the team benches, rather than on the
oak planking of the bleachers. He told them that the team
had already done their wind sprints and stretches and they'd
be out for a scrimmage momentarily.

Once Swetsky and MacNeice were settled, Swetsky filled
MacNeice in on what he knew about Mercy's basketball
coach. Knox had been a McGill University basketball player
chosen for the national team until he blew an ankle in train-
ing, missing the Pan American Games. Though he was tall,
a few inches over six feet, he would have been below aver-
age height on most elite teams.

MacNeice glanced over at Knox. In his Mercy polo shirt
and warm-up pants, he still appeared fit.

Swetsky was looking up at the championship banners
hanging from the rafters of the gym.

"Bring back memories?" MacNeice asked.

"Big time."

None dated to his own era, he told MacNeice, because
back then, this was a new school. It took them a few years
to get their sports programs together. "Having followed the
city tournaments for years, I knew this team was in the top
three. Just before you got to the house, I also Googled Knox.

He's been consistent. Every season he's coached them, the Mercy team seems to have the potential to win it all."

The doors swung open from the locker room and the players ran into the gym. They immediately formed two circles at either end of the court, tossing the ball rapidly from one to the other. Dylan Nicholson and Tom Smylski were in the circle to the right. When someone dropped the ball, the others yelled, "Mercy!" and the next player tossed the ball faster until it was essentially a line drive to the next player.

Knox blew his whistle, the lines unwound and each player took a layup at the net. Knox paced outside of the action, encouraging and sometimes correcting either the shooter or passer. These drills lasted fifteen minutes. When Knox blew his whistle again, the players stripped off their warm-up suits, tossed them onto the bench and took positions at centre court, where they began doing two-man drills, tearing off toward the net, passing the ball between them as they attacked. If the man taking the shot missed, the second man attempted to tip it in or take a jump shot.

Returning to the line after dunking the ball, Dylan looked MacNeice's way for the first time and nodded. Smylski noticed and said something, and both boys looked at the detectives.

"Focus. Focus. Focus," Knox yelled.

The two tore off again toward the net, and this time Smylski took the shot. Though he seemed to hang in the air and could easily have dunked the ball, he waited until he was arcing downward before flipping the ball casually into the hoop as if it was the simplest thing in the world.

"Cut the showboating, Smylski," Knox yelled.

"Yes, coach."

Dylan gave him a low-five.

Moments later, the scrimmage began. Freshmen or third-string players moved to the home and visitor benches, where they stood to watch the action. MacNeice could hear Swetsky coaching under his breath: "Good, good, good." "Take the shot." "To the guard—pass to the guard." Several times, Swetsky was ahead of the coach on a call.

Knox was focused on the players, but he was also watching the two detectives. At first, it was just passing glances, but then MacNeice noticed him standing, hands on his hips, looking at him through a cluster of players. When MacNeice caught him, Knox nodded, then looked at the clipboard he was clutching in his right hand.

The practice ended at six. Dylan gave a brief wave to MacNeice before disappearing into the locker room. Knox came over to usher the two men out of the gym, but neither stood to leave. "Have you got a few minutes, Coach Knox?" MacNeice asked.

"Well, no. Normally I'd go over what we did and the corrections I want to see."

"I understand. It won't take long. Perhaps your assistant coach could fill in."

Knox reluctantly pulled out a chair and sat opposite them. "The assistant coach is the shop teacher. He's just started—well, you know that, of course."

"Good scrimmage, coach," Swetsky said. "Initially, I thought you had a two-man team, but judging by their ball control, you've got quite a few strong players. Great passing and hustle all-round, which makes it difficult to double up on Nicholson or Smylski and shut them down."

Knox nodded his thanks. "They're good, but there's a long way to go. And four of them are graduating next year, so I've been getting them to work with the younger players. Hopefully, we won't feel like we're starting over."

"But that must be an annual concern," MacNeice said.

"It is. Tomorrow, I'll mix them up, get Dylan and Tom on opposing sides. I haven't wanted to do that recently, since Dyl's been through so much."

"What was it like, having David Nicholson as an assistant coach?" MacNeice asked.

"Look, I already spoke to your detectives. Nicholson was only assisting because his kid was on the team."

"How long had you known David Nicholson?"

"I'd been here for two years when the Nicholsons arrived."

"How would you describe your relationship with him?"

A long pause. "It was okay. He loved the kid. Though even that, I personally found…a bit creepy. He didn't give Dylan much space. But that was none of my business."

"And his wife, did you also know her?"

"I did. She was an amazing woman, a great teacher—a natural. It was a blow when she disappeared. And it's worse, now we've heard what happened to her."

The door to the locker room opened and the assistant coach stuck his head out and called, "Coach, are you going to speak to the team, or should I let them go?"

"Let them go. I'll follow up at tomorrow's practice."

The door closed and MacNeice said, "I know Dylan told you that his father was responsible for her death—were you shocked to hear that?"

Knox looked out to the court, studying the gleaming urethaned surface broken by circles and straight lines— white, red, and blue—the elegantly rendered rules. "Frankly, I always thought Nicholson was a creepy control freak. But Dylan…that kid is so healthy. He's balanced…smart. You saw him out here. He's passionate, fair, shares the ball, has an eye for where the play is going, and manages to find himself—more than anyone—in a position to capitalize . . . either by scoring or assisting."

Knox stopped abruptly. "I don't know—maybe he takes after his mother. Maybe four years with her was enough to set him on this path." He shook his head as if to erase what he'd said. "Look, I teach mathematics, not psychology."

"Still, that you think Dylan takes after his mother is an interesting observation. Thank you for your time, coach." MacNeice stood up, helping Swetsky to his feet. They came around the table and, as MacNeice offered his hand to Knox, he said, "Your first name is Al—is that short for Allan?"

"No, it's Alexander."

"Do you have kids of your own, coach?"

"No. Thankfully, my wife and I divorced before we had kids . . . Sorry, that didn't come out right."

MacNeice smiled and said he understood what he meant. "How long ago was that?"

"Thirteen years this September 18." Knox's voice was flat, matter of fact.

"If anything else occurs to you about David Nicholson, anything you'd like us to know, here's my card. Please call me."

They shook hands at the gym door. As he let go of Swetsky's hand, Knox told him he'd be welcome to come out again. "I can use guys who know what they're doing. We can't pay, of course, but it's clear you love the game."

Pulling away from the Mercy parking lot, Swetsky said, "Dylan's a star—royal jelly all the way. Smylski's good, could be great: physically he's got all he needs."

"And the coach?"

"He's a math teacher. Maybe creativity's not his thing. He sees the players like geometry in motion. He's built a well-trained and disciplined starting line, but what the juniors and freshmen are making of it, I can't tell. I think the key is having a chance to go head to head with the seniors, not to sit there watching them play. But he's a winning coach and this was one off-season practice, so what do I know."

MacNeice said, "It's interesting that the coach divorced roughly around the time the Nicholsons were together at Mercy. It's a major leap, of course, to link the two events, but Knox clearly resented David Nicholson posing as a coach so he could watch over his son. And one other small point stood out: his first name is Alexander."

"So?"

"Sandy is a common diminutive for Alexander. We've gone through that school looking for anyone with a name that begins with S, because Nicholson refers to someone by that initial in the diary he kept."

"Jesus. Does Knox fit the profile?"

"He does. Nicholson would have had to be unconscious, but Knox is big enough to manhandle him onto that wagon... Mission accomplished: I didn't even have to ask whether you could be involved. He invited you himself. And, as you're still on medical leave, will you start attending practice?"

"I'm in, absolutely."

Pulling up in front of Swetsky's house, MacNeice noticed his wife at the door. By the time he stopped at the curb, she was striding down the front stairs. "Brace yourself, John."

"Her bark is worse—no, come to think of it, her bite is much worse. I'll blame it on you."

As Swetsky got out of the Chevy, his wife was standing at the end of their front walk with her arms folded. With his big paw on the roof, Swetsky ducked back into the car and whispered, "I won't tell her there's a second grenade." He slapped the roof and shut the door.

[31]

I T WAS 7:50 P.M. WHEN HE SHUT THE CHEVY DOWN, NEAR SAMANTHA'S apartment. He sat in the car, frozen by the thought of Fiza. While there'd never been anything explicit said between them, he couldn't help feeling that he'd cheated on her. And Fiza's frosty but civil response didn't change that. Worse, though he was looking forward to seeing Sam, the week had gone by without her crowding his thoughts. Yet this was the first person he'd slept with since Kate's death. What kind of sense did that make? It was just after eight when he buzzed her apartment, then climbed the steps to her door. When it opened, Samantha greeted him wearing a long black cardigan. As she slid her arms around him, he realized that was all she was wearing.

All his reservations flew, and he was about to pick her up and carry her into the bedroom, when she said, "Hey, let's slow down a moment. I've ordered in from Thai Village. I've chilled the champagne ... I thought you were the delivery guy, and even the delivery guy takes his time." She smiled up at him as she pulled her sweater down to mid-thigh.

MacNeice smiled back, but he felt foolish and was thinking, *I'm too old for this.*

The doorbell rang and Sam reached past him and pressed the buzzer to let the delivery man in.

"Can you get it? I'm not decent."

MacNeice patted his pockets for his wallet. He was retrieving it from the inside pocket of his jacket when there was a knock at the door. He opened it and looked up at the broad, smiling face, saying, "How much is it?" He didn't have time to register whose face it was, before the impact and the brief but not unpleasant sensation of falling backwards.

"Aye, the blow is extremely crude but spectacularly effective. Ye may be interested ta know, ah learnt tha growin' up in Clydeside and not in the service of Her Majesty." Bishop was wearing a grey T-shirt and black jeans. Squatting in front of MacNeice, he appeared immense, a gorilla studying a caterpillar. "It's better if ye doan close your eyes, MacNeice. They swell shut if ya do." He lifted MacNeice's head so they were looking directly at each other. "MacNeice—ah know the name. Your family is from Perthshire, just north of Glasgow. Your clan motto is 'By courage, not by craft,' aye, but nae t'day." He studied the detective's face then let his head drop again. "You'll feel a mighty pounding behind those eyes. Ah'm afraid ah've split the bridge of your nose, but otherwise, you'll survive."

He showed MacNeice two bloodied pencils, then dropped them on the floor. "While ye were out, I shoved 'em up yer nostrils. Then ah snapped them together like chopsticks ta reset your nose. You'll have a fine straight beak, laddie—no charge for the medical services rendered."

MacNeice could taste the blood in his mouth. His nose was already so swollen it intruded grotesquely into his sight-line. Disoriented, he attempted to scan the room.

"Auch, your lady friend—a wee bit underdressed for the occasion but not unattractive."

He towered over MacNeice's chair. "Don't trouble yourself, MacNeice. She's trussed up, but not a feather of tha pretty head is outta place." He pointed and MacNeice painfully turned his head to see Samantha gagged and sitting on a chair in the doorway of her bedroom, her arms and legs tied in precisely the same way he was. The cardigan was twisted, exposing one breast and her entire lower abdomen, and she was trying to wiggle so that less of her was bare. Her eyes were wide with shock and fear.

The plastic ties cut into his wrists and his ankles, which were tethered awkwardly to the rear legs of the chair to ensure he couldn't get his footing without toppling face-first onto the wood floor. Using his tongue, he tried pushing the cord out of his mouth to speak, but gave up and shook his head in frustration—which only served to increase the pain in his head and the flow of blood into his throat.

"We have a wee bit a business ta attend ta, am I right, Detective Superintendent MacNeice?"

The big man took him by the hair and shook his head up and down. When MacNeice tried to pull away, Bishop shoved his head hard against the wall.

"Ma name is Bishop. But ye know tha. Ye bin makin' a bit a fuss o'er me, detective. Jacko Bishop. Ah go by Mars—the candy bar, not the god, eh—and Bishop's not ma real name, of course, just another amusing *nom de guerre*."

He retrieved another chair and placed it in front of MacNeice. Bishop watched him straining to see Samantha over the man's shoulder.

"Aye, ah'd prefer she was more modest too." He walked past her into the bedroom, emerging with a blue blanket. Glancing down at her breast, he looked at MacNeice and smiled. "Ah'm sure ye agree, the more plump and firm the better." He tilted his head to look at the breast again. "Very pretty, Miss." He pulled the cardigan closed and dropped the blanket on her legs to cover her groin. Turning away, he said, "There, tha' should help ye to concentrate, detective."

MacNeice tried to speak past the cord but started coughing.

"Auch, cough it up, man. Ye need ta get tha out. Ye've already made a fine mess of your shirt. Here." He pulled the cord out of MacNeice's mouth and told him to spit the blood onto the floor. "It's only blood and spit," he said. "Ye've yet to cough up an organ." He shoved the cord back in MacNeice's mouth.

"Ma stay in your fine community is at an end and ah need ta be on my way. I took the liberty to pay for yer dinner— aye, with a bonnie tip ta boot." He picked up the plastic bag of Thai Village takeout from where it sat by the front door, put it in the oven and turned the gas on to 250 degrees. "Tha' should take care of it."

Returning to the living room, he sat down, crossed his arms and studied MacNeice. "The smell is somethin' terrible, d'ye nae agree? Ah mean, as a Scot, ye cannae possibly enjoy the foul smell of tha." He shook his head slowly in disbelief and looked at his watch. "By the time those wretched vittles are alight, we'll be finished and I'll be gone. Ta business then." He rubbed his hands. "A wild guess, Detective Superintendent: ye're lookin' at me for the deaths of Duggie Langan and his Scandinavian sweetheart. As well, tha bonnie wee girl, Sherry—ah dinna remember her last name."

MacNeice's eyes went to the tattoos on Bishop's arm.

"Ye recognize these, do ye?" He pointed to each word in turn, emphasizing the syllables. "Belfast—we took as good as we gave, and they lost. Herzegovina—treacherous cunts, the Serbs. But they have their reasons, eh?" He put his index finger on the next name and shook his head. "Mogadishu—ah was in the employ of the Queen, but only barely. Queensberry rules never made an appearance there. By Iraq and Afghanistan, ah was a soldier of fortune and, for the love of God"—he moved his finger to the last tattoo— "the Congo's no place for gentlemen soldiers, paid or no." He took a deep breath and pointed to the SAS tattoo above the place names. "Do ye also know this insignia, detective? Jus' nod if ye recognize it."

MacNeice nodded.

"Aye, so now ye know, or think ye do, that Her Majesty spared no expense nor worldly resource in the making of me." He was smiling broadly. "And what Queenie didn't teach was taught ta me long before in Glasgow.

"Ah'm being reassigned abroad, but before ah take my leave, ah felt you deserved the truth about my stay here."

MacNeice blinked to indicate his interest in hearing the truth. The intense pain in his head wouldn't allow him to nod again.

"Ah encountered my friend Duguald in Liverpool. My employer had no immediate work for me, so Duggie arranged passage on the same freighter. Ah'd never been ta sea. Aye, it was boring as shite. Thought ah'd come along ta take in the local sights here in bonnie Dundurn till my call came.

"I liked Duggie well enough, and everything would have been fine, except ah picked up a short-term contract to do some local security work. Ah will na say who my employer was or what, if any, instructions he gave mae ta act as ah ave."

But Bishop did insist it was only after many complaints about the "thieving mick bookie" went unheeded that Bishop responded, and then only reluctantly. "Duggie was a good lad, eh. Irish ta the core, mind ye—needed a chin smackin after a few pints—but a good lad."

Still, he had a job to do. "Ah bought anchors to sink Duggie, but when ah arriv't tae pick him up in ma rented truck, he was walkin' out with Anniken. Ah offered them a lift home and saw immediately tha Duggie knew home was not the destination.

"Ah parked out by Princess Point, a bonnie place to die. Getting outta the truck, ah drew ma weapon…this one." He reached under the T-shirt to reveal a large calibre semi-automatic. "We went inside the cargo area and ah closed the door."

The cargo space was empty but for the anchors, the line and the packing tape. Duggie tried to talk him out of it. Seeing that was futile, he switched tactics and begged Bishop to let Anniken go. "It dinnae please me ta refuse him, but there ye have it. Ah couldna let her go, now could ah?"

Bishop carried on with his narration. "Ah knew he hadn't touched her yet, and so ah says, 'Duggie, that's a beauty right there, a true, untouched beauty. Ah want ye tae at least see her.' Ah told Anni to take off her clothes, and when the lass refused, ah smacked Duggie with mae weapon. She was shiverin' with fear but started ta undress. At first, Duggie was wiping away the blood pourin' from the top of his haid, but then he looked over at her. She was a beauty indeed.

"Ah snapped her neck — she felt only a heartbeat of pain. Then, and only because he was behavin' very badly, screamin' and lunging at ma, ah garrotted poor Duggie. Ah used an anchor for each and tied them with clever knots, assuming tha would do the trick. Alas, the creatures of your dusky bay got the better of mae."

Bishop and Duggie had gone fishing in Byrne's boat; he knew where it was moored and that the key for the motor was on Duggie's Irish harp key-chain. When he took them across to Cootes, it was well after midnight; and when he dumped them over the side, he thought he'd said goodbye forever.

Smoke was starting to come out the sides of the oven door, but the fire alarm had not been triggered. "Sherry... Auch, ah have ta admit, ah lost it there. We made spectacular love on her bed and when ah awoke, she was on top of me, running her fingers over ma tattoos. That's when it started."

Interpreting the confusion on MacNeice's face, he mimicked her, hitting a squealing falsetto. " 'Oh my God! Like that is so fab! Like really! Like awesome, like-like-like-like really — oh ... my ... God.' " He shook his head. "Ta ma mind, Detective Superintendent, ye have serious problems with your education in Dundurn. There was a university diploma on the wall of her boudoir. And yet, for a half-hour or more after I woke, she continued ta blather. Ah couldnae stand it and couldnae shut her up. My head was poundin' from so many blue drinks and ah snapped. Ah felt like a right shite about it, but there it is."

He reached over and pulled the cord from MacNeice's mouth. "Ye ave questions, MacNeice?" He dropped it under his chin and waited.

MacNeice cleared his throat. "Why the tape on the girls' eyes?"

"Oh aye, the tape . . . pure superstition. Ah'd a fixer in Afghanistan who said it released the soul from the body . . . or some such thing. Ah'm not normally given ta such twaddle, but ever since, ah've taped them. Not for Duggie, though. By the time ah had him on the bay, his face and eyes were so black and swollen, ah just wanted ta be done wie him."

Bishop stood up, glanced back to the kitchen, where the smoke was billowing above the stove. Samantha was also looking, her eyes welling with tears. "It appears, miss, ye didn't install a smoke alarm near your cooker. Ye better hope this one is working." He pointed to the detector in the living room ceiling. He tried to shove the cord back in MacNeice's mouth, but MacNeice jerked his head away.

"One more question: Why did you come here to tell me this? You could have just left."

"Aye, but as ye can see, ah don't lack for confidence. Ah'm also a wee bit fatalistic — we have ta be in our line of work, do ye na think?"

Seeing the surprise on MacNeice's face, he added, "Ye and me are like rugby players. You're city, ah'm international. There's more at stake in my game — failure is fatal — but the pay packet's thicker." He smiled like a man who liked his chances. Putting on his coat, he added, "Ah honestly feel terrible about Anni, a bonnie wee girl, and Sherry too. Actually, MacNeice, to be truthful, ah just wanted to confess my sins to a fellow traveller."

He shoved the cord back in MacNeice's mouth, then winked and headed for the door, where he stopped to say, "Don't bother looking for me on the motorways or water-ways. Just imagine ah was the grim reaper tha' came ta town, then left. We won't meet again, MacNeice."

The fire was now crackling in the kitchen. The moment Bishop stepped out to the landing, the smoke curled into the living room and travelled swiftly across the ceiling toward the door. Bishop leaned back into the apartment and gave a casual salute to Samantha.

As the door closed, the smoke detector came to life with a painfully loud *blurp, blurp, blurp*. MacNeice shoved his head back against the wall, trying to get the chair onto its back legs so he could use his feet. It was to no effect—the chair legs were too close to the wall. Finally, he managed to get the sole of his left shoe, then his right, flat against the wall. He pushed off sharply, forcing his head and shoulders forward for momentum. The chair tipped and fell, smashing his knees, then his forehead, on the floor. He was face down on the carpet with no ability to move to either side. The blood rushed to his head, into his mouth, and out his nose. He was going to suffocate if he didn't do something fast.

On top of that, smoke was curling around MacNeice's head. He used whatever lung capacity he could command to exhale, sending spittle and gore whistling past the cord and onto the floor. But when he attempted to inhale, he took in smoke and choked, which left him with no capacity to breathe in or out. He blinked hard, the smoke searing his eyes. The last thing he saw were the flames rising in the kitchen. Then it hit him: he'd always wondered how his life would end, and here he was, upside down, literally out of breath, choking on his own blood.

[32]

BRIGHT... *SO BRIGHT. SO COLD... IT'S FREEZING.* HE COULDN'T TELL if his eyes were open or closed, but his thoughts searched for Kate. He imagined blinking—but was he blinking? The light was so intense. *Why would God take me away only to blind me, and why is it so bloody cold?* Kate hated the cold; her request to be cremated was, in part, a final claim on warmth.

Beyond a mechanical wheeze, he couldn't hear anything, but he felt no pain and his body felt weightless. He assumed he was floating upwards. *Kate... Kate, I'm here.* He was certain she'd hear him, but he couldn't feel his mouth move—was this how it worked? You think you're speaking, but you're not. He blinked several times because he didn't want to miss the first sight of her—she'd be wearing white. She always chose white. A summer dress, French and flowing. *But it's so cold here. And that wheeze—is that me?* He held his breath, listening. The noise continued. Was he actually holding his breath? He couldn't tell. Were his eyes open? He thought so, but when he blinked, it was the same: white, very white.

"HE'S SUFFERED HEAT and smoke inhalation damage to his upper respiratory tract," Dr. Munez said to Aziz as he looked into the ICU cubicle where MacNeice lay. A breathing tube was inserted in his mouth and down his throat, the other end attached to a respirator. He had IVs in both arms. "Clinically, he was dead when the firefighters arrived, but the scans indicate there's no brain damage. He's heavily sedated so he will tolerate the respirator, and he's on antibiotics and cortisone—steroids—through the intravenous drips." The immediate concern, he said, was not brain function, though there was evidence that he'd received a concussion either due to the fall or a blow inflicted prior to it. "The very real concern now is clearing the carbon monoxide built up in his lungs."

The doctor told Aziz there was the potential of a fatal chain reaction, a shutting down of MacNeice's ability to take in oxygen. "After that, pneumonia follows quickly and, well . . ." Seeing the shock on her face, he added, "It's only been twenty-four hours, detective; we just need more time. We'll take him off the respirator in a few days and see if he can breathe on his own. If he can, we'll move him to a step-down unit. He won't likely be able to speak for a while—imagine a severe case of laryngitis. Being optimistic, I'd say he's going to be in hospital for at least a week or two."

"What's the condition of the woman who was found with him?" Aziz asked.

"Ah . . . she had been gagged too, but she was upright, bound to a chair, and didn't have the added complication of a broken nose. The ground floor door had apparently been left open so the dense smoke that enveloped your colleague mostly passed her by. She suffered some damage to her upper respiratory tract, however she's already in a step-down unit."

Aziz was still focused on MacNeice. "He has a broken nose?"

"Sorry, yes. What made his breathing difficult was the fact that it was broken at the bridge, but, ironically, it may have saved his life."

"How so?"

"He couldn't breathe, you see. There was so much blood in his nasal passage, mouth and throat that he was filtering some of the smoke and lethal particulates. Mind you, in the end he couldn't breathe at all."

"Was the woman . . . interfered with?"

"Ah, no. There appeared to be no physical interference other than the bruising caused by the ties on her wrists and ankles."

"Is she conscious?"

"No. While she's off the respirator, we're keeping her sedated to minimize the stress on her throat and lungs. We're going to keep her asleep until tomorrow morning, then wake her."

Munez excused himself and left Aziz alone. She moved closer to MacNeice's head and immediately regretted it. His face was pale and puffy, and his eyes were swollen shut, the colour of purple plums. She put her hand on his shoulder—it felt cold. Too cold. She removed her hand.

WAVING TO THE cop sitting in his cruiser, Aziz climbed over the police tape surrounding Samantha's apartment. Vertesi and Williams were on the way, but she'd have at least ten minutes alone. Even before she left the sidewalk, she was hit by the acrid smell of burnt plastic and wood. Reaching into her pocket, Aziz took out several tissues, covered her nose and mouth and stepped inside. She climbed the stairs, which were covered with fine black ash, and paused at the threshold of the unit.

To the right, between the living room and bedroom, was a chair on its side. Next to it lay a soiled blue blanket; plastic ties were scattered where they'd been cut from the woman's wrists and ankles. A knotted blue gag-cord was looped over the bedroom door handle.

To her immediate left was another chair. The bloodstains smeared on its seat had for the most part been diluted by firehoses and left to form a large pink pool on the floor. Two pencils and four plastic ties were thrown against the wall, likely by the force of the hoses. A bloodied blue cord was tangled around a leg of the chair. She tucked the tissues in a pocket and kept her hands there. Though there was abundant smoke and water damage, there was no sign that the fire had actually reached the living room. However, the kitchen was destroyed. The laminates were buckled and blistered, and whole cupboard units were charred and cut through by axes. Their contents lay scattered and crushed on the floor. A champagne bucket had melted on the counter, and kernels of dark green glass, like a cache of emeralds, had been blown everywhere when the bottle exploded in the heat. They crunched noisily underfoot as Aziz walked to the staircase leading up to the office and roof patio. While charred, it was still intact.

Back in the living room, she picked up MacNeice's coat and held it to her chest. Moving reluctantly to the bedroom, she stopped and looked back from the vantage point of the overturned chair. Whatever happened, MacNeice's lover had had no choice but to watch. Aziz stopped at the bedroom door, looked in and saw that the bed was untouched.

Aziz could hear Vertesi and Williams thumping up the stairs. She put MacNeice's coat back on the sofa. When they came in, Williams touched Aziz's arm briefly before he walked past her to squat, looking at the bloodied chair. Vertesi went into the kitchen and stood there, hands in his pockets, staring around at the damage. "Weird," he said.

Using his pen, Williams picked up and studied the cord. "What's weird?" he asked.

"Like we've just learned Dad's been having an affair — weird."

"Anyone know who she is?" Williams asked, putting the cord down.

Aziz descended the staircase from the mezzanine office. "A journalist. Apparently, a good one."

"Fair enough. Boss deserves the best." It was an absent-minded comment that Vertesi immediately regretted.

Williams turned to Aziz as she passed by. She glanced at him and smiled briefly.

"Ah, Mac's coat," she said, taking the keys from the pocket. "I'll check on the car." She was out the door a moment later, walking quietly down the wet stairs.

Williams went over to the doorway of the kitchen. " 'Boss deserves the best' — well done, Rocky."

"I knew it was wrong the moment it left my mouth, but what the hell. The guy almost dies up here in some woman's apartment, a woman none of us knew existed. Don't you think that's weird?"

AZIZ FOUND MAC'S holstered service weapon locked away in the Chevy's glove compartment, sitting on top of a tattered volume of e. e. cummings's poetry. She opened the book to the slip of paper marking "dive for dreams" and recognized MacNeice's scratched star in the corner and his underlining of the last two lines:

> *dive for dreams*
> *or a slogan may topple you*
> *(trees are their roots*
> *and wind is wind)*
>
> *trust your heart*
> *if the seas catch fire*
> *(and live by love*
> *though the stars walk backward)*

Aziz said the lines out loud before putting the book back and locking the compartment. Stepping out of the Chevy, she locked the doors and looked up at the apartment's windows. The rain that had stopped the day before had begun again in earnest, pelting her face until tears were indistinguishable from water.

[33]

"**L**ISTEN, AND DON'T TRY TO SPEAK," AZIZ SAID.
Four days had passed, and while there was no sign of pneumonia, this was the first day MacNeice was fully conscious and breathing entirely on his own. His voice was a whisper. When he tried to push it, he started coughing so badly he felt sharp pains in his back. Dr. Munez had told him, "That's your lungs complaining. If you insist on speaking, you'll only slow down your recovery."

MacNeice hadn't been debriefed, nor had he been told how Samantha was, beyond Dr. Munez mentioning matter-of-factly that she had been discharged the evening before.

He'd been dozing when Aziz arrived, and while he was getting used to the shock on people's faces — Wallace, Swetsky, Williams, and Vertesi — he wasn't prepared to see her. It was morning, the step-down unit window faced east, its pale blue curtains were drawn and she was a silhouette.

Whispering, he asked, "Are your eyes smiling?"

"I told you not to speak... and yes, they are."

He nodded, and closed his eyes. She was being kind. Wallace and Swetsky had made a point of telling him he looked like a raccoon or worse. The white of his left eye was crimson after he'd blown a blood vessel during a coughing fit.

Aziz proceeded to brief him, all business. "Sherry Berryman's roommate called to say that several friends had seen Sherry dancing with someone who looked like Bishop at the Boogie Bin."

MacNeice nodded.

"The bouncers, bar girls, and several customers confirmed that a big man danced through the night with her. They described tattoos, names that ran down his arm, though the only ones anyone could recall were the words *Iraq* and *Afghanistan*. There was also a negative blue × on his chest. No one went near the big man because he seemed so intimidating, especially after he stripped off his sweater. They said Sherry was drunk and falling all over this stranger more than twice her size."

MacNeice wanted to tell Aziz that he already had a confession from the big man himself, but she raised a hand to stop him, so he closed his eyes and listened.

"A waitress said he'd finished his tenth blueberry martini before grabbing his sweater and leaving with Sherry. The bouncer who hailed the cab added that she climbed on top of him the moment he shut the taxi door."

Aziz had tracked down the driver, who confirmed dropping them at the apartment. "He said he was worried they were actually going to do it in the back seat and leave him with a mess to clean up. But every time he glanced back in the mirror, the guy was looking at him, so he decided cleaning up was preferable to pissing the guy off."

"That it?" he asked, his eyes still closed.

"Samantha told us about him too, but she said she couldn't hear most of what he said to you, and she couldn't recall his name or even if she had heard it."

MacNeice opened his eyes, took the pen and pad off the enamel table and wrote, "Jacko 'Mars' Bishop." She took it and looked up at him.

"Mars?" she said.

"After the candy bar, not the god," MacNeice whispered, struggling to suppress the rattle in his chest. He motioned for the pad and wrote, "Bishop confessed to killing Kallevik, Langan, and Berryman, before setting the apartment on fire. I don't think he intended to kill us—but he wouldn't have lost any sleep if he had."

Over the next half-hour he wrote notes to Aziz about the SAS, Bishop's service tours and the record of his service and contract work tattooed on his arm. He whispered that Bishop had said he was leaving for another assignment, and began coughing again. When he recovered, he wrote on the notepad: "Try Ex Affairs/Bishop not his real name/ tattoos/a good physical description—esp. SAS."

Aziz took the note and stood to leave. MacNeice whispered, "Samantha was discharged yesterday. I haven't heard from her."

She smiled at him. "Samantha was relieved to hear you are recovering."

He made a move to sit up but couldn't, and fell back, coughing hard. She held his shoulder until it subsided.

"Samantha told Vertesi she's going to stay with family till the apartment's refinished. She'll call you when she can."

Aziz did up her coat and paused at the door to wave like Queen Elizabeth — something she hoped he'd find funny — but his eyes were closed.

THREE DAYS LATER, Samantha still hadn't called.

MacNeice was washed, shaved, and dressed in the clothes Vertesi had retrieved from the stone cottage. He was sitting in a chair by the window, waiting to be discharged. While his breathing was still shallow and even a slow walk around the ward left him winded, MacNeice felt desperate to get out of the hospital and back to work.

If Bishop was still in Dundurn — which he doubted — he wanted to be the one to find him. If he wasn't, he'd press for his extradition from wherever he'd gone. Looking down at the knotted plastic bag containing his soiled clothing, MacNeice considered whether to have it cleaned or just dump it in the trash because he couldn't face the smell of it.

A half-hour later an orderly wheeled him down the long corridor to the elevator, the bag of smoky clothing riding on his lap. A melody entered his head as he was pushed into the elevator, something inspired by the rhythmic *thump, thump, thump* of the chair's small front wheels — a piece of gum was perhaps stuck to one. "Bum bum bum bum bum...," he hummed to himself as the elevator descended, wondering what it was.

"Sir?" the orderly asked, looking down at him.

"Sorry...just a piece of music stuck in my head."

Idling at the curb was one of the department's Chevys, sleek black under the steady rain. As the orderly pushed him through the front doors, Williams emerged and jogged over to help.

"Just take the bag, Montile. I'm okay," MacNeice said. He thanked the orderly and got to his feet. He walked to the car hoping that he looked strong enough for what he was about to ask.

The wipers cleared away the blur to reveal another grey morning in Dundurn. Descending the hill to Main Street, Williams stopped at the intersection, signalling a turn to the east.

"Not home, Montile. Take me to work."

"Boss . . ." Williams kept his foot on the brake and looked over at his passenger.

"Work." Wanting to avoid a debate, he turned to look out the window. Though his voice was hoarse — vaguely reminiscent of Brando in *The Godfather* — its tone was nonetheless resolute. Williams turned off the indicator, checked his side mirror and accelerated through the intersection.

Parking near the rear entrance, Williams came around and opened the door for him. With great effort, MacNeice pulled himself from the car. When Williams handed him the plastic bag, he walked over to the trash bin and dropped it inside. "I believe I'll take the elevator."

"No problem. I'll fire up the espresso machine."

That sounded wonderful to MacNeice. He hadn't had coffee of any kind in a week.

At the cubicle MacNeice managed the hellos efficiently, conveying with a few words his complete disinterest in talking about how he was feeling. He settled into his chair and looked up at the whiteboard, searching for something new. When Williams handed him the coffee, he closed his eyes and inhaled. Bliss.

An hour later he was exhausted. He was about to leave, when the telephone on his desk rang. Ryan picked it up.

"It's Dylan Nicholson, sir." MacNeice nodded that he would take it.

"MacNeice."

"You sound bad," said Dylan. "You're probably too sick to come, sir, but my mom will be buried tomorrow. I was just thinking…"

"Do you want me to be there with you?"

"Ah…yeah. Yes, sir. Children's Services said it would be okay if…"

"Why don't I pick you up?"

THE FLOWERS IN his living room, put there, he suspected, by Aziz, were open—twelve, deep burgundy tulips, each exposing six fat black anthers dangling on the ends of delicate stamens. Fragile and dying, they nonetheless reached out to the large window and the forest beyond.

He was hungry, but too exhausted to cook. He retrieved some ancient biscotti Marcello had given him, poured a double grappa, and sat by the cottage window to look for birds. When biting through the biscuit proved too difficult, he dipped it in the grappa until it was soft. That proved to be delicious. He poured another drink.

After two doubles and several biscotti, he moved to the sofa and propped up a cushion so he could gaze out the window. The rain had settled into a light but steady mist that hung in droplets from branches and buds—tiny sparkling crystal balls that in turn grew too big, fell and disappeared from view. Chickadees flitted between the trees closest to the window. He imagined for a moment that they knew he was in rough shape, and that they would stand by him in the lonely stone cottage, no matter the weather. *How pathetic*, he thought. *Now, I'm relying on chickadees to keep me going.*

[34]

WOODLAND CEMETERY, ELEVEN A.M. THAT SUCH A SMALL CLUSTER of solemn mourners was gathered at Jennifer Grant's graveside only added to the heaviness of the scene. Most were huddled under umbrellas, perhaps praying not for her salvation, but for a short service.

As MacNeice approached with Dylan by his side and Vertesi close behind, he studied the black silhouettes against a grey sky. He was having difficulty breathing and couldn't risk taking a deep breath for fear of coughing.

The scene was a set piece: a dozen people gathered between two mature maples, leafless branches shivering in the rain. Dylan had his head down, his new black coat, purchased for him by Children's Services, buttoned to the neck. Under it, he wore dark blue cotton pants, pressed with a sharp crease, probably by Dylan himself. On his feet were black crosstrainers, a reminder to everyone that he was a kid and that what was unfolding shouldn't be.

The Anglican minister stood under a large umbrella held by a woman behind him, who wore a large Tilley hat that shed the rain onto the shoulders of her coat.

Dylan's mother was being interred in the plot her parents had purchased for themselves, never thinking their daughter would precede them. The funeral, at least, had caused Dylan and his grandparents to meet in order to discuss how it would go. Dylan had successfully argued that her remains be cremated and that there be no church service or visitation.

His grandparents were standing close to the minister, huddled under an umbrella beside their surviving child, Robert, who stood out in the rain, his head protected by a black baseball hat. As beads of water gathered at the front of the peak, he'd look down to the grave and they'd drop off. Tom Smylski and his mother stood together under another umbrella, Tom grim-faced and focused on Dylan. Next to Tom was Coach Knox, head down and casting only brief glances in Dylan's direction. Next to him, Mercy's principal and vice-principal stood erect, dignified and patient in the rain.

To the right, separated from the others, stood Graham McLeod, glistening in his weather-beaten Barbour and brown wide-brimmed hat. He nodded at MacNeice before turning his attention to the small rectangular hole in the ground.

With everyone else gathered on one side, Dylan chose to stand on the other, MacNeice and Vertesi on either side of him. Dylan glanced about briefly before catching the minister's eye and nodding for him to begin. Instead of opening

the book, the minister recited from memory a poem by
Mary Elizabeth Frye that MacNeice recognized as the one
Kate's mother had read at her funeral.

> *Do not stand at my grave and weep.*
> *I am not there. I do not sleep.*
> *I am a thousand winds that blow.*
> *I am the diamond glints on snow.*
> *I am the sunlight on ripened grain.*
> *I am the gentle autumn rain.*
> *When you awaken in the morning's hush*
> *I am the swift uplifting rush*
> *Of quiet birds in circling flight.*
> *I am the soft stars that shine at night.*
> *Do not stand at my grave and cry;*
> *I am not there. I did not die.*

Next, the minister opened his book, and as the familiar
words of interment rang out, the boy's shoulders started
shaking. He hoisted them up—hoping perhaps it would be
mistaken for shivers in the rain—and the rain coursed down
the back of his neck where his coat collar gaped. MacNeice
took off his scarf and wrapped it around the boy. Without
looking up, Dylan whispered, "Thanks."

MacNeice put his hand on Dylan's shoulder and pulled
him to his side. At first the boy resisted, but then he surren-
dered to the needed comfort. Across the way, everyone who
didn't have their head down was watching him, and before
long, most of them were weeping too.

Jennifer's parents and her brother appeared frozen
in anguish, unable or unwilling to look away from the
small hole in the ground. McLeod turned away from the

grave, toward the horizon, possibly unable to face the final reminder of his own failure to save her. Even the minister's helper was moved to tears, her hand trembling, sending a shower off the edge of the umbrella that narrowly missed the Book of Common Prayer and splashed onto the minister's shiny black shoes.

Only Alexander Knox, the only adult here who knew Dylan well appeared stoic. With his hands thrust deep into the pockets of his coat and the rain streaming down his face, he stared at the small pit and its surrounding carpet of synthetic grass, brilliant green in the grey, brown, and black surroundings. As the ashes were being lowered into the ground, MacNeice caught an exchange of glances between the coach and Jennifer's brother. Though brief and non-verbal, it was something private, a split-second communication that both could assume had gone unnoticed.

When the service was over, MacNeice suggested a trip to the Secord Dairy with Tom Smylski and his mother. No one said anything on the drive. Once inside the dairy, however, the boys ordered banana splits. When they were finished, they asked for two more. Tom's mother rolled her eyes in mock shock but didn't object. As they dug into their second sundaes, the two friends chased funereal gloom with sugar-induced nervous laughter. Mrs. Smylski shook her head, uncomfortable or embarrassed that the detectives might consider the behaviour inappropriate. But MacNeice understood. Dylan's hysterics were likely the first time he'd laughed since life, as he knew it, had ended.

After they dropped a very sleepy Dylan at his foster home later, the image of Knox at the cemetery still haunted MacNeice. Taping a man with a live grenade at his throat and wheeling him into a park to be discovered by chance by anyone—a mother with a baby stroller, a couple of teens, or firefighters, paramedics and cops—suggested someone frozen to the core. Rationally, he didn't believe a high school basketball coach could work up the hatred for it, but his intuition and experience suggested otherwise.

As Vertesi pulled up in front of the stone cottage, MacNeice asked, "What would Dylan's basketball coach have in common with a greengrocer in Dundas?"

"Knox lives up on the east mountain—that's a long way to go for a cucumber."

MacNeice got out of the car and watched as Vertesi reversed out of the gravel driveway, negotiated the potholes and broken pavement and disappeared down the road. It was late Friday afternoon and the rain had stopped. There were even faint patches of pale blue sky breaking through the cloud cover. He closed his eyes, cautiously breathing in the smell of damp undergrowth. Chickadees and juncos chattered in the trees about him. He heard a tractor-trailer gearing down for the lights at Main and Mountain. MacNeice listened, loving the music of it—*clung-chunk, verrrr; clung-chunk, verrrr; clung-chunk, verrrr*—until the highway was quiet and the songs of eternally positive birds reasserted themselves. He opened his eyes and, for a moment, the world seemed brighter.

HE WAS INTO his third grappa when the phone rang. It was Wallace, asking whether he was ready for full duty or still needed time. "I'll be fine after the weekend, sir."

"The British consul-general has requested your presence this Monday at his residence in Toronto—ten-thirty a.m. You are to meet a British colonel, one Sir Giles Tremain

Lyttelton CBE, of the Special Air Service. If that mouthful means anything to you, perhaps you can enlighten me?"

MacNeice told Wallace that Aziz had called the British embassy to ask about the whereabouts and history of Jacko Mars Bishop. "As he is a triple murder suspect who served in the SAS and told me that the name he was using was false, we gave the embassy a detailed description, including the list of tattoos and that he likely was from Glasgow. We also provided three black and white photographs taken from security cameras that tie him to the murder of Sherry Berryman."

Wallace said, "If you're not feeling strong enough, Mac, I can send Aziz along to meet Sir Mucketyduck."

MacNeice laughed. "I'll go, and take Aziz with me."

He'd just put down the phone when a vehicle braked outside. MacNeice went to the door to find Marcello retrieving a stack of aluminum foil containers from the trunk of his car. He carried them past the detective. "Fiza dropped by. She said you were here but probably surviving on Kraft Dinner. Here you go: lasagna, ricotta ravioli, roasted root veggies, and grilled garlic rapini. You can freeze the pastas." He disappeared into the kitchen and just as quickly reappeared to shake MacNeice's hand, bumping his shoulder.

MacNeice offered him a grappa.

"No, *grazie*. I have to get back—we're booked solid tonight. You take care, eh. We miss you."

Within minutes Marcello had come and gone, but the smell of food had taken over the house. Cutting a generous slice of lasagna, he was struck by how lonely he felt.

He opened a bottle of red wine and poured a large glass. Across from him, the other chair was tucked tight to the table. With his foot, he shoved it out and—call it a trick of the wine—for a moment he could believe someone was about to sit down. Not Kate surely. And now, not Sam.

He could hardly blame her. She had almost died because of him and her apartment was in ruins. "Fair enough," MacNeice said aloud, and cut another piece of the pasta.

Still, this cottage he loved, this nest that had known years of overwhelming tenderness, seemed unbearably cold. Filling his glass again, he set his mind to fighting the drift the wine was taking him in. After rinsing the plate, knife and fork, he put them in the dishwasher. He poured another glass of wine and went into the living room to lie down on the sofa and count his blessings.

Just after midnight, he was awoken by the telephone. How long it had been ringing he couldn't tell, but when he picked it up, his voice wouldn't work. He coughed and tried again to say hello.

On the other end of the line, a voice said, "Mac . . . is that you?"

He swallowed hard—his throat was dry, his head spinning. "It's me . . . yes, it's me." He couldn't tell if his words were loud enough to be heard on the other end.

"I'll be right there." The line went dead.

He put the phone down and sank into the sofa. Had he dreamed the phone rang, dreamed his voice hadn't worked? Who was the voice?

There was an empty grappa bottle and glass on the coffee table. *Is it possible*, he wondered, *that I finished a nearly full bottle of grappa in one evening?*

He went into the kitchen and splashed water on his face. He was awake. Or was that a dream too? Was this alcohol poisoning? The cork for the red wine was sitting on the counter; he picked it up and shoved it into the bottle — that small act had to be something only an awake person would do. While his head hurt, he knew it wasn't due to the concussion or the broken nose. Even fine grappa in quantity can give you a hangover. He went back to the sofa.

When morning came splintering through the trees into the living room, it flickered and teased the thin skin of his eyelids until he opened them. He let his head fall to the right and once again saw the empty grappa bottle. He was still wearing the black suit from the funeral. Certain now that he was awake, he nonetheless still felt disoriented.

No one had come. He must have been dreaming. Swinging his legs to the floor, MacNeice pushed himself up to face the window. On a branch he kept meaning to remove for fear it would swing in the wind and smash the pane, was a female cardinal. She was watching him, turning her head from side to side, masked eyes behind a vermilion beak. Seconds passed before the male — fast flashing red — passed by and out of sight. The female didn't appear to notice but he knew she had — the two were inseparable. She flew off when MacNeice stood up.

He put the glass in the dishwasher and took the bottle out to the recycling bin beside the driveway. Returning to the door, he saw a small folded piece of paper on the threshold and picked it up. He went to the kitchen, turned on the espresso machine and sat down at the table.

"Knocked several times. No answer. Walked around to the garden, saw you asleep on the sofa — happy to see you were okay. Fiza"

[35]

NESTLED IN THE HEART OF ROSEDALE, THE HOME OF THE BRITISH consul-general wasn't any more stately than its neighbours. The only signals that its inhabitants weren't investment bankers, plastic surgeons, or corporate lawyers were the security cameras, the high black iron fence, and the small handsome coat of arms above the gate and over the front door.

Andrew Portman met them there. A career diplomat in his mid-forties, the consul-general was accustomed to dealing with much kinder issues than multiple homicides, yet Portman appeared buoyant — and proper. He took their coats, handed them to an attendant and waited for him to leave the foyer before he said anything more.

"Thank you for coming on such short notice. I'll take you into the drawing room to meet with the colonel after I establish the ground rules."

"Mr. Portman, why are we meeting here at your residence and not downtown at the consulate?" Aziz asked.

"Ah, you're British," he said with a smile.

"I'm a Canadian now."

"Quite. Well, detective, Colonel Lyttelton requested we meet in a less formal environment."

"By which you mean secret and confidential," MacNeice said.

"I prefer the term *less formal.*" The smile was gone. "Your meeting will last one hour and thirty minutes. All questions are permissible, with the understanding that some may go unanswered, for national security reasons. The colonel is in the city for this meeting only, following which he will fly home to London." Portman's smile returned and appeared sincere; he wanted to avoid any diplomatic missteps. "Are we clear?"

They nodded and Portman took them into an elegantly appointed sitting room and on through a set of oak panelled doors to the drawing room. Lyttelton was standing by a large window, looking out to the garden.

"Detective Superintendent MacNeice and Detective Inspector Aziz, please allow me to introduce Colonel Sir Giles Lyttelton."

Lyttelton swung around and walked smartly toward them. Crisp handshakes done, Portman said, "I'll take my leave, then." Stepping backwards, he pulled the oak doors closed behind him. Lyttelton motioned for them to sit down.

A trim man just under six feet, the colonel wore a tailored dark blue suit, a red tie with tiny gold SAS heraldic crests on the diagonal, and a white shirt with a crisp cutaway collar.

His shoes were deep burgundy and polished to glass. It occurred to MacNeice that Lyttelton would be impressive in his regimental dress uniform, though this Savile Row number was a close second.

The pleasantries that followed, primarily focused on Aziz's English accent, were brief. Lyttelton positioned himself on the window side of the refined Edwardian mahogany table, which meant MacNeice and Aziz sat opposite. The remaining chairs had been moved off to line the wall. There was a large manila envelope on the table in front of him.

Clever, MacNeice thought. The colonel would be in silhouette and they'd be squinting at him against daylight. He was free to study their brightly lit faces while remaining unobserved—a military brain choosing his opponent's position on the field of battle.

"If you don't mind, colonel, I'll just close those curtains." Before Lyttelton could object, MacNeice had levelled the playing field.

The colonel was handsome and masculine, an echo of earlier British adventurers and explorers. He had sharp, falcon-like features, a narrow nose and piercing eyes, with flesh drawn so tight over his cheekbones that two vertical lines dropped to his chin like cables anchoring a suspension bridge. Close-cropped salt and pepper hair was swept severely away from his temples and forehead. It was clear the man was a hunter, a single-purpose creature.

"Shall we proceed to the matter at hand," Lyttelton said. It was a non-question delivered with a brief, squinty smile. He took off his jacket—trim torso, flat stomach—and draped it crisply over a nearby chair.

He pulled a file folder from the envelope, opened it and pushed a photograph of a man in a dress uniform across the table. Jacko Mars Bishop. "His name is Robert Gordon

Buchanan." As they studied the image, a prototype of the warrior portraits released to the media whenever a soldier was killed in action, all MacNeice could see was the man who had terrorized him and Samantha and left them for dead. "The finest soldier in the finest regiment I know," Lyttelton added.

"Buchanan re-enlisted twice and served his full term," he went on. "He was decorated several times for valour. In Yugoslavia, for example, during the 1990s war, with one wounded comrade in the back of his Land Rover and only a young recruit beside him, Buchanan faced down a Serbian captain and twenty heavily armed troops. He led forty-three Croatian female students and their six female teachers to safety in a UN compound." With each citation he mentioned, Lyttelton pulled out another document to prove it.

MacNeice and Aziz waited and watched. When the file folder was empty, Lyttelton set it aside to reveal another. This one he didn't open, just placed both hands flat on top of it. MacNeice noticed a ring with the SAS seal on the baby finger of his right hand.

"You served with him, colonel, throughout his time with the SAS?" MacNeice asked.

"I did. And I tried to persuade Robert to stay in, but as you know, there's no shortage of conflicts in the world." Her Majesty's forces were facing redeployment back to the UK after Afghanistan. Buchanan, he said, "was extremely well trained and not the least bit interested in sitting at home. He wasn't alone. It's not unusual for NATO forces to lose some of their finest to private defence contractors. They usually say they're leaving for the larger income — we cannot compete on that level — but they're really pursuing the action. I've come to think of them as similar to elite athletes," he said reflectively. "The men know they have a period of time to use their physical and intellectual talents, and be well compensated. In the forces, that would mean patiently climbing the ranks until you have enough pay and pension to buy a decent home when you retire. But that's a pittance to what a man of his calibre could earn in the same period with a mercenary outfit. Assuming you exit alive, you would indeed live well."

MacNeice glanced deliberately at his watch and noted that twenty minutes had passed. "My experience of Bishop — or Buchanan — is not as inspiring as yours."

Lyttelton had caught the gesture. "Right. Let's turn to your homicides. After reading the materials provided and seeing the CCTV images, I am not disputing that Bishop was Buchanan. It's not unusual for these men to have several identities and to wander the world between assignments. Nor is it unusual, sadly, that they find it difficult, while wandering, to avoid getting into hot water."

"Hot water?" MacNeice's jaw tightened, fury rising in his face.

"By that, detective, I mean that mostly we hear of them wreaking havoc in a bar in Thailand, crashing a motorbike in Spain, or throttling a prostitute in Calcutta. What you have here, however, is so rare I might refer to it as unique."

"Neither DI Aziz nor I are unaware of Buchanan's expertise. I've personally experienced it first-hand. We're also aware that the killing of two innocent women and a young man — civilians — was not what he was trained to do. The psychotic transformation of this man is not our concern. Apprehending him for these murders is."

Lyttelton stiffened. He studied MacNeice's face, then glanced over at Aziz. "I am not an apologist for murder,

detective superintendent. I am offering you another, perhaps parallel, reality. There are, at last count in my regiment alone, and in the towns and villages in which we
served together, at least twenty friendly combatants and
another two hundred civilians that owe their lives to Robert
Buchanan."

"Yes, but you see, colonel, I'm only concerned with the
three homicides Buchanan committed in Dundurn. We're
here to seek his extradition and arrest, and your assistance
will be deeply appreciated."

Lyttelton looked down to the folder under his hands
before returning his gaze to MacNeice. "Sadly, I can't help
you. Major Buchanan was killed in Nigeria on Thursday
last week."

MacNeice sat back in the chair and exhaled.

Aziz leaned forward. "Can you prove it?"

"I can. Buchanan's broker had been contracted by a
French-Nigerian mining complex, Or-Afrique S.A., to provide security for the evacuation of French nationals due to
political unrest in the country's northern provinces. The
team Buchanan led was experienced but underequipped and
without support. Worse, explosives supplied by the Nigerian
army, intended to secure the perimeter of the compound, for
the most part failed to explode. Many were killed."

Glancing over at MacNeice, who was still silent, Aziz
pressed: "But do you actually have proof that Buchanan died
there?"

"Yes, we do." Lyttelton opened the remaining file folder.
It contained two affidavits and a packet of black and white
photographs. Before he passed them across the table, he
looked solemnly at MacNeice. "Buchanan was known to
his seven subordinates as Angus Robertson. One of these
transcripts" — he laid his palm on the paper — "is by the sole

survivor of his team, a wounded former US Marine named
Mostacci, currently recovering from a stomach wound in
a Marseilles hospital. The other affidavit is from Madame
Monique Fillion, wife of Or-Afrique's last man in Nigeria.
The photographs were taken from a camera mounted in the
evacuation helicopter."

Lyttelton eased the documents across the table.

Once they were in their hands, the colonel stood and
picked up his jacket. From his pants pocket, he produced a
flat silver case from which he removed two cards. "If any
more questions arise, don't hesitate to contact me." Lyttelton
laid the cards on the table. "Unless you have further need of
me, detectives, I'll be off." Putting on his jacket, he picked
up the empty military file, tucked it smartly under his arm,
and walked around the table to Aziz. He shook her hand and
then MacNeice's. A moment later he'd disappeared through
the side door of the drawing room.

Aziz picked up the first of the transcripts as MacNeice
peered somewhat numbly at the photographs. Whatever
he was about to discover paled against the satisfaction he'd
been robbed of—he'd never see the man he knew as Jacko
Mars Bishop in court.

The first photograph, taken from the door of a helicopter,
revealed two buildings under attack, with fires alight in an
infield and dark figures either running and firing, or lying
flat and twisted on the ground, likely dead. The photograph
had a narrow bar at the bottom right with "03. 24. 13. / 21:34P
/ EV-2." He glanced at the bottom of the next photograph,
each was dated and timed sequentially.

The helicopter must have been taking fire, because in
the second print the point of view had swung about, presumably to the advantage of an on-board machine gun. In
the corner of the photo, he could see a white X painted on

the roof of one of the buildings. There were three figures near the small stairwell and someone was lying at the edge of the roof, firing out toward dark figures caught in pools of light at the perimeter.

He picked up another photo. Two minutes had elapsed, and the helicopter was about to touch down, blowing dust and bits of debris everywhere. To one side of the image, smoke was rising from the twisted wreckage of a tower. More dark figures were running and firing at the building. In the next photo, the helicopter was on the roof. There were two figures — women — huddled against the stairwell shack wall, cowering from the powerful wash of the rotor blades. Beside them was a body wrapped in white fabric.

The following print sent a chill down MacNeice's spine. A large man stood in the stairwell doorway. Like a giant, he filled the void. The women were getting up: the big man was firing off to his left and the women covered their ears. Realizing Lyttelton had provided him with a storyboard, MacNeice fanned the rest of the photographs out on the table.

In the next, the big man had picked up the wrapped body. As he carried it over his shoulder, he shielded the women and kept firing; they were running toward the helicopter camera. In the next photo, the big man was close to the camera, dropping the wrapped body inside the chopper. He was yelling something, presumably to the crew chief inside. MacNeice's heart was racing as he studied the face of Major Robert Buchanan, Jacko Mars Bishop and Angus Robertson.

In the following images, Buchanan, with his back to the camera, was running to the stairwell door, where another man had fallen. All about him, the roofing gravel was spitting with the incoming fire. In the next, Buchanan was back at the helicopter, the wounded man on his shoulder.

Buchanan again appeared to be yelling something, this time to his left, possibly to the pilot.

In the next, Buchanan appeared to have been running back to the stairwell door when he was hit and launched sideways, struck in the hip or abdomen. MacNeice picked up the next. The helicopter was lifting off, twenty feet or so above the roof. There were dark figures pouring out of the stairwell door, firing toward the chopper. Buchanan lay off to the right side, firing back at them.

MacNeice's heart sank when he picked up the last photograph. No longer interested in the helicopter, the dark figures had fanned out in a semicircle and were concentrating fire on Buchanan. His assault rifle had been cast aside and clouds of dust and blood rose from his body and the gravel all about him. Anniken Kallevik, Duguald Langan, and Sherry Berryman's killer was literally being ripped to pieces.

MacNeice got up and walked over to the windows. Pulling the curtains apart, he looked out to the garden, aware that his heart rate had shot up dramatically. Behind him, Aziz was reading the second transcript—she hadn't spoken. He didn't have the stomach to read, at least not now. The pictures had done enough. Buchanan had saved the lives of hundreds, and in those grainy black and white prints, it was clear he had died saving several more. The man had been capable of giving life, but terribly proficient at taking it.

So, there was nothing fundamentally sinister about Bishop. Had they met prior to his running amok in Dundurn, MacNeice might have enjoyed his company.

Bishop was a bullet in a chamber, but it was the hand on the trigger that had made him lethal.

MacNeice swung around and said, "Pack it up, Fiza. Let's go talk to Paul Zetter."

[36]

CHET BAKER'S SAD AND TENDER BALLADS FILLED THE CHEVY ALL the way from Toronto to the turnoff for Dundurn. Aziz knew MacNeice loved music, but she knew he also used it to discourage conversation and to find some silence in himself.

Crossing the bridge above Cootes Paradise, she noticed him looking for the little bay. It was impossible to see from that height. He coughed, cleared his throat and said, "I'm not sure how to measure two hundred lives or more saved against the three taken here in Dundurn." He did a U-turn and headed for the botanical gardens, driving down to the inlet where they'd carried Anniken Kallevik's frozen body to the shore only weeks before.

Stopping where he had parked that day, he said, "I'll just be a minute."

As Aziz waited in the car, he walked to the shore and stopped to stare in the direction of the marina Anniken and Duguald had left on their final boat ride. Looking down at the water lapping softly onto the stony shore, he thought even the bay seemed exhausted, unable to summon the energy to break a wave, let alone disturb the pebbles from their sleepy algae beds. MacNeice knelt down and picked up the flattest stone he could find. Standing, he turned it so his thumb and forefinger held the edge. Intent on skipping it to the end of Cootes and into Dundurn Bay, he wound up and sent it flying low across the water.

It skipped twice, three times, then curved up on an angle and swung off course before careening downward and slicing through the surface. MacNeice's head hurt from the effort and he was having difficulty breathing. Behind him, he heard the passenger door of the Chevy open and clunk shut. Bishop had slaughtered three people, MacNeice thought, but in Britain and elsewhere, he'd be remembered for saving hundreds. He was a hero.

"You looked like you were trying to throw that all the way to the marina."

"I was. But I put too much on it." He coughed. "Sorry, Fiza." Though what he was sorry about remained unsaid.

"Have you heard from Samantha?"

"Not a word."

She didn't respond, and he looked up at the hills on either side of the tiny bay. Anniken's body was on the way home for a proper burial, where once again she'd be surrounded by loved ones. Duguald would likely be interred locally with only his uncle to see him off.

But out here, very soon, the world would green, and kids would look for jack-in-the-pulpits and trilliums, chase frogs and turtles, or fish for sunfish and be terrified when they hooked carp in the shallows. Kayakers would swing in for a respite from Dundurn Bay's chilly winds, and again lovers would come for kisses and more.

MACNEICE AND AZIZ entered the offices of Canada Coil and Wire at 2:51 p.m. No one was in the reception area, though they noticed a woman in a floral dress glancing back at them as she entered the washroom down the hall. Since the door to Zetter's office was open, they walked in, startling the man behind the desk.

"Who the hell are you?" he said, standing up.

"Sit down," MacNeice said. "I assume you're Paul Zetter."

"Yeah, so you know me. Who are you?"

"Detective Superintendent MacNeice. This is Detective Inspector Aziz."

Zetter sat down, gathered the papers on his desk into a pile and turned them upside down as the two detectives sat across from him. He was a pale, thin man with pockmarked skin, whose eyes narrowed as he studied them.

"Do you know why we're here, Mr. Zetter?"

Zetter shrugged. "I haven't a clue. Why don't you enlighten me after you show some identification."

When that formality was over with, Aziz put the photos of Anniken Kallevik and Duguald Langan face up on the desk. Zetter didn't move, nor did he look at them right away. When he finally glanced at them, his eyes skittered away after a moment. Aziz laid a photograph of Sherry Berryman next to the others. That one, he didn't bother to look at.

"These are the bittersweet moments in an investigation, Mr. Zetter. They are precious—but brief," MacNeice said.

"I have no idea what you just said, pal. Nada. Zip. Next?"

Aziz put the SAS dress uniform portrait of Buchanan down beside the others. Zetter leaned forward. "He's big, but I don't know him."

"I think you did. You knew him as Jacko Mars Bishop."

"Did I?"

"Yes," Aziz said.

MacNeice was looking at the overturned stack of papers. "Tell us about your business."

Zetter sat back in his chair and smiled at MacNeice. "The import and export of coil and wire. These days, more import than export."

"Due to the closing of the steel mills?" Aziz said.

"That, yeah. The Chinese and Indians — among others — can deliver faster and cheaper than we ever could."

"By the looks of it, you run a lean operation here." MacNeice looked around.

"We've got the reception and my office, and with the warehouse and the yard, maybe fifteen thousand square feet . . . Yeah, it's lean."

"Pays well though, does it?"

"Why, you want in?" Zetter put his elbows on the desk. "What's your point, detective? You want to see my books? I promise you they've been looked at by smarter guys than you."

"I'm sure they have. What I'm interested in, however, are your off-book expenditures and income."

"You two got some nerve — do you even know who I am?"

MacNeice said, "You're a businessman who hires muscle. One of the men you hired is Bishop. Bishop is responsible for three murders and two attempted murders."

"What the —"

"I'm not finished. The only question we still need to answer is whether Bishop did two of these murders on your orders."

"You're seriously whacked. You should seek help."

"Perhaps I should."

Zetter stood up. "This is fucked. I want you two outta here now, and" — he shoved the photos across the desk toward Aziz — "take this shit with you. You think I don't have contacts? I know people. I'll call the mayor. I don't need this shit." He reached for the phone.

MacNeice stood up. "We'll go, but before we do, could you tell me why an importer of coil and wire requires personal security?"

Aziz reached over and collected the photos, putting them back in the folder.

"Charge me with something or get out." Zetter's hand was still on the phone, but he made no move to dial.

"Consider yourself under suspicion in the deaths of three people, Mr. Zetter. Do not attempt to leave Dundurn."

As they left the office, the woman in the floral dress was sitting behind the reception desk. By the look on her face it was clear that she'd heard most, if not all, of the exchange.

MacNeice stopped in front of her. "Your name, please?"

"Gloria . . ." Her voice quavered. "Gloria Zetter. I'm Paul's wife."

"You're also his receptionist?" Aziz asked.

"I run the office."

"For chrissakes, Gloria," Zetter screamed.

It was as much of an assault as a smack across the face. Gloria went red with humiliation and turned back to her computer — which hadn't been switched on.

In the car, Aziz asked MacNeice why he hadn't pressed Zetter further.

"No need. We have a confession from the killer, who's now dead. Gloria Zetter is listed as partner and chief financial officer, though I wonder if she's aware of his gambling on horses or exactly why he needs heavies around him. We'll come back to him, but for now we'll track his movements."

"You think he'll bolt?"

"Absolutely, and as quickly as possible."

"You think he's up to more than gambling, don't you?"

"I do. He takes people for boat rides — perhaps across the lake. I could imagine there are women on that boat to amuse his clients."

"Drugs."

"Possibly, or just prostitution. Enterprises for which you occasionally need heavies."

"I'll get a surveillance team on him."

[37]

MacNEICE WAS EXHAUSTED. HE HAD JUST FINISHED BRIEFING
Wallace on rattling Paul Zetter's cage and the meeting
with Colonel Lyttelton. He gave him copies of the images
and the written transcripts from the survivors in Nigeria
for his press briefing. Before he left, MacNeice told Aziz to
call him if anything broke.

It was only 5:30 when he walked through the door to the
cottage. He put the keys down on the table under the Bill
Brandt photograph of a nude on a stone beach. He patted
her bum and kicked off his shoes. Propping himself up on
a pillow on the sofa, he lay down to watch for birds, and
fell asleep.

The call from Aziz came at 10:56 p.m.

Paul Zetter and his wife had been detained while trying to board a plane to the Bahamas. A pair of shorts, one change of underwear, a Hawaiian shirt and a shaving kit were all he'd packed, perhaps because he had $456,920 nestled at the bottom of his suitcase. Zetter had argued that it was a family ritual to take a March break—though he and Gloria had no children. The couple were now waiting for MacNeice in separate interview rooms.

When MacNeice arrived, Aziz could see he was struggling.

"You and I will take Mr. Zetter first." His voice was raspy, barely a whisper. "I think it's good to keep his wife on ice for the moment."

Zetter was a little less cocky, though he still denied knowing Bishop. "But I did hire several men to guard the yard. There's always theft and graft in the coil and wire business."

"The names of the guards?" Aziz asked.

"I can't remember. I always pay them in cash, so I have no record of them. Why was I arrested?"

"DS MacNeice told you not to leave Dundurn, because you are under suspicion and may be charged as an accessory to murder," Aziz said. "And you were trying to leave."

"MACHT4. Your silver Mercedes?" MacNeice asked.

"Yeah, so?"

"Bishop was seen getting into your vehicle."

"Says who?"

"Says me. I saw him get into your vehicle and drive away from the Block and Tackle Bar."

Aziz put the photograph of Bishop/Buchanan in front of him again.

"I want to talk to my lawyer," Zetter said, taking one of their cards from his pocket and using it to pick his teeth.

"As is your right, Mr. Zetter." MacNeice stood up. "And our right is to impound your yacht and vehicle. They will be swept by Forensics, as will your home and offices."

Aziz stood. "A constable will be in shortly to escort you to a telephone." She followed MacNeice out of the door.

GLORIA ZETTER WAS another story. Terrified and deeply embarrassed at being escorted in handcuffs through the airport, she immediately claimed she knew nothing about her husband's business affairs. That changed when MacNeice reminded her that she was her husband's business partner.

"Sure, but I don't know what he does beyond the coil and wire business. Pauly keeps that away from me — and I don't wanna know."

"But you have met the so-called security men."

"Well... yeah, I guess."

"Tell me, is theft in the coil and wire business so rampant that you need three security staff to protect it?"

"I don't know."

"Well, how many break-ins did you suffer and how much was stolen before your husband hired these men?"

"I can't recall."

"Can you recall ever hearing of theft at your warehouse?"

"No, but..." She shifted in her chair. "Do you do things like plea bargains here?"

"You mean in the homicide interview room." Aziz was surprised to hear the question so soon.

"Mrs. Zetter, if you tell us all you know about the deaths of these three people," MacNeice said, putting the photos on the table, "and how your husband was funding his bets on the horses with Duguald Langan, something can be worked out."

Gloria sat forward, sighed and then started talking. "Pauly was a bookie himself a long time ago. It's not easy to steal in the coil and wire business—really not easy. Basically, we ship whatever we can source locally very quick. And when our product comes from Asia, we ship that real quick too—that's how we get paid." She turned to Aziz. "Miss, can I have some water, please?"

"Certainly. And it's detective, not Miss," Aziz said, pressing the pause button on the recorder.

When they were alone, MacNeice studied the woman across from him. She was slightly overweight, but not unattractive. Though it wasn't hot in the interview room, her forehead glistened. "You look tired, Mrs. Zetter. It must have been a rough night."

"Yeah, you got that right."

Aziz returned with a large paper cup of water. "Here you go." She sat down and turned on the recorder.

"The heavies?" MacNeice asked.

She put the cup down and wiped her mouth with her hand. "He hired them to ensure bets and debts are collected."

"You're saying that Paul was taking bets?"

"For years he hadn't been. But then the Irish guy came along and he was doing so well. Pauly wanted in on the action."

MacNeice put the photograph of the man she would have known as Bishop on the table in front of her. Gloria shivered and looked away.

"That guy was trouble from the start. I seen it comin' and I said so. Pauly asks him to do somethin' and that wacko does it and then some." She shifted, crossed her legs and adjusted her dress so it rested neatly above a dimpled knee. "We were gettin' beat on bets by the Irish kid who gets off a boat and, just like that, he's a bookie, like fairy dust. We thought it was 'cause of his winning personality — he had that in spades."

She was nodding as she recalled their reaction to him. "Pauly says, 'Bishop came off the same boat. He'll rein him in the moment I say so,' and so we go on and, just like I warned him, the kid has a touch. He's taken over the yacht club, he's got guys up and down the north end." She sipped her water.

MacNeice was going to prod her, but realized she was not done talking. She leaned forward to signal she was going conspiratorial on her husband.

"Pauly tells me he tried to negotiate with the Irish, ya know, like bring him on as part of our team, to lighten our load. But no — in his mind, he was there first." She lowered her voice as if she was afraid to say it too loud. "Pauly tells Bishop, 'Straighten that kid out. He plays with us or he don't play.' That's all he said, I swear to Holy Mary — I was there when he said it. So off Bishop goes — alone, mind you — and next thing we hear, Irish has left town. Then they're fishin' bodies outta the bay. Why he off'd them we never knew. Then he goes to the dance hall, and he offs that little girl... Sherry, Cherry — what's her name?"

"Sherry Berryman," Aziz said.

"Yeah." She shrugged and pointed across the table at Aziz. "I tell ya, this guy comes to dinner — watch out, eh — you may not make it to the ice cream. I was scared — oh shit, was I scared. Then he comes in, asks me for his payout. He says — and this is God's truth, cuz I wrote it down, eh." She wiggled in her chair, trying to make herself more comfortable. "He says, 'Family Zetters' — he makes *Zetters* sound like "Zeeters" — 'I must take my leave of your rusty wee town and bid a-doo' — whatever that means — 'as duty calls and I must away.' Anyway, we paid him and pretended we'd miss him." She shuddered theatrically.

"Did you know anything about what he did before he got here?"

"Naw, he never said anything. One day though, I'm watching him take off that heavy sweater he was always wearin', to put on a Canada Coil and Wire T-shirt, and his tits were bigger than mine—but solid, eh—and tattoos everywhere, so I just knew he was trouble. Jesus, there's a Mom's worst nightmare, eh?" She tucked in a strand of hair that had broken free of her blond, but vaguely pink, hair.

"Gloria, we have already begun forensic searches of Paul's car, the yacht, and your house. Do you want to tell us what we might find?"

"I don't know."

"Well, during the sailing season, we're told, Paul would take parties out on that boat and wouldn't return for hours."

"Yeah, he loves it. I hate it, makes me feel sick." Gloria screwed up her face to suggest gagging with seasickness.

"We'll need the names of the other guards."

She feigned not knowing, shaking her head slowly from side to side. At last she said, "Larry Cornelli and Jimmy Albert—good guys really. They're listed in our annual report as drivers. Never killed anyone, that's for sure...least that I know of."

"Is there anything else, Mrs. Zetter?"

"We're in the coil and wire business. It's legit. Beyond that, we're just bookies, y'know? We're not into rough stuff beyond smacking bad debts outta people, and even then, that's rare." She put a hand to her chest. "My heart almost broke when I heard about those girls. Tore me apart—I knew Bishop did it and I couldn't say squat...till now. I told

Pauly I was gonna leave him for that, for that and lotsa other reasons." She leaned across the table toward MacNeice. "Am I gonna be okay here? Pauly will be really pissed to hear me singin' like this."

"Your co-operation here today is appreciated, Mrs. Zetter. However, you'll likely be charged as an accessory to murder. Your lawyer will guide you through it. Detective Aziz will have your statement printed out for you to sign. If you have anything to add, now is the time to do it."

She blinked at him like she'd been kicked in the head, but she had nothing more to add.

MACNEICE MADE HIS way back to Zetter's interview room to find him sitting with his lawyer. MacNeice turned on the recorder and announced the beginning of the second interview.

"Counsel, please state your name."

"James Dempsey."

"Mr. Zetter," MacNeice said, "you've had time to reconsider your statement. Have you anything else to add?"

Zetter looked at his lawyer, who spoke for him. "Mr. Zetter will not be saying anything further at this time."

"In that case, I am charging you with counselling murder in the deaths of Anniken Kallevik and Duguald Langan. Further charges may be laid, pending the forensics reports on your vehicle, yacht, home and office."

MacNeice stood up with some difficulty. Turning to the lawyer, he said, "You'll inform Mr. Zetter as to what happens now. A constable will be in shortly to take him to a holding cell."

BACK AT THE stone cottage, MacNeice wasn't sure which he wanted more: some of Marcello's lasagna or simply to lie down. Even though it was late, he settled on the lasagna and put it in the oven.

The phone rang but he didn't even consider answering it. He was fed up with talk, fed up with listening—even to himself. A half-minute later, his cellphone rang. He looked at his watch, 9:52 p.m., and looked down: *unknown number*. He let it ring until it stopped.

When his cell rang again, he picked it up. "MacNeice."

"It's Sam."

He sat back in the club chair and took a deep breath. "How are you?"

"I'm fine, but that's not why I'm calling."

"I'm listening."

"I wanted to tell you myself that tomorrow the *Globe and Mail* is publishing my story about what happened that night."

"Okay..."

"I don't need your permission, Mac, though I would like it. I'm a journalist, though, and you turned my home into a war zone. Quite apart from my feelings for you, I felt the need, the responsibility, to tell the story."

"So what are your feelings for me?"

"Don't, Mac. Honestly, I can't..."

"Can't what? Forgive me or risk having a relationship with me?"

There was a long pause before she answered, "Both."

He could smell the lasagna and went into the kitchen, the phone to his ear. Before he was able to come up with a response, she said, "I'm sorry. I wanted to give you a heads-up about the article—I hope you understand."

"Do I understand?" He pulled the foil off the meal.

"Mac, I don't want this to be hurtful or spiteful. I'm just trying to..."

"Sam, thank you for calling." He wasn't sure whether she said goodbye because the phone was already on the counter, its screen glowing before slowly dimming to black.

TWICE HE DIALED Aziz's number and hung up before the call went through. At least that was what he thought.

When his phone rang at 11:30 and he saw her name, his heart jumped into his throat. He was terrified what he might say, or ask. "MacNeice."

"You called me twice. Are you all right, Mac?"

"Ah, no, yes, sure — no, I'm fine. Must have been pocket dialing."

"Right." Her voice sounded sleepy but unconvinced.

"Did I wake you?"

"No, I was reading."

"What are you reading?"

She laughed. "Mac, what's going on?"

"I remember, years and years ago, Kate took me to the museum in Toronto, where her quartet was playing." He stood up and looked out the window into the darkness. "While they were practising, I wandered about and ended up in the textile gallery. I didn't care about textiles, I was just wandering..."

"Mac?"

"I saw this quilt... Actually no, I didn't care about the quilt until I read its caption. It was titled, *Keep Me Warm One Night*."

Silence. He could hear her getting out of bed or off the sofa.

"So Samantha called," she said.

"Yes. She's written an article about what happened. It'll be in the *Globe and Mail* tomorrow . . . She just wanted me to know."

"I'm sorry."

"Don't be. I'm the one who should apologize to Sam for unwittingly bringing her into this . . . world. But I also owe you an apology and I know, I've said that before." He heard her sharp intake of breath. "I don't want to open this up," he said. "I just wanted to say that I'm sorry for everything. That's it . . . and now I feel awkward."

"I accept." She laughed briefly, and clearly with some effort, but it took the tension out of the air. "Have you been drinking grappa?"

"No, not tonight."

WHEN MORNING CAME, he remembered the call but not what he said. For the first time since the fire, MacNeice climbed onto the workout bike and peddled for his life, hoping it would bring colour back to his face and that he could do twenty minutes before falling into a coughing spell or a splitting headache. He managed it. As poor as he felt, his body responded as if he'd actually had a great night's sleep.

AZIZ LOOKED UP from the espresso machine. "I can see you're feeling better."

"I am. After we talked, I fell asleep. Fiza, I apologize that it was so late —"

"Stop it. You're allowed to be shaky — you've had a serious head injury." She smiled at him, took her coffee cup and went back to the cubicle.

He looked at his watch—8:42 a.m. His legs were tingling from the exercise, but otherwise he felt stronger than he had since before the fire. He made himself a coffee.

"You good?" Swetsky said when he saw MacNeice leaning against the wall of his cubicle. "What a pair we make, eh?"

"I'm fine, John," MacNeice said.

Swetsky looked at him skeptically.

"Okay, I'd be lying if I said I didn't want Bishop, but he's gone and it's over. There are accessory charges to deal with, but now I can focus on the Nicholson case."

Swetsky shoved a chair toward MacNeice. "Vice-principal Brion, lovely lady, came to practice yesterday and asked me—on behalf of the coach, apparently—if I'd accept an official role as assistant coach. That's protocol, apparently—Knox couldn't ask me directly. Anyway, I said sure. Fact is, I'm having a blast."

He could see that MacNeice was waiting, so he went on. "I've cranked Knox up on purpose. Any of the guys I play with wouldda popped me by now for my attitude. But this guy's strange. He goes almost purple, leaves the court and heads into his office. Then he comes back five minutes later as if nothing happened. I actually think Knox is a great coach. All I'm criticizing him about are tactical differences. The thing is, he's good precisely because he's extremely controlled. Those kids know the fundamentals better than any teenagers I've seen. They're actually pretty to watch. But, put a scrambling gutsy team from the projects on the court with them, one that claws their way to the net, and they'd have their hands full."

Seeing he had MacNeice's full attention, Swetsky went on. "Dylan and Tom are the only ones with any creativity. Whether they make the play or not, if it looks like they're playing like street kids, Knox will holler something about hot-dogging or showboating, telling them to stick to the basics. I think spontaneity pisses this guy off; it's not his thing. Control is." Swetsky put his hand up. "Does that ring a bell for you?"

"David Nicholson," MacNeice said. "Dylan must take after his mother, given the men he's been surrounded by. Take the job, John. You love basketball, and we have a long game to play here." He slapped Swetsky on the shoulder and took his cup back to the servery.

AZIZ WAS BUSY finishing a report on the interview with Lyttelton when Vertesi let out a whistle. "What is it, Michael?"

"Good news," Vertesi answered, then said, "Boss, take a look at this." He held up the front page of *The Standard*. Below the fold there was a sidebar with a photograph of Markus Christophe. The headline read: "Anniken Kallevik Travelling Companion Married in Oslo." Vertesi read the item out loud.

> *Markus Christophe was married yesterday in a small civil ceremony that was attended by the sisters of Anniken Kallevik — close friends of the bride. Kallevik, 27, a graduate student from Hamar, Norway, was travelling the world with Christophe and had stayed on in Dundurn, Ontario, to work at the Royal Dundurn Yacht Club. She was strangled and her body disposed of in Cootes Paradise, where it was discovered in early March of this year. A member of the wedding party was quoted as saying, "The Kallevik family is, of course, very much in our hearts." The wedding took place shortly after the interment of Kallevik's*

remains. The consul-general of Canada to Norway was
present at the burial on a cold, windswept hillside in
Hamar, but declined to make a statement.

MacNeice swung around to the whiteboard to stare at the photo of Markus next to Anniken. Off to the right, someone had taped the official portrait of Major Buchanan. Behind MacNeice, his phone rang. Glancing around, Vertesi saw that he wasn't going to answer, and picked it up. "Yes, sir," he said. "One moment, I'll see if he's in." Swinging about on his chair, he said, "Boss, it's Wallace. Are you in?"

He nodded and sat down heavily. "MacNeice."

"You're the toast of Toronto, MacNeice," Wallace said. "Did you know about this *Globe* article?"

"Yes, sir, I heard about it last night."

"I'm going to put you on speaker so you can listen to the message Mayor Maybank left for me."

There was the sound of clicking, then a pause...

Wallace...you know how I feel about Mac, so I don't
have to sugar-coat what I'm about to say. This is one
of the first times in my memory that news from the fair
fucking city of Dundurn has ever graced the front page of
the fucking Globe and Mail. While I'm happy Mac got
laid—he deserves to get laid—he didn't need to fuck a
reporter, much less one with this kind of influence. Look,
I'm happy he survived the fire okay, but to be honest,
seeing this article, I cannot say the same for this, this...
[the sound of shuffling newspaper] Samantha Stewart—
Christ, even her name sounds like an alias to me. He got
screwed, but he didn't have to screw all of us. You know
how difficult it is to convince people, corporations, to

*move to Dundurn? We're still the rectum of the universe
for a lot of folks. And now? Now we'll be known for rabid
Scots running around snapping the necks of our citizens,
and head-butting and almost torching our top cop. I am
not happy.*

Wallace picked up again. "I don't need to add anything to that, I think. But, should your old pal Mayor Bob call, tell him I dressed you down for your poor choice in women."

When he put the phone down, everyone but Aziz was watching him.

"You all right, boss? Was that the mayor having a shit-fit?" Williams asked.

"It was..." His chest tightened and he worked hard to relax his breathing before the rattle rising in his chest took over.

Aziz swung around to face him. "We all read the piece, Mac. You're presented as courageous—even fearless—and Bishop just sounds bizarre. Sam says he was a gentleman to cover her up with a blanket and to not touch her. Nonetheless, he left you both for dead." Aziz was going to stop there, then added, "Samantha wrote that she was terrified that you had died in that chair—that's the reason she gives for ending the relationship."

MacNeice nodded several times, and then he looked toward her. "He didn't leave us to die." He got up to tap the image of Bishop on the whiteboard. "I think he knew how long it would take for the firefighters to get there. While he hadn't anticipated I'd knock over my chair—and maybe he should have—I don't think he wanted us dead. He could easily have killed us both and disappeared. No one would have known. No, he wanted us to know what he'd done. I just don't know why."

Aziz said, "Maybe he was tired of it . . . of that life. Maybe he wanted the truth to be told—and not just the valour and heroics. Lyttelton would have turned him into a poster boy for recruitment.

MacNeice stared at the whiteboard. Turning to Williams and Vertesi, he said, "Okay, let's get going. Arrest William Byrne and Melody Chapman for perjury and as accessories in the murders of Anniken Kallevik and Duguald Langan. When you've got them in lock-up, arrest . . . " he flipped through pages of his notes, "Larry Cornelli and Jimmy Albert, the heavies that worked with Bishop in Paul Zetter's operation. Talk to Vice about potential bookmaking charges, but I want them in a lineup on a potential charge of assault and battery on Freddy Dewar. Freddy can take a good long look at them."

"I love it. A roundup, just like the old days." Williams grabbed his notebook and cellphone.

Vertesi stood up and nodded at MacNeice, then followed Williams out the door.

MacNeice picked up his coat and turned to Ryan. "Find the connection between Robert Grant, Jennifer's brother, and Alexander Knox. There is one. I don't know what it is, but I'm confident you'll find it."

Ryan cracked the knuckles of both hands. "I'll call you as soon as I've found something."

"And find as many photographs of Dylan Nicholson as you can—close-ups, head and shoulders."

MacNeice turned to Aziz. "Let's head out to Dundas and do some vegetable shopping."

[38]

JUDGING BY THE EXTERIOR, GRANT GREENGROCERS WAS THRIVING. Smartly dressed middle-aged women vied for positions in front of impeccably arranged vegetables and fruit under the broad dark-green awnings. A young man was offering tastings of locally produced chutney and savoury sauces on toast. The shop's logo, an oval festooned with vines, was displayed proudly on his apron.

"Tell us, Daniel," MacNeice looked up from the name tag on the apron's pocket, "where we will find Robert Grant?"

"Upstairs in his office. I'll take you. Excuse me, ladies," he said. "I'll be right back."

Leading them up the stairs at the back of the store, he added, "It was originally a dentist's office."

Robert Grant looked up from his desk. "In those days, at least in Dundas," he said, "it paid to be versatile. Downstairs he was the chemist, up here, the dentist." He stood to greet them, recognizing MacNeice but appearing uncertain why.

"I'm Robert Grant." He offered a hand, first to Aziz.

"I'm Detective Inspector Aziz and this is Detective Superintendent MacNeice of Dundurn Homicide."

Grant thanked Daniel and hastily ushered him from the office, closing the door behind him. Unsure of what to do next, he asked if they'd like tea or coffee. Before they could answer, he invited them to take a seat in front of the desk.

"Uh, we have a promotion on chai teas...organic."

"That won't be necessary, Mr. Grant." MacNeice sat down in the barrel-backed captain's chair.

"Please call me Robert." He chuckled awkwardly, moving the order forms on his desk to the side.

"I saw you at your sister's interment," MacNeice said.

Grant squinted as if he was trying to remember and then said, "Sure, right, you were with Dylan. I noticed you didn't look well."

"I'm fine now," MacNeice said. "You were interviewed by two of my detectives, but I wanted to talk to you myself."

"Certainly, whatever I can do."

"Tell us about your sister's disappearance and the reactions you had to it at the time."

Grant furrowed his brow. "I already told those detectives this story...and I'm not sure what else I can add."

MacNeice made no attempt to hide the fact that he was studying Grant, and the man moved the order forms back to the centre of the desk, crossed and uncrossed his hands, all the while smiling nervously. To his credit, he had the presence of mind to wait MacNeice out.

"How well do you know Alexander Knox?" MacNeice asked at last.

"I'm sorry . . . I'm not sure I do. Knox?"

"Take some time to consider your answer." MacNeice smiled, hoping it would either relax the man or make him realize he was on the threshold of a serious mistake.

The cellphone in MacNeice's pocket buzzed, and he excused himself and left the room. In the hallway, overlooking the ancient pine stairs with its descending wall of framed black and white photographs—the corner shop through history—he answered Ryan's call.

"Sir, Al Knox and Robbie Grant played together on Dundas High's Raiders basketball team for three years. Under Robert's photo in the yearbook, underneath his '#1 Goal for My Senior Year,' it says, 'Keep Knox away from my sister.' Also, I've got three great shots of Dylan, two from his yearbook, one from *The Standard's* coverage of last year's high school championship game."

MacNeice thanked him and put the phone away. Back in Grant's office, he asked, "Again, any recollection of Alexander Knox?"

"As I said —"

"You played on the same team together for three years, Dundas High School's Raiders. I believe he had a crush on your sister?"

Grant suddenly looked flattened, but MacNeice carried on. "Knox was at the funeral, and I saw you acknowledge him. Shall we start over?"

"I haven't seen him much since we graduated."

"Are you certain that's true or do you want to think about that as well?"

Grant's back straightened and his face flushed red. "I told your two officers everything I know—what else do you want from me?" He abruptly stood up and walked over to the window. Neither detective moved.

"Not everything," MacNeice said. "You didn't mention Knox, his relationship with you or your sister."

"Did you blame David Nicholson for your sister's disappearance," Aziz added.

"I did."

"Why did you change your mind?"

"I didn't." He glanced over to the fireplace mantel, where a Kodachrome of a teenaged Jennifer looked back from a silver frame. She was wearing a turquoise bikini and smiling broadly with her hands on her hips—by the looks of it, down at Burlington Beach.

"Did you know David Nicholson before your sister met him?"

Grant sat down again. "No, none of us knew him. They met at college. My parents said he was just what Jenn needed."

"Did Knox know him in college too?"

"I don't think so. They were all in the same place, getting degrees that would lead to teaching, but Nicholson was into things like the chess and debating clubs. Al was into playing ball."

"How serious was the crush Knox had on your sister, the one you referred to in your yearbook?"

"It was kid stuff. You know, he'd be at our place for a soda, and Sis was there. They'd flirt a bit."

"Was he known as Sandy or Al in high school?"

"Both. At the time he probably thought 'Al' was more macho for an athlete. But his parents called him Sandy and eventually everybody did. Jenn never called him Al. He was always Sandy to her."

"Were you aware that Nicholson beat Jennifer before she left for California?" MacNeice asked.

"I was, but I thought it was just a smack—her wild side bumping up against his steady-Freddy."

"It was something more than a smack, Mr. Grant. It was sufficient enough for her to leave her son."

"But I didn't know that." He shook his head as if to erase the comment. "It was the hardest thing to accept when she left, because she loved Dylan. Up to that point, Nicholson always seemed a bit distant from the child, but Sis was mad about him, always teaching him and protecting him. She was crazy about Dylan."

Aziz couldn't suppress a comment. "So, even though you referred to her as 'wild,' the probability of her deserting him seemed far-fetched to you."

"For sure. No way she'd leave that kid, unless..." He looked over at the photo of his sister. "... unless she was on drugs or alcohol. She called—this was a week or so after she got to California. She wanted me to check on Dylan, to make sure he was eating properly, wearing clean clothes. She told me to take him a book, tell him that his mom loved him, that she'd be home soon, that kind of thing. The day I went there, David had actually made cookies."

MacNeice had been looking at the photo of Jennifer in the bikini, and turned back to Grant. "You were in the Royal Dundurn Light Infantry Reserve for three years. Can you tell us about it?"

Grant appeared confused by the question. "I don't see what that has to do with Jenn, but I was a student and it was a summer job. I joined because I didn't want to work here. I wasn't sure that I wanted this life," He smiled, "You know, the one I'm living now."

Aziz said, "For a year you did a lot to try and find your sister, but then you gave up. Why?"

"After a while it seemed clear Jenn wasn't coming home because she didn't want to. She wasn't being found because she didn't want to be."

"In the reserve, were you taught how to use a grenade?" MacNeice was looking directly at him. "I'm certain I wouldn't forget being a teenager and throwing a grenade, but if you can't remember, we can find out through DND."

"Yes, we were taught how to use grenades. But I really don't know what you're driving at here. You think I killed Nicholson? My sister's dead, at the hands of her husband and we—all of us who'd judged her poorly—have to live with that. What could my high school reserve service have to do with this?"

"Maybe nothing," MacNeice said, and stood up to terminate the meeting. "Thank you for your time."

ONCE IN THE Chevy, MacNeice looked back at the thriving grocery business. "Can you hear it or feel it? The fizz beginning on that second floor."

"Is that why you ended the interview?"

"Yes."

"So you think he and Knox conspired to murder David Nicholson.

"I think he was involved."

"Then why stop the interview? Why not press him harder?"

"Because Grant is on the phone to Knox right now."

The difficulty was that, as far as the police knew, neither man had knowledge at the time that Jennifer had been harmed by David Nicholson other than what Grant referred to as the "smack" that sent her off to California. Both men would have been all too happy to report him to the police had they known about the basement on Ryder Road.

"So why would they go to such extremes so many years later?" MacNeice asked.

Aziz said, "Who knows. Are we off to Mercy for an interview with Knox?"

MacNeice executed a slow U-turn back toward the city. "Not exactly."

"Was this visit a shot in the dark?"

"Partly... but more about the fizz." Just as he was about to add that it was a good day for a drive because it wasn't raining, the rain began again, softly at first, but within seconds, it turned into a deluge.

MACNEICE PASSED MAIN and Aberdeen, dropping down the hill and past the entrance to the division parking lot. Aziz didn't bother to ask him where he was going, because she knew well before he turned up the street toward Our Lady of Mercy High School. Shutting down the engine, he looked out beyond the chain link fence to the building but said nothing. The sound of rain filled the space between them.

Moments passed before he said, "Look over there, second set of windows to the right of the exit doors... that's Knox's office."

Aziz glanced toward the school. MacNeice watched it as if he was waiting for something dramatic to happen.

"Do we go speak to him?"

"Knox is all about controlling outcomes. Swetsky hasn't been able to push him over the line, so it's doubtful that I could... So, we wait."

Grant was probably on the phone to Knox, who was reassuring him that this was just a fishing trip and the cops had no evidence—otherwise, they would have arrested him. "He's watching us from that office," MacNeice said.

"You can see him?" She swung her head to look at the building.

"No, but I can feel him. More precisely, if I were him, I'd be looking out that window."

From all she'd heard about Knox and learned about basketball, Aziz was prepared to make a few wild guesses of her own. "A basketball coach trains young men to fight for ball control and to score more points than their competitors. If you're right, Mac, his identity may be entirely dependent on his ability to determine outcomes. If he's smart, he's already worked out the 'what happens if' scenarios."

"So you're saying he's one step ahead of us?"

"Basically. If he has done this, Knox would have his escape planned just like a marmot creates multiple exits through an underground tunnel system. In his case, escape might include using the second grenade on himself."

"Because prison means he loses his authority."

"Precisely. He's likely to be most dangerous when this loss of control is imminent."

They sat for a few minutes in silence before MacNeice eased the Chevy up the side street and past Mercy's entrance, turning left on King, toward Division uptown.

VERTESI AND WILLIAMS hadn't returned, though Ryan said there were three people already in the holding cells and the duty sergeant had said legal aid was on the way for two of them—the heavies—and a James Street lawyer had already arrived for Melody Chapman. "They haven't found Byrne yet."

"Any other news?" Aziz asked.

"Well, the chief meteorologist has warned that this record rainfall will continue till the end of March... and that local communities have the responsibility to manage local reservoir capacity."

Aziz managed to grin for him.

MacNeice returned just then with espresso for himself and Aziz. He was studying the whiteboard as Ryan continued. "And this came in from the Al Jazeera online newsfeed:

> Late yesterday, Nigerian national forces retook Sunke, the center nearest OR-Afrique's mining interests. It had been under control of the province's Islamic insurgents, Boko Haram. The mutilated bodies of members of an independent security team were retrieved from a ditch and flown to Niger, where they will be repatriated to their country of origin, at the expense of their employer. Arrangements are underway in Glasgow for the return of one, a local hero, Major Robert Buchanan. The highly decorated former member of the elite SAS brigade led the security force and died while trying to save his comrades...

Realizing the cubicle had gone silent, Ryan shut up.

Aziz turned to MacNeice, who was taking the images of Anniken, Duguald, Markus, Sherry, and Buchanan off the whiteboard. He placed each one on the filing cabinet, resting his palm on the images for a moment as if they might otherwise fly away. Lyttelton, he was certain, was doing damage control on Frankenstein's image, eclipsing the random acts of savagery with those that produce medals for bravery.

MacNeice sat at his desk and studied the Nicholson case images. He finished his coffee, put the cup down and opened his notebook. Flipping through the pages, he stopped when he found a telephone number.

He placed the call and the phone rang several times. MacNeice glanced at the time, 1:25 p.m., and noted it on the page. He was about to hang up when a woman answered.

"It's Detective MacNeice calling. Is Dylan there, please?"

"Well, he's just on his way out for a slice of pizza with Tom, but I'll see if I can catch him for you." She sounded engaged and bright. MacNeice wondered what it was like for Dylan to be in a house with someone who was actually maternal.

"Hey, sir . . . What's up?"

Knowing that Dylan's lunch hour was fleeting, MacNeice cut to the point. "Can you recall how long you've known Coach Knox?"

"Since I came to Mercy. Why?"

"I'm just tying loose ends together. Did your dad ever mention the coach prior to your going to Mercy?"

"No, I don't think so . . ."

"How would you describe their relationship before your dad became an assistant coach?"

"To be honest, my dad wasn't much of a coach. He didn't know anything about the game when he began, and some of the guys made fun of that."

"Have you ever asked Coach Knox about why he agreed to let your dad help?"

"No . . ."

"Sorry to bother you, Dylan. I'll let you get to your pizza. Say hello to Tom for me."

"Yessir, I will."

MacNeice swung away from the desk to see Aziz looking his way. "I know... I'm walking a fine line."

"Yes, you are. Do you think he'll mention your interest to Knox?"

"I hope so."

MacNeice studied the photographs some more. Maybe Knox had recognized Dylan's potential and wanted to nurture him, even if that meant accepting his father as an assistant coach in a sport he knew nothing about. But that wasn't something a dominant person focused on perfection would normally do.

Perhaps Nicholson brought something extra, a special skill that would contribute to the Panthers' success — but that seemed highly unlikely. So maybe Knox owed Nicholson, or Nicholson knew something about Knox that became leverage for whatever he wanted.

Ryan swivelled around in his chair. "Sir, those photos of Dylan are in the folder on your desk."

He opened the file. Of the yearbook photos, one was blurred, showing Dylan with Tom outside the gym; the other was his Most Outstanding Player portrait. Tousled hair spilled over his forehead and, though he was working hard to look serious, his smile gave the impression that he'd been holding his breath. In *The Standard* photograph, he was sweating, his shoulders glistening, hair stuck to his forehead. It was from an interview following the Panthers' city championship victory. He seemed deliriously happy.

MacNeice realized then that Nicholson's coaching wasn't about basketball — it was a struggle between two men for the control of a teenager.

[39]

"**R**YAN, FIND ZENO TRAKAS FOR ME.**"

"Yessir," Ryan said, and turned to his computer, his fingers hammering in the speedy rhythms MacNeice found musical.

MacNeice took the staff photo of Knox and moved it next to David Nicholson's face on the whiteboard. According to Nicholson's diary of his wife's imprisonment, it appeared "S" had had an affair with Jennifer. Had that knowledge been enough to blackmail Knox for a job as assistant coach? On the other hand, was the fact that Nicholson knew about the affair enough for Knox to want to blow Nicholson up?

He tapped the photos several times and started over: S has an affair with Jennifer and Nicholson finds out. Nicholson wants more than revenge; he wants pain and suffering— "Well that fits," Jennifer would say if she could. But how do you inflict pain on a man who's bigger, fitter and very physical? Psychological pain wasn't good enough.

Jennifer Grant didn't stand a chance—a free spirit stuck between two control freaks. Knox is a natural head-game player.

Perhaps Nicholson wouldn't have known that off the top, but he'd have found out fast. Whatever he had on Knox had to be head-game proof. MacNeice took the red marker and dropped an arrow below Knox's portrait. Below it, he wrote, "Sex, drugs, and rock 'n' roll," without knowing why.

"Boss, Trakas on three."

MacNeice went back to his desk, noticed Aziz watching him, and said, "Fasten your seat belt."

Trakas was somewhere in traffic. "This better be good. I don't take fucking phone calls from you, understood?"

"Very clear. You're not going to like my request, so I'll make it clear for you: I am the Detective Superintendent of Homicide, Detective Trakas, and I want to speak to Luther Tirelle. Understood?"

He could hear cars streaming by and the Doppler effect of a semi's horn arcing and fading. Trakas was standing on the side of a highway. "Non-negotiable even if you were Wallace."

"We may get to Wallace, but I'd like to avoid that for your sake. He is in a cutback frame of mind and we've had two retirements in Records, which he wants to fill with one man."

He let that hang in the air for a moment. "I don't need to know what line Tirelle is on or where in the world he picks up the phone. But I need five minutes of his time, and I need it now."

"I'll call you back." The line went dead.

MacNeice put the phone down.

"Sorry for the language, sir, but that was frickin' A cool," Ryan said.

"Byrne's in a holding cell," Williams announced as he rounded the corner of the cubicle. Vertesi was behind him; both men were carrying legal boxes, which they deposited on their desks. "What was frickin' A cool?"

The phone rang again; Ryan picked it up, turned and nodded to MacNeice, and put the phone on speaker.

Trakas said, "MacNeice, you are going to pretend you don't know anything about the guy you're going to speak to, just that you know he knows where the grenades went and why. What else do you need from him?"

"I want to know what his buyer—I believe his name is Knox—was into that was serious enough to want to blow someone up."

"Okay, you're someone I owe who knows...Who's Knox?"

"Tirelle's basketball coach."

"Jesus. Okay, so you want to know who had what on him that he needed to buy a couple of grenades—that about it, detective superintendent?"

"That captures it."

Trakas took MacNeice's cellphone number, confirming first that it didn't have a message on it. "As far as Tirelle is concerned, you don't have a name, so don't use one. Stay by the phone—understood?"

"Understood."

Vertesi looked about after Ryan hung up. "What's going on?"

Aziz tried to explain the call, the trip to Dundas, sitting outside the school and staring up at Knox's office, and finally the conversation with Dylan. "Shakespeare, fair and foul, chaos, harmony, discord, climax—now you understand as much as I do."

"Wanna hear what we did today, Mommy?" Williams lifted the top off the banker's box.

MacNeice's cellphone rang, and everyone shut up. "Hello," MacNeice said.

The combined three-cell conference call came with an echo, as a male voice asked in a thick Jamaican accent, "Oom I speakin' wit, mon?"

MacNeice didn't answer.

Trakas's voice: "No names, we agreed."

The Jamaican made a hissing sound, sucking air through his teeth. "Then wot you want?"

"Two grenades came to Dundurn," Trakas said. "A guy used one on another guy. Do you know why the bomber decided to scatter him?"

MacNeice could hear the sound of several voices over the line and wasn't sure whose phone they were coming from. He assumed Tirelle's. A dog barked.

"Mon, 'e say...Knox, thas 'is name, was a client...and 'is sport coach...Huh?" The man paused as he got some clarification from a voice in the background. " 'is basketball coach."

More talk in the background, another dog barking somewhere, and the sound of Trakas coughing. MacNeice waited.

"Mon caught Mr. T in a toilet wit Coach Knox an' 'e treaten 'im wit it."

"What are you saying, exactly?" Trakas asked.

More voices, this time laughing or hooting. When the voice came back on the phone, it was all the speaker could do to control his laughter.

"Other mon — Nicholson — 'e say 'e caught the coach 'aving sex wit' Mr. T, but..." He started laughing again, as did everyone in the background. "It was ganja, mon, not sex 'e was afta...'i-grade semi sensi..." The speaker was listening again. "Weed...big quality too, 'e say." He added matter-of-factly, "Dis nex one be the las' question, 'cause 'e don' like ... Whass?" Everyone started laughing again. " 'E don' like dis pop quiz." More laughter.

When it subsided, MacNeice asked, "How long had he been supplying Knox with weed, and did he ever ask for anything heavier?"

There was a long pause, and then a new voice came on, with a Canadian accent. "That's two questions." Behind him someone applauded. "But all right. First things first. Knox and I, we thought Nicholson was a joke, him assuming I was giving head when I was dealing some serious shit to my best customer. Straight through high school, it was ganja and hash. Second question: he didn't go harder, not because he wouldn't have—that dude's wound pretty tight—but I wouldn't sell him any. For my own sake and his, I kept him functional. Okay, this conversation's over." The line went dead.

A moment later, Trakas called back. "That better be it, pal, because that right there is some scary fuckin' shit. From now on, you don't know me. Oh, and start dicking around targeting me for cutbacks, and I'll jump ship to work for the other side, where they know the meaning of loyalty. So chew on that, DS MacNeice." He hung up.

Williams waited a moment before speaking, waving a hand over his head to dispatch imaginary cologne. "We've hauled all the cattle into the barn, boss. What's next?"

"Bring Robert Grant in for an interview," MacNeice said, and he went over to the whiteboard. He took down the staff photos of Jennifer Grant, David Nicholson, and Alexander Knox and carried them back to his desk. He put Dylan's basketball photos in a row above the others, retrieved a magnifying glass from the drawer, and started scanning the faces.

Aziz was writing up their first interview with Robert Grant. Several minutes passed before curiosity got the better of her and she stopped to watch MacNeice, head close to the desk as he studied each photo, humming something to himself. She thought she would wait for him to surface before asking what he was doing, but she couldn't.

"What's that?"

Without looking up, he said, " 'My Funny Valentine.' "

Aziz crossed her eyes at him, but he was so engrossed, he didn't notice. She decided to wait him out.

Next, MacNeice took a pair of scissors to a sheet of department stationery and cut it into two-inch strips. He laid a couple of the strips over Dylan's *Standard* interview photo, isolating the eyes and another couple over someone else's face—she couldn't see whose—also isolating their eyes. Carefully, he lifted that photo with the strips in place and put it directly below Dylan's. He sat up, stopped humming and looked again at the images through the magnifying glass. Then he turned and smiled at Aziz.

"What have you found?" She slid her chair next to his.

He handed her the magnifying glass. "See for yourself."

"The soft curves of Dylan's face, his nose, cheekbones and hair all come from his mother. But his eyes are interesting," she said.

"You wouldn't notice it if he wasn't smiling or if his hair was in the way, yet his eyes are neither his mother's nor Nicholson's."

Aziz took the strips of paper off the second photo, revealing Alexander Knox. "My God." She put a hand to her mouth.

Then she studied all the photos for evidence that might prove him wrong, but she couldn't find any. Jennifer's eyes were wide and the orbital bones around them were shallow, making her face appear open and sunny. David Nicholson's orbitals were more rectangular, which made his eyes also seem somewhat rectangular, or at least less teardrop-shaped. Knox's smile in his staff photo lifted his cheeks, emphasizing his hooded eyes. There was no mistaking the similarity between Dylan's eyes and Knox's when both were smiling.

MacNeice constructed another theory: S has an affair with Jennifer just before or after her marriage to Nicholson. Does Nicholson discover it when Jennifer announces she's pregnant, or is he convinced the child is his? Does Jennifer tell S she's pregnant by him? It would be years before Nicholson caught Knox in the toilet with Luther Tirelle; if Nicholson knew that Dylan wasn't his son, he'd have caught Knox in a perfect trifecta of shame — drugs, sex with a student, and impregnating a colleague's wife. Knox would be powerless. What would a man driven by a need to dominate do when he realized he was forced to submit to any request from a man he actively hated?

If he denied having sex in the toilet with Tirelle and told the truth about buying marijuana from him, there'd be no upside — he'd be driven out and ostracized — with people suspecting he was engaged in both. If it came to light that he'd had an affair with Jennifer Grant on or around the eve of her marriage to Nicholson, he'd be considered a scoundrel.

Pure speculation, MacNeice thought, *but pure nonetheless*. Nicholson would have a hold over Knox and his ransom was Dylan. To drive the point home, after Dylan made the team, Nicholson demanded to be an assistant coach, knowing that his lack of knowledge or interest in the game would show his contempt for Knox, and also how close he'd stick to his son — even if Dylan wasn't actually his. Aziz put the magnifying glass down. "Do we order a DNA test?"

"Not yet . . . It's just a theory," MacNeice said.

WILLIAMS AND AZIZ conducted the session with Robert Grant, asking many of the same questions that she and MacNeice had asked him before. No longer the gentleman grocer, Grant was angry about being hauled into the station and he showed it.

"Tell us, Mr. Grant, about your days playing basketball with Al Knox," Aziz said.

"I don't know what to tell you. I mean, we get together for Glory Days, an annual reunion of the team."

"That's progress," Aziz said. "We've gone from you not knowing Alexander Knox to your knowing him in high school but not seeing him since to now annual get-togethers." She looked up at him. "Is it becoming clear to you why you're here?"

Grant shook his head. "No. Nor do I understand why you're so interested in Knox."

"Why do you think David Nicholson was asked to be assistant coach when it appears he knew nothing about basketball?" Williams asked.

"Was he asked?"

"Good question... Was he?"

"I don't think so. Given how seriously Al takes the game, I doubt it."

Aziz cut in. "Did Knox ever discuss his affair with Jennifer just before she married David Nicholson?"

Grant shot out of his seat. Williams told him to sit down and answer the question. He did sit, showing his discomfort by folding and unfolding his arms. At last he said, "I don't know anything about that... It was none of my business what Al or Jenn did."

"Well, he was your friend and teammate and she was your sister—I think that makes it your business," Aziz said.

"Look, you do remember that I, we, her remaining family, are victims of David Nicholson?"

"So tell me why a man like Knox would tolerate an assistant coach like Nicholson. Any thoughts on that, Mr. Grant?"

"I want to call my lawyer."

"Actually, we're done with you," Aziz said. "I think we've got what we need."

"MICHAEL, MONTILE, FOLLOW Grant," MacNeice said when Aziz and Williams returned to the cubicle. See where he goes. If he heads to Mercy or over to Knox's place, stay well back, but when he leaves, let him know you're there—be subtle but obvious."

[40]

GRANT TRAVELLED EAST IN HIS VAN, CATCHING THE LIGHTS ON MAIN. At Sherman, he suddenly peeled across three lanes to head north, doubling back on King all the way to Dundas, where he parked in the grocery shop's lot. He got out of his van and checked to make sure the store had been locked up, before he walked up the street to his home. It was 7:14 p.m.

Vertesi called MacNeice. "Either he made us right away, or he called from the van and found out Knox wasn't home. Do you want us to stay near and see if he has any visitors or decides to head out again?"

"Yes, but out of sight. This is a bit of a slow cooker, but it is cooking."

When he hung up, MacNeice ordered an unmarked car to sit overnight outside Knox's bungalow in the east end, with instructions that he be called if Knox left, and then requested a search warrant for Knox's office and house. Saying good night to Aziz, he left to head home, taking the stairs two at a time, a first since the fire.

HE DIDN'T KNOW how long the phone had been ringing, but when he swung his arm over to answer it, he was certain he'd just fallen asleep. He put the phone to his ear.

"Mac?" It was Aziz.

He sat up in bed and saw the time. It was 7:39 a.m. He'd slept through the night. "Yes."

"I'm in a cab coming to you. Grant's on the move. He came out of his house twenty-five minutes ago, and looked around before walking quickly to the store, where he got into the van. He's heading toward Dundurn, and Williams and Vertesi say he hasn't spotted them trailing him."

"I'll be ready," MacNeice said. He threw some water on his face and quickly got dressed, and then the phone rang again. It was Vertesi.

"You were right about Grant, Mac. He's just pulled up in front of Mercy and went in through the gym doors at the back. We've got a sightline to the van, the front door, and the side of the building. What's the plan?"

MacNeice could hear Aziz's cab labouring up the hill. He didn't believe Knox would have the second grenade at the school, but he didn't want to find out with another explosion.

"Stay put and out of sight. If Grant bolts, stick with him. Aziz and I are on our way." Twelve minutes later, MacNeice pulled up behind Vertesi and Williams's car on a side street near the school, and they all settled in to keep watch. By 8:45, most of the students were inside, and the stragglers were either jogging to the front doors, or standing about on the sidewalk, smoking cigarettes, presumably waiting to hear the bell.

At 8:47, Grant came out of the gym and ran for his van. He tore off, scaring a teenager out of his way by blasting on the horn.

Vertesi nodded MacNeice's way and powered the Chevy around the corner in pursuit.

"Let's go see what Grant stirred up," MacNeice said. He and Aziz climbed out of the Chevy and walked toward Mercy's front entrance.

DYLAN THOUGHT HE was in trouble when Coach Knox came out of the office and came toward him with his head down. Dylan had been shooting hoops in his first period spare, and the only broken rule that came to mind was that he was wearing a hoodie in the gym.

"Do you trust me, Dylan?" Knox came close and took the boy by the shoulders.

"Sure."

"What I'm going to ask you to do will seem strange, but I need you to trust me — it's important." He turned and began to lead Dylan to the exit doors. "There's something you need to know — I mean about your parents . . . and me."

"Is this what Detective Superintendent MacNeice asked me about?"

Knox stopped for a moment, but then said, "Possibly, yes." He threw his hip against the crash bar, opening the door. Above them, the Mercy Panthers' championship banners fluttered in the draft.

Outside, a light rain was falling and Dylan pulled the hood over his head. His coach was wearing only sweatpants and a short-sleeved polo with the team's logo on it. Walking the boy around the football field, he said, "I've got something special stored in a secret cupboard in that concrete shaft that leads to the storm sewer. It's the only place I know where it would be safe. City workers haven't been down there for years."

Dylan frowned at him doubtfully, but just then the team's equipment manager passed by; the men nodded to each other. When the equipment manager was out of earshot, Knox said, "Trust me on this, Dylan, it'll be all right—I promise." He dug in his sweatpants pocket and took out a key chain with a number of keys on it. He picked one out and showed it to the boy. "I removed the city lock on the cupboard a while ago and put on a lock of my own."

He half smiled and climbed the six steps to the top of the storm sewer riser, where he lifted the overflow grate and held it up for the boy. Dylan hesitated, but then he climbed in.

"Climb down to the bottom. There's plenty of room to stand up down there. Don't worry, there aren't any rats, and I'll be right behind you."

MACNEICE OPENED MERCY'S massive faux Gothic door for Aziz and stepped inside behind her. They were met by Celestine Brion, who'd spotted the unmarked cars idling on the side street. She wanted to know why they were there and asked how she might help, though actually what she wanted was the drama to stop so her school could return to normal.

"We're here to interview Coach Knox," MacNeice said.

"Well, his first class isn't until...," she looked up at the caged clock on the wall, "9:45. Why don't I bring him here and we'll meet in my office."

"We'd prefer to speak to him alone."

She seemed surprised by that. "I don't understand. Is there a problem I should know about?"

"No, ma'am, there isn't," MacNeice said, and stepped around her, leaving Brion to stare at their backs as they headed down the corridor.

The coach wasn't in his office or the gym. They opened the double doors leading to the football field and looked outside. There was no sign of him, but hurrying toward the building to get out of the rain was a man struggling with two overstuffed ball bags that appeared more awkward than heavy.

"Have you seen Coach Knox?" MacNeice asked as the man drew close.

"He's with Dylan Nicholson. I passed them on the field."

"Where were they headed?" MacNeice asked.

"That was weird. Coach climbed up that concrete pillbox—the sewer thing—and then both of them went down. I didn't even know the school had access to that."

MacNeice turned to Aziz. "Call it in—all services, including the bomb squad."

The teacher, startled, said, "What's going...?"

"I don't know," MacNeice said, "but you'd be wise to go inside and stay there." He gently pushed the teacher in through the double doors.

MacNeice looked toward the parking lot and took out his phone. "Ryan—very quickly now—patch me through to the person responsible for the east-end storm sewers." He started walking toward the graffiti-covered pillbox just beyond the football field, Aziz keeping pace.

"Hold on, sir." Ryan's voice was replaced by intermittent digital burps.

Less than a minute later, someone answered, "East Mountain Reservoir, Duane Simpson. Who's this?"

"Detective Superintendent MacNeice, Dundurn Homicide. What's the flow currently coming through the downtown east-end storm sewers?"

"Surges every half-hour. Why, what's up?"

"Can you stop them?"

"The reservoir up here is a few inches from disaster. Short answer: no way."

"Have you made the public aware of this?"

"Do you tell your neighbours every time you flush the toilet?" Simpson couldn't hide his irritation. "We're doing our job, detective — flushing till it stops raining or we get it stabilized."

"When was the last surge?"

"Exactly thirty-six seconds ago."

"How long will it take to reach Mercy High, near Main?"

"Twelve to fourteen minutes."

"How much water can we expect?"

"Well . . . it's a surge, so it'll fill that sewer and last about ten minutes. What the hell's going on down there?"

"We have two people in that sewer."

"What the — get them the hell out of there! The water'll hit there at thirty, thirty-five miles an hour. It'll be like getting hammered by a train in a tunnel."

"Emergency services are on the way," Aziz said to MacNeice, her ear to her own phone.

MacNeice put his cell in his pocket and looked at his watch. "We've got roughly ten minutes before it floods."

They ran through the rain to the concrete structure. MacNeice wasn't sure what would happen next, but he didn't want to be caught up in his coat and jacket, so he took them off. He could feel his heart pounding. Though his breathing had returned to normal, he still felt like there was a fifty-pound weight on his rib cage.

Glancing back, he saw that Brion and Principal Westbrooke were marching toward them, accompanied by the school's security guard. Students and teachers were peering from classroom windows, and several teens late for class had turned to follow the administrators, willing to risk the consequences rather than miss out on something exciting.

The circular grate was closed. MacNeice lifted the cover onto its back and looked down. He could see Knox and Dylan at the bottom, standing on the sewer's narrow walkway. Knox had glanced up at the sound, and when he spotted MacNeice, he wrapped his arm firmly around the boy's neck. Below them, the water was running at a steady but unthreatening pace.

"Leave us alone, detective," Knox called. "I won't harm him...I just need time to explain." His voice boomed off the circular wall of the shaft.

Dylan looked confused and scared, clutching a piece of paper in his right hand. "He says he's my father," the boy yelled. "He's even got a letter from my mom."

Knox said, "You don't have to read it now, Dylan. I know it by heart: 'Sandy, I don't know what to do. I've missed two periods now. David and I are getting married next Saturday. He doesn't want children right away. Please, please call. Jenn.'" The coach looked up at MacNeice. "I didn't call her back. I've had to live with that."

Knox was gripping something in his right hand like it was a baseball. MacNeice knew what it was.

He looked back at the approaching phalanx of administrators and students—there were now more than a dozen people closing in on them. He grabbed Aziz's arm and pointed her toward them. "Get them back to the school."

He stepped on the ladder and looked down the shaft. "Put the grenade away, coach. I'm coming down."

Dylan tried to pull away, as Knox shouted, "Don't. I swear..."

MacNeice took another step and then another. Beside the first rung on the ladder, MacNeice saw the foam insulated mechanical cabinet where Knox had likely stored the grenade and maybe the letter. He stopped when he heard the unmistakable sound of Knox pulling the pin.

"Coach, this sewer's going to be hit by a storm surge in a few minutes. Put the pin back. Come on, we'll go up together." He started descending again.

"You think talent like Dylan's could come from that man? In the last three years, I've nurtured and been more of a father to him than that twisted freak ever was."

"Put the pin back, coach. You don't want to harm Dylan."

Knox shook his head. For a man fixated on control, he was quickly losing it.

Aziz appeared above them. As MacNeice took another step downward, she climbed over the edge and began to descend.

"I'm warning you both," Knox screamed. "Don't come any farther."

MacNeice took another step. If he squatted, he figured he could just reach the top of Dylan's head, though the boy was held tight in the crook of Knox's arm.

Dylan's panicked eyes sought MacNeice's as Knox looked down. He seemed to be considering whether to step off the walkway and into the water. As MacNeice took another step, he jumped, pulling Dylan with him. The water was almost to their knees.

"Nicholson was a monster—I should receive a medal for what I did," Knox yelled, as Dylan struggled. "I'm sorry, so incredibly sorry for the police officer who died. I thought he'd be unwrapped by thugs in the park...that I'd be doing Dundurn a favour."

Knox's hand was shaking. "Nicholson just clung to Dylan. He was rubbing it in my face."

"He also knew about your relationship with Tirelle."

"Nicholson didn't have a clue. I'd had enough of the mocking and his pathetic need to..."

Dylan lunged for the ladder, but Knox yanked him back. MacNeice considered reaching for his side arm but it was on his right hip. By the time he had it aimed, the coach would release the lever on the grenade. He looked up at Aziz. She was almost even with MacNeice on the ladder on the other side of the tunnel access, and directly above Knox. She glanced at the Glock inside her jacket. She had the same problem. Reaching, drawing, flicking off the safety — all Knox had to do was open his hand. MacNeice shook his head.

"Coach, what's the plan here?" MacNeice said.

Knox looked north along the sewer. "I have one...trust me."

"Does it include Dylan?"

"What do you mean?"

MacNeice moved down another rung. "I can't let you take Dylan. Let him go. Once we're all out, we'll close the cover and walk away."

Knox shook his head, trying to decipher what MacNeice was trying to pull. He looked down the tunnel and back up to find Aziz level again with MacNeice.

Before they heard it, they could feel it trembling in the metal rungs.

MacNeice put his hand against the concrete wall of the shaft and felt it there too, a subtle but growing tremor followed by indistinct white noise. "Coach, that surge is coming. Put the pin back and give us Dylan. I promise we'll leave you alone."

But Knox was cornered and just shook his head, drawing the boy closer to him.

The white noise had become the roar of something unforgiving approaching fast, pushing everything ahead of it, including the sound, so it was impossible to determine how close it was. Dylan struggled to get free, but what had looked like a protective embrace had turned into a headlock and Dylan was choking.

"Don't hurt your son, coach. Put the pin back before it's too late and we'll help you up the ladder."

"I can't." The water was now above his knees, driven by what was coming. Knox turned and looked north down the tunnel, measuring perhaps how long it would take to run to the next vertical shaft. The roar grew louder by the second, the ladders were rattling and the sewer water, now above the walkway, was passing by in angry waves.

Knox may have been thinking about the humiliation of giving up, maybe about the trial, the disgrace and the media frenzy or the rest of his life in prison. The man was frozen.

MacNeice had to scream to be heard over the noise. "Put that pin back. Don't do this." Lowering himself on the ladder, he put a foot on the submerged walkway.

With the water slamming furiously at their legs, Knox finally made a decision. Keeping an arm around Dylan's neck, he fumbled with the pin, trying to put it back, but he couldn't see the hole in the grenade's safety lever without letting go of the boy. Knox was shaking from panic; he looked up at MacNeice, who reached down and called, "I'll do it. Give it to me, just keep the clip closed."

"No," Knox screamed.

On his next attempt, the pin slipped from his fingers and disappeared in the rush of water. He looked helplessly at MacNeice, his eyes filling with tears.

MacNeice yelled, "It's okay. Just hand it to me."

Knox let go of Dylan and lifted his arm to pass the grenade. That's when it hit.

A wall of grey-black water slammed into them. Instinctively, Aziz reached out and grabbed Dylan's hoodie. She had threaded one arm through the ladder rungs and held on to his hoodie with both hands. The force of the water slammed her against the wall but she hung on.

MacNeice leapt, grabbing the rung above Aziz. He edged down the ladder until he was pressed against her back, trying his best to hold her as she held the boy.

The water was boiling up toward the escape hatch, threatening to swallow them. Aziz was able to keep her head above the water only because her arm was locked around the step. Dylan's weight and the force of the current pulled on her elbow joint and the pain was excruciating. "Mac, the hoodie's coming away."

MacNeice took a deep breath and disappeared below the surface, clutching the ladder with his left hand. Buffeted by the water, she could feel his body slamming against her lower legs.

Then it happened: she lost her grip on the hoodie. Desperately, she reached into the current, but there was no boy.

She screamed and smashed the water with her fist.

MacNeice's head appeared, his face contorted with effort. He met her eyes, trying to communicate what—did he have Dylan? Coughing, he took a breath and disappeared again.

Aziz reached down and found MacNeice's shoulder; she took a deep breath and ducked under, following MacNeice's arm to where his fist was clutching Dylan's belt and jeans. She was trying to find something to grab hold of when there was a flash and deep boom from somewhere farther down the sewer.

Knox had let go of the grenade. For an instant, the black water turned pale brown. Whatever damage it had done was lost on her. When she finally caught hold of Dylan's leg, she was out of breath.

Aziz thrust herself backwards, determined not to let go of him. She could feel MacNeice's body pinning her to the ladder but could no longer feel her left arm wrapped around the rung. With the last of her strength, she pulled against the current, shoving herself upwards. Her face broke the surface, and suddenly a firefighter appeared above her. He reached down and clamped a large hand on Aziz's shoulder.

"I've got his leg—get the boy out first," she screamed. In seconds, the firefighter was on the ladder behind her, reaching under the roiling water for Dylan.

He groped for a second, then turned his face sharply up to hers. "There're two people down there."

She wiped the hair from her face and yelled, "MacNeice. He has the boy. Hurry!" She was yelling as loudly as she could but wasn't sure he could hear her words, though he nodded. Above her, another rescue worker was quickly descending on a rope line.

The firefighter snapped a safety line to the rail, inhaled deeply and threw himself beneath the surface. He quickly had hold of Dylan and the doubled-over form of MacNeice. Pulling hard, he hoisted them both to the surface.

"I've got the kid," he yelled to his partner. "I can't hold them both. Grab the detective."

The man on the rope line swung to where he could throw his arms around MacNeice. His partner hauled the boy up the ladder, as more hands reached in from above, ready to help.

The rescuer on the rope line yelled at Aziz, "I'll be right back—don't go anywhere." He smiled at her, and she managed to smile back. She wasn't capable of going anywhere. She had the shudders, her left arm was numb and her right, looped around the rung, was throbbing as though she'd wrenched it from its socket.

For what seemed like minutes, MacNeice's face hung less than a foot from hers. His eyes were closed and his lips had turned purple. He was unconscious, dead weight. Then an unseen team reeled in the line and the rescuer walked him up the wall, keeping MacNeice's legs free of the ladder.

Aziz watched the two ascending as if by magic as darts of rain fell toward her. At the top of the shaft, several arms broke the circle and the two men disappeared from view.

In seconds the rescuer was back, gesturing that he would drape her over his shoulder. Reluctant to relinquish her shaky purchase on the rung, she hesitated, and then let go, collapsing on him. As he lifted her up, she was fixated on the torrent below. It remained a deafening, menacingly indistinct blur, like standing too close as a speeding bus passes by.

At the top, he set her down on the concrete platform. Exhausted, she closed her eyes. Rain washed away the grime and, for the first time since she was a girl, Aziz prayed.

Nearby, Dylan was on his back. His eyes were closed and the rain was pelting his face. They'd bared his chest, and three paramedics worked in turns doing CPR. His skin was so pale it was almost translucent. Ten feet away, she could see MacNeice's legs but nothing more. Firefighters and paramedics surrounded him and there were open medical kits on either side.

Aziz kept praying. *My Lord, forgive me and admit us to Your mercy; You are the most Merciful of all those who show mercy.*

A firefighter approached on the run. "I heard there's someone else in the sewer."

"Yes," Aziz said, and then corrected herself. "No...he's gone. That explosion...he was holding a grenade."

The firefighter shook his head. "Okay, so let's get you off there. Put your arms around my neck and just relax—I've got you." Like a sleepy child being lifted by her father, she hung on to him and he carried her to an ambulance in the parking lot.

"I'm not leaving," she said with difficulty as he set her down, her teeth chattering with the cold.

"That's fine with me, detective. I just wanted to get you out of the rain and under a Kapton blanket. You've got a nasty laceration on your scalp—probably hit by something coming down the sewer. The paramedics will take care of it, but you're gonna need a tetanus shot."

She could see the ring of cops keeping Mercy's staff, straggling students and worried neighbours away. Two members of the bomb squad rushed out of a black van in the parking lot and were met by a uniform who must have told them they'd missed the show. Disappointed, they removed their cumbersome gear and stowed it in the vehicle before walking over to the concrete pillbox to see the shaft.

A paramedic wrapped a foil blanket around her. Disregarding the cut to her head, Aziz stood up and started making her way toward MacNeice.

She'd only staggered a few feet when there was a menacing rumble in the distance, like something massive was being sucked from existence.

Those who weren't engaged in saving the lives of Dylan and MacNeice turned in time to see the distant goal posts shudder and lurch before dropping from sight. Swallowed whole. A teen in a Mercy melton jacket shouted, "No fucking way!" as others about him gasped. Moments later, the entire goal line—from the posts to the bleachers—folded into the ground, leaving the bleachers' steel supports hanging over an abyss. Dark grey water shot skyward, arced and then fell to fill the muddy gap. The field soon flooded to the thirty-yard line and a grey tide raced around the surrounding track.

"What the hell was that?" the firefighter shouted.

"The grenade," Aziz said wearily. "I guess it shattered the sewer wall and the surge undermined the field."

He turned to her. Blood was running freely from her temple to her chin, where it bled into the wet collar of her jacket. A plume of red spread along the grey threads. Taking her gently by the shoulders, he said, "Ma'am, why don't you sit down. You're bleeding." Whatever she was going to say next was lost in violent sputtering and hacking. A paramedic had rolled MacNeice onto his side and he was purging himself of the water that had invaded his airways. In seconds, he was given oxygen tabs and one of the firefighters had draped a foil blanket over him and slid a makeshift pillow under his head. When he was finished coughing and spitting, he rolled onto his back and lay still.

Nearby, a paramedic had positioned defibrillators on Dylan's bare chest. Shouting for clear, the paramedic hit the switch, sending an electrical charge through the boy. His body bucked violently. There was a sickening pause that seemed to deflate everyone, and then Dylan coughed, sending a ragged stream of grey water into the face of the paramedic holding the paddles.

The firefighters laughed in relief, and Dylan's eyes opened wide with fear. He stared at the men and women around him and tried to sit up. One of the firefighters eased him back down so the paramedic could slip oxygen tabs in his nostrils. The firefighter covered him with another foil blanket and Aziz heard him say, "Stay on your side, son. You've still got some sewer in you." He rolled Dylan over so he was facing MacNeice. He seemed shocked to see the detective lying on the grass, covered in tinfoil, looking back at him.

The firefighter holding Aziz asked her what she wanted to do.

"Take me to MacNeice," she said. He nodded and put an arm around her waist and carried her forward, her feet dangling several inches off the ground.

MacNeice was staring skyward when she appeared above him. He blinked several times, then studied her face with a look of wonder. He smiled before letting his eyes close.

She turned to the firefighter, who still held her off the ground. "Lay me next to him, please. Can we keep the blanket?"

"Sure thing, but don't get too comfortable. The paramedics will be taking the three of you away as soon as they get their gurneys out here."

He put her down next to MacNeice, tucked her silver blanket around them both, then covered them with a heavy wool DFD blanket. MacNeice turned in her direction, scanning the details of her face. The tightness around his jaw, which had been there since the fire at Samantha Stewart's, was gone. His eyes were watery, whether from tears or rain, she couldn't tell. But his smile, when it came, was what she imagined she'd see if she ever woke up next to him. She smiled back.

He raised his hand and let it pass lightly and softly over her cheek. Somehow, he seemed to know the difference between a raindrop and a tear.

[41]

AFTER TWO DAYS IN THE HOSPITAL MacNEICE WAS SENT HOME. Though he didn't feel the need for any more rest, he was nonetheless happy to be out of the public eye, dodging the press conferences that had been taking up much of Wallace's time since Coach Knox had exploded in the sewer.

He knew about those conferences, because on his first day home, he'd turned on the television to be confronted by school portraits of Alexander Knox, David Nicholson, and Jennifer Grant—the same ones he had taped to the whiteboard. Wallace confirmed that the latest tragedy signalled the end of the investigation into the fatal bombing in Gage Park. After that, the network cut away to a reporter standing near the concrete sewer shaft. As the reporter spoke, the camera panned to the other end of Mercy's football field, where two bulldozers were busy lifting broken sections of concrete and soil and sod from the wide gash. MacNeice turned the television off.

He took out a Nina Simone CD and slipped it in the player. He turned down the volume and waited for the satin chords of "I Put a Spell on You." Until he'd met Kate, MacNeice had only known the song as sung by its creator, Screamin' Jay Hawkins. The original was more voodoo than love, more Halloween than bedroom. Simone's take was the perfect fusion of sex and longing.

Crossing the room, he settled onto the sofa and lifted his eyes to the skeletal canopy of the pre-spring forest. He wasn't prepared for the coyote that walked casually in front of the large window, pausing to put its snout toward a pane, sniffing as if a fine scent had betrayed the presence of the weary man inside.

Its coat was lush despite the winter, its eyes wise from several millennia of living rough. He sat up slowly and reached for the camera on the side table. The coyote turned, wary but not intimidated. It lifted a leg and calmly peed against the cottage wall. Before MacNeice could level his camera, it trotted casually across the patio and out of sight.

The chickadees, juncos, and the pair of cardinals had remained frozen on their branches while the coyote was near. MacNeice watched them, each tilting an eye to the ground. Perhaps in their birdbrains they worried that the beast might be gifted with flight, and for birds maybe stranger things had happened. When they started hopping about again, calling to each other and dropping down for seeds that had fallen from the feeder, he knew the coyote was out of range.

Life and death appeared among the trees outside the cottage. Insects eaten by larger insects, or by birds, and birds by bigger birds — or by house cats. All hunted for opportunity, but none had the breadth of appetite of that coyote. On a good day, it dined on mice, rabbits, groundhogs, birds, eggs, kittens, or lapdogs; on bad, it managed with frogs, toads, fish, turtles, salamanders, garter snakes, roadkill, and garbage. Getting shot or trapped by cops or angry farmers, or being whacked on the highway, were the only things that kept coyotes from dying in bed surrounded by family. Did a robin or a cricket ever die of old age?

What happened to the three teachers from Our Lady of Mercy High School lacked all of the primal qualities MacNeice saw through this window. Their humanity had been reduced to zero, until all that remained was raw bone.

In the few hours that David Nicholson had had to reflect, bundled tightly onto a woody wagon, he knew there was little chance he'd be unwrapped safely. If he had been lucky, he might have had a moment to say what was tucked beneath his chin; instead he had a few seconds of easy breathing while he waited to die. He might also have assumed his real crime would have gone undetected until the sad little house was knocked down for the development of another vineyard.

Accustomed to game plans, Sandy Knox had left what happened to Nicholson to chance, inadvertently setting his own bar for torture. He would have suffered the consequences if Nicholson had been rescued in Gage Park; he should have anticipated what had happened, when it wasn't thugs but first responders who arrived to deal with the bundled man in the wagon.

In the quiet of the cottage, MacNeice wondered what triggered Knox to pick up the phone and call Tirelle. His best guess: Nicholson was a sadist. He'd planned a different punishment for Knox than the one he inflicted on Jennifer.

Sandy's would be slow and everlasting, and *Dylan was the weapon.* Nicholson allowed Knox to believe that the boy was his creation. When Dylan showed signs of becoming a phenomenon, Nicholson began pulling the rug from under Knox, who finally decided that a decade of pain was enough.

MacNeice was still grappling with the terrible journey Jennifer Grant had taken to her death. She must have known the moment she entered the house on Ryder Road that she wasn't coming out, but it was unlikely she could have anticipated the horrors that awaited her there.

He hoped Dylan would survive in spite of the terrible tragedy of his parents. Would his dreams be defined by his mother's death, by the shallow concrete grave, her soiled wedding dress? Would the twisted knot of his two fathers eventually unwind and be his own undoing? Under the weight of these thoughts, MacNeice closed his eyes and eventually began to drift.

A feeling of warmth touched his face. He opened his eyes to find the sun had broken through the cloud cover. A sparrow on a nearby branch took the opportunity to fluff its feathers. It reminded him of the way Tuscan women shake their duvets before draping them over the railings of narrow balconies to air for the day. He closed his eyes again, happy to wander once more through Tuscany with Kate at his side, both of them grateful to be alive.

BY MID-APRIL, APART from the occasional shower, the rain had finally stopped. Many described the rest of spring as the most beautiful in living memory. It seemed like nature had taken a deep breath, and in the exhaling it released an excess of colour, birdsong, and intoxicating scents. Gardens sprung up overnight and, following almost three months of rain, farmers and fruit growers throughout the region—usually given to cautious predictions—spoke about the prospects of record harvests.

Driving past Samantha Stewart's flat, MacNeice saw the For Sale sign planted in the narrow garden beside the door. She had moved to Toronto and wouldn't be coming back other than to see her family. She wouldn't be calling MacNeice and there weren't going to be any tender letters exchanged between them. He understood why. So much of what had happened since the night he almost died in her flat was a blur. What remained in focus was the aftermath of pain and exhaustion and the cost to his relationship with Aziz.

He could recall how his chest ached as he ran toward the storm sewer, how weak his legs were as he lowered himself down the shaft. He remembered leaping across to Aziz, taking a deep breath and going under to grab hold of Dylan's belt. It was like being caught beneath a terrible black surf. He was aware of his legs against hers; he remembered being reassured to feel her there, as if he'd survive being under as long as he could sense her body against his.

There was a moment when he felt the air being punched out of his chest, when he lost the strength to pull against the current. There was nothing he could do but hang on. If he were to die, he would do so holding on to the boy.

In the ambulance later, he'd asked where Aziz was. The paramedic who was attaching monitoring equipment to his chest looked up. "That woman who was lying next to you?"

"Yes."

"She's on her way to hospital too."

"Will she be all right?"

"All I can say, sir, is that when she was lying next to you, she looked pretty happy." That was something MacNeice would remember.

INITIALLY, THE DEATH of Alexander Knox was considered a suicide. From her hospital bed, Aziz clarified that he was actually handing the grenade to MacNeice when the surge swept him away. He and the grenade had travelled over a hundred yards underwater. Knox was probably dead from drowning by the time it exploded.

It took two days before the city could drain the sewer: the collapsed concrete walls, soil, sod, and gravel had effectively dammed the system. Subsequent surges were diverted west of Mercy, but it took another day to find Knox's body. His torso and legs were intact, lodged against the grill at the bay end of the system. But that was all they found. A deadly combination of forces — the blast and the surge — had carried everything else through the exit.

Robert Grant no longer needed prompting to talk. He told Vertesi and Williams that his role was simply to get David Nicholson to come to a house that actually belonged to Knox, on the pretext that the family had several things of Jennifer's that Dylan might be interested in having.

"Why?" Williams's voice was low and grave.

Grant appeared puzzled by the question. Williams glanced up from his notebook and waited for him to answer. "I disliked David immensely. I thought he was lying about Jenn and I hated that he took Dylan from our family. It was as if we were the ones that had chased her away to California."

Grant hadn't known about the affair or the letter his sister had sent Knox about being pregnant with Dylan.

Knox had convinced his old friend that he just wanted to get Nicholson alone and persuade him to stop pretending to be a basketball coach and let Knox do what was necessary to groom Dylan's talent. While Grant didn't entirely believe him, he hadn't noticed the wagon or the duct tape and, even if he had, it wouldn't have meant anything to him.

"And the grenade?"

Knox knew Grant had been in the reserve. He had asked him about grenades, how they worked, how much time you had after pulling the pin — information he could easily have gotten from the Internet. Knox never told Grant that he had one, just said it was something he was curious about. The grocer was still incredulous: "Where did he get a grenade?"

At trial Grant was convicted as an accessory in the murder of David Nicholson and an accessory to manslaughter in the death of Constable Szabo. His lawyer wasn't out of the courthouse before he announced there'd be an appeal.

Paul Zetter was convicted as an accessory in the murders of Anniken Kallevik and Duguald Langan. In his defence, Zetter claimed he had never told Jacko Mars Bishop to kill anyone, but he admitted that he'd asked him to solve the problem of Langan getting greedy. After Langan disappeared, Zetter moved in on his bookmaking clients, happy to remain ignorant of Bishop's solution. Furthermore, when DS MacNeice came calling at Canada Coil and Wire, Zetter had told Bishop there was a homicide cop looking for him.

Zetter's thugs were charged and convicted for assaulting Freddy Dewar. The Crown's chief witness appeared in court in a navy blue blazer with two rows of merchant marine service decorations. Dewar had identified both men from separate lineups; additionally, before they stepped into the light, he'd described a ring on the third finger of one, and a tattoo on the right hand of the other.

Gloria Zetter was given a six-month suspended sentence. No hard evidence existed that connected her to her husband's illegal activities. Melody Chapman and William Byrne were charged with and convicted for obstruction of justice and illegal gaming, but both were acquitted on the charges of accessory to murder.

[EPILOGUE]

FEBRUARY 23, THE FOLLOWING YEAR: THE REGIONAL BASKETBALL Championships.

The Panthers were ahead of the Hawks by sixteen points in the dying minutes of the final game of Dylan Nicholson's senior season. Interim Coach John Swetsky, who had taken a leave of absence to help the team, was on the sidelines. Dylan was next to him, a towel draped over his shoulders. Swetsky had pulled him from the game because it would have been unsportsmanlike to run up the score.

Keeping his promise, MacNeice was in the stands. Minutes before, he had watched Dylan on a breakaway, running down the court, then pivoting around a defender—his hair flying wildly—launching through the air and turning to dunk the ball behind him. He'd landed, looked up and smiled briefly at MacNeice, then ran the length of the court to block a shot.

Swetsky swung awkwardly around to scan the stands. Though he was moving without the cane, he was still unsteady. When he caught MacNeice's eye, Swetsky threw both fists triumphantly in the air, then mimicked the elegant hand movements of a standing jumpshot.

MacNeice understood. Swetsky had finally taken his shot. By helping Dylan, Swetsky's own fears had disappeared like raindrops in a fire. MacNeice swallowed the emotion rising in his throat and then he stood and applauded both man and boy.

[ACKNOWLEDGEMENTS]

My much-loved grandfather, Joseph MacIntosh, might have said, had he read this book, "Auch, for the love of God, laddie — where do these stories come from?" His son Ian, a mountain of a man, gripped my hand as I left for art college and said, "Remember boy, the only culture in Ontario — is agriculture."

Though both are long gone, I still remember what I learned from them. Tenderness from Granddad, strength from Uncle Ian — their DNA runs through MacNeice's veins. For research, I've tapped several of my health science sources, doctors Dody Bienenstock, John Bienenstock, Rae Lake, Karel O'Brien and Gerry O'Leary. I'm grateful to Donna Wolfe for checking my transcription of a Clydeside dialect and John Michaluk, for an unforgettable tour of the waterfront and the remains of Hamilton's Brightside. Similarly, I also want to thank Bill Gordon for his personal history of life at Stelco.

These stories emerge from dreams, a life of curiosity, observations of light and shadow, a profound love of beauty and a respect for blackness. They come to life with the help and generosity of my first readers. First among them is my partner in life, Shirley Blumberg Thornley. Without her, MacNeice would not have happened. I'm grateful also to Bruce Westwood, Chris Casuccio and Kristine Wookey of Westwood Creative Artists for their ongoing support. And to Anne Collins, of Random House Canada, my champion and whip-cracker. MacNeice and I are blessed to have her in our corner.

I want to thank my family: Marsh, Andrea, Daniela, Lucas, Ian, Sophia, Chuck and Kathryn, for their patience, love and support.

I'm grateful to Richard Halperin for allowing me to use an excerpt of his poem, "Beauty." As great poets do, he's gently lifted a hidden truth from the shadows to the light.

Finally, thank you to everyone at House of Anansi Press—especially Scott Griffin, Sarah MacLachlan, Douglas Richmond, Maria Golikova, Alysia Shewchuk, Sara Loos, and Joshua Greenspon—for bringing this book back into print and introducing MacNeice to a new audience.

COMING SOON
from House of Anansi Press

Available Now

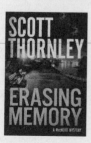

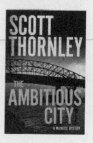

SPIDERLINE

www.houseofanansi.com

SCOTT THORNLEY grew up in Hamilton, Ontario, which inspired his fictional Dundurn. He is the author of four novels in the critically acclaimed MacNeice Mysteries series: *Erasing Memory*, *The Ambitious City*, *Raw Bone*, and the forthcoming *Vantage Point*. Thornley divides his time between Toronto and the southwest of France.